the Man in 3B

OTHER NOVELS BY CARL WEBER

the Man in 3B

CARL WEBER

GRAND CENTRAL
PUBLISHING

NEW YORK   BOSTON

Grand Central Publishing
Hachette Book Group
237 Park Avenue
New York, NY 10017

www.HachetteBookGroup.com

Printed in the United States of America

RRD-C

First Edition: January 2013
10 9 8 7 6 5 4 3 2 1

Grand Central Publishing is a division of Hachette Book Group, Inc.
The Grand Central Publishing name and logo is a trademark of Hachette Book Group, Inc.

The Hachette Speakers Bureau provides a wide range of authors for speaking events. To find out more, go to www.hachettespeakersbureau.com or call (866) 376-6591.

The publisher is not responsible for websites (or their content) that are not owned by the publisher.

Library of Congress Cataloging-in-Publication Data
Weber, Carl, 1964–
    The man in 3B / Carl Weber.—1st ed.
        p. cm.
    Summary: "Meet Darryl Graham, or as his new neighbors in Jamaica, Queens call him, The Man in 3B. He is the man every woman wants and every man wants to be, so inquiring minds want to know. Unfortunately, in Darryl's world, what you know can hurt you, and when he winds up dead, those inquiring minds become the prime suspects."—Provided by the publisher.
    ISBN 978-1-4555-0526-5 (hardcover)—ISBN 978-1-4555-2250-7 (large print trade pbk.)—ISBN 978-1-4555-0523-4 (ebook)   1. Apartment houses—Fiction. 2. Neighbor—Fiction.   3. Murder—Fiction.   4. Triangles (Interpersonal relations)—Fiction.   5. African Americans—Fiction.   6. Jamaica (New York, N.Y.)—Fiction.   I. Title.
    PS3573.E2164M36 2013
    813'.54—dc22

                                                                    2012025861

This book is dedicated to my grandmother, Sarah Weber,
who will be one hundred years old in June 2013. I love you, Nana.

Acknowledgments

First off, I'd like to thank all the people at Grand Central Publishing for the warm welcome, especially my new editor, Latoya Smith, and the director of publicity, Linda Duggins. Moving in any capacity is difficult, but you've made the transition very pleasurable.

Next, let me thank the woman who orchestrated the deal, my good friend, second mom, and agent, Marie Brown. We've worked together for almost fourteen years, and I hope you know that I not only value your opinion, but most importantly, your character. I love you, Marie. Thanks for being there when times were tough and others weren't around.

I'd like to thank Martha Weber and Joylynn Ross for all your help in getting *The Man in 3B* finished. This may have been the toughest project I've attempted. Without your late-night hours reading and editing, I might not have ever finished.

Oh, and let's not forget you, the reader. Without you, I'd be nothing, so thanks. See you in a few months for *The Family Business 2*. Enjoy.

the Man in 3B

Prologue

September in New York City

It was one of those muggy Indian summer nights, where Detective Sergeant Dan Thomas of the 113th Precinct in Queens sat at his desk thinking about his latest case. He was now in his third hour of overtime, and it didn't look like he was going home anytime soon to splash around in his new pool with wife number two as he'd promised. He'd just left a horrific crime scene, where a local man had been found dead in his apartment, burned beyond recognition. Both his partner and lieutenant had already come to the conclusion that this was probably some unfortunate accident, or perhaps even a suicide, but Dan's gut told him different. It told him this was a homicide, and in all his years on the job, his instincts had never led him astray. So instead of heeding the advice of his lieutenant and letting the case go until morning, Detective Thomas sent his partner to the fire marshal's office to see if she could find out the exact cause of the fire. He also had a couple of uniformed officers bring in some of the dead man's neighbors for routine questioning. Maybe one of them would be able to shed light on the situation. Thus far, they'd only turned out to be concerned citizens, singing "Kumbaya" and praising the deceased as if he were the next messiah, but Detective Thomas wasn't convinced.

Nobody's this well loved, he thought.

"Dan," his partner, Detective Keisha Anderson, called as she entered the squad room waving a folder. She was panting, as if she'd literally run the entire way from the fire marshal's office. "I gotta give it to you, partner. Your instincts were right on as usual. Fire marshal said it was definitely not an accident. They can't tell exactly what started it right now, but someone used an accelerant to start the fire so they could contain it to one room."

Thomas nodded his approval. "Nice work, Anderson. Those idiots over at the fire marshal's office usually take two weeks to get us anything relevant. What'd you do, promise to sleep with one of them?" Thomas laughed.

"Nope, promised you would," his partner replied with a laugh of her own. "Big, burly guy named Sullivan. He said he likes to be on top, so you're catching tonight, not pitching." Thomas gave her the finger, and she shot back, "Hey, just thought you might wanna be prepared."

Anderson handed Thomas the file, then sat on the arm of a nearby chair as she waited for him to read it. When he finished, Thomas looked up, trying to hide a vindicated smile that spread across his thin lips. He'd call the wife and tell her the pool would have to wait. Once again, his intuition had been spot-on.

He looked over at his partner.

"So where do we go from here?" she asked as Thomas got up from his chair.

Thomas didn't say a word. He gestured for Anderson to follow him as he headed toward another room. Once inside, he pulled back a curtain that revealed a large picture window, which served as a two-way mirror.

"You wanna know where we go from here, Anderson?" Thomas asked as he stared at the five people sitting on the other side of the glass. "For starters, we're going to drill each one of them until we find out who the murderer is."

Walking away from the glass, Thomas retrieved a small notepad from his suit jacket and began flipping through pages. His partner watched the five suspects. They were all eating fried chicken from Popeyes and drinking soda and coffee ordered by the lieutenant and paid for by New York City taxpayers.

"I don't know, Dan. They all look like one big, happy family." She shrugged. "What makes you think one of them is a murderer? I mean, there's still the possibility of suicide."

"Possible, but not probable. This guy didn't kill himself, and my gut tells me one of them did the job for him."

Thomas walked back over to the window next to Anderson, and they observed the group on the other side.

"What do you mean? What do you see that I don't? To me they all look pretty normal, more like the guy or girl next door than killers." Anderson's eyes went from the group to Thomas and then back to the two-way mirror again.

"Maybe, but you've been on the job long enough to know that looks can be deceiving. I see five people who are hiding something."

"Hiding something like what? They all look content."

"If you had just lost a member of your 'big, happy family,' as you put it, would you still be sitting here, smiling and laughing while enjoying your food? Or would you be genuinely broken up about it?"

She scanned the group again. "Yeah, I guess you're right. I never thought of it like that. The only one remotely upset is the kid."

"Mm-hmm," Thomas said. "It's like when the troublemaker of the family dies. Everyone shows up at the funeral for protocol. Do you see any tears being shed for that man in there, Anderson?"

"Nope, I haven't seen anything more than a few crocodile tears. All I see is a bunch of people getting fat on the city's dime." She folded her arms. "So, who do you think looks good for it? They can't all be in on it."

"No, but my guess is that it's one of the two ladies. A gruesome murder like this could only be a crime of passion. It's not an easy thing to light a person on fire and burn them to a crisp. Not unless you really hate them."

Anderson nodded her agreement. "Which one?"

"Take your choice." Thomas glanced down at his notepad, then at the very scantily clad woman at the end of the table. "The neighborhood gossip said the deceased had a history with them both. Word is the pretty young thing over there is a schoolteacher, but I ain't never had a teacher who looked like that."

"Me neither. What was her connection to the deceased?"

"From what I'm hearing, jilted lover."

"Now that, my friend, would give her motive," Anderson reasoned. "But if that's the case, why are you even looking at the other one?"

"You mean the fat ass?" Thomas said without missing a beat.

"Dan!" Anderson snapped at his lack of political correctness, then added under her breath, "Although she does have one hell of a donkey butt."

"No, I'm not saying she's a fat ass. That's what the deceased called her in front of the entire neighborhood this morning."

"Damn. I'd kill a motherfucker for that shit myself."

This time Anderson managed to get a laugh out of Thomas. "Exactly my point."

Anderson shook her head and then moved on to the next suspect. "If I had to put my money on somebody, I'd put it on him." She pointed at the handsome man sitting next to a young college-aged kid. "You do realize that Cliff Huxtable over there is a fireman. And who would know more about setting a controlled fire than him?"

"Nobody, except maybe a fireman's son." They both turned toward the boy.

"Isn't he like some straight-A genius or something like that?"

"Mm-hmm, and so was the Craigslist Killer. That same gossip I spoke to said that he and the deceased spent a lot of time together in the deceased's apartment—until they had a falling out."

"What about him?" Anderson pointed to a thin, light-skinned man in his late twenties wearing a well-tailored suit and a silk tie. He had a plateful of chicken in front of him but never took a bite. "Why does Mr. Shirt and Tie look so nervous?"

"Him? Not sure, but he's the jilted lover's current boyfriend, and I hear him and our victim had a lot of beef over the girlfriend."

"Ohhhh. I've handled more than my share of love triangle cases. He could easily turn out to be our number one suspect." She shook her head uncertainly. "I just don't know, though . . ."

"What's there to know?" He looked his partner in the eye. "Like I said, one of those people in that room is a murderer. Now all we have to do is figure out which one."

Connie

1

I stepped off the bus and briskly walked the eight blocks home, carrying two heavy shopping bags filled with groceries for my husband's birthday celebration, for which I planned to go all out. I could have gotten off the bus at the corner of Guy R. Brewer Boulevard and 109th Street about a block from my apartment, but I'd heard some weight loss expert on *The Today Show* the other day explaining how if you get off one stop before yours and walk the rest of the way home every day, you can lose up to ten pounds per year. Sounds crazy, right? I'm not even saying that I believed her, just that I was so desperate to lose the fifty-plus pounds I'd gained after my wedding that I was willing to try anything. I'd tried every diet book, tummy-buster DVD, and weight loss infomercial gimmick there was, all with no results. With money being so tight now, walking was a lot cheaper than buying another set of DVDs or a gym membership.

I had to do something to lose this weight. I couldn't even get my husband, Avery, to look at me in a sexual manner, and the Lord knows I missed his touch.

About halfway down my block I saw anchorwoman Nancy Williams staked out in front of my building, reporting the six o'clock news. Some folks watched CNN; others ABC or CBS; many got their news from 1010 WINS radio; but the women of my neighborhood got our local information from Nancy Williams and the 109th Street news team of gossips. Along with Nancy was her number one investigative reporter, Lily Nixon, our building super's wife. Nancy's weather girl, Ms. Bertha Dunbar from 1B, could tell you the next day's weather just by how her bones felt. They were surrounded by three other neighbors from our building and a couple of girls from across the street.

"Hey, y'all," I greeted as I stopped in front of them, trying to catch my breath after my walk. They greeted me in their usual friendly manner, but the looks that passed between them told me something was up. Either they were trying to decide if they would include me in the latest gossip, or they were trying to decide who would be the one who got to break the story.

"Okay, what's the latest?" I asked Nancy. I knew it wouldn't be long before she spilled her guts because Nancy couldn't hold water. "Or should I be afraid to ask?"

"Be afraid," Nancy quipped.

"Be very afraid," Pam from across the street added with a smirk.

"Humph! It's our men that should be afraid." Lily laughed as the women around her traded high fives and *uh-huhs*.

It was starting to look like it would take a while for them to deliver the news, so I set my heavy bags down on the stoop. "What in the world are y'all talking about?"

"Three-B." Nancy pointed in the direction of the third-floor apartment on the right. "Or should I say, the man in 3B. That's what we're talking about."

I looked over at Lily. "So y'all finally rented it, huh?" I asked, wondering why that was such a big deal. Lily's answer told me there was much more to the story.

She practically purred when she told me, "We sure did, and I hope this one stays forever. It's about time we had some new eye candy around here."

"Here, here," a couple of the women chimed in unison.

"I'll tell you what," Nancy added with a devilish grin. "I'm willing to chip in if he falls behind on his rent, just as long as he's willing to work it off. If you know what I mean." She wiggled her rear like she was about to take it from behind.

"Well, if that's the case, then count me in too," one of the women cosigned with gyrating hips. "And hell, he ain't even gotta do any work. I'll take care of everything." They all busted out laughing.

I shook my head and joined their laughter. "I take it our new neighbor is a man?"

"He's more than just a man. He's the man that's gonna have the water and electric bills on this place going sky-high," Jewell replied with deadpan seriousness.

"Excuse me? Why's that?" The last thing I needed was for our bills to be going up.

"Because, honey, that man's so fine, we gon' be going through our wet panties like drawers is goin' outta style. We gon' be doing laundry and taking cold showers more than ever."

The cackling and high-fiving resumed.

"Nancy, you and Lily ought to be ashamed of yourselves," I said with a smile. "You're married women for crying out loud." I felt bad for their husbands. I mean, how bad were things at home if they were lusting over the new guy in 3B like that?

I grabbed my bags before making my way up the steps and opened the door.

"I may be married, but I ain't dead," Lily quipped.

"That's right," Nancy said. "Go on with your bad self, but I guarantee you'll be right out here with us once you get a load of what we're talking about."

"I seriously doubt that. I got a man, and he's all I need to get me through the night," I answered before disappearing into my apartment building. I meant what I said about Avery being the only man I needed. I just wondered sometimes if he still felt the same way about me.

Out of habit, I walked toward the elevator, but then remembered the advice of the woman on TV and headed for the stairs. Carrying those two heavy bags, I huffed and puffed up three flights. By the time I reached the landing to enter the third floor, my chest was heaving and I was so out of breath I thought I was going to pass out. My vision was so blurry that the number three on the door almost looked like thirty-three.

This is ridiculous, I thought. *How the hell did I ever let it come to this? Those were only three flights of stairs, not ten!* I hauled my sweaty self through the doorway, leaning against the wall as I trudged down the hall to my apartment. In front of my door, I let both grocery bags fall out of my hands as I struggled to catch my breath.

"Hey, are you okay down there?" a man's voice called from the other end of the hall.

It sounded like Benny, the young college kid who lived in 3C, but I was still too damn out of breath to lift my head and find out as I fumbled through my purse for my house keys.

"Miss? Are you okay?"

As he got closer, I finally looked up, and I thought my eyes were playing tricks on me because I swear I was staring at a god or maybe an angel or something.

"You okay?" he asked again.

My vision was fine now, and this incredibly handsome figure stood before me. I could only nod.

If this was who Nancy and her news crew were talking about outside, they hadn't told no lies, because this brotha was finer than fine—the kind of fine where you turn to stare and walk right into a damn wall! He was tall with a skin fade and a perfectly manicured beard—a combination of Tyrese, Teddy Pendergrass, and Michael Jordan all wrapped up in one. He was wearing a jogging suit that fit him like it was tailor-made, and I could tell he was pure muscle underneath it. He wore an earring in his left lobe and an expensive watch on his wrist, but the piece of jewelry that stood out the most was the thick gold chain and a Star of David pendant he wore around his neck.

"Umm...are you okay?" he asked for the third time before I finally realized this gorgeous man was waiting for me to speak.

"Good Lord, I've died and gone to heaven! And you're...you're an angel, aren't you? God sent me an angel, and he's fine as hell."

Did I really just say that? How embarrassing. Now I was not only sweaty, but my face was also probably bright red. I had this terrible habit of saying really stupid things when I was around handsome men, and this was probably one of the best looking I'd ever seen. If I had my wits about me, I might have been able to play it off like I was joking, but I was so flustered by this guy I could barely think straight.

"Well, I wouldn't say all that." He chuckled and flashed a smile with teeth so white I swear they lit up the hallway. "This place is nice, but I wouldn't call it heaven, and the closest thing to an angel I've seen is you, pretty lady. Now, are you all right?"

Pretty lady! Was he flirting with me? He couldn't be flirting with me. Men like him didn't flirt with me. But it sure sounded like he was flirting with me. *Get it together, girl. You're a married woman.* I willed myself to snap out of it and start making some sense before he thought I was a complete lunatic.

"Oh, there's nothing wrong with me. Just getting a little exercise. I probably should have taken the elevator instead of the stairs. These bags are a little heavier than I thought. I think I might have overdone it." I closed my mouth when I discovered that now I had gone from being unable to speak to rambling like an idiot. Miraculously, he didn't seem to notice my crazy behavior. In fact, he was still flirting.

I swear to God I felt my knees tremble when he leaned in close to me and whispered in my ear, "A woman who likes to keep in shape. That's very impressive. But between me and you, everything already looks to be in shape." He pulled away. "So don't hurt yourself, you hear me? I can't go having my new neighbor all sick and laid up. At least not until I get some food in my house so I can make you my homemade chicken soup and nurse you back to health."

Thank goodness that wall was there to hold me up.

"Baby, I don't care if that soup comes out of a can..."

Oh no. What the hell is wrong with me? I'm a married woman. Connie, get yourself together, girl, before you make a bigger fool of yourself than you already have.

"I'm sorry. I didn't mean to call you baby. It's just I call my husband—"

He stopped me. "Your husband? Listen, I apologize for my forwardness. I'm not trying to cause any trouble, especially since I just moved here. I'm really sorry. I didn't see a ring."

So it wasn't in my head. This gorgeous man had been making a pass at me. I had to smile. My ego hadn't had a boost like this in years.

"I stopped wearing my rings a few years ago when they got too tight. You know, um, I'm not quite the same size I was on my wedding day."

His eyes traveled down my body, and unlike the way Avery looked at me lately, this guy seemed to like what he saw. Damn, it felt good to be admired that way. I tried to switch to a more neutral subject before I got myself into trouble.

"You, uh, must be the new man moving into 3B that I've heard so much about."

His pleasant, happy face became stern. "What exactly have you heard? I just got the keys twenty minutes ago. I haven't even moved any of my stuff in yet."

I was a little taken aback by his reaction. "Oh, nothing bad," I said to reassure him. "I just heard that there was a new man moving into 3B, that's all. We look out for each other around here, but everyone kinda keeps to themselves," I lied.

"Oh, I see. That's good, 'cause I'm kind of a private person, and I like to keep a low profile myself."

Hah! With that face and that body, no way you're keeping a low profile.

Fortunately, I hadn't spoken out loud this time, but I still felt the heat on my cheeks. This man had me thinking all kinds of crazy things. It was time to get out of there, because there was no telling what I might say or do next.

"Well, neighbor, it was nice meeting you. I guess I better get these groceries inside and start dinner," I said, hoping to escape whatever power he seemed to have over my good sense.

His eyes were all over my curves once again, and I swear he looked like he wanted to pour chocolate over every single inch of me and lick it off. Or maybe that was just the fantasy I was having in that moment. Either way, I thought I would melt into a puddle right there in the hallway when he took my hand, kissed it, and said, "Well, pretty lady, your husband's a very lucky man."

"Uh . . ." I'd lost the power to speak again. All I could do was give him a stupid grin—and yet he still looked at me like he thought I was something special. This was one sexy mutha.

"I'll see you around, neighbor," he said.

I nodded, wishing he would stand there and hold my hand forever.

"By the way," he said, "I didn't get your name. Mine's Daryl. Daryl Graham."

I finally regained the power of speech and said, "I'm Connie Graham."

"Hey, how 'bout that? We could be related. Is Graham your maiden name or married name?" He stared at me and waited for an answer, but I'd barely heard his question because I was so wrapped up in those sexy-ass eyes of his.

"Huh?" I whispered. "Did you say something?"

"I said your name's Graham, just like mine. Maybe we're cousins or something."

I said my name was Graham? Oh. My. God. There must be some kind of correlation: the sexier the man, the stupider I become.

I tried to laugh it off. "Oh, you must have heard me incorrectly. My last name is Mack. Connie Mack."

I'm sure he knew I was full of shit. There's no way someone could mistake Mack for Graham. He knew I'd just called myself Connie Graham, but he was so sweet he let it slide so I wouldn't be more embarrassed.

"Yeah, I probably heard you wrong. Well, Connie Mack, I'll be seeing you around."

He kissed my hand once again, and then he floated off into heaven. Or maybe he took the elevator or the stairwell. Heck, I don't know. All I knew was that I had to hurry inside, so I could make dinner before my husband got home. I'd planned on giving him the blow job of his life as a birthday present, but now that Mr. 3B had me all worked up, we were going to have to rethink things 'cause Connie Mack was gonna need a little something herself.

Benny

2

I was looking out my bedroom window, laughing at the neighborhood women ogling the new tenant in 3B as he came out of the building. He headed toward the U-Haul truck that was parked in front, and every pair of eyes on that stoop was glued to him like he was a big, juicy steak and they hadn't eaten for weeks. I watched as he gave them a friendly nod, then disappeared into the back of the truck. Don't get me wrong. He was a handsome enough man, but those sisters were losing their minds with the way they were acting, especially now that he was out of sight. If they knew I was watching them as they flashed their breasts or wiggled their asses at him when his back was turned, they'd probably keel over and die.

But all that came to an abrupt end when my father, Ben Senior, came walking down the block. Normally when he approached, the women of the neighborhood were all quick to speak. Some even flirted with my old man, but today they had nothing to say. No need for leftovers when fresh meat had arrived, I guess.

Ms. Nancy, as I called her out of respect, who had led the women in their antics, practically sprouted angel wings when Pop approached. Not that she was an angel by any stretch of the imagination. Ms. Nancy had been seeing Pop behind her husband's back for quite a while. Considering how often she'd sneak up to our apartment in the middle of the night or after her husband left for work, I'd say she was pretty smitten. She knew my dad didn't play that junk, and if he had seen her lifting up her shirt the way she did, they'd be over. I think she could already sense that he'd been looking for an excuse to kick her to the curb.

What she didn't know was that one of the other ladies who hung around our stoop, her friend Ms. Pam, had been making overtures toward Pop for quite a while. Ms. Pam was a thirty-five-year-old bombshell that all the older men on our block had been trying to get with. From the way she and Pop were giving each other eye signals, it looked to me like tonight was the night he was going to seal the deal—that is, as long as Ms. Nancy didn't pick up on it and find some way to cock block.

As you can probably tell, my father is a ladies' man. He is also a New York City fireman. Even more importantly, he is my hero. There were not a lot of men like Pop, and although I had a hell of a lot of respect for his uniform, I had even more respect for him as a man. He'd raised me by himself since I was eight without one complaint. He'd sacrificed his entire life for me, and I'd never wanted for anything growing up. As a kid, I told him and everyone who would listen that I wanted to be just like my dad.

"Nah, son, I don't want you to be like me," he'd tell me. With his hand on my shoulder, he'd look down at me and say, "I want you to be better than me. I want you to use that brain of yours and make me proud." I looked up to my father then, and now at twenty years old and in my second year of college, I still looked up to him.

Turning my attention back to the street, I watched my father give one last signal to Ms. Pam. He seemed to purposely ignore the other women on the stoop as he headed toward the truck, probably going to introduce himself to our new neighbor.

Instead of watching it all from the window, I decided to go downstairs to be part of the action.

"Benny, come here, son," Pop said when he saw me come outside. "I wanna introduce you to another Knicks fan." Our new neighbor was wearing a Knicks jersey. Pop was a die-hard fan.

I carefully maneuvered my way past the ladies to avoid getting cursed out, then walked over to the U-Haul truck, where my father was standing next to our new neighbor.

"Benny, this is Daryl Graham. Daryl, this is my son, Ben Junior. We all call him Benny."

"Nice to meet you, Benny." Mr. Graham had been holding a big box. He placed it back in the truck and shook my hand with a firm grip.

"Pleasure's all mine, Mr. Graham," I replied.

"You can call me Daryl," he said, then turned to Pop. "Very polite young man you have here, Ben. He's pretty tall too. He play any ball?"

Pop put his hand on my shoulder. "Benny here played forward in high school. Had a full ride to Hofstra too, but we turned it down."

Daryl looked confused, and I couldn't say I blamed him. I mean, how many people turn down full scholarships?

Pop explained, "You see, Benny here's a little bit of a brain. He got a full academic ride to Fordham University up in the Bronx, so he traded in his sneakers to pursue a degree in electrical engineering. He's doing pretty well too. I'm proud of him."

"As you should be." Daryl nodded approvingly and turned his attention to me. "So, how's college working out for you, Benny?"

"Pretty good. I'm maintaining a 3.8 grade point average."

Pop spoke up. "It would have been a 4.0 if it wasn't for that schmuck racist who taught psychology. Not one black person got over a B."

"Pop, he doesn't wanna hear all that." I shot him a look and he raised his hands as if to surrender.

"All right, all right. I'm sorry, son," he said as he reached into the back of the truck and picked up the box Daryl had been holding. "I hope you don't mind, but that movie's gonna have to wait. I just volunteered to help Daryl carry his boxes upstairs."

"Oh, man, I didn't realize you had plans with your son," Daryl said. "Listen, Ben, I can take care of this. Last thing I wanna do is come between you and your son." He looked at me. "You do know you're one of the lucky ones, right? I lost my dad when I was about fifteen."

I liked this dude. "As a matter of fact, I do. But it's cool. There are lots of ways a father and son can spend time together—like helping a new friend move into his apartment." I smiled and leaned in to take a box from the back of the truck.

Pop tilted his head in the direction of the women on the stoop and said, "Too bad you couldn't get your little entourage over there to help. You'd probably be finished by now."

"What entourage?" Daryl asked.

"You mean to tell me that you didn't notice you have an audience?" Pop clarified.

Daryl glanced in their direction and shook his head. "Man, I'm not even paying attention to them. Only thing I'm worried about is unloading this truck."

"Well, their lazy asses ain't gonna help you. I can tell you that. I got a week's salary that says not one of them offered to lift a finger to help you out."

My father looked to the women on the stoop. Their ears were deaf to anything he had to say, but their eyes were still clearly focused on Daryl. Lucky for Pop that his snide remark had gotten by them. The women in our building really knew how to stick together when they weren't stabbing each other in the back.

"Now that you mention it, no, they haven't offered," Daryl said.

"Take my advice when it comes to the women in this building. Hit it and quit and don't get too attached 'cause all of 'em ain't nothing but a bunch of gold diggers and whores."

Daryl had nothing to say but nodded his understanding. I couldn't read his expression, but somehow I got the feeling Pop had gone a little too far calling them whores.

"Anyway, let's get this stuff upstairs," I suggested to change the subject.

"You look like a strong young man so why don't you start with this?" Daryl transferred a heavy box from his hands to mine. "I'll grab something off the truck."

As Pop and Daryl went into the truck to unload more boxes, I looked down and realized what I was carrying.

"Oh, wow! Is this the new system Bose just put out?" I called out.

"What do you know about that?" Daryl asked, exiting the truck. My dad followed behind him, his arms full.

"My boy's a bit of a tech nut," Pop answered for me. "If it's got circuits and wires, he knows about it."

"Well, that's all right," Daryl said. If I hadn't just met the guy, I'd say he sounded almost like he was proud of me. At the moment, both Daryl and my father wore the same smiles on their faces. "And that's good to know because I'm not. Maybe if I throw you a few ends, you can help me out with setting up some of my equipment. I'm sure a college kid like yourself can use a little money from a side hustle."

"No doubt," I answered as Daryl led the way into the apartment building.

The elevator arrived and we all piled on. I was the last one in, closest to the buttons, so I pressed three and we headed up.

I looked over into the box Daryl was carrying and couldn't believe what I saw on top of it. "No way. Please tell me that is not the new iPad."

"Oh, that?" Daryl said nonchalantly. "Yeah, a friend hooked me up. I haven't had time to figure that thing out yet."

"I told you my son's a mechanical genius. I bet he'll have you operating that thing like a champ in no time," my father said, putting in a good word on my skills.

"I don't know about a genius," I said, looking over my shoulder at Pop, who still had a proud grin on his face.

As the elevator doors opened, Daryl said, "I have a friend who hooks me up with all that stuff."

He said it so casually, but it didn't come across as bragging. I liked that about him. There was nothing worse than a man who tried to make another man feel inferior by flaunting his worldly possessions. And then he said something that made me like him even more.

"You're free to come mess around with my stuff whenever you have time. I'm sure you could teach me a thing or two."

Pop put his hand on Daryl's shoulder. "Oh, I'm quite sure he could. Benny is a techie, a mechanical genius, a gadget geek . . . you name it.

I hope you meant it when you said he could come over, because I have no doubt he will."

Daryl stopped in front of his apartment door and turned to face us. "One thing you'll learn about me is that I mean everything I say." He looked at me. "I mean it, son. Feel free to come over anytime."

I couldn't wait to get my hands on some of Daryl's stuff.

Avery

3

It was a good thing I wasn't driving, I thought as I walked home from Jiggles strip club, drunker than I'd been in a very long time. "Happy fuckin' birthday to me," I muttered as I stumbled down the sidewalk toward home.

Yes, it was my birthday—my fiftieth, to be exact—and I had spent it alone at Jiggles, ogling the tits and ass of some of the best-looking women I'd seen in a while. Most men would leave a place like that and head home to their wives, where they would make love in the dark, fantasizing that it was a stripper underneath them. Me, I couldn't stomach the thought of touching my wife, not with the way she had let herself go. It was more than the fact that I was turned off by fat women. Her weight gain pissed me off because her ever-expanding waistline was a symbol for how much everything in my life had gone to shit. Every time I looked at her I was reminded of how far I'd fallen.

See, five years ago I was on top of my game, well on my way to becoming a millionaire as the top-selling mortgage broker for Option One right here in Queens; but when the bottom fell out of the housing market, I became a casualty of my own success. One day I'm the darling of the company, making six figures, newly married to one of the finest women you'd ever wanna see, rocking his and hers Mercedes, and living in a big-ass house out on Long Island. Then the next day, the housing market is in the toilet and they're letting me go without notice. I think that was the first time, other than when my kid was born, that I actually shed tears as a grown man, but trust me, it wasn't my last.

With the economy the way it was, the job market was so tight that I couldn't get a job at McDonald's, let alone another mortgage company or bank. By the time my unemployment ran out, both of our cars had been repossessed. I can't begin to tell you how much of a loser I felt like, standing there with my wife, watching those bastards tow away our cars. By that time, I was four months behind on an upside-down mortgage, and like half of America, I just gave up and stopped making payments altogether. Six months later the bank foreclosed on our house and sold it on the courthouse steps for half of what I paid for it. Things were so bad that I ended up filing for bankruptcy. It was an awful time in my life, one I don't think I could have ever prepared for. I mean, who prepares to be a goddamn loser?

My wife, Connie, tried to be supportive. She'd say things like, "You'll find another job. Things will get better. You just wait and see."

She was trying to remain upbeat, but by that time, I was so damn depressed I could barely even look at her, let alone listen to her perky, Susie Sunshine encouragement. It got to the point where I was basically ignoring my wife, and she started drowning her sorrows in junk food.

While I was losing all the material things in my life, my once sexy, superfine, curvy spouse was packing on the pounds—lots of them. She said she'd only put on fifty pounds since I married her five years ago, but I was willing to wager it was more like seventy-five to a hundred. Once upon a time I couldn't wait to get home just to look at her, and now I was embarrassed to walk down the street with her fat ass.

Yeah, I know I sound insensitive, but I don't do fat. Never have. That's why I left my first wife, and Connie, as supportive as she was about our financial situation, knew that. Sometimes I wondered if the real reason she wanted me to find a new job was so I could support her Dunkin' Donuts habit.

Connie was right about one thing, though. I did eventually find another job about eight months after my unemployment ran out. Now instead of closing deals on million-dollar homes, I was selling furniture at Cheap Sam's for ten dollars an hour. Oh, I got commission too, which this past week brought my check to a whopping $602.83 after taxes. I used to pull in two grand a week minimum. Considering the fact that my rent on a bullshit apartment in a halfway decent neighborhood was $2,000, we were barely making ends meet.

That's why I knew Connie was gonna go ballistic when I got home and told her I only had a hundred dollars in my pocket. Most of my paycheck was in the hands of the strippers at Jiggles now. At the time, all I could think about was that a brotha deserves a good lap dance on his birthday, but now I was dreading another fight with a wife who was big enough to pin me to the floor if she wanted to.

As I walked across the overpass to the Van Wyck Expressway, I stopped and looked over the railing at the cars whizzing by below. I wished I was in one of the cars, speeding away from Queens, away from this life that I hated.

"Ha!" I said as I put a foot on the railing. "Who am I kidding? What life? Shit, I died when the housing market crashed."

Before I knew it, I was standing on the railing, ready to jump. You know what they say: Alcohol is like liquid courage, and those six vodka and cranberries I'd had were making me think I could go through with it. I could jump off the bridge and end my poor excuse for a life.

I took a deep breath and lifted one leg. "Good-bye, cruel world," I said, laughing at the cliché.

"Hey!"

The voice that came from behind startled me so much that I almost lost my balance and fell over the side. I put my foot back on the railing and turned around to see a man about my age offering an outstretched hand.

"Mister, don't do it," he said. "Trust me, it's not worth it. Whoever or whatever it is that's bothering you is not worth dying over."

Believe it or not, I chuckled. "How would you know? You have no idea how fucked up my life is."

"I know because I was standing on that very same railing a year ago, ready to jump."

I stared at him for a second as I tried to read his face. Was he bullshitting me? If he was just saying that to talk me down from the edge, then I was not in the mood. "Look, I don't have time—"

He cut me off. "I got turned down for partner in my accounting firm, found out my old lady was cheating on me with my best friend—who was a partner—and that I had cancerous polyps in my colon. All in one day. Trust me, if anyone wanted to die, it was me."

Even if he was up here, I thought, *that doesn't mean he understands what I'm going through.*

"Why'd you stop yourself? Didn't have the guts?"

He smiled and shook his head. "No, a fifth of Jack Daniel's will give you the guts to do just about anything. But as I stood right there thinking about why I was going to jump, I realized a few things."

"Like what?"

"Like that bitch I called a wife was just that—a bitch—that colon cancer is treatable, and that there are plenty other ways to make money if I'm willing to put in the hard work."

I looked at him, wondering if it had really happened that way. If right before he went splat on the Van Wyck, he'd had some great moment of clarity and found the will to live again. And even if it did happen like that, I still wasn't sure I wanted to be talked out of jumping.

Dude was determined, though. He kept on with his speech. "More importantly, I thought about how my being dead would affect my kids. All I would be doing is passing the burden on to them, all because I was having a bad day, got drunk, and killed myself. I love my kids. I'd never do anything to hurt them."

He was starting to get to me. That was some deep shit he was talking.

"You got any kids, man?" he asked.

"Yeah, I got a daughter. I'm really proud of her. She's a schoolteacher."

"You love her?"

"Of course I love her. She's the most important thing I got in the world."

"Then why in the world would you leave her this burden? Look, man, I don't know what's got you up there, but ask yourself one question. Would you do it if you hadn't had a few drinks?"

I wasn't sure about the answer to that, but I was sure about one thing: "I'm a complete fucking failure. I hate this life. I just want it to be over."

He nodded his head sympathetically. "I can relate. But what you have to understand is that dead is dead. Once you step off that bridge, there is no do-over, and you're not coming back, and your daughter's gotta deal with the pain. Did you know suicide runs in families?"

My heart raced as my alcohol-soaked brain tried to process everything. A few more inches and I'd be on top of one of those cars down there. I couldn't help but wonder if it would hurt or if I'd die instantly. And what if I didn't die? What if I just ended up some helpless, disfigured vegetable who had to wear grown-up diapers the rest of my life? With my sad, pitiful luck, that's probably exactly what would happen. Yeah, I might have considered myself to be a dead man walking, but now that I gave it some thought, I knew he was right. Dead was dead, and there was no coming back from that. I took another look over the edge, and all of a sudden, I was afraid.

"What the hell am I doing?" I asked myself.

"You're doing the right thing, brother. Just take my hand so I can get you down from there."

I took his hand and he guided me down to the sidewalk.

After I'd calmed down a little, I asked him, "Was that the truth? Were you really up there a year ago?"

He looked at the railing. "Yeah, I was really up there. You still wanna die?"

"Not right now. I can't promise how I'll feel next week, a month from now, or even tomorrow, for that matter, but I thank you for your words today."

"Not a problem. Here's my card. I'm here anytime you wanna talk. Name's Martin Cain, but my friends call me Cain."

I took his card and put it in my pocket. "Nice to meet you, Cain. I'm Avery Mack."

"Avery, you mind if I give you some advice before we go our separate ways?"

I shook my head. "Not at all. Seems like you got all the answers anyway, right?"

"First off, stop worrying about what everyone else thinks. Secondly, start living for you and what makes you happy, because that's what everyone else is gonna do." He patted my shoulder and started to walk away. "Call me when you're ready to talk. I think we've got a lot in common and we can help each other out."

Krystal

4

"I can't believe you're really going through with it," I said as I stared across the table at my best friend. Monica and I were having lunch in the outdoor section of B. Smith's restaurant in the waterfront resort town of Sag Harbor. Monica had just dropped the bomb on me. Instead of spending the night in our summer rental, curled up in front of the TV, drinking cheap champagne, eating chocolate-covered strawberries, and watching the newest episode of *Mob Wives*, she was going to play peek-a-boo with her jailbird ex-boyfriend Rodney, who I couldn't stand.

Now normally I wouldn't give two shits what Monica did in her room behind closed doors. I mean hell, she was a grown-ass woman, and this wouldn't be the first time she had male company. The thing that was getting my panties in a bunch was that her fiancé, Wayne, who she was marrying in three weeks and who I happened to like a lot, had just left this morning to go back to the city.

Monica peered over her knockoff Gucci sunglasses, showing off her hazel eyes that set off her bronzed skin and light brown weave perfectly. She was a big girl, but she carried her weight well, and her gigantic titties and ass attracted men of all races.

"Damn right I'm going through with it! Rodney's got some of the best dick I've ever had, and his head game is off the charts. Can you say multiple, multiple, multiple orgasms?" she sang. The expression on her face made me think she was about to have an orgasm just talking about it.

I shook my head. "Girl, I heard you and Wayne last night. Didn't you get enough then? I mean, damn, it sounded like y'all was going at it all night long."

"We were." She smiled proudly, sitting up in her chair as she pushed her sunglasses back on her face. "And under normal circumstances, yes, it would have been enough, but..."

"But what? You gonna sacrifice your future for a fuck with a man who just got outta jail?" I gave her this look that said, *Have you no shame?*

I could not understand what had gotten into my friend. All she ever talked about was how she couldn't wait to get married so they could live together and Wayne's dick would be at her disposal all the time. Now out of the blue she was talking about that degenerate Rodney like he was Valentino himself. She was starting to sound like those whores from back home that we were always talking bad about.

She rolled her head on her shoulders sister-girl style. "Don't look at me like that. I know what you're thinking, and under normal circumstances, getting some from Wayne would be more than enough. But Krystal, Rodney's what you call a game changer, and well, I can't pass up a chance to be with him. Life is too short. Every time he touches me, he takes me to places I've never been." She said that shit with so much emotion that I almost wanted to try Rodney out myself.

"Girl, I know you didn't have me pay five hundred dollars for a bridesmaid's gown, and you're not going to get married. My God, Monica, Wayne loves you. He just bought you a house. He wants to spend the rest of his life with you." I sat back in my chair and folded my arms. Like I said, I liked Wayne. He was a nice guy and he didn't deserve to be hurt.

"What are you, crazy? Of course I'm getting married. I love my boo." She was moving her hands as she spoke, and her huge titties were bouncing up and down to emphasize every word she said. "Rodney is just, just... you know... *the one.* I know he ain't marriage material, and I damn sure wouldn't leave Wayne for him, but I can't help but sleep with him. Besides, I might not get another chance to be with him the way he keeps violating parole and getting locked up."

Now I was really confused. Was she actually going to risk her relationship and health to sleep with a guy that wasn't even, as she put it, marriage material?

"Do you even hear yourself, Monica? You sound like you've lost your mind. Is he worth it?"

"Yes, he's worth it, and yeah, you're right, I probably have lost my mind. I know I sound crazy, but I'm still going through with it because he's the one."

I wanted to grab her by the neck and choke her. "You keep talking about him being *the one*. What exactly is *the one*?"

She sighed. "He's *the one guy* that can ring your bell without even trying. He makes your palms perspire and your insides moist just thinking about him. Every woman has one, but most of us want to run when he comes around because we know we're about to do something we shouldn't. But you can't resist. It's like you're a drug addict and you're trying to quit...so you tell yourself one more fix and I'm done."

She looked at me like I was supposed to respond. I only folded my arms and raised my eyebrows like I thought she was crazy.

"Oh, come on now. Don't act like you don't know what I'm talking about."

I stared at her silently for the next five minutes as she continued to try to explain herself. Finally, she gave up and changed the subject to the shoes of a woman who had walked past our table. I'm sure she thought that I was judging her. Funny thing is, I was actually a little jealous.

"Daryl Graham," I finally mumbled as she continued to rant about how ugly the woman's shoes were. The words came out of my mouth almost as if I was afraid to say them. I wasn't even sure she'd heard what I said until she abruptly halted her rambling.

"Dow Jones?" she replied.

"Daryl Graham," I repeated, annoyed by her mispronunciation.

"Darnel who?" She waved her hand like his name was insignificant. "Who the hell is he, and what does he have to do with those ugly-ass shoes she's wearing? Please don't tell me he's the special-ed designer who made them."

"No, he doesn't have anything to do with those shoes." She looked clueless, and I contemplated changing the subject for a second before I finally admitted, "Well, for lack of a better word, he's *the one*."

She peered over her sunglasses. "Excuse me?"

"Daryl Graham is *the one*. He's my version of your Rodney."

Monica leaned forward in her chair like she was ready for some juicy details. "Where the hell did this Daryl Graham come from, and why haven't you told me about him? I done heard about Sam, J.R., Slim, and some dude named Michael, but you ain't never told me about any Darnel." She actually sounded hurt.

"His name is Daryl, Monica, okay? Daryl. And there wasn't much to tell. We were seeing each other when you were away in the navy. It didn't work out, and you were nowhere to be found."

She lowered her head. "Yeah, I know. I'm sorry I was MIA back then." Monica and I didn't talk much about the time she spent in the navy, probably because it was the best time of her life and the worst time in mine—including my short-lived time with Daryl, which I'd totally fucked up.

"Look, I know it's too little too late, but you wanna talk about it?" she asked.

I looked my friend directly in the eyes as I tried to figure out why I hadn't ever mentioned Daryl to her. Maybe it was because she'd never seemed interested in that time in my life. Maybe it was because I didn't want to share my time with Daryl with anyone. Or maybe I'd let the best thing that ever happened to me slip right through my fingers, and I thought she'd laugh at me. Truth is, everything between him and me happened so fast and seemed to end just as quickly. Whatever the reason, I guess it was time I told my best friend about the one that got away.

"Yeah, I guess I owe you that much," I said as I began to explain.

Connie

5

Before I walked out of my apartment, I turned one last time to look at my husband snoring on the sofa. It wasn't the same fake snoring I'd heard from him last night when I wanted to get intimate and he claimed to have a headache. It broke my heart to think he'd pretend like that to avoid making love to me. I was already upset that he'd had the audacity to come home after midnight the other night with some cockamamie story about how he'd attempted suicide and was rescued by some man named Cain. I let it slide because it was his birthday, but he must have really thought I was stupid, because I was sure the only person he knew named Cain was some stripper named Candy Cane, and she was probably the one who fleeced him out of his share of the rent money.

With all that being said, I still loved the man's dirty drawers and wanted to make things work between us. Somehow I was going to have to get my sexy back, and the bottom line was it all came down to my weight. It had to be, because every other area of our marriage was covered. Shit, what more could a man ask for? He had a faithful wife who kept a clean house, made all his favorite meals, and was willing, ready, and able to take him for a ride on the love train anytime he was willing. It had to be my weight.

"Avery, honey, I'm going out for a while. I'll see you later." I shook him once and he stopped snoring, but he never lifted his head.

"Where you going?" he mumbled, his head still buried in a pillow.

"I'm going for a run. I'll make you some breakfast when I get back." I was feeling good until he turned his head and raised an eyebrow.

"A what? You're going for a what?" The skeptical look on his face made me second-guess myself. Maybe I had set too lofty a goal.

"Okay, maybe not a run, but a jog," I replied confidently, which only caused him to stifle his laughter.

"Okay, a light jog, all right?" Then before he could say another word or make another gesture, I said, "A walk, dammit. Just a walk, okay? Do you think I can do that?"

"Look, I don't care what you do as long as your fat ass does something."

"What's that supposed to mean?" I asked, holding back tears.

"If you don't know what it means by now, Connie, I don't know what to tell you. I'm going to work, so I won't be here when you get back."

"Why? I thought this was your Saturday off. I was hoping we might go to a movie or go out to lunch. It's beautiful outside. We never do anything together anymore."

"Look," he said, "I'm having a hard enough time coming up with my share of the rent. I need the overtime. I'm trying to get them to give me Dave's management position when he leaves next month. Besides, do you know how expensive movies are these days? We can't afford to go to the movies."

"I don't know why not. I'm sure it's cheaper than a lap dance," I mumbled under my breath.

"What'd you say?"

"Nothin'. I said, 'I love you, honey.'" I bent over and kissed him. "Think I can get some tonight? It's been almost three weeks."

He glanced at me with this less than sympathetic look on his face. "We'll see, if I don't have a headache."

Dammit, had it really come down to this, me begging my own husband for some dick?

"Forget it. Just make sure you have your share of the rent when you come home." My good mood totally ruined now, I shot him an evil glance, then headed out the door straight for the elevator.

It wasn't until I got to the first floor that I realized I should have taken the steps to get warmed up; but by the time I stepped out onto the stoop, I saw that things were already heating up.

"What in the world are you ladies doing out on the stoop this early in the morning?" I asked, checking my watch. It was a little after seven on a Saturday morning, and half the women of the building were sitting out there in their housecoats, coffee cups in hand. "Surely there aren't any breaking news stories already."

"Girl, please. You must think we're stupid," Nancy snapped to her coanchors before directing her next comment at me. "We out here for the same reason you are." She looked me up and down. "Only thing is you got one up on us."

All eyes were on me as I stared at her, puzzled. "What in the world are you talking about?"

"I'm talking about that sweat suit you wearing. It's new, ain't it?"

That damn woman knew more about my wardrobe than I did. What, was she sleeping in my closet? "Yeah, it's new," I told her. "What about it?"

She shook her head and grinned at me. "You can play dumb if you want to, but all I wanna know is when did you take up running?"

One of her coanchors chimed in, "Right after she found out Mr. Graham up in 3B takes his morning run around the park about this time."

"You know what? You ladies are a mess." I shooed my hand at their silliness. I had no idea Daryl took morning jogs. "This ain't got nothing to do with our new neighbor and everything to do with me and my husband. I'm trying to look good for him."

"Mm-hmm, we hear you," Nancy said sarcastically.

With a smile on my face, I headed to the park, shaking my head at the women and their antics.

I got started on the walking trail and realized quickly that this was not going to be as easy as I'd thought. I was starting to feel tired after only the first few steps. Lucky for me, there were resting spots every so often. Well, they weren't really resting spots. There was equipment for joggers to stop and stretch on, but for me, they were resting spots. All I did was lean on the equipment and pray to God I didn't collapse.

"Hey there, pretty lady."

The words I heard coming from behind gave me a sudden burst of energy. My body, which was initially slumped over the piece of outdoor workout equipment, suddenly perked up like a twenty-year-old's nipples. I'd know that voice anywhere. I'd know those words anywhere. Not many people referred to me as a pretty lady—not even my own husband. And only one man had a baritone voice like that. Daryl Graham.

"Hi there, neighbor," I said as he approached. I was actually surprised to see him. Even though the ladies back at my apartment building had told me Daryl took morning runs, my mind had been on other things—like how to reignite my marriage, or even more basic, how to catch my breath.

"Look at you. First I see you taking the stairs instead of the elevator, and now you're getting your workout on in the park. You really are serious about getting in shape, aren't you?" He bent over to tie his sneaker.

"Yes, I am." I felt my cheeks getting warm, but I didn't even know why I was blushing. I seemed to lose all sense of control whenever this man was around.

"How far are you going? A mile? Two miles?" He began to stretch. Unlike me, he was using the equipment for its intended purpose.

"I was going to try and make it around the entire park. That's five miles."

He raised his eyebrows and let out a low whistle. "Impressive. I usually jog about a mile, maybe two, but five? That's a little too ambitious for me."

I blushed again, but this time I knew why. I was embarrassed. "No, no, I don't plan on jogging it. I'm going to walk it." Avery's cutting comments from this morning rang in my head.

"Oh, I see." Unlike my husband, Daryl looked supportive. "Maybe I'll walk it with you. If you don't mind."

"I can't think of anything that would make me wetter—I mean, I'd like *better*. Jesus Christ. I'd like that," I said. Gentleman that he was, Daryl acted as if he hadn't even heard my obvious faux pas.

We began our walk, me and the most handsome man I'd ever met.

"I haven't seen you around much. I guess you don't hang out on the stoop like the other ladies," he said as he gave me a charming smile.

"No, I have a job and a husband to take care of. I don't have time to be sitting around gossiping all day."

"Preach, sista!" He laughed, raising his hand as if he were in church. "Do any of them work? Every time I come outside they're out there. It doesn't matter what time."

I answered, "Oh, I'm sure a few of them have jobs, but from what I hear, they all like to sit on the stoop because they like the view." I glanced over at him, thinking, *And I can't really blame them.*

He looked puzzled. "Really? Not much of a view if you ask me. Maybe they see something I don't."

"Maybe." Was it possible this man really didn't know the effect he had on women? I couldn't help myself; I busted out laughing.

He turned to face me. "What's so funny?"

"Nothing," I replied, trying to contain my laughter. "Just a personal joke you wouldn't understand."

There was an awkward moment of silence where I just stared down at my tennis shoes; then I tried to break the tension by changing the subject to something more mundane. "So, uh, where are you from?"

"Born and raised in Queens," he said proudly. "Been in Queens all my life. I used to live in Jamaica, down by the projects."

"Southside? Whoa, that's a pretty rough area."

He shrugged. "Not really. No rougher than any other hood in the five boroughs."

"I suppose."

"What about you?" he asked. "You always live in Queens?"

"No, been here about three years. My husband and I moved here a few years ago from Long Island."

"Speaking of your husband, I haven't had a chance to meet him yet."

"Well, he's pretty busy with work. He's a salesman for Sam's."

"Cheap Sam's Furniture? I got my living room set from them."

I nodded.

"How's that working out for him?"

"It's not. He hates it. It's just something he's doing until a management position opens up or the housing market picks up again. He used to be a mortgage broker doing real good for himself. And now he's just..." I lowered my head. Thinking about all the changes going on in our life right now saddened me. Avery was so bitter. "He's just miserable."

Daryl stopped walking and put his hands on my shoulders. He waited until I raised my eyes to look at him before he asked, "Is everything all right? I'm sorry. I didn't mean to pry."

"No, it's nothing like that at all." I had this sudden urge to reach out and hug him, to thank him for the kindness he was showing me. I couldn't remember the last time a man was so interested in hearing what I had to say. For some unexplained reason, I felt like I could trust this man even though I hardly knew him.

"Mr. Graham—Daryl—can I ask you something?"

"Sure."

I swallowed my pride and asked, "What does a man really want out of a woman?"

I half expected him to start laughing, probably because it's what Avery would have done if I had asked him that question. But Daryl stayed quiet and considered his words before he answered, "The usual. A woman who is sexy, sophisticated, classy, kind, giving, sexy, gentle, submissive to a degree...and did I say sexy?" He chuckled, but when I didn't laugh with him, he realized there was something deeper going on.

He said simply, "Why do you ask?"

And with that single question, the floodgates opened. I started walking again so I wouldn't have to face him. Daryl kept his stride beside me.

With tears rolling down my cheeks, I said, "I know I shouldn't be confiding in someone I just met, but my husband doesn't look at me the same. Sometimes he won't look at me at all. And he sure as hell doesn't want to touch me. But I think you just answered my question for me. As a matter of fact, I don't even know why I asked. What man doesn't want a sexy woman by his side? And I sure as hell ain't sexy no more with all this weight on me."

"Ah, I get it." I could see him piecing it all together in his head. "That's why you take the steps and now you're out here exercising. It's for your husband."

"Yes. I've put on a few pounds since we got married a few years ago. I'm almost sure that's the reason for the change in our marriage," I admitted.

"Well, exactly how much weight have you gained?" He paused. "If you don't mind me asking."

I didn't mind. I was the one who'd brought it up. "I don't know . . . forty, fifty pounds." I shrugged, knowing that it was exactly fifty-two pounds and five ounces.

"Can I keep it real with you?" he asked, sounding hesitant for the first time.

"Please do." I sighed anxiously, fearing that this gorgeous man was about to tell me I was huge and disgusting. But I needed to hear the truth. It was the only way I could fix things in my marriage.

"That is quite a bit of a weight gain for a brotha to have to contend with." His words hurt, but then he softened the blow with, "But if he loves you, at the end of the day, he should just see it as more of you to love. I mean, hell, it should be him out here with you, not me. If you were my woman, that's how I'd see it."

There I went blushing again. "Speaking of which, why don't you have a woman? A nice guy like you, seems like you'd have them lined up on your doorstep." Technically speaking, if one counted the news crew, he actually did.

"Oh, I've got my share of friends. You'll see them coming through from time to time, but there's no one serious."

I hate to admit it, but my heart leaped at the idea that he was single.

His phone rang, and he raised his hand politely. "One second. Let me get this."

"Hello," he said, then stopped in midstride, as if whoever was on the line had surprised the hell out of him. "Yeah, wow, it has been a long time." He covered the phone. "Connie, can you give me a sec?"

I nodded and walked on ahead in order to give him some privacy. About five minutes later, he caught up to me. I couldn't quite gauge the look on his face.

"Everything okay?" I asked.

"Ex-girlfriend wants me to visit her tomorrow."

I felt a momentary twinge of jealousy, which bothered me. Why should I care about his ex? "Is that a good thing or a bad thing?" I asked.

"I don't know. A while back I thought we were gonna end up married with a house full of kids, but in the end she hurt me pretty bad."

I was touched by his openness and sincerity. It had been a long time since I'd witnessed a man exposing feelings other than anger and disappointment. It made me want to protect him.

"Sorry to hear that. What happened?"

We stopped at the next stretching station and sat down on a beam designed for balance exercises.

"Let's just say she turned out not to be who I thought she was." He looked away, clearly reliving some old hurt. "Now she's asking me to forgive her."

"Can you?"

He shrugged. "I want to, but I don't know if I can trust her. What I do know is that I loved her. Don't know if I'll ever stop."

I felt my eyes tear up again as I thought, *I wish Avery could love me that way.*

After a few sad, silent minutes between us, he took a deep breath and stood up. "Okay, enough about me and my past loves," he said, sounding renewed. "Do you really want to get rid of those extra pounds and get in shape?"

"Of course."

"Then let me help you. I exercise almost every day. And if I'm not tooting my own horn, I'd say it works out for me just fine." He flexed his muscles and struck a Mr. Universe pose. "Let me help you find what works for you."

"You're going to be my personal trainer or something?" I laughed, but it was more to cover my insecurity rather than my thinking anything was funny. With Avery's negative comments still in the back of my head, I wasn't sure I believed I could really lose the weight.

"Actually, yeah, if that's what you want to call it. I'd be your personal trainer."

I didn't want to insult him, and I truly appreciated his offer, so I got serious, even though I was scared. If I tried and then failed, I'd feel even worse than I already did. "Sure, that would be ... great," I said halfheartedly. "But how much is it going to cost me? My husband and I are on a pretty tight budget."

He thought for a minute. "You cook?"

I held my arms up and looked down at my ample figure, as if to say, *What do you think?*

He smiled at my joke. "Then let me think about a favorite meal you can prepare in return for my services."

Seeing him standing there, looking at me with not a hint of disgust in his eyes, I felt inspired to at least make the effort. I don't know what it was about Daryl, but he made me feel like I was worth something, like this shouldn't only be about Avery. Like I owed it to myself to get healthy.

"You've got a deal." I reached out and shook his hand. "When do you want to start?"

"Heck, we're already here at the park standing by a piece of exercise equipment. What do you say we get started now?"

And start we did. That man worked me out on every piece of equipment along the walking trail. Over an hour had passed by the time we headed back toward the apartment building.

"Daryl, I must say, my body is tore up, but you know what?" I stopped walking and faced him. "It feels good."

"Glad I could make you feel good." Maybe I was just imagining it, but it sounded like his voice became just a little deeper.

What they say about exercise raising the endorphins must be true, because that one little comment had me, a faithfully married woman, thinking all kinds of naughty things about other ways Daryl could make me feel good. Oh yes, I was going to enjoy working out.

Krystal

6

"Okay, I'll see you tomorrow morning, Daryl. Bye."

I was so elated when I hung up that I almost jumped out of my chair and did a jig. It had been three days since Rodney came to visit Monica. Three days during which I had to listen to her scream, beg, and plead for more at the top of her lungs. Three days since she reminded me that I too had a "Rodney" in the form of Daryl, who could have me anytime he wanted. I'd spent the better part of those three days on Facebook, reconnecting with old acquaintances and friending people I would have much rather forgotten, all in a quest to track Daryl down. I'd had absolutely no luck finding him until this morning, when I got a text from a mutual friend down south who had Daryl's phone number.

My life had been so screwed up after I stopped seeing Daryl that I'd tried to block him from my mind and pretend the relationship never happened, but now that I'd had that talk with Monica, it all came rushing back. Now Daryl was all I could think about.

You see, I was a real mess when I met Daryl. I'd just lost my mom to some very suspicious circumstances. The police and my father called it a suicide because of the e-mail my mother supposedly sent out before her death, but no one could ever convince me my mother killed herself. Sure, she was a little depressed, but what woman wouldn't have been when she found out her husband was trading her in for a younger, much thinner model? She never would have left me alone in this world. She loved me too much for that.

I couldn't get anyone to listen to me, including my dad. Don't get me wrong. I still loved my dad, but two months after my mother's death, he was already gallivanting around with a woman who was only seven years older than me. I had no doubt that she was with my father because of his money. The way I saw it, that hussy had plenty of motive to kill my mother. I still can't stand that bitch to this day.

My mom's death hurt me in ways I can't even explain, and I hated everything and everybody, including myself. I was in so much pain during that period of time. I dropped out of St. John's University during the first semester of my sophomore year and turned to drugs and thugs to numb the pain. Cocaine, Ecstasy, and bad boys with even badder reputations—that's all I desired out of life for the better part of two years.

But all that stopped and everything changed when I met Daryl. He was the first man to act like he really cared about what was going on in my life. I could talk to him, let him know what I was going through, and he actually listened. To this day, I have not met anyone who was a better listener . . . or a better handball player.

I'll never forget the first day we met when Daryl walked up behind me at the handball court over by Rochdale Village.

"Excuse me," he said. "If you got next, can I be your partner?"

I was on the court playing handball, waiting for this guy named Flex so we could go back to his place and get high on E. I'd just gotten my ass kicked by this bitch Angela and her sister Carmen because of this scrub named Johnny that I was playing with. I hated the idea of losing to those chicks again, so I barely even paid attention to Daryl's looks, just his stature, which was tall and athletic. Besides, to me he kinda looked a little corny, all decked out in his New York Knicks sweat suit with a gold chain around his neck. Who the hell did he think he was anyway, Carmelo Anthony?

I asked him, "You any good?"

"Good enough to beat their asses." He glanced over at the sisters.

"A'ight, we'll see." I gave him the once-over, then nodded. Hell, he had to be better than Johnny's scrub ass.

We played the next game as partners. Daryl hadn't lied at all. He was good enough to beat the sisters—and everyone else who challenged us that day. Our triumph on the handball court became an invitation to a celebratory drink, which I had no problem accepting since Flex had stood me up. A couple of free drinks would probably take the edge off. Who knew? Maybe I could even get Daryl to purchase some get-high.

Over drinks, I found out Daryl was about as knowledgeable and deep a man as they come, but I still didn't see any type of love connection. Oh, he was nice enough, and now that I had a chance to look at him up close and personal, there was no doubt he was fine. But he seemed a little too square for my taste. I was into roughnecks. The rougher you were, the more I liked you, and Daryl's preppy behavior seemed far from gangster. Or so I thought until these two dudes named Damon and Stork rolled up in the bar.

Now, if you're from South Jamaica, Queens, you know who Damon and Stork are. They're probably two of the biggest thugs Queens has ever produced. They were involved in everything from armed robbery to drug dealing. For a girl like me, who had a thing for thugs, just the sight of them made me wet. So when they walked over to the table, I was pretty much ready to leave Daryl by his lonesome and get with some real men.

"Yo, ain't you Daryl Graham?" Damon's eyes got small as he pointed his finger at Daryl.

They were standing about two feet from our booth, looking menacing as they waited for Daryl's reply. My poor heart started beating outta my chest. I was looking for a place to hide because Damon and Stork never went anywhere unless they were strapped. If Daryl said the wrong thing, it was about to be on and popping in that bar.

"Yeah, I'm Daryl. What's up? Do I know you?" He must have had no idea what was about to come, because he said it so nonchalantly it was almost condescending.

I pushed my chair back so they wouldn't get any of his blood on me.

"Yooooo! Stork! You know who this is?" Damon shouted. He

turned to his partner, then pointed at Daryl. His eyes were large with excitement as he gestured wildly. "This is Majestic's man, Daryl Graham, from over there by 40! This nigga is a legend."

Stork's entire demeanor softened. "Get the fuck outta here. That's Daryl Graham, *the* Daryl Graham?"

"Yeah, man, *the* Daryl Graham." Damon was smiling at Daryl, looking like he wanted to ask for his autograph. "You don't remember me, but I'm Majestic's little brother, Damon."

Daryl studied him for a second, then said, "Damn, yeah, I remember you, but you ain't so little no more. How's your brother doing? I miss that cat."

Damon hesitated. "He's upstate right now, but he's a'ight. I'm trying to put together some ends so I can send him a package next week."

Daryl reached in his pocket and pulled out a wad of cash. I watched as he peeled off five hundred-dollar bills like it was nothing.

"Put this on the books for him and tell him I said what's up. If he needs anything, tell him I said to holla. He knows where to find me."

There was a silence between them, and for a split second, I thought I saw Damon sniffle back some tears.

"Thank you, man. Thank you." Damon took the money, then gave Daryl one of those one-armed brotherly hugs that guys do. Stork did the same. Daryl was only about four or five years older than us, but they were treating him with the respect of an elder.

"Yo, ma, take care of our man," Damon said to me before he left.

I'd known those brothers for about five years, and I'd never seen them show respect to anyone the way they had to Daryl. And they weren't the only ones. I was so wrapped up in wanting to hook up with Flex and getting high that I hadn't noticed it until that moment, but Daryl had a way about him. He was the kind of guy who made all the women want him and all the men fear him. Even wearing that corny-ass sweat suit, his presence couldn't be ignored. He was larger than life; he dominated the room. All of a sudden I was totally turned on. Daryl was everything I wanted—a preppy thug.

I ended up spending the night with Daryl...and the next night and the next until it was known by everyone that I was his and he was mine. He wouldn't tolerate my drug use, and to be honest, I had no desire to use drugs when I was with him. Within a week I was drug-free.

I'd learned a lot of things the hard way in my dealings with the losers, drug dealers, and thugs, but Daryl taught me something none of them even had an inkling about. Daryl taught me about love. Oh, I knew how to have sex. A sista knew how to work her hips and make a nigga throw his back out, but what I didn't know was what it was like to make love. Even better than what he taught me, Daryl gave me something I'd been sorely missing ever since my mother died. Daryl loved me. I know he did.

At least he did until I screwed up everything.

Avery

7

"Your destination is on your right. You have arrived," the mechanical GPS voice announced as I pulled in front of what could only be described as a McMansion. I double-checked the address to be sure I wasn't at the wrong place. Sometimes those GPS devices get confused and take you to the wrong address. I'd had that happen a few weeks ago when I was going to Fourth Avenue in East New York, Brooklyn, and ended up over the bridge on Fourth Avenue in Manhattan.

"Whoo-wee!" I whistled as I got out of the car and walked along the long driveway to the front door of the huge brick colonial. The house looked like it had come straight from the pages of *House Beautiful* magazine. There was a Mercedes sports coupe and a Bentley in the driveway. Kind of reminded me of my old life when I had money.

"Who is it?" a sultry female voice called through the intercom when I rang the bell.

"It's Avery Mack. I'm here to see Cain."

That's right. I was there to see the same Cain who had talked me down from that railing on the bridge. We'd been corresponding via phone and text for the past few days and struck up what appeared to be a genuine friendship. The man should have been a motivational speaker because every time I hung up after one of our conversations, I felt all amped up and energized, like I could do anything. I hadn't felt like that since before I lost my job.

When the mahogany double doors opened, the vision before me almost literally took my breath away. The woman standing before me was so beautiful that I gasped involuntarily. She resembled Nicki Minaj with her pink hair, tiny halter top, and low-cut capri pants. I could see a butterfly tattoo between her large, symmetrical breasts that were on full display. I struggled to tear my eyes away from her cleavage to look at her eyes as she tipped down her designer sunglasses and fluttered her long, fake lashes at me.

"So, you're Avery?" she asked with a smile.

"Yeah, that's me." I swallowed deeply, trying to keep my cool, even though I was feeling weak in the knees over the simple fact that this gorgeous being knew my name.

"I'm Holly. Cain didn't tell me you were so cute." She pivoted around on one foot and started walking away, then turned her head to look at me over her shoulder. "C'mon in."

I gladly followed. Her stilettos clicked on the marble floor as her ample hips swayed back and forth. I could see another butterfly tattoo on the top part of her right butt cheek, which was visible over her low-cut pants. She had one of the nicest asses I'd ever seen. Kind of reminded me of Connie's ass back in the day. The damn thing almost had me hypnotized as she sashayed in front of me. I had no idea what I was getting into, but I found myself more alive and excited as a man than I'd felt in years.

"Cain's out back by the pool," she said. "He's been waiting for you, and so have we." She walked through French doors to the backyard, where a large, kidney-shaped pool and waterfall sat in the center of a parklike yard. I felt like I was on an episode of *MTV Cribs*. I was so busy checking out the view that I didn't think to ask who she meant by "we."

"Avery," Cain called out. He was stretched out on a white leather chaise with a beautiful bikini-clad woman on each side, like he was Hugh Hefner. One woman was Asian with long hair, and the other one was a platinum blonde Marilyn Monroe throwback. The Asian one plucked an olive from a dry martini and fed it to Cain while the blonde rubbed lotion on his legs. I had to admit my new friend Cain was becoming more fascinating by the minute.

Cain stood and gave me a brotherly hug. "Welcome to my casa.

Mi casa es su casa." Cain turned around and smacked the blonde woman on the ass just hard enough to get her attention. "Cindy, hon, can you go get Avery a martini. No, scratch that. Make him a virgin piña colada." She kissed his cheek and headed toward the house without another word.

Cain turned back to me. "I would offer you a drink, Avery, but alcohol doesn't seem to agree with you. You might wanna lay off it for a while."

He was only half joking, but I couldn't blame him for saying it, considering how drunk I'd been the night we met. "Yeah, you're right. It's probably for the best."

Cain nodded. "Holly, Kim, you girls go help out Cindy. I wanna talk to Avery alone for a while."

"But what about the party?" the pink-haired sister asked, looking genuinely disappointed. "I was hoping to get to know Avery."

"We'll get the party started after Avery and I talk. It will be just a few moments, promise."

They gave him no further argument, like he was a king and they were his loyal subjects. Before she left, Holly gave me a seductive wink and a smile, and all the blood rushed to my groin. I don't think I need to explain what was going through my head.

I looked at Cain. He was chuckling. "She's beautiful, isn't she?"

"Yes, very. She's not your daughter or girlfriend or anything, is she? If so, I was just looking." I hoped he didn't think I was trying to be disrespectful, because I would flip if someone my age looked at my daughter the way I'd been looking at Holly.

"No, no." He motioned for me to sit down. "We're all friends here. Friends with benefits, I might add, and from the way Holly was looking at you, she wants to be your friend. I'm sure you're going to *benefit* before you leave here."

"She's a little young for my taste. I've got a daughter about her age." Although there was no denying how sexy Holly was, I wasn't lying one bit when I said I preferred my women a little older. I'd been lusting over Jerri, this fine-ass thirty-seven-year-old bookkeeper from work for a while now. We'd been flirting back and forth for the past few months, ever since I found out she was getting divorced. Unfortunately, she put up the stop sign big time when one of the bigmouth sales associates told her I was married.

"You like 'em a little older. I can understand that, but are you saying you'd kick Holly outta bed?" He gave me a cross-eyed look.

I lifted my eyes in the direction of the women's retreating backsides. Damn, Holly did have a nice ass. I could still smell her perfume wafting on the air. "No, I'm not saying that at all. I'm just stating a personal preference in women."

Cain said, "I'll have to remember that next time I invite you over. Make sure I have some of my more mature friends stop by."

"Now that'll work. I like 'em thick, not fat. I got fat at home," I joked halfheartedly.

"Well, that's a relief. For a second there I thought I was going to be hanging out with a damn prude." Cain sat down on a chaise next to me. "Besides, my friend, you need to live a little, expand your horizons. I know I don't have to tell you that you're not getting any younger. Take it from me. There's nothing like some twenty-something-year-old pussy to keep you young." He flexed his arms to display his well-toned muscles.

At that point, I was more than willing to test out his theory, especially since I'd already made up my mind that if the opportunity presented itself I was going to fuck the hell outta Holly's fine ass. But before I got myself all caught up in Cain's little world, I needed some answers.

"Cain, what am I doing here? Don't get me wrong. I appreciate your hospitality, but you said you had something you wanted to talk to me about face-to-face." It's not every day a man gets invited to a mansion where beautiful women are ready to screw him. Some things are just too good to be true, and this was feeling a little like one of those times. I mean, could this guy really be doing all this simply because he felt bad for me?

Cain leaned back in his chair and studied me for a minute. I couldn't read his expression to know if I'd offended him. Finally, he said, "I do have something to talk to you about." He sipped his martini. "I only wanted to loosen you up and make sure your head was screwed on right first."

I didn't say anything. I needed to see where he was going with this.

"How you doing anyway, man? You all right?" he asked. He was saying the right things, and his face wore the appropriate look of concern, but I wasn't a hundred percent convinced that it wasn't an act. Of course, I barely knew the guy. This was the first time I'd ever met him face-to-face when I was sober. Even though he'd saved my life, I wasn't about to let this virtual stranger become my shrink.

I chose to keep my answer short and to the point. "I'm doing better."

"Okay, I'll accept that for now," he said, then tried to pry more out of me. "How's work going?"

"Work sucks." I shrugged. "But I can see a light at the end of the tunnel. It looks like I'm next in line to be promoted to store manager. With any luck, I'll be making another twenty, thirty grand, and that will point me in the right direction."

"Hope it works out for you." He said it sarcastically, and I got the distinct feeling he didn't believe things were going to work out in my favor. "How about your marriage? How's that working out for you?"

This time I was more honest. "It isn't. My wife's not a bad woman, but I have nothing in common with her anymore. Heck, most nights I hate to go home after work." I lowered my head. "She's so big. I'm physically repulsed by the woman." It was embarrassing having to admit this to a man who was surrounded by gorgeous women with *Playboy*-worthy figures.

He shook his head. "Wow, that's not good . . . not good at all."

"Tell me about it."

"If it's like that, why stay married? Why don't you ask her for a divorce?"

"Where the hell am I gonna go?" I asked. "I can barely pay my share of the rent now."

"Avery, you sound miserable. You haven't been thinking about killing yourself lately, have you?"

"Nah. I'm good. I'm not that guy anymore."

Cain actually laughed at me. "You can't lie to me, Avery. Did you forget we've both been down the same road? I know what it's like to want to end it all. That doesn't just go away. Deep down, you still feel like your life isn't worth shit. Like you have no real purpose, and if you died tomorrow, it would be more of a blessing than a curse." He spoke with total confidence about thoughts I'd barely even admitted to myself. I felt like he was reading my mind.

"Tell me I don't know what I'm talking about," he challenged. "Tell me you woke up today looking forward to going to work."

I couldn't tell him anything because he already had the answer, and I hated it. "What are you, some type of priest or something?" I asked. "Is that why you asked me here? You planning on saving my soul?"

"No, I'm no priest. Far from it. But I do want to give you an opportunity to truly change your life, give you a reason to live."

He stood up and started pacing beside the pool as he continued, "I wanna help you feel important again. Like the man I'm sure you used to be."

"Nice speech, but I don't see how you expect to do that, especially in this economy. Unless you're a magician or something."

"Avery, look around you. Look at this house. Look at these women. You think they do that for no reason?" he asked. Then he answered his own question. "No, they like hanging out with a rich and powerful motherfucker who drives a Mercedes, takes them out to fancy restaurants, buys 'em Birkin bags like he's buying sodas, and takes them on exotic vacations."

Something wasn't adding up about Cain's story. I asked, "How did you get all this? I thought you told me you were turned down for a partnership last year." How could a man with all of this have stood on the same bridge I did, ready to jump, only a year ago?

The look on his face told me he understood my skepticism, but he didn't seem offended. "I did lose my job. But when I stepped off that ledge, I decided that instead of ending my life, I was going to change it. So I put away the negative and made a plan to achieve all the things I wanted out of life. I think it's time you did the same."

I wanted details. If what he was saying was true and I could be living large like this in a year, then I definitely wanted in. "So what exactly did this plan of yours entail?" I probed.

Cain sipped the last drop from his drink and gazed down into his glass like a tea leaf reader looking into the future. "First, I told my boss he could kiss my ass."

"I'll say this much about you—you have some balls." I felt energized by the idea of saying, "Fuck you," to the powers that be. Plenty of days I wished I had the guts to do that at Cheap Sam's. "What about your cheating wife?"

"Oh, that bitch. I got rid of her two-timing behind as fast as I could. I gave her everything: the house, the car, my best friend, and the fucking dog. I didn't want anything other than closure. Luckily my kids were grown, so I could just walk away." He sat back on the chaise, looking like a man who was totally at peace with his life. "I got rid of the job, I got rid of the wife, and I got rid of the cancer. See, they all fed on each other."

"What do you mean?"

"When you have negative people in your life, they become like a cancer. In fact, I'm in remission now that I've kicked all this craziness outta my life and started living for me."

The more I heard, the more I was intrigued. It was like watching one of those late-night infomercials, the kind where they show Average Joe and his wife, who bought a DVD and learned the secret to success. The kind where a motivational speaker makes you believe Joe and his wife went from living in a trailer to living in a beachfront mansion. Shoot, if it could happen to them, why couldn't it happen for me? That's how Cain was making me feel.

"What's the secret formula?" I asked. If this was one of those infomercials, I'd already be dialing the 1-800 number.

Cain leaned forward dramatically. "You wanna know what it is?"

"I do." I was on the edge of my seat. "What?"

"You've got to live like you're dying. That's the only way you're going to enjoy life. Act as if you only have one day to live."

He leaned back again and let that thought sink in for a minute. Then he asked, "What choices would you make?"

I couldn't answer right away. I'd heard the cliché before, "live like you were dying," but I'd never really thought about what that would mean in my own life.

"I gave you two pieces of advice the other day: stop worrying about everyone else and what they think, and start living for what makes you happy." Cain looked around his spectacular yard as if to send the subliminal message, *All this could be yours.*

"Now," he said, "let me give you some more advice. They say that money is the root of all evil. Well, call me the devil because I'm here to offer you plenty of money."

"Doing what?"

Cain laughed off my question and said, "Come on in the house. I want you to taste the good life. Then, after you go home and sleep on it, you'll give me a call—when you're ready to start living again."

Benny

8

I watched in amazement from my bedroom window as Ms. Nancy gently kissed her husband before he made his way past the other ladies sitting around the stoop and into the truck that carted him off to work. That lady sure deserved an Oscar for the performance she'd just given, acting like the dutiful, loving wife. She knew good and well that by the time he hit the Belt Parkway, she would be knocking on our door, and by the time he got to work, she would be in Pop's bed, having her head knocked up against the headboard. This was their routine whenever Pop shifted from the day shift to the night shift.

Like clockwork, there was a knock on the door. I stuck my head in my father's bedroom. He was sprawled out across his queen-sized bed with a sheet covering half his body. "Pop, I'm pretty sure that's Ms. Nancy at the door. Want me to let her in?"

He lifted his head and glanced at the clock radio, then immediately shut his eyes again. He had barely been home from work two hours, and he obviously needed more sleep. He wasn't going to pass up this opportunity, though.

"Might as well," he said. "It's been over a week, and she ain't gonna let me rest until she gets some."

"Didn't you have Ms. Pam up here yesterday?"

He lifted his head and opened one eye to look at me. "What, are you keeping score for me or something?"

"Nope, just worried about you. You keep messing with all these women and you might end up dead from a heart attack—or worse,

one of their husbands. Besides, you ain't no spring chicken no more,"
I joked.

"What!" He threw a pillow at me, fully awake now. "I'll have you
know, if they'd let me, I could handle both those broads at the same
time."

"Okay, player-player. Look, I'll see you sometime tonight. I'm
gonna head up to Fordham. See if I can get a couple of my classes
changed before the semester starts next week."

"A'ight, son. I'll see you tonight. You good on cash?"

"Yeah, I'm good."

I left his bedroom and went to let in Ms. Nancy. She was standing
there in the doorway, fidgeting like a crackhead looking for a fix.

"Hey there, Ms. Nancy."

"Hey, Benny. Your daddy home?" she asked with a smile.

I nodded politely, though I wanted to laugh. That woman knew
darn well that he was home. Shoot, she knew everything happening
on our block and in our building at all times. When it came to Pop,
she knew his schedule better than he did.

"He's down in his room." I stepped out of the way and she sashayed
down the hall. I had to give it to her; I could see what Pop saw in her.
She had a nice figure for a woman in her forties.

By the time I got downstairs to the stoop, all the old hens had
taken their horny tails back inside their apartments. They'd been
spending more time outside than usual these past few days. It didn't
take a rocket scientist to figure out that they were hoping to catch a
glimpse of Daryl from 3B. Without Ms. Nancy to keep them all riled
up, though, I guess they'd decided to take a break.

I headed out of the apartment building in hopes of getting to the
Bronx without incident. I'd made it down the steps and was just about
to break toward the bus stop when I heard the sound of screeching
tires.

"Yo, college boy! Let me holla at you a second."

"Shit," I mumbled.

I knew who it was without even turning toward the car. His name
was Leroy Johnson, and he and his boys were some local thugs I'd

gone to high school with. Recently they'd become my worst fucking nightmare come true. Now, I wasn't no punk, but I also wasn't a fool. Leroy and his bunch of hoodlums weren't something to play with.

Leroy had been trying to jump me into his gang ever since I graduated high school two years ago. He'd been coming at me a lot harder lately because, as he told me, they had "some things in the works that required a brainy brother." I'd been ducking him the better part of the summer, purposely laying low with hopes that they wouldn't spot me. With any luck, they'd get arrested or wind up dead before I had to tell them no. Unfortunately, my luck had just run out.

"Ay, yo, Benny, did you hear my man talking to you?" That was one of Leroy's boys, probably the one they called Muscles. He'd gotten the nickname for the reason you'd expect; he was the most muscular son of a bitch I'd ever met.

The thought of running back in the building came to mind, but that was dead when I heard the car doors slam. If I tried to run, they'd be able to cut me off in a flash. So I turned toward the voices. It was Leroy and Muscles all right.

"Benny, where you been?" Leroy asked.

"I been around," I said, shrugging meekly.

"Yeah, well, we ain't seen you," Muscles said.

I turned my attention to Muscles and flinched when I saw the black teardrop tattoo underneath his right eye. I wasn't anybody's gangbanger or thug, but I knew the legend behind those teardrop tattoos. I sure didn't want to be the reason for him getting another one tattooed underneath the existing one.

"I been around, y'all. Ask anyone." I was trying to keep it together, but my voice cracked.

Leroy smirked, patting my shoulder condescendingly. "You know what, Benny? Don't worry about it. The fact that you're here now is all that counts. Where you headed?"

"Oh, I'm, uh, just headed up the block to the bus stop," I stammered, praying that they were going to let me go. "I gotta go up to my college and do a few things."

"Then it looks like I'm right on time," Leroy said. "What do you say I give you a ride and we can, you know, talk about *that thing*? Did you get a chance to look it over?"

"Oh, yeah, well, about that..." *Damn, damn, damn!* If only I'd left a minute earlier, I might have dodged this bullet. The last thing I wanted to talk about was "that thing."

I was in a spot, but I tried to stay calm and think my way through it before I said the wrong thing. *Okay, Benny, you gotta think like Pop. How would he handle this?*

One thing I knew for sure was that my father wouldn't back down. I took a deep breath, then straightened out my back, holding my head up high. "Look, Leroy, I'm sorry, but I made up my mind. I just can't come through for you on that, man."

Every muscle in my body was tense as I waited for him to react. At first he stood there and stared me down. It probably surprised him when that wasn't enough to make me change my answer. He glanced at Muscles, who looked like he was about to rip my head off, and then back at me. I nearly pissed myself when he roared out in laughter.

"Do you hear that, Muscles? Benny here is a riot." The veins in his neck seemed to throb with each wave of laughter. "He's a straight-up comedian. He's got his chest all pumped up, talking about he's made up his mind."

Muscles joined in the laughter for a second, and then just like that, Leroy stopped. He glared at me and said, "You know, you might be real smart with computers and shit, college boy, but you ain't as smart as I thought you were. 'Cause if you were, you'd know that I do all the thinking around here."

Muscles took a step closer. He looked like he was itching to kick the shit out of me.

"Let me make myself clear," Leroy continued. "I wasn't asking you a damn thing. I was telling you. Now, get your ass in the car before I put my foot in it."

I took a breath, then let it out slowly, trying to keep my composure even though I felt like I was ready to pass out. "Look, Leroy, I really do appreciate you guys including me in your plans and all, but I'm not getting in your car or robbing no jewelry store with you."

"Who said anything about you robbing a jewelry store? You just gonna be the lookout after you disable the alarm system," Leroy explained simply.

Knowing I was somewhat of an electronics whiz, Leroy and his boys had approached me a few months back about this alarm system they were supposedly buying. They said they were going to open a bodega and wanted to see if it was a reliable alarm system. They had the model number and the whole nine. Stupid, naive me looked at it as a challenge to see if I could disarm it. It turned out to be a simple system. I told him he shouldn't buy one because a guy like me could disarm it in a heartbeat. Stupidest thing I'd ever said.

That's when Leroy told me about his real plan. They were going to rob Goldberg Jewelers, the biggest jewelry store in Queens, and I was going to disarm the alarm system for him.

"Nah, man, I'm sorry, but I can't be a part—" Before I could finish my sentence, I felt the full force of Muscles's huge fist in my gut. I doubled over and struggled to catch my breath. I'd had my share of school yard scrapes, but I'd never been hit that hard in my entire life.

"Dammmmn, that shit hurt, didn't it? I know that shit hurt," Leroy mocked, grabbing his stomach. "Now, if you don't get your ass in the car, I'm gonna have my man Muscles do more than that to your face."

"I bet you don't."

I'd like to say that I'd found the courage to speak those words, but they didn't come from me. They had come from behind me.

Muscles and Leroy turned toward the voice. "Oh yeah, and who the hell are you, his daddy?"

"As a matter of fact, I am," Pop responded as he made his way out of the apartment building and onto the stoop. All he needed was some theme music, and he would have looked like Shaft in a wife beater and jeans. "And now that you know who I am, who the hell are you?"

"We're a couple of your son's buddies from high school. Isn't that right, Benny?"

"Buddies? I don't think so. I know all my son's friends," my father said, "and trust me; you're no friend of Benny's. Now get the hell away from my kid!"

"Sounds like you calling me a liar, old man, and I hate being called a liar." Leroy took a few steps toward Pop as I felt Muscles grab the back of my neck, jerking me straight up.

Pop stood his ground. "I don't care what you like. I want you to get the hell away from my son and get the hell outta here."

"You hear that, Muscles? College boy's daddy wants us to leave," Leroy said with a smirk. "I guess we better go then."

Muscles let go of my neck, and for a split second, I thought they were actually going to leave.

"You okay, son? I was looking—" Pop never finished his sentence because he was damn near knocked off his feet by a haymaker.

"Pop!" I tried to run to his aid, but Muscles slammed me down on the concrete. He kicked me in the ribs a few times to make sure I stayed put and then went to help Leroy stomp the shit out of my father.

I was struggling to get up, praying they weren't going to kill my father, when out of nowhere, Daryl appeared on the scene. He spun Muscles around and punched his privates like they were a speed bag. Muscles doubled over, and Daryl planted a foot in his face so hard that Muscles fell right to the ground. It was like watching a superhero take out the villain in one of those comic books turned into a movie.

Once Daryl finished with Muscles, he turned his attention to Leroy. He pulled the Thug Master off my father and slammed him to the sidewalk so hard that he had to have seen stars. Down but not totally out, a bloodied Muscles came charging at Daryl like a bull; but just like a matador, Daryl managed to move quickly to the side and get the raging bull in a headlock.

"If you don't get out of here and take your friend with you, I'm gonna break your fucking neck," Daryl seethed through gritted teeth.

Muscles wasn't about to give up that easily. From his bent-over position, he was able to get some leverage and started lifting Daryl off the ground. Daryl still wouldn't release Muscles from the headlock. He started pounding his fist into Muscles's face.

They tussled to the ground, where Muscles tried to pull out a gun. Things could have turned tragic in a heartbeat, but instead, Daryl quickly wrestled the gun away from Muscles and turned it on him.

Daryl aimed the gun at Muscles, who still looked like he was going to try to jump bad again.

"I wish you would," Daryl spat. "'Cause to the cops, this ain't gonna look like nothing but self-defense."

I don't know if it was his words, the menacing look, or the gun in Daryl's hand, but Muscles stopped dead in his tracks.

"Obviously y'all don't know who you're fucking with, so you might wanna ask somebody." Daryl threw up something that looked like a gang sign, and Muscles's eyes became large. I couldn't be positive, but he almost looked like he had a little fear. "Now, like I said, you might want to get your boy and get the hell out of here."

Muscles helped Leroy up off the ground, and they leaned on each other as they limped to their car.

As we watched them drive away, my father said, "Daryl, I don't know what to say except thanks." His face was bruised and he probably had a few broken ribs, but thank God, he was alive. "You saved me and my boy."

"Don't thank me," he replied. "That's what neighbors are for."

From that moment on, Daryl Graham was no longer just my neighbor. He was my new hero.

Krystal

9

Wow! was the only thought that ran through my mind as I tried to savor the last spasms of the best orgasm I'd ever had. Of the many, many orgasms I'd had that day, it was hard to pick the best, but yeah, I'd say this one was it. Daryl had always been good in bed, but he'd actually taken things to the next level this time. There's something to be said for reunion sex, I guess.

I exhaled slowly, then looked down to see him sliding up from between my legs until his lips met mine. I could taste myself as he kissed me, and I bit his lower lip. My hands roamed over the array of tattoos along his muscular shoulders and back. The feel of his Adonis-like body pressed against me sent mini-tremors down my spine...and to that special place that he'd so masterfully pleased with his lips and tongue only a few moments earlier.

I gasped as he positioned himself between my legs, sliding into my slippery canal with ease. He was my own personal Kryptonite, making me weaker the further he pushed himself into me.

We'd barely even said hello earlier. He kissed me at the front door of my vacation rental and then swept me off my feet. I didn't protest at all when he carried me into my bedroom and undressed me. The way he looked at me, I felt like I was the most precious thing in the world, and I belonged to him and only him. He kissed me from head to toe, paying extra-special attention to all my erogenous zones.

And to think I was scared to death of how he would react when I first opened the door.

Truth be told, I almost hadn't recognized Daryl at first. He'd filled out and gained a little weight, not to mention the fact that he'd gone from cornrows to a faded haircut and beard. Not that I'm complaining. He looked sexy as hell with a beard.

"Has anyone ever told you that you're the greatest lover ever?" *And that your dick is the absolute perfect fit for this pussy?*

He moved his hips and hit that spot inside me, making me gasp and jump. "Yeah, just one that I can remember."

"Who was she?" I asked, suddenly feeling a little jealous.

"It was about five years ago," he answered without missing a beat with his gyrations. "Fine little thing. A college girl, if I remember. She kinda reminds me of you."

I finally caught on. "Well, dammit, she sure as hell didn't lie."

He kissed me gently and then pushed up on his arms. I looked up into his eyes as he hovered above me, grinding his hips to get even deeper. I smiled when I saw the Jewish star pendant hanging from a chain around his neck.

"Is this the one I bought you? I can't believe you still wear it." I reached out and touched it, running my hand along its edges.

"It sure is."

He stared at me with this adoring expression, as if there was more he wanted to say but couldn't. I knew how he felt. I also had a lot on my mind, remembering how the whole world seemed to fade into the background whenever we were together.

How did I ever give him up?

I spoke to him in a whisper, looking deep into his eyes. "I'm so sorry. I didn't mean to hurt you. If I could do it all over again . . ."

He shook his head, then placed his lips over mine, kissing me quiet. "I know. It's okay. I forgave you a long time ago."

"How?" I asked. How could he forgive me when I'd committed the worst of sins? This man, this wonderful man, had saved my life, gotten me off drugs and back in school. Meantime, I had taken away the one thing, the only thing, he'd ever asked me for without even giving it a second thought. You don't forgive a woman who does that, and you damn sure don't forgive a woman who aborts your child against your wishes. Do you?

I didn't even know I was pregnant at the time, but it didn't take Daryl long to figure it out. He knew my cycle like clockwork, and when I didn't have my period on time, he made the declaration that I was with child and needed to take a pregnancy test. When I protested and said it must be something hormonal and I was probably just late, he went right down to the drugstore and picked up a First Response test kit. You should have seen his face when he saw the double pink lines—like he'd won the damn lottery. He was too hyped to even notice my disappointment.

"This doesn't scare you at all?" I'd asked.

"No. You're gonna be a great mom," he kept repeating. "A great mom."

What Daryl didn't know, or perhaps wasn't ready to hear, was that I wasn't going to be a great mom because I wasn't going to be a mom at all. I didn't want or need a baby then or now. I wished I could sue the damn pharmaceutical company that made my birth control pills, because I'd followed their instructions to the letter and they'd literally ruined my life. Hell, I was only twenty-one and had finally gotten back into school. I couldn't have a baby—not then.

A few weeks later, I pretended to go to class when actually I was going to a women's clinic in Long Island to have an abortion.

I knew Daryl would never be able to forgive me, so I had my lie all planned out. I told Daryl I'd had a miscarriage and we'd have to try again; meanwhile, I started taking a stronger birth control pill. He was pretty devastated, but things finally went back to normal—until my credit card bill came in and he questioned the charge to Planned Parenthood. I'll never forget the look of hurt and pain on his face. I was sure he'd never forgive me when he walked out that night and didn't return.

And now here we were, making love again.

"Do you really forgive me?"

At first, he didn't give an answer in words. He just kept kissing me as we made love. Finally he said, "I forgive you because I love you."

"And I...love...you," I moaned as I savored the feeling of him deep inside my walls.

"Besides, we can always make another baby, right?"

He gave one final thrust that hit the right spot, and I could barely breathe, let alone speak. A beam of bright sunlight danced through my mind as I arched my back and exploded in ecstasy.

When the waves of pleasure finally subsided, I lay there with my eyes closed, spent. I felt happier than I'd been in a long, long time until I realized Daryl hadn't collapsed in exhaustion beside me. In fact, I felt him still hovering over me. I opened my eyes and saw him staring down at me with a less than satisfied look on his face.

"What's wrong?"

"You didn't answer my question," he said.

"What question?" I wasn't being facetious. In the throes of passion, I hadn't really been concentrating on his words. I was too busy enjoying the way he made my body feel.

"I said we can always make another baby. I want to know if you agree."

Talk about killing that after-sex glow. "Daryl, do we have to talk about this now?" I didn't want to think about a baby. I wanted him to make love to me over and over and over again.

He rolled off of me and looked up at the ceiling. "Yes, I think we should talk about this now. I mean, you said you love me, and I told you I love you, which means we never really stopped loving each other. And we only broke up because you had an abortion. I need to know if there's a future in this or if this is only a onetime thing. If it is, I'm cool with that, but I need to know."

"Look, I'm not going to hurt you ever again," I assured him, kissing the top of his head. I was becoming slightly irritated but trying to hide it. All I wanted to do was cuddle and savor this moment. I hate to admit it, but I was willing to say whatever I had to, to make sure he didn't get up and leave. "We can have as many babies as you want, as long as you continue to make me feel like this."

I felt Daryl finally relax as he pulled me into the crook of his arm.

"This is where I want to be," I said as I kissed him.

"You sure this time?"

"Mmmm-hmm." I nodded, suddenly feeling sleepy. I just wanted to conk out and doze for a while. That's what good loving will do for you.

Unfortunately, Darryl still wanted to talk. "I want us to start a family, babe. See, I got a new place. Maybe you can move in. I'd like to buy a house in a year. I just need a little bit more time." He was sounding more excited with each word. How the hell did this man have so much energy after all the sex we'd had?

"Aren't you getting ahead of yourself?" I asked, fighting to keep my eyes from closing. This was probably the time I should have told him about my life and the things that were going on in it, but I was too damn tired.

"Maybe, but we've got a lot of time to make up for. So what do you say? Wanna move in?"

"That sounds like a plan," I murmured. "But we can talk about that over lunch. Right now I need a nap."

"I guess I knocked you out, just like old times, huh?" he said, his voice full of pride. I wasn't mad at him for being proud, though. He still had the touch; in fact, he was even better. I was feeling weak as a kitten.

"Yep, you sure did."

He pulled the duvet over my shoulders and wrapped his arms around me again. With a happy sigh, I drifted off to sleep.

Benny

10

"Hey, Benny, what's up, my man?"

I looked up from my Kindle to see Daryl coming up the stairwell, carrying a bag of groceries. It was good to see him. He'd been kind of MIA ever since he saved our asses from Leroy and Muscles the other day.

"Nothing much, Daryl. How you been? You're looking mighty chipper." I stood from where I was sitting on the stairs to greet him.

"I don't know about chipper, but I'm happy as hell. Been spending time out in the Hamptons with a friend, getting a little sun, some rest, and a little something else." He came up the steps and gave me a pound and a snap.

He noticed the e-reader in my other hand. "That one of those Kindles?"

"Yeah, it's a cool little gadget. I was reading this biography about Steve Jobs, the founder of Apple. Pretty interesting stuff."

"Reading in the stairwell?" he said with a laugh. "I heard of people reading in the bathroom. Matter of fact, I do that myself. But you're taking it to another level."

I shrugged. I was used to people around here calling me nerdy, so I didn't know whether he was making fun of me.

"Your pops is right. You really are a big brain. That's good, man."

"Thanks." I relaxed, knowing for sure now that it was a compliment.

"So, big brain, why you in the stairwell instead of the comforts of your own home?"

"Oh, yeah, well, Pop has *company*, so I'm just chilling out here until he's finished. I'm, uh, you know, tryin' to give him a little privacy."

"I heard that. Seems likes your pops be having a lot of company," Daryl said with admiration in his tone.

"Yeah, he does," I said with a halfhearted laugh.

I guess Daryl picked up on the fact that I wasn't too enthusiastic about Pop's extracurricular activities. "That's cool," he said. "You don't have to hang out here in no stairwell. Not when I'm around at least."

He walked past me to the entry to the third floor. "Besides, don't I owe you an ass whipping in that new *Madden 2013*? You were talking junk about my Cowboys, weren't you?"

Madden 2013 versus reading in the hallway—it was a no-brainer. With Kindle in hand, I followed Daryl to his apartment. Within minutes, we were sitting on the sofa with controllers in hand, going at it in a game of *Madden*.

"A'ight, youngin', I guess you do have some skills," Daryl admitted after I scored on him for the third time.

"I can do a little something," I said as I continued to whip his butt. "But what I wish I could do was fight like you. What was that you was using the other day on Leroy and them, some type of martial arts?"

"Something like that. I used to do a lot of MMA back in the day, and I have a black belt in karate."

"MMA?"

"Mixed martial arts. You know, like the UFC?"

"You used to fight in the UFC?" No wonder he'd kicked Leroy's ass so easily.

He lifted his hand. "Nah, I never fought in the UFC, but I did have a couple fights for their competitor, PRIDE."

"Get the hell outta here. Really? Did you win?"

"Six wins, one loss," he said proudly.

"That's pretty good. Why'd you stop?"

"Other than the fact that I got knocked the fuck out in my last fight, it's a big commitment. I was making more money in my day job anyway." He paused for a minute and looked away, like he was remembering something. "Plus, when someone puts their hands on me or mine, I have a tendency to hold grudges and want to kill them."

"Yeah, I can understand that. That's how I feel about them dudes Leroy and Muscles. But they're gonna get theirs. My day is coming."

He offered, "I could teach you a few self-defense moves if you want."

This guy was so cool. I didn't know too many adults, other than my father, who seemed genuinely interested in me. I decided in that moment to confide in him something I hadn't even told my own father. "Nah, I got something better than karate moves. I got a guy who's gonna get me a gun next week."

Daryl hit pause on the game and put down his controller. He looked at me and said, "Whoa . . . slow your roll, young brother. Those cats ain't worth it and carrying a gun ain't you." I was surprised that he raised his voice and even more surprised he was against me having a gun after the way he punked Muscles. "Let me give you a little advice. Never let anyone change who you are inside. You're no thug. What the hell do you need a gun for?"

Was he serious with that question? He saw the way Leroy and Muscles were coming at me. "To protect me and my pops," I replied defiantly. "They ain't never gonna do that to us again."

"Look, Benny, if you want, I'll teach you how to protect yourself, but you don't need no gun."

"Why?" I pushed. "You got a gun, don't you? Tell me you don't have a gun." I stared him dead in the face, waiting for an answer.

"Look, the world I deal with is different from yours."

"Oh, really? You trying to tell me the world you supposedly live in is worse than what happened to me and Pop?"

He hesitated for a second. "Nah, I can't say that, but let me ask you something. What do you know about guns?"

I shrugged my shoulders. "Nothin' yet."

"Exactly my point. All a gun's gonna do is get you thrown in jail, and trust me, that's not a place you wanna go. Now, you don't have to worry about those cats no more. I took care of it."

"How?" Something about the way he said it made me understand that he was talking about more than just the ass whipping he'd delivered the other day.

He shifted his eyes briefly in my direction as if I shouldn't be questioning him. I got the message and sat back on the sofa.

"You're gonna have to trust me on that, Benny, but it's taken care of. You have my word on that."

"Okay, I trust you," I said, knowing there was no use in arguing with him. I knew he meant well, but I was still going to buy a gun, and no one—not my pops, not Daryl, or anybody else—was gonna stop me.

"Thanks. I appreciate that. Now tell me something. What was that all about anyway? Why were they after you?"

I really didn't want to talk about it, but if I owed anyone an explanation, it was Daryl. "They wanted me to rob a jewelry store with them," I admitted.

"You?" Daryl looked confused. "They wanted you to rob a jewelry store with them? No offense, Benny, but that doesn't even sound right."

"It does if you need someone to deactivate the alarm system."

Out of the corner of my eye, I could see Daryl nod like it made sense now. "You're that good with computers that you can crack passwords and stuff, huh?"

"Yeah, I guess," I answered, tired of talking about this. "We gonna get back to the game?" I picked up my controller, ready to play again.

When he didn't answer, I looked over at him. It was clear that his mind was not in the game but elsewhere.

"Hey, can you excuse me for a minute? I wanna get out of these clothes." He stood up with a strange sense of urgency. He nearly fell over the coffee table as he left the room. "Feel free to hit the fridge. There's some soda in there. There's beer in there too."

"I'll grab a soda if you don't mind," I said, standing up. "I can't drink beer legally for another three weeks. And trust me, you don't want my pops breathing down your neck over one beer."

"All right, then, help yourself to a soda," I heard him say as he disappeared into his bedroom.

Each apartment was pretty much the same, so I knew my way to the kitchen. I grabbed a can of soda, cracked it open, and guzzled half of it.

"Here."

I turned around. Daryl was standing there in jeans and a T-shirt. He was holding a box, which he stretched out to me. "This is for you. I hope you know what you're doing."

"What is it?"

"A Glock 9 millimeter semiautomatic."

"For me?" I was confused. Was this some sort of reverse psychology trick he was trying to pull? "I thought you said I shouldn't have a gun."

"I did, and I still feel that way, but I could tell by your eyes that you weren't listening to me. You were still gonna buy a gun, weren't you?"

I nodded slowly, embarrassed that he could read me so well. "How can you be sure those guys aren't gonna come after me again?" I asked in an attempt to explain myself.

Daryl didn't answer my question. Instead, he said, "You buy a gun on the streets, Benny, it's probably gonna have a body on it. I know this gun is clean because I bought it myself at a gun show down in Virginia. Least this way, you ever get caught with it, you're only doing a year for gun possession."

Wow. Pop would have never seen things this way. Having Daryl was like having a cool older brother. "Thanks, Daryl."

I opened up the box, grinning like it was Christmas morning.

"Don't thank me," he said. "I'm doing this against my better judgment. Your father ever finds out I gave you this and I'm the one who's gonna be dead. Now, let's go." He took the box out of my hands and threw it into a knapsack.

"Where are we going?" I asked. He was already halfway to the door.

"You ever fire a gun?"

"No," I said honestly, following him.

"Well, there's no reason to own one if you don't know how to use it. This isn't a video game, Benny. This damn thing can take a man's life or get you killed. If you're gonna carry, you need to know the proper way to handle it."

I nodded but didn't say anything. Having the gun would make me feel safer, but Daryl's words kind of brought me back down to earth. Carrying a gun was no joke.

"I've got a friend who owns a junkyard over there on Liberty. I just gave him a call, and he said we can do a little practicing over there. Let's go. I wanna be back home before dark so I can get some rest. I'm supposed to be back in the Hamptons at nine in the morning."

Avery

11

My confidence was high as I returned home from work. After hanging out with Cain and the girls, I'd made the decision to take hold of my own future. I'd had a taste of the good life, along with some very good pussy, and I wanted it for myself. So I'd been working my ass off, despite the fact that I hated my job, to prove that I should get the promotion to manager.

And it had finally paid off. I'd gotten a call from my boss, Dave. He wanted to see me to discuss his transition to the main office and my replacing him as manager. I still had to go through the formal interview process with the store's owner, Sam, but neither of us was worried about that. Things were finally looking up.

"Hey, you must be Avery," I heard someone say as I placed my key in my door. I turned to see some dude that looked like he'd just jumped off the cover of *GQ* magazine. "Nice to meet you."

I shot him a wary look. "Do I know you?"

"Oh, my bad, partner." He leaned in with an extended hand, looking all cheery and shit. "Forgive me. I'm Daryl, your new neighbor in 3B. I met your wife. She's a really nice lady. You're a lucky man."

What the fuck was that supposed to mean? I almost asked him but decided it wasn't worth it to kill my good mood. At least I knew how dude knew me.

"Nice to meet you, neighbor," I said, giving him a short handshake, then turning away to let him know I wasn't interested in small talk. I didn't want dude to think I was the buddy-buddy kind that he could stop by and borrow a cup of sugar from. Not that I planned on being around this dump too long after I got my promotion.

"Nice meeting you too," he said hesitantly, probably sizing me up as well. "Listen, is it okay if I work out your wife?"

"Excuse me?" I straightened my back and turned to look him in the eye.

"Oh, sorry. Maybe that didn't come out right. Your wife's trying to lose weight. I told her I'd be her personal trainer if it's all right with you."

"She's a grown-ass woman. She can do whatever the hell she wants as long as it doesn't cost me anything." I waited for him to respond, but he only stood there with this dumb look on his face. "Now, if you'll excuse me, I just got finished working all night and I'm tired." I turned away from him and unlocked my door.

"Well, then I guess I'll see you around," he said.

Neither one of us bothered with a good-bye before I went into my apartment.

Inside, I heard soft music playing and noticed the light of a candle flickering against the ceiling, a sign that Connie was probably up. Before I could figure out a way to avoid her, she came out of the kitchen with her hands behind her back like she was hiding something. Unfortunately, she couldn't hide those rolls of fat that were hanging out of the negligee she'd squeezed into. I felt like I wanted to hurl.

"Hey, baby, you're home. Happy birthday," she said in a singsong voice.

"Birthday? It's not my birthday. You know damn well my birthday was last week," I reminded her.

"I know that, silly."

She walked toward me with a mischievous grin on her face, her hands still behind her back. She was trying her best to walk seductively, but I was repulsed nonetheless. I mean, whose idea was it to make lingerie in plus sizes? Who honestly thought anything that big could be sexy? A big woman can be cute, charming, or even precious, but sexy ain't nowhere on that list.

"I know your actual birthday has come and gone." Now she was right up on me, all up in my face. I had to give her credit; she did smell good, but that sure didn't mean I was turned on.

She pulled back and winked. She was still hiding something behind her back, and from the crazy look in her eyes, I was starting to think she was about to pull out a knife and stab me.

"But it's you who still needs to come. I never gave you your birthday present...," she said with what she probably thought was a sexy voice. To me, it sounded like nails on a chalkboard. "I know you've been wondering when you were gonna get your birthday blow job. Well, honey, the time is now...and when I get finished, you can reciprocate if you want to."

I know there are plenty of men out there who would be dropping their pants the second their wives offered to give them head. Hell, I would have been one of those men a few years ago, because in that area, Connie truly did have skills. But great oral skills or not, I couldn't do it anymore. I just couldn't. I couldn't pretend that I wasn't repulsed by the idea of making love to her, let alone reciprocating oral sex as she'd suggested. I couldn't continue to fake it.

Now, before you go thinking I'm the biggest asshole on earth, let me explain. I wasn't only thinking about myself. Connie deserved better too. I was sure there was a man out there who would love every pound of her—one of those chubby chasers or something. Unfortunately, I wasn't that man. Therefore, I was not the man for Connie. And if I truly loved her once like I claimed to, it was time I told her exactly how I felt and gave her the opportunity to move on with her life.

"Connie, we need to talk," I said with a sigh.

"Oh, we're going to talk all right, but it's going to be my lips doing all the talking, if you know what I mean." That's when she finally pulled her hands from behind her back, revealing a can of whipped cream. "And I've got a little extra something to say." Before I could respond, she grabbed me by the hand and led me over to the couch. "Sit!" She was trying her best to sound authoritative, like a plus-sized dominatrix. Still not sexy. Still not happening.

"Connie, please. Seriously, there's something I need to—"

"I said sit!" she demanded, pressing her hand up against my chest, forcing me to fall back on the couch. I threw my head back in exasperation, but I think she mistook it for ecstasy, because she dropped to her knees and began to pull off my sweatpants and boxers. I reached to pull my pants back up, but she actually slapped my hand.

"Stop it, Avery." She took hold of my manhood and put it in her mouth.

Okay, I'm not gonna lie. It felt good. It felt damn good, and there was no stopping her now. Besides, it was a birthday blow job, which meant it was all about her pleasing me. Therefore, I didn't have to reciprocate, did I?

I guess I'd forgotten how good she was, because I was getting close to that release point faster than I would have expected. It was hard to believe she was making me feel that good with her mouth. A couple of times, I had to look down just to make sure it was her mouth making me feel that way. But that's when I'd almost go limp, spotting a bulge of fat or something. Then I'd throw my head back and remind myself, *Don't look at her body; just look at her face. Matter of fact, don't look at anything. Just lay back and enjoy the moment.*

She worked her tongue like a snake, every now and then squirting the whipped cream on me and sucking it off. She did this until finally I jerked, twitched, and damn near had a seizure as I came.

With my head still thrown back and eyes closed, I sensed her standing up, her huge shadow over me. I opened my eyes to see her posing with a victorious look on her face. She was completely naked.

"Now, what was it you wanted to tell me?"

I took a deep breath and announced, "Connie, I want a divorce."

Nancy

12

It was just another typical day with me sitting on the front stoop, participating in my favorite activity—running my mouth with the girls about this and that going on in the neighborhood. There was nothing I loved more than gossiping with them, except, of course, for getting busy with Ben. So when he walked by and gave me the signal to meet him upstairs at his apartment, I didn't waste any time making an excuse to leave the girls and heading up for my weekly lesson in "fire prevention." Ben's a damn good fireman, if you ask me, and for the past few years, he'd been putting out my fire on the regular. I was sure none of the ladies believed me when I said I was going to make dinner for my family, but I really didn't give a damn what they thought. All I cared about was that Ben was waiting for me with his extra-long fire hose.

I had my hand raised to knock on Ben's door when it flew open.

"Oh, hi, Little Ben," I said in a nice tone. I was determined to be extra nice to my lover's son even though he always acted stank toward me.

"It's Benny." He rolled his eyes, throwing his backpack over his shoulder. "Looks like I have perfect timing. I'm leaving and you're coming." He yelled into the apartment, "Pop, you got company. I'm out."

He brushed by me, slightly bumping my shoulder. If he was anyone else, I would have given him a piece of my mind, but I was not about to mess up the good thing I had going with my man just because his son was a disrespectful little shit.

I entered the apartment to find Ben sitting on the couch. I had to stop and stare. For a man in his midforties, Ben kept himself in remarkable shape, and his stamina was like no other man I'd ever been with. Even more importantly, Ben appreciated a more seasoned woman like myself, which was way more than I could say for Charles, my husband of seventeen years. Ben made me feel like a woman should feel, special and appreciated. If I had to do it all over again, he was the one I'd marry.

Believe it or not, I would have preferred to honor my vows rather than have an affair, but Charles didn't love me. Charles loved some twenty-five-year-old big-tittie secretary named Brenda. That cradle-robbing son of a bitch had been screwing her ever since she started working with him five years ago. When I found out about her, I asked him to stop—hell, I begged him to stop—but he didn't or wouldn't. Now he spent most of his time with her, sneaking in the house after midnight on the regular. Rumor was that they had a baby together. Can you believe that as nosy as I am, I'd never looked into it to verify if there really was a child? I decided it wouldn't do me any good to know the truth. I was determined to stay in the marriage for the sake of my own children. They loved their father, so the two of us played nice for the public. He even gave me a kiss every morning on the stoop to keep up appearances for the ladies—right before he went to work to be with his bitch. Most days, my time spent with Ben was the only happiness I felt.

"Hey, love, how's it going?" I asked as I walked over to the couch and sat next to Ben.

"Pretty good." He wrapped his arms around me in a warm hug. "How are things with you?"

"They were going pretty good—until I went to knock on your door and ran into Benny. You know, I don't think that son of yours likes me very much. I mean, it's like he always has an attitude when he sees me."

"Oh, Benny's a good kid."

I rolled my eyes. "He may be a good student and all, but he could stand to learn a few lessons about how to respect his elders," I said, coming dangerously close to starting a fight that would ruin my chances of getting any.

Just as I expected, Ben defended his son. "Look, why don't you try to understand where he's coming from, Nancy? I'm always preaching to him about making the right choices, and then he sees me making—well, you know..."

"No, I don't know. Why don't you say it?" I folded my arms over my chest and twisted up my mouth. I knew exactly what he was trying to say, but if he was going to take his son's side over mine, I was not about to make it easy for him.

He looked me up and down. "You're a married woman."

Okay, yeah, that was true, but what the hell did Benny care? It wasn't like I was creeping on his father. That kid needed to loosen up a little bit. I'd never seen someone his age so damn uptight.

"I get all that—kind of. But I don't think it's any of his business." I said it as kindly as I could because I was still hoping to get naked within the next ten minutes, so I couldn't risk agitating Ben.

"Well, actually, it is his business," Ben corrected me. "He's my son. I'm his father. He looks up to me, Nancy. And you have to admit I spend a good amount of time with you. Take away the time I spend working, and well, I guess lately there hasn't been a whole lot of father-son time. Maybe he feels like you're taking time away from him." Ben stared off momentarily. "Which probably explains why he's been spending more and more time with Daryl over in 3B."

"Do I detect a little jealousy in your tone?" I questioned.

Ben snapped out of his daze. "Who, me? No, it's just that Benny needs a man he can look up to in his life and maybe I haven't been there the way I should. He shouldn't have to go to a neighbor when he has his father."

Shoot, I could have kicked myself. Why in the world did I bring up this subject? Now Ben was getting all sappy on me, boohooing about his parenting duties. If I didn't get him out of this funk, there was no way we were having sex.

"Yeah, I guess you're right," I said, taking his hand. "At the end of the day, if we want our kids to do the right thing, then we have to set the right example. But you're only human, Ben. And you're a damn good father."

Ben looked over at me with a gleam in his eyes. I thought it meant we were about to get busy until he jumped up from the couch.

"Do you really believe that—what you just said about setting the right example?"

"Yeah, of course, I mean—"

"Good," Ben said, cutting me off. "Stay there. I'll be right back."

"Ben, what's wrong? Where are you going?"

He didn't reply, but I heard him shuffling around in his dresser drawers, and then he reappeared in the living room with something in his hand.

"I've been thinking," he started. "It is time for us to do the right thing, and the right thing is you leaving your husband."

It took a few seconds for his words to sink in, and by then he'd already opened the box in his hand to show me an engagement ring inside.

"Ben? What is this? What are you talking about?"

"We need to make this right. Yeah, this might have started off as a sex thing, but I think both you and I know it's deeper than that now. You've said it yourself that I'm the most important man in your life. If that's true, then let's do it."

"Ben, I can't leave my husband," I said sadly.

"You can't?" he said, closing the box. "Or you won't?"

Damn. Now I knew for sure I wasn't getting any today.

Connie

13

I wished I had something to cover myself up with as I stood there naked and exposed, taking in the vile words my husband had spoken to me.

Had I really heard him right? No, I couldn't have. I know he didn't just say, "Connie, I want a divorce." Especially not after what I'd done for him. This might sound vulgar, but I could still taste him in my mouth, for God's sake. My jaws were locked in an open position, and it was only partly from the shock of his words. I mean, I'd sucked his dick for ten minutes straight. I knew I'd be feeling the pain in my jaw for days, but my heart? He might as well have cut it out of my chest.

Dear Lord, this couldn't be happening.

"This is a joke, right?" I asked as I covered myself with the negligee I'd thought would turn him on. "You didn't say that you want a..." I couldn't even say the word.

"Yes, I did. I said I want a divor—" I slapped his face hard and then attacked him with a few choice words of my own.

"I heard what you said, you rotten, no good son of a bitch. Don't you think you could have said that shit before I sucked yo' little, shriveled-up dick?"

He looked down at his manhood, which was still sticking out. "Hey, my dick is not little." Leave it to Avery to be more concerned about his dick than the fact that he'd just hurt me to the core. He took it even further, I guess trying to destroy any shred of self-esteem I might have left. "But I guess compared to your big ass it would be."

His insult hurt, though not as much as you might think. You see, he'd said things like that a million times before—maybe not verbally, but through his actions. I'd let it slide so many times, made excuses for his cruelty in my head, but no more. My humiliation became a rage coursing through my veins.

"You know what, Avery? So many other sisters would've left your miserable ass the second you got that pink slip, but I've been here supporting you, allowing you to mope around while I waited on you hand and foot. Yet I put on a few pounds and now you want a divorce? Your love for me couldn't withstand a few pounds? Really? You've got a damn good woman in me, but your shallow ass don't even realize it." I can't describe how angry I was as he sat there on the couch looking crazy. "You should have said that shit a long time ago."

"I've tried. I've wanted to, but—" He went to stand up, and I forcefully pushed his ass right back down on that couch. There was no stopping me now.

"But what? You were too busy letting me suck your dick?" The more I thought about how he laid back and let me suck his dick—and swallow!—when he probably knew all along he was going to ask for a divorce...oh, it was on.

"I wanted to tell you a long time ago."

"Then you should have!" I had so much tension building up inside that I started pacing to release some of it. My only other option would have been to strangle him, and no way was I going to jail for his worthless ass.

He stood slowly, as if making sure I wouldn't run over and tackle him, which I was trying very hard not to do. "Baby, who are we kidding here?" he said cautiously, then picked up steam when I didn't haul off and hit him. "I didn't have to say it. You know there's been a distance growing between us for some time now. I love you. You are a good woman. You've always been good to me. It's just that I want something different in a woman."

I stopped pacing and turned to him. "Nigga, is you crazy?" I roared, the ghetto rising up out of me. "All I've done for you...If you wanna be real about things now, I'm the one who should have asked for a divorce when your sorry ass made us lose our house and cars.

And you wonder why I picked up weight. Stressin' over whether or not I was gonna have a roof over my head."

I couldn't help the tears that filled the rims of my eyes. Before I knew it, I was storming off toward the bedroom.

"Wait, Connie. Where you going?" he asked, taking a few steps toward me.

"Where am I going?" I mocked. "To get my gun so I can blow your muthafuckin' head off. That's where the fuck I'm going," I raged. The next thing I knew, he was behind me, holding both of my arms to keep me from moving forward.

"Get off of me!" I yelled, turning around to face him as I broke loose from his grip. By now, hot tears were pouring down my cheeks onto the cleavage that my husband apparently found so unappealing. I could see now that there was no pleasing him. He didn't want me. My man wanted a divorce. I was hurt, embarrassed, and pissed the fuck off all at the same time, a mix of emotions like a tornado brewing inside of me.

"I know you're hurting," Avery said. "I'm hurting too. As a matter of fact, the other day, on my actual birthday, I was honestly about to commit suicide."

"Then you should have had the balls to do it," I said even though I doubted it was true. "You would have saved me the trouble of having to clean up your blood and brain matter from my living room floor." On that note, I resumed my trek to the bedroom to retrieve my gun.

"No, Connie, don't! Wait!" he pleaded, once again grabbing my arms.

"Get off of me!" I pushed away from him so forcefully that he almost toppled over. My own strength surprised me—and scared me a little. I realized that if I didn't get myself under control, things could turn out very badly for me. God knows the neighbors had probably already heard the commotion and called the police.

Squeezing my eyes shut, I took a few deep breaths and counted to five, then opened my eyes and pointed to the door. "Go," I said as calmly as I could. "Get the fuck out of my house."

He looked surprised. I guess he hadn't expected things to go quite like this. Can't say I blamed him, considering how long I'd been taking his shit without any complaint.

"Well, can I at least get some of my shit?" he asked.

I turned my back on him and walked toward the kitchen. "Get your shit and get out of my house. I don't ever wanna see you again."

I stayed in the kitchen, slamming around pots and pans as I thought about all the disrespect I'd suffered over the years. And then the final indignity of announcing he wanted a divorce right after he busted a nut! Oh, I was fuming—until I heard the door slam as Avery walked out.

That sound echoed in my head like a gunshot, replacing my anger with fear. What the hell had just happened? I looked down at my body, at the extra rolls of flesh around my middle that Avery had convinced me were so unappealing. Suddenly I wondered what other man would ever want me?

I ran to the bedroom and what I saw made my heart drop. The closet door was open and Avery's side was totally empty. Every dresser drawer was hanging out, and there was nothing in them. All of Avery's clothes were gone. This fool was serious!

I threw on a robe and bolted out of the apartment, down the stairway, calling out, "Avery! Avery, come back!"

Outside on the stoop, I looked frantically up and down the street. There was no sign of Avery or his car. Tears welled up in my eyes again, but this time there was no rage. It was pure sadness.

What have I done? How could I let my man walk out of my life? I've got to get him back.

"Connie?"

I turned around to see Daryl standing there, looking very concerned.

"Everything all right?" he asked. "I heard you yelling."

All the tension of the night caught up with me, and I suddenly felt exhausted. I pulled my robe tighter around me and sat down on the stoop. "Have you seen my husband?" I asked pitifully.

"Yeah, I met him about an hour ago when he was going in your apartment." He sat down beside me. "Is everything okay?"

I couldn't help it. I broke down and let the tears flow. "He left me,"

I blubbered. "Avery wants a divorce. I can't believe my life has come to this."

"Shhh. Don't worry, Connie. These things have a way of working themselves out. I promise." He put his arm around me and rocked me as I cried on his shoulder.

That little bit of kindness meant more to me than he could ever know.

Krystal

14

"Damn, Daryl, why are you doing this to me?" I moaned, hitting my fist against the wall in frustration. Was it possible to want someone and hate him all at the same time? I'd been feeling this way ever since Daryl called to tell me he wasn't coming to see me this morning, basically ruining my day. Call me spoiled, but after a week of steady visits, I'd become accustomed to him slipping into my bed to soothe the fire burning inside of me each morning. Today that fire was burning hotter than ever, which is why I was really pissed that he'd blown me off because his neighbor had a slight emergency.

Well, hello! Earth to Daryl: me being horny is an emergency too. A big-time emergency! You don't just fuck a girl silly every morning for a week, then cut her off cold turkey, especially not when she's admittedly addicted to the dick. My ass was so horny I was about to climb the walls. Yep, I needed a fix.

I'd tried to convince Daryl to leave his friend and come take care of me, but that wasn't his style to abandon someone in need. On the outside, he had that sexy thug swagger, but on the inside, he had the heart of a Boy Scout. It was one of the things about him that I had fallen in love with when we first met.

My sexual frustration was what had brought me to the shower to cool off in the first place, but even with the lukewarm water flowing down my body, I still couldn't put out the yearning between my legs. As I directed the spray from the showerhead between my breasts, lustful memories filled my head: Daryl on his knees in that very same shower, his head between my legs, doing what he did oh, so well. I'd always been a sucker for some good head, but nothing could compare to the way he worked his tongue.

Cut it out, Krystal, I scolded myself. Fantasizing about oral sex wasn't exactly a good way to get Daryl off my mind, and I definitely needed to get him off my mind—not just because he wasn't there to satisfy me, but because it was time to break things off with him. I was starting to get too attached. I only had a week left on my rental, and then it would be time to go home to reality, to my life without Daryl—the life I was afraid I was starting to forget.

Unable to take my mind off lustful thoughts, I positioned the showerhead lower and leaned against the wall. The water spraying against my coochie felt so damn good that there would be no stopping me now until I had an orgasm. I closed my eyes and imagined the stream of water to be Daryl's silky tongue lapping against me. I slid my hand down to massage my clit, imagining it was his touch.

"Mmm," I moaned as I pleasured myself with soft, gentle strokes. Within moments, I was almost there...until I was interrupted by the sound of the front door opening. I was sure it was Daryl keeping his date with me after all. Sure, he was a little later than we'd originally planned, but he was still right on time as far as I was concerned. As long as he got into the shower and helped me finish this orgasm, everything was good.

I heard his footsteps nearing the bathroom. I got wet, or should I say wetter, when I heard him enter the bathroom. He didn't say anything, which was actually kind of sexy, like he wanted to do a little role-playing. Fine, I'd play along and be the unsuspecting woman who gets surprised by a stranger in the shower. Hell, I'd even make it a little more interesting. I'd pretend that the stranger caught me in the act of playing with myself.

I heard the sound of his zipper and then his pants falling to the floor. I leaned against the wall and resumed the stroking of my clit. The thing is, I was so turned on at this point that I actually came after just a few strokes. With one long, low moan, I exploded, my clit throbbing and my legs nearly giving out.

"Damn, baby, what kind of shower you got going on in here?"

I got the shock of my life when the shower curtain opened and I saw not Daryl, but Slim. He was standing in front of me butt naked with his member at full attention.

Okay, call me a hypocrite if you want. I'd jumped in Monica's shit for cheating on her fiancé, and now here I was doing the same thing to Slim, my affectionate, kind, and caring boyfriend who would do anything in the world for me. That's why I'd been trying to force myself to forget about Daryl. Okay, maybe I wasn't trying so hard, but what's a girl to do when she's getting some of the best dick she's ever had?

"Oh my God, Slim. What are you doing here? Aren't you still supposed to be working in Virginia?" I asked, suddenly feeling very embarrassed and a little guilty about the orgasm I'd had while thinking about another man—one who could show up on my doorstep at any minute.

Slim laughed. "A better question is what are you doing in here?" He stepped in the shower and planted a deep kiss on my lips. "Never mind. I know exactly what's going on. I guess somebody missed me. Two weeks is a long time to go without." His hands roamed up and down my naked body. "I couldn't take it either, so I had to come home and get some. I missed you, baby, and the way you make me feel."

He moved his hand to where mine had been minutes earlier. After only a few strokes, he lifted me up by my ass and pressed me against the wall, sliding his manhood into me as deep as it would go. At first, I wasn't into it. My mind and my body had been set on Daryl's long, thick dick; but I was so sexually charged from masturbating that I got into what Slim was doing pretty quickly.

"Oh, Slim," I moaned. "Fuck me, baby. Fuck me until I come all over you."

"That's right. Didn't I tell you Daddy would take care of you? You know he always has what you need."

He went in and out of me like a piston, and within a few more strokes, I felt myself nearing another orgasm. Unfortunately, after only two more pumps, I felt him begin to jerk inside of me.

No, not yet, I thought as I began throwing my hips back at him, trying to quicken my climax. *I'm almost there. Not yet...*

"Come on, baby, keep it up," I encouraged. "Momma's almost there."

"Damn, baby. Shit, yeah. Ohhh. Krystal, baby. Ahhh. I love you, boo."

I opened my eyes and stared at his face. His expression of ecstasy was exactly what I needed to send me over the edge. We came together and shared the moment with our lips locked.

Slim pulled me away from the wall and slid me back down until I was on my feet. He kissed me one last time and said, "Do you have any idea how good you make me feel?"

As bad as it sounds, I couldn't bring myself to say, "You make me feel good too," because I was busy thinking about the fact that if Daryl had been in the shower, I probably would have had three or four more orgasms by now. Instead I said, "I think so."

"I love you, Kris," he said, opening the shower curtain and reaching for a towel.

"I love you too." That one I could manage to say, and I meant it too. Slim wasn't Daryl in the bedroom; he couldn't make me come rapid fire without breaking a sweat, but then again nobody but Daryl had ever done that. What Slim could do—and had done—for the past five years was take very good care of me. We met not long after Daryl walked out, and ever since, Slim had given me everything I needed, both materially and emotionally. That's probably why I was feeling so bad all of a sudden as I realized how far I'd let myself stray. I'd only planned on seeing Daryl for a one-night fling, and now I was craving him the way an addict craves her next high.

Slim picked up his clothes and went into the bedroom while I rinsed myself off and then followed him inside. "I thought you weren't coming back until next week," I said as I entered the bedroom.

"I finished up my business a little early," he replied, taking me into his arms. "Besides, I missed you, baby."

"Did you bring me something back?" I asked eagerly. Whenever he went away, I could always expect him to bring me a package.

"Of course I did," he said with a sexy grin. He picked up his pants, which he'd thrown across the dresser, and pulled out a familiar small, light-blue box. "You know I always got what you need."

I happily took the box from him. This was definitely not the first time he'd brought me a blue box, and I always loved what was inside, but this time the surprise was even better. "Slim? Is this what I think it is?" I squealed when I opened the box.

"That's right, baby. That's exactly what it is." He wrapped his arms around me. "You like it?"

I lifted the ring out of the box and slid it on my finger. "Oh, Slim, it's beautiful," I cried. "Does this mean...?"

Slim nodded and held my hand in his. "We've been together for quite a few years, and I know you've wanted to get married, so I figured it's about time I made you a legitimate woman. It's a carat and a half."

"Slim...I..." I was at a loss for words, that's what I was. I was not expecting this at all. I'd been trying to get Slim to commit for the past two years, and I was starting to think this would never happen. Well, now it had happened, and his timing couldn't have been worse. I mean, I'd been so damn strung out on Daryl this past week that I'd practically forgotten I was supposed to be in love with Slim.

Thankfully, Slim didn't seem bothered by the fact that I could barely speak. I guess he figured I was too mesmerized by the bling. So he filled the silence for me. "I went over to the furniture store and spoke to your pops," he said. "I asked him for your hand in marriage and all that jazz, like you said you wanted."

Now that was a sign that Slim was serious. He and my father got along, but Slim never went out of his way to talk to my dad.

"What did he say?" My father wasn't much of a talker. It wasn't that he didn't like Slim; he'd become more withdrawn in general ever since he lost his job and had to start selling cheap furniture.

"He said the decision is up to you, but if you said yes, he'd be proud to have me as a son-in-law." Slim put his hands on my waist and looked into my eyes. "What do you think? Krystal Mack, will you marry me? I love you. You know I'll always have what you need, baby."

Slim was right. Everything I needed and had wanted for the past five years was right in that pale blue box—at least until Daryl came back into my life a week ago. I glanced at the box, then looked up at Slim, who was waiting expectantly for my answer.

After waiting so long for this proposal, I didn't know what the hell to say now that it had happened. I actually considered trying to stall him, buy myself maybe another week or two so I could enjoy a little more time with Daryl before ending it completely. I wanted to quit my habit gradually, not have to do it cold turkey. There was only one problem with that. If I said no or even asked for a little more time, Slim was not the kind of man who would put the offer on the table ever again.

As Slim stood there waiting, I quickly weighed the pros and the cons in my mind. Both men were good providers. Daryl was a much better lover, but it's not like Slim was a slouch in the bedroom either. Plus, Slim was easier to talk to than Daryl, who used to get a little moody and withdrawn. Then there was the religion thing. Daryl was an Israelite, and he'd always made it very clear that if we ever got married, he expected me to convert.

I looked down at the blue box in my hand and thought about the many similar packages Slim had brought me over the years. That's when I realized the most important distinction between them. Daryl had been a little too controlling in our relationship, always telling me what he thought I should or shouldn't be doing, what was good for me and what was bad. Slim, on the other hand, always brought me what I wanted, no questions asked. Like his favorite line, he always had what I needed.

Aside from a few good orgasms, there was no question in my mind about what my answer should be.

"Yes, Slim. Yes, I'll marry you."

Avery

15

I walked confidently through the doors of Cheap Sam's with my head held high and my chest stuck out like I owned the damn place. Granted, it might not have been my name hanging on the sign outside, but once I had my meeting with Dave and he made my promotion to manager official, everyone who worked there was going to know that I was the new HNIC (Head Nigger in Charge).

Like my man Cain said, it was time to live like I was dying. In the past week, I'd given Connie's fat ass the boot, moved temporarily into a room at my parents' house, and was about to seize the promotion I'd been coveting for two years. I was feeling alive again and had a newfound confidence to go along with my generally good mood. Cain's advice—along with the young, tight pussy he'd provided at his house—had given me a whole new outlook.

I must have been radiating confidence because even Jerri, the store's fine-ass bookkeeper, was giving me the time of day again. I'd been trying to get with her for a while, but things had cooled off ever since she decided she didn't do married men. At least that's what she claimed, but lately it seemed like she was always around, smiling up in my face, like all I had to do was ask and she'd give up the pussy.

She was sitting behind the counter, waving at me when I walked in. I strolled over to her, and the closer I got, the prettier she got. Damn, I wanted to fuck this woman.

I leaned on the counter like I was John Shaft. "Hey there, Jerri. What's cooking, good looking?" I said cockily, eyeing her up and down.

"Hey, Avery. How you doing?" She batted her false eyelashes.

"I'm good." I smoothed over my mustache.

"You know, Avery, there's something different about you lately," she remarked, raising an eyebrow.

"Yeah, well, I've been thinking a lot about you. Maybe that's it."

Jerri smiled, clearly loving the attention. "What you been thinking about?"

"How you and me need to go out to dinner and see a show."

Her face lit up. "I would love to go out to dinner..."

"Cool," I said, but she put the brakes on a little.

"But are you sure your wife won't mind?"

I chuckled at her attempt at playing hard to get. "You don't have to worry about that. Me and my wife just separated. I'm a single man now."

Her smile became even wider. "So, do you have your own place and everything?"

"Well, not exactly. I'm kinda staying with my parents right now, but I'm working on some things." In my mind, that was a minor technicality. It was only a matter of time before I had a place of my own again, but to Jerri it was obviously more of a hurdle.

"Oh," she said kind of under her breath with a frown. "Well, I'll be honest with you. I'm looking for a man who's a little more stable. I ain't got time to be taking care of nobody."

I took a step back. "Well, damn, woman. There's no shame in your game, huh?"

"Avery, I'm a high-maintenance woman. I need a man who has a future, and well, you're just a salesman who lives with his momma." She frowned.

Ouch. If any other woman had said it, I would have flipped out on her ass, but the thing is, I was so hot for Jerri that I was willing to let it slide. "Not for long," I told her. "I guess you ain't heard that I'm about to be the manager of this place."

Her eyes lit up again, probably because as the bookkeeper she knew everyone's salaries. "Is that why Sam and his son are here?"

"I suspect so. I've got a meeting with Dave now. Guess Sam and his son are going to sit in."

"Well, don't let me stop you, Big Daddy," Jerri said as I took a step toward the door marked MANAGER. "Oh, and Avery?"

With my hand on the knob, I turned around to get one last look at her. "Yeah?"

"If what you say is true and you get the promotion, I'll be open to going out with you and celebrating anytime you're ready."

"Now that's what I'm talking about!" I grinned, adjusted my tie, then turned around and walked into Dave's office.

Dave was sitting at his desk. Across from him was Sam, who kind of reminded me of Colonel Sanders. Next to Sam was a young, freckle-faced kid in his twenties, whom I suspected was the owner's son.

"Avery, my man, glad you could make it. Have a seat." Dave stood, gesturing toward the chair to the right of his desk.

"Thanks. Glad to be here." I shook everyone's hands before I took my seat next to the kid.

Dave started the conversation. "Well, Avery, as you know, I'm going to be headed to the main office to become general manager."

I nodded, anxious to get the formalities over with so they could offer me Dave's job.

"So," Dave continued, "Sam here wanted me to talk to you about the future of this store and the transfer of one management team to another."

I spoke up, ready to deliver the words that I'd been practicing for this moment ever since Dave told me he was leaving. "First of all, Dave, let me congratulate you on your promotion. This store's loss is the entire company's gain." I glanced over at Sam, making sure I had his attention. I wanted him to understand I was a team player. "Secondly, whatever I have to do to make the management transition smooth I'll do. I don't have to tell you I live and breathe Cheap Sam's Furniture." Pretty good speech if I do say so myself.

Dave didn't seem nearly as impressed as I thought he'd be, though.

"Uh, thank you, Avery. I appreciate your kind words," he said, then shot an awkward glance at Sam. "And as far as your work ethic, I agree with you wholeheartedly. I even went to Sam and told him you were the man for this job." Dave's eyebrows were pulled together in this weird, remorseful expression. What the hell was going on?

"And? What did you think, Sam?" I asked, pushing ahead as if I weren't getting a really bad feeling about this whole thing.

"Ahem." Sam cleared his throat nervously. "I said that he was probably right, but..."

I tried to remain calm, even though I knew nothing good ever came after the *but* in a situation like this. This time was no different.

"But we're going to go in a different direction filling that position right now."

"Huh?" I felt like all the blood had been drained from my body.

"Avery," Dave spoke in a rush. "I know this is a little bit of a surprise, but we do have big plans for your career. You just have to be patient a bit longer."

"Who's going to be manager?" I asked. If he told me it was one of those assholes I worked with on the sales floor, I was prepared to hit the roof. I was ten times more valuable to the company than any of those fools.

Dave's eyes went to the young kid, who had yet to say anything. "Avery Mack," Dave said, "I want you to meet Sam Junior. Sam wants you to train his son to run this store. Figures he should start at one of the stores for a year or two before we move him over to the main office."

"He's a smart kid. He just graduated from Boston College, and he's eager to learn," Sam added, patting his son on the back. "I'm sure it's not gonna take long for you to teach him all you know."

I was so thrown off guard by this announcement that for a second I was totally disoriented. I shook my head as if it would clear my confusion. "Wait—what?" I uttered at the same time that the kid stood up and held out his pasty hand for me to shake.

"It's going to be nice working with you," he said. "And once my father moves me up to the vice presidency, I'll make sure that you get this management position."

Oh, hell naw! This was not happening. No way was I going to accept this snot-nosed rich kid as my superior. That damn job was supposed to be mine!

I looked down at his hand, which he dropped to his side when he figured out I wasn't going to shake it.

"Kid, let me ask you a question," I said in a controlled voice. The young boy nodded. "What exactly is a pillowtop mattress? And how would you distinguish it from, say, the Sealy Posturepedic Solon Plush Euro Top mattress?"

"I don't know," he answered blankly.

"Exactly." I looked pointedly at Sam and then back to his son as I continued, "Tell me the difference between contemporary furniture and classical furniture."

"Ah, I'm not really sure," he stammered, and I had to laugh.

"And you want to be a manager in a furniture store?" I turned to Dave. "He's not even ready to be a stock boy."

Dave, of course, didn't have the balls to agree with me in front of the boss. He just shrugged his shoulders and avoided eye contact.

I turned back to the boss. "Sam, please. I know he's your son, but he can't run this store."

"That's why you're going to be here to train him," Sam answered, totally unfazed by the lack of knowledge his son had demonstrated.

"Are you crazy?" I bellowed. "Man, I'm not training that kid to take my job. That's bullshit!"

"You're sliding on a slippery slope, Avery," Dave warned, but by now I didn't give a crap.

I felt my pulse pounding, causing the carotid artery in my neck to bulge out. I was enraged, and after years of being beaten down, I wasn't going to take it anymore. No more swallowing my pride only to make a few lousy dollars. Finally, my fury found its voice. "You know what, Dave? Fuck you and your Uncle Tom ass." I gave him the finger, then turned to Sam Junior and said, "And fuck you too, you little pimply-faced bastard." Finally, I turned to the owner. "Oh, and Sam, a very special fuck you to you, you Kentucky Fried Chicken–looking motherfucker. You can take this job and fuck yourself. I quit!"

I held both my middle fingers up as I backed out of the room, slamming the door behind me.

Jerri came strutting up to me, looking excited. "Well, did you get the promotion?" I could practically see dollar signs in her eyes.

"No, I didn't get it! Matter of fact, fuck you, you stink-ass, gold-digging whore!" I left her standing there with a dumb look on her face as I stormed out of the building for the last time. Even though I'd just quit my job, my adrenaline was at an all-time high. If this was what it felt like to live like I was dying, then I wanted more—lots more.

Benny

16

I sat at my computer, putting the finishing touches on my latest blog entry. As I hit save, I started thinking about the night ahead of me, wondering what it would bring. Whatever it was, I knew it would be fun. It's not every day a guy turns twenty-one. I planned on making the best of it by going out to a club, getting drunk as hell, and with any luck, getting laid. I knew the latter was a stretch, but a guy could dream, couldn't he? As I wrapped up my journal entry, I heard a knock on my bedroom door.

"Come in," I called out, knowing it could be only one person.

My father stuck his head in the door.

"Hey, Pop. What's up?"

"Nothing much, son. I'm getting ready to head on out." He entered the room with the same depressing look he'd had earlier, when he got the call to go back to the firehouse for the night shift. "I'm sorry about tonight."

"It's all right. I'll see you in the morning." I tried my best to sound disappointed, but I wasn't at all. With him out of the way, I was sure I would have a much better time. I loved my pops like a friend, but he was still my parent, and there are some things you don't want your parents to see. I was hoping to get into some of those things tonight.

"No, it's not all right. It's your twenty-first birthday. For years I've been telling you that when you turned twenty-one, I was going to take you out and get you drunk for the first time."

I held back a smile. The look on his face was so pitiful I almost wanted to tell him not to feel bad because I'd been drinking for years.

"Don't worry about it, Pop. It's all good. We're gonna get drunk together one of these days."

"Well, anyway, here you go . . ." He handed me an envelope.

"What's this?" I asked.

"Open it and see," he urged.

I pulled out the card and glanced at the inscription inside, but I was much more interested in the smaller plastic card inside the envelope.

I held it up, and Pop said, "It's one of those Visa gift cards. I saw the way you were eyeing Daryl's iPad, so I figured I'd give you one." He patted me on the back. "Happy birthday, son."

"Thanks, Pop." I got up and gave him a quick hug.

My father's eyes wandered over my shoulder. "Who's that you got as your screen saver?"

I shrugged. "Oh, that? That's Daryl. I got his picture off the Internet."

"Three-B Daryl?" He sounded confused.

"Yep."

He leaned in to get a closer look. "Oh, shit. That is him, isn't it? He looks like a boxer or something."

"MMA," I said. "He used to be some kind of Mixed Martial Arts champion back in the day."

"Get the heck outta here. No wonder he kicked those guys' asses by himself like that. I was starting to think I was getting old."

"You are old." I laughed. "Hey, speaking of Daryl, maybe I'll see if he wants to go grab a beer with me tonight."

My father hesitated, clearing his throat before he said, "You spend an awful lot of time with Daryl, don't you?"

"Yeah, we've struck up a pretty nice friendship. I like him a lot. Why, you jealous of our friendship?" I teased.

"Who, me? You're my son. What do I have to be jealous about?"

"Exactly. I mean, considering I never say anything about your friendships and all the time you spend with Ms. Pam, Ms. Karen, Ms. June, and Ms. Nancy, I don't see why you would be jealous. Me and Daryl are just friends. You and those ladies are—"

"I get your point." That was enough to get him to drop the subject.

It actually made sense that he was jealous, considering the fact that I was hanging out at Daryl's a lot, playing video games and stuff. Daryl talked to me like a man, unlike Pop, who seemed to forget sometimes that I wasn't a little kid anymore. Sometimes I got so frustrated that I'd been thinking about moving into the dorms at Fordham or getting my own apartment. Pop seemed to be a little threatened by my friendship with Daryl, but I wondered what he'd think if he knew that Daryl was the one who convinced me not to move out. He said I should have a talk with my father instead. I still didn't have the guts to do it.

"I'm gonna have a birthday surprise for you later in the week," Pop said. "You have a happy birthday until then."

About a half hour after Pop left, I knocked on Daryl's door. I knew he'd be home, because he always seemed to be around at night whenever I stopped by.

"Hey, Benny, come on in, man." He waved me in unenthusiastically. I could tell from the start that he wasn't in the best of moods. "How's things?"

"I'm doing a'ight, Dee," I replied as I plopped down on his sofa in front of the TV. "Tell me you haven't been in your pajamas all day."

Daryl looked down at his clothes, which consisted of a T-shirt, pajama bottoms, and slippers. He frowned as if it had finally dawned on him that he was dressed for bed. "Yep. Haven't even made it to the shower yet."

"What's up, man? You sick?"

"Nah." He sat down on the recliner and picked up his cell phone from the end table. All of a sudden it was like I wasn't even in the room. He punched in a few numbers and placed the phone to his ear. I watched his jaw tighten as he waited for the call to connect. Dude was seriously tense. He looked beyond pissed when, getting no answer, he finally pulled the phone away from his ear, hit end, and slammed it back down on the table. "Dammit!"

"Daryl, everything all right?"

He didn't answer right away. It took a minute for him to come back from wherever his head was at. "Oh yeah. Yeah, dude," he finally said. "I'm okay. Just got a lot on my mind the past few days."

"You sure?" I asked. "'Cause you sure don't look okay."

Again he hesitated.

"Look, man, you know you can talk to me, right? I mean, you listened to me talk about my pops plenty of times before," I assured him.

Daryl looked at me and shook his head. "No, man, as a matter of fact, I'm not all right. I'm fucking pissed," he admitted.

I felt bad that he was upset, but I have to admit that it felt pretty cool to think that Daryl saw me as an equal, as someone he could confide in—not like some little kid.

"What's going on?" I asked.

"You remember the other day when I told you I was supposed to be going out to the Hamptons to see a friend?"

I nodded. "Yeah, the morning we ended up helping Ms. Nancy clean up when the pipes burst in her apartment. You said you had to cancel on your friend."

"Exactly." He picked up his phone again and stared at the screen, but he didn't make a call this time. "Well, I've been trying to call ever since, and I ain't heard a peep from her. First she wasn't answering her phone, and now it's disconnected."

"I mean, I'm no expert in the love department or nothing, but it sounds like someone is trying to send you a message." I was joking, trying to lighten his mood a little, but the look he shot me could have melted ice.

"My bad," I apologized. "So, what're you gonna do? You got no other way to get in touch with your girl?"

He shook his head. "She's not my girl. She's a friend. Someone I thought I could trust. Someone who wouldn't play games."

If this person wasn't his girl, he sure looked broken up about her getting ghost on him. But what did I know? My expertise was in electronics, not relationships.

"Wish there was something I could do to help," I offered.

As if an idea had suddenly come to him, he whipped his head in my direction and said, "Y'know, maybe there is."

"Happy to help," I said. "What is it?"

"You're good with computers. You think you could track down a cell phone signal?"

I shook my head. "I'm good, but not that good. I don't have the equipment to do something like that. We'd have the FCC all over us."

He stayed quiet for a minute before he came up with another idea. "Well, what about hacking into the account for the number I have? Maybe if I can see who she's been calling, I can find her."

"Yeah, man, I could probably get into the account," I said. My father would kill me if he knew what I was agreeing to do, but what the hell, I was helping out a friend.

"Cool. I'll go get my laptop," he said.

I stopped him before he could leave the room. "Uh, not tonight, man."

"Why not?"

"It's my twenty-first birthday. Hacking something like that is complicated and time-consuming if you don't want to get caught. I'm trying to go to the club and get my drink on," I said. "I actually came by to see if you wanted to go with me."

Daryl's shoulders drooped like he was totally disappointed. Damn, he must have been really strung out on this chick if he couldn't even wait another day for me to hack her account.

"C'mon, Dee. Go get dressed. It'll do you some good to get outta here. I'll get her phone log for you tomorrow."

He waved his hand, trying to look like he wasn't pressed. "Nah, man. That's not it. It's just..." His eyes wandered around the room like he was searching for an excuse. "Didn't you tell me your pops wanted to take you out?"

"He's working tonight. Besides, he's not exactly the best person to be with if I'm trying to meet someone, if you know what I mean."

"Why not?" Daryl asked, looking slightly more relaxed. I guess talking about my issues with Pop—for the millionth time—helped him get his mind off the disappearing chick. "From what I see around the building, your father seems like a pretty popular guy. He might be able to give you a few pointers."

"I wish," I said. "It's just, you know, sometimes he doesn't know when to back off. Shoot, in high school it was so bad I stopped even trying to get with any girls. I mean, it's pretty embarrassing trying to walk a girl home when your pops is trailing behind you in his car the whole way."

Daryl let out a low whistle. "Yeah, I'd say that's pretty bad."

We laughed and joked for a while longer about the silly shit my father used to do, but all in all, I couldn't complain. He might be a little overprotective, but Pop had taken good care of me ever since my mother died.

"What do you say, man?" I asked. "You gonna come with me or what?"

"Why don't you ask some of your friends?" he said.

That kind of hurt a little. Was he saying he didn't consider us to be friends after all?

"You know," I said, trying to sound like it didn't bother me, "if I didn't know better, I'd say you were trying not to hang out with me."

I guess that got his attention, because at least this time he didn't totally try to brush me off. "No, man. That's not it. It's just that I'm a little tired, and I haven't even had a shower today. Why don't you run out and grab us a six-pack or something? I can whip your ass at some *Madden*."

It was closer to what I wanted but still not good enough. "Aw, man, I don't wanna stay in tonight. I'm *twenty-one*! Don't you remember what it was like when you reached the drinking age? I want to go out to a club, throw back a few drinks with my boy, and who knows? We might both get lucky."

He shook his head. "It's getting late."

"Late?" I walked over to his living room window. "It's not even ten o'clock yet. We've played video games until three o'clock in the morning." I turned to face him and asked, "What's really going on?"

"Maybe we can do it tomorrow."

"Tonight's my birthday, not tomorrow. I'm only gonna turn twenty-one once." I hate to say it, but I was starting to sound like a whiny little kid, even though the law said I was officially a man now.

"Look, I'm sorry. I can't go out with you tonight," Daryl snapped, catching me a little off guard. I'd never seen him catch an attitude like that before. Well, I had something for him if he wanted to bitch up on me.

"Yeah, well, I guess I can't hack that number either." I stood my ground, waiting for him to respond. I wasn't sure whether he was going to give in or tell me to get the fuck out of his apartment.

After some uncomfortable silence, he said, "Hey, Benny, I'm sorry. I apologize. I didn't mean to snap at you like that. It's just that..." His words trailed off, and then he finally said, "Hell, I guess I should tell you the truth."

He bent down and raised his pants leg to expose a large black bracelet around his ankle. "I can't go out with you because I'm on house arrest."

To say I was shocked is an understatement. You couldn't have paid me to believe that Daryl, the guy who I'd looked up to practically like a superhero, was actually a convict.

"Man, what did you do?" I blurted out, then instantly felt bad.

I could see from the look on his face that Daryl was hurt. "Look, Benny, you're a cool kid and all. I really enjoy kicking it with you, but I'm going to have to ask you to back off on this one, okay? There are a lot of things you don't want to know about me."

I nodded, staring down at the device that was locked around his ankle. I had so many questions. Not knowing which ones he'd choose to answer, I started with the basics. "How are you out all the time if you're on house arrest?"

"I'm on house arrest from sundown to sunup for the next six months."

"Oh...I know you don't want to tell me what you did, but tell me one thing: you're not a murderer, are you?"

He actually smirked. "No, man. Murderers are in jail. I'm only on house arrest."

I looked down at his ankle, fascinated by the device that was attached there. "Hey, can I see that thing?" I reached out to touch it even before he gave me permission. I messed around with it for a minute, then sat back on the floor.

I asked, "If I told you I could get that thing off of you, then would you go out to the club and have a beer with me?"

"Dude, please. There's no way we can work around this. It's either a six-pack and a game of *Madden* on your birthday or a drink out at a bar tomorrow during daylight hours."

I pushed forward with my plan. "I've never met an electronic device that I couldn't manipulate."

"Yeah, but I don't want to manipulate my way onto Rikers Island."

I wasn't ready to back down. This bracelet was just the kind of challenge I liked. "C'mon, *friend*. Trust me. Compared to a jewelry store alarm system, this thing would be a piece of cake."

Krystal

17

I was back home in the apartment I shared with my father and step-mother after spending a few days in Pennsylvania, where Slim and I went shopping at the outlets. We bought a bunch of things for our new place, and then I'd come back to Queens to pack the last of my stuff to move in with Slim.

I'd gotten out of the Hamptons rental as soon as possible, because staying there after Slim's proposal would have been a recipe for disaster. Eventually Daryl would have shown up, and I was definitely not prepared to deal with that—ever. There was no reason for Slim to know about my fling. As far as I was concerned, my week with Daryl was something I would remember forever but never talk about again.

From the way Daryl was acting, it was obvious he didn't see things quite the same way I did. He blew up my phone for days after I disappeared. I turned off the ringer, but it seemed like my purse was vibrating constantly with Daryl's calls. It got so bad that Slim noticed and started asking questions. I finally slipped away for an hour, found a Verizon store, and had my number changed.

I felt a little bad about the way I was doing Daryl. I should have at least given him an explanation, but I couldn't talk to him. Truthfully, I was afraid that hearing his voice would make me want to see him again; seeing him would make me want to kiss him; kissing him would lead to fucking; and fucking would lead to disaster. So I was moving on, and Daryl would have to do the same. He'd eventually understand that I was doing him a favor. Daryl deserved better than me.

I put Daryl out of my mind the best I could as I finished packing. Even though I was just moving to an apartment downstairs, it felt good to know I'd finally have my own place. I'd be close enough to keep an eye on my dad without having to share a space with my fat bitch of a stepmother.

"Avery? Is that you?"

Speaking of my stepmother...

"Avery?" she called out again.

I stacked two full boxes on top of one another and headed out of my room.

"No, it's not Avery," I whined in a mocking tone as I entered the living room. I'm sorry, but I hated Connie. "It's me." I rolled my eyes and sucked my teeth, and she gave the same right back to me.

"Anyway, when my dad gets home, tell him to come down to my apartment. I'm in 1A."

She stared at me with this dumb expression on her face, like she was waiting for me to say something else.

"What?" I snapped.

"Haven't you heard? Your father doesn't live here anymore." She didn't elaborate, just stood there looking stupid.

"What do you mean? Where the hell is my father?"

"Your dad left me, Krystal." She swallowed as if she was choking back tears. "He asked for a divorce."

"Yes!" I pumped my fist in the air and did a little victory dance. "Yes, yes, yes!" I can't begin to explain how happy I was at that moment. Let's say that if I ever doubted it before, at that moment, I knew there was a God.

Connie's eyes were shiny, like she was about to cry, but I didn't give a shit. How the hell did she expect me to take the news? I hated her guts for what she'd done to my mother, and I'd always made that very clear to her—when I bothered to speak two words to her. Over the years, we'd probably only had two or three real conversations, and it felt damn good to know that this could very well be our last one.

Connie finally fixed her lips to ask me, "What are you trying to say?"

"Ha! Do you really need to ask me that?" I replied. "It means that I'm happy my dad finally wised up and got rid of your fat ass."

She shook her head and sniffled. "Why do you hate me so much, Krystal? What have I ever done to you but be nice?"

"You married my father, that's what you did."

"I've never been anything but good to both you and your father. I let you live at my house, for crying out loud."

I looked around the little-ass apartment and laughed. "I'm supposed to be thankful you let me live in this dump? Shoot, I'm payin' you rent anyway, so you ain't *let* me do shit."

Connie's tears dried up real quick, and she threw attitude right back at me. "You spoiled little bitch. What, you think you're supposed to be allowed to live rent-free?"

"If you hadn't been around, that's exactly how I would've been living. You don't think Daddy told me you were the one making me pay rent?" I shook my head in disgust. "And all you been paying is the light bill. That's a damn shame."

"Light bill? Are you crazy?" She damn near exploded, but I knew that heifer was faking.

I sucked my teeth and said, "Don't act like my father hasn't been paying all the bills around here."

She didn't reply, but her face kept getting redder. I half expected to see steam start coming out the top of her head.

"All you ever wanted him for was his money, you gold-digging heifer," I said, accusing her of the same thing I always did. Our arguments always came to this point, and it usually bothered her when I called her a gold digger. This time, she only laughed it off.

"His money? What money? Your father ain't got shit," she snapped. "And if he does, it's news to me. He ain't paid a bill around here in months. If I didn't love h—"

"Love! You don't love him! You never did, you gold-digging piece of shit. My momma told me about you, you fucking whore!"

"Whore? You better watch your mouth and remember who you're talking to," she threatened with fire in her eyes. "I'm not the one who was being passed around from thug to thug, worrying your father to death. That was your crazy ass." She'd turned the tables on me and hit a nerve. I felt exactly like I did when I was a teenager and Connie first came around. I felt like shit.

She kept going, trying to inflict more damage. "You are good and crazy, you know that? Just like your pill-popping momma."

Now she'd crossed the line. I took a step toward her and roared, "Don't talk about my mother, bitch."

She laughed. "Bitch, huh? Well, at least I'm not a liar, am I?"

"I ought to whip your..." I took a step toward her, expecting her to back down. I was actually a little confused when she stood her ground. Usually Connie was a weak bitch.

She folded her arms over her huge belly and smirked at me. "Ha! You can come over here if you want to, but you ain't got your daddy to hold me back now." She dropped her arms to her sides and clenched her fists. "And this weight sure makes a girl heavy-handed."

"You know what? You're not even worth it." I was too cute to be walking around with a black eye from my stepmother, so I backed off. "My daddy deserves to be happy, something you never could do for him. That must be why he's leaving your fat ass, huh?"

Her fists opened and her shoulders sagged. I could see I'd taken all the fight out of her, so I took another jab. "My mother made him happy, and you couldn't stand that, could you? That's why you had to get rid of her."

Before I headed back to my room to get some boxes, I said, "Both you and I know you killed her, Connie. And one day, one day, I'm gonna prove it."

She looked unfazed by my threats, probably because she'd heard them so many times before. I'd always believed she had something to do with my mother's death, but I'd never been able to get anyone to listen to me. "And another thing, if anything happens to my dad, I'm coming for you. And that's not a threat, it's a promise."

"I hope you got all your shit," she said, "because I'm calling a locksmith when you leave." She was so furious that I could see her hand shaking as she pointed to the door.

I laughed. "Ain't shit in here I would want unless I was having a garage sale."

"Hey there, sis! Guess who's twenty-one?"

I was heading out to the U-Haul truck to help Slim with his last couple of boxes when I looked up to see my neighbor, Benny, stepping into the lobby with his arms outstretched for a hug. After the run-in with that fat bitch Connie, it was good to see a friendly face. Benny was a nice, cute college kid who liked to call me his big sister. He was real smart and a late bloomer, who was finally coming into his own. The booze on his breath wasn't the thing that shocked me most about running into Benny, though. The thing that made my heart pound and my knees go weak was seeing the man who was following behind him.

"D-Daryl? What are you doing here?" I asked when I finally found my voice. For a second, I was so shocked it was like I forgot how to speak.

"I live here," he replied. His eyes said a whole lot more, but I guess he didn't want to curse me out in front of the kid.

"No, you don't." I was starting to feel faint.

"Um, do you two know each other?" Benny asked, but his question went unanswered by both of us.

"You can't live here. I live here." I leaned against the wall for support.

"Not here, as in right here in the hallway, but in this apartment building. My apartment, the one I was telling you about, is on the third floor. I live in 3B." I was definitely getting light-headed, and the feeling got even worse when Daryl brought up the fact that I'd disappeared on him. He said, "I've been calling you."

"Yeah, I know" was all I could say. I didn't really want to go into details in front of Benny, and I think Benny picked up on that. Not to mention the fact that Slim, who was unloading the truck, would probably be coming through that door at any moment.

As Daryl and I stared at each other saying nothing, Benny cleared his throat. "Well, uh, I guess you two do know each other." He turned to Daryl. "Look, Daryl, man, I'm gonna head on up. I'll meet you back at your apartment so we can put that thing back together."

Daryl handed him the keys, and then Benny headed off, hollering back at me, "See you later, sis."

"Yeah, Benny, uh, see you later." I said it in a whisper. I doubt he even heard me. "Does he know about us?"

"I don't think so, but he's not a stupid kid. Besides, so what if he does? I'm not even sure there is an *us*. What's going on, Krystal? Where the hell have you been?"

I just stared at him, wishing I had a lie I could tell him.

"I've been trying to call—"

I didn't let him finish, because we'd already been through that, and I didn't have the answer he wanted to hear anyway.

"Do you really live here?" I asked.

"Yes." He nodded. "Now, can you please tell me what the hell is going—"

He stopped midsentence when he saw Slim walk up behind me and wrap his arms around my waist.

"I see you've met our new neighbor," Slim said.

Oh, God. This is not happening, I thought.

"Uh, do you two know each other?" I asked, feeling as stupid as I probably sounded.

"This is Benny's friend," Slim said. "We met outside by the truck. Did you know Benny's twenty-one? He wants to go out for a drink later this week."

"Are you two together?" Daryl asked. His tone was loud but even. Slim probably didn't even notice anything was wrong, but because of our background, I knew Daryl was shocked—and pissed. It was probably taking all his self-control not to go off on me and kill Slim.

"Oh, uh, yes, this is my fiancé, Slim," I replied, forcing myself to sound upbeat.

I saw Daryl's shoulders slump ever so slightly and I felt terrible. I really didn't want to hurt him, and I definitely hadn't planned on ever telling him about Slim. When I left the rental house, I thought I was leaving Daryl and the affair behind. Little did I know that by running away from the Hamptons, I would be running into Daryl—literally.

As much as I wanted to run away again, I had to stay put and act like nothing was out of the ordinary. "Slim, this is—"

"Daryl, right?" Slim interrupted, unaware of all the tension that was going on between us.

"Right," Daryl answered stiffly, his eyes darting in my direction every few seconds. "We met outside."

"Slim, Daryl's an old family friend. He was there for me when my mother died." With my eyes, I begged Daryl not to go there.

"Is that right?" Slim asked.

"I always seem to be there when she needs me." Daryl nodded with what I considered a condescending smile. "So, Krystal, you did say he's your fiancé, right? How long you two been engaged?"

Slim placed his arm proudly around my shoulders. "Yeah, I finally popped the question the other day. Even went and asked her old man for her hand in marriage. Trying to make an honest woman out of her. Know what I mean?"

"Oh, I know exactly what you mean." Daryl chuckled and shook his head. I could feel my stomach begin to churn. "Nothing like an honest woman."

Daryl was getting dangerously close to busting me in front of Slim, and I was terrified. Damn him, he was enjoying it too. I did not need this drama.

"Anyway, we have to finish up here..." Slim hinted that it was time to stop catching up with old friends, and I couldn't have agreed more.

"Oh yes, for sure. Besides, looks like we're going to be neighbors." Daryl glanced in my direction, probably to be sure he was making me squirm. I managed a nervous, tight smile as he continued to put on his show. "So we'll have plenty of time to shoot the breeze. I'm looking forward to that spades game."

"That's what's up," Slim said. "I'll talk to Benny and arrange it."

Daryl said, "On the real, though, holler at me so that we can go grab a beer or something. I'm sure we have a lot in common."

"I'ma do that. If my girl Krystal here is down for you, then you must be an okay dude."

"Feeling's mutual, my friend. If Krystal vouches for you, you must be a'ight," Daryl said. He looked at me with a grin on his face, and then he walked away. His act was over. I could only hope there wouldn't be an encore.

"He seems like a cool dude," Slim commented as Daryl walked up the stairs.

"Yeah, real cool," I replied. "You could almost call him cold."

Benny

18

I was about to plop down on the sofa and turn on the TV when Daryl finally walked into his apartment with a scowl on his face. The look didn't surprise me, considering the tension between him and Krystal in the lobby. It was pretty damn obvious the two of them knew each other, and it was also apparent from the way they were ignoring me and talking in code that they had some kind of issue to work out. I didn't know what was going on, but I was too hungover from my birthday celebration to try to figure it out. That's why I got the hell out of there when I did. It looked like things had gotten even worse after I left, given Daryl's mood when he came in the apartment.

"I can't believe she played me like that," Daryl huffed. He looked even more pissed off and hurt than he had last night when he found out his Hamptons friend changed her number.

"Played you how? What's up with you two anyway?" I wasn't sure I really wanted the answer, because not only did I consider Krystal a friend, but her man Slim was cool too. "Please tell me you're not banging Krystal."

He sat down next to me and said, "Let's just say we've got history. A long history."

I looked at him and raised my eyebrows. "History, huh? Spit it out, man."

"Benny, she's the woman I was going out to see in the Hamptons."

"Get the fuck outta here. I didn't think Krystal was like that." I was expecting him to say they used to date or something, but you couldn't have paid me to think Krystal was cheating on Slim. They always seemed so devoted to each other.

He laughed. "Neither did I."

"Damn, I guess she did play you."

Daryl shot me a sarcastic look. "You think?"

"Look, I know you're pissed, but maybe you could keep that shit on the low. That guy unloading the truck outside is her boyfriend. He's also a friend I'd like to keep. As you know, I don't have many of them around here."

"Fiancé," Daryl snapped irritably. "He's her fiancé."

"Really? Well, that's news to me, but let me give you fair warning as my friend. Slim ain't nobody to play with."

Daryl stood his ground. "Benny, I don't know if you realized it or not, but I'm nobody to play with either."

"Daryl, man, you need to chill. This is no time to get in a pissing match over pussy. I like Krystal and all, but she ain't worth it. She's been with Slim for like five years." I stood up and patted my buddy on the shoulder. "There are plenty of other fish in the sea. It wasn't like you couldn't have brought home any of a dozen of those women from the club last night."

He took a calming breath. "You're right. I don't know why I'm stressing over her. Obviously she ain't nothing but a—"

I cut him off. "Don't go there, man. You and I both know you're talking in anger. Don't let her take you there."

He laughed, this time genuinely. "Look at you giving me advice. You're taking this I'm-twenty-one-and-a-man shit seriously, aren't you?"

"I'm supposed to." I folded my arms. "That's what friends are for."

"Yeah, you're right. Thanks for being there." He pulled me in for one of those brotherly hugs.

"I'll always be there for you, bro."

He leaned back and said, "Now, listen. We need to get that thing back around my ankle. I know you're good, but I'm home now, and I'm feeling a little paranoid."

He had finally agreed to let me take off his ankle bracelet last night so we could go out to celebrate my birthday. It had taken me the better part of an hour to figure it out, but I'd finally bypassed the relay signal on Daryl's home-monitoring device, looping the signal from the device to his home phone. That way the connection was never broken, and it was safe to take it off without alarming the authorities.

You should have seen the look on his face when I'd finally laid the device on his coffee table. He was a little nervous, but once he realized the device was still working as if it were on his ankle, he broke out in this big grin and said, "I'm really impressed, Benny." That made me feel good—almost as good as when I handed my ID to the bartender later that night and purchased my first legal drink. Yeah, overall it was the best birthday celebration I'd ever had.

Now it was back to reality, and the first order of business was to get Daryl hooked up again before he had a heart attack.

"No problem," I said. "All I have to do is clip it on and redirect the signal back to the relay, but I'm still a little tipsy. You got any Coke or coffee to help me sober up? I don't wanna make a mistake. It's a little more complicated than it sounds."

"No, no mistakes. That's the last thing I need," he said. "I don't drink coffee, but I have a six-pack of Pepsi in the fridge and a 5-Hour ENERGY in the cabinet. That should be enough caffeine to get the light-headedness outta you." Daryl spoke as he headed to his bedroom. "I'll be right back. I wanna put on some loose sweats before you put that thing on my ankle."

"Cool. I'll grab that Pepsi if you don't mind," I said.

"Help yourself," I heard him say as he disappeared into his bedroom.

I walked to the fridge and grabbed a can of soda, cracking it open and guzzling down a few swallows. As I turned to head back to the living room, I noticed a book sitting on the counter next to the refrigerator. I already knew Daryl was a reader, because I recalled carrying in several boxes of books when my dad and I had helped him move in.

Picking up the book, I read the title out loud, "*Both Sides of the Fence* by M. T. Pope." I began flipping through the pages and then read the description on the back of the book. It described the story of a married man on the down low. Sounded pretty scandalous.

What the hell is Daryl doing reading this book?

I put the book down, picked up my drink, and headed back to the living room. Still a little curious about Daryl's choice in reading, I strolled over to his bookcase to see what other types of books my new friend was interested in reading.

I browsed the shelf, noticing all kinds of nonfiction titles, books about sports and history and stuff like that. But then my eyes landed on a white book, and the title caught my attention. I pulled it from the shelf and stared down at it. "Whoa, shit!"

"That's a pretty good book." Daryl startled me and I dropped it. Good thing I had set down my soda or I'd owe him a carpet cleaning. I looked up at him. He was wearing a robe instead of the sweats he'd said he was going to change into.

"You've read this?" I held it up, the cover now facing him so that there'd be no mistake about which book I meant.

"Yeah." He spoke casually, as if the book I was holding was the Holy Bible and it was normal for everybody to have read it.

"You've read *On the Down Low* by J. L. King?" Again I had to be clear that we were talking about the same thing.

"Yeah. It gave me a lot of insight into that lifestyle. You should read it," he replied, shrugging and then heading over to the couch. I watched him position himself on the sofa, placing his ankle on the coffee table. "Okay, genius, put this thing back on."

Still a little shocked, I put the book back on the shelf, then walked over to the couch and sat down next to Daryl, staring straight ahead kind of dumbfounded.

"What are you waiting for?" Daryl asked.

I picked up the device and knelt down on the floor next to the coffee table. I'd said I wanted to sober up, and I was definitely no longer drunk. I just couldn't figure out why my hands were shaking.

"You okay there, Benny? You look a little nervous, man."

I looked up at him, embarrassed. "Uh, yeah. I'm all right, but could you pull your robe a little tighter? I'm getting an eyeful of your privates, and it's not exactly what I wanna see when I'm trying to concentrate. Know what I mean?"

"Oh, my bad. Sorry about that." He pulled his robe closed, but I couldn't shake the image of the biggest dick I'd ever seen in my life—and I don't even think he was erect. Now I'd been in my share of locker rooms playing ball, but I'd never seen anyone working with anything like that.

"So, um, Daryl, how long did you say you were in jail?"

"Not sure if I did," he replied. "But I did eighteen months in Otisville, New York, a fed joint. Why?"

"Nothin'. Just asking."

"Look, man, I told you. I'm no killer or anything like that. I just got caught up in some shit I had no business being in."

I didn't answer him, only kept my head down and my attention focused on the ankle bracelet.

Daryl tapped me. I looked up at him and he winked. "But I am gonna kill you if you don't get this thing back around my ankle."

"Almost done," I said with a nervous laugh.

It took me around thirty minutes in total to put on the device and rewire everything.

"You up for a game of *Madden*?" Daryl asked when I finished. "I been practicing." He picked up a game controller.

"Uh, look, you know what? I'm really tired," I said, putting my tools in their case.

"Aw, man, who you fooling? You just don't want me to finish getting in that ass."

Exactly. I swallowed hard and stood up. "No, for real. And you know how my pops can be. I better get going so I don't have to deal with him."

Daryl put down his controller. "Well, all right, I guess you're gonna be the party pooper. I hope you had a good birthday."

I made my way to the door. "I had fun. A little different than I expected, but nice. Look, Dee, I'll get with you tomorrow, all right?"

"Cool," Daryl said as I exited, then closed his door. I turned and looked back at the door, wondering was it possible Daryl was on the down low?

Connie

19

Ten pounds! I'd lost ten pounds since Daryl had started training me, and I felt like a new woman. I was exhilarated, rejuvenated, and renewed after stepping off the scale this morning at the YMCA. I hadn't felt proud of myself for anything in so long. It sure as hell beat tired, weighed down, depressed, and lonely, which was how I'd been feeling the past few weeks since Avery walked out and asked for a divorce. Okay, I still felt lonely, but other than that I felt as good about myself as I had in a long, long time.

"Hey," Daryl said as I was inserting the key into my door. We'd just come back from our Saturday morning workout. "You've really been doing well. I'm impressed."

"Thanks. I hope that Y scale didn't lie."

"Scale's not lying. I can see it in your face." He smiled. "That's the first place you start to see weight loss. I really am proud of you."

"Daryl, you've been a good friend during a really bad time. I don't know what I would have done after Avery left if I didn't have you to talk to—" I stopped because I could feel myself getting emotional.

"Hey, that's what friends are for. To be honest, it's his loss. You keep doing what you're doing, and he'll come running back, begging on his hands and knees. You'll see," he said as he headed toward his apartment. He slid the key in the lock and said, "By the way, me and Benny are going fishing on one of those charter boats this afternoon. Would you like me to bring you some fish?"

I turned to face Daryl before opening my door. "You catch, I'll cook 'em. How's that sound?" I winked at him, surprising myself.

I suppose those few little pounds I'd dropped had kicked in a little confidence. I was becoming the old me again.

"Sounds like a plan. I'll see you later, neighbor." He gave me his trademark charming smile, then went into his apartment.

"Bye, handsome," I mumbled to myself as I entered my apartment.

"Where you been, Connie?"

"Jesus!" I screamed, practically leaping a foot off the ground. Avery was sitting in a chair across the room. "Avery, dammit, you scared the shit outta me."

"Sorry. Didn't mean to." His words sounded gentle and kind, something I wasn't used to. I was surprised by his smile and the confident aura he gave off. Kind of reminded me of the old Avery, the man I fell in love with so many years ago. "How've you been, Connie?"

"Well, considering my husband's been gone almost two weeks, I guess I'm doing okay. I missed you, Avery." I walked toward him, tears filling my eyes. I touched his arm and ran my fingers down his forearm. As much as he'd hurt me, as much as I'd tried to make myself hate him, that simple touch sent a jolt of electricity through me.

Before I even had time to think about what I was doing, I'd dropped to my knees in front of him and reached for his zipper. I knew what he needed. I knew what would make him stay.

He placed his hand on mine to stop me. "Connie, please. I didn't come over here for that."

"Then what are you doing here?" I was confused and humiliated at the same time. How could he not feel the same spark I was feeling? I got up off the floor, wishing I could escape this room, maybe wind back time so that I was back out in the hall, feeling good about myself.

He nodded toward the duffel bag next to him. "I had to get a few more of my things...plus, I wanted to give you this." He reached down beside him and picked up a manila envelope that was folded in half. He extended it to me.

"What's this?" I asked, dread filling my heart as I took the envelope from him.

He kept his eyes glued on the envelope, as if he couldn't bear to look me in the eyes—or didn't want to. I looked back down at the envelope and ripped it open, pulling out the papers inside and giving them a quick glance.

"Are you serious? You still want to go through with this stupid divorce thing?"

"Connie, I'm sorry, but nothing's changed," he confirmed. "I told you I was here to get a few things." He made a noise that sounded like a chuckle, and it felt like a knife in my heart. "What? Did you really think I was here to move back in with you?"

"Well, yeah," I said.

Now he gave me an all-out laugh that made me want to slap him. My embarrassment transformed into pure anger.

"This is stupid, Avery," I shouted. "You don't have to do this. You've made your point. The same thing I used to get you, I didn't use it to keep you. I know I've let myself go, but I realize that now, and I'm making strides to correct it."

"Is that so?" He looked very skeptical.

"Yes. I've been working out and eating right. Hell, I've already lost ten pounds." I ran my hands down my body, my eyes pleading with him to at least notice the weight loss, as minor as it was, and see that I was trying. I wanted him to understand that I was bound and determined to be the woman he'd fallen in love with, both inside and out.

He didn't notice or at least he didn't act like he did. It was like Avery looked right through me. "Look, Connie, just read over the papers, sign them, and give them to your attorney. I think you'll see I was fair in what I'm willing to give you out of this divorce."

"Ha! What you're willing to give me? This is a joke," I blurted, pissed off that he seemed to think he was doing me a favor. "You ain't got nothing. If anything, the judge might make me pay alimony to your broke ass."

I could see his anger rising, and I realized that things were near the boiling point. A moment ago, I was determined to show him how much I wanted our marriage to work, and now I'd let him get the best of me and I was hurling insults. I had to dial back my anger before things got physical.

I softened my voice. "Look, Avery, I'm sorry. I didn't mean that. I'm just so angry because I'm trying really hard here." And I was trying—trying really hard not to break down in front of him. "I don't want to give up on you, Avery. And I don't want you to give up on me. I really don't. Can't you see? I've already lost ten pounds," I said again, hoping this time he'd see it.

He stood there for a moment, looked me up and down, then said, "Sorry, but I'm done. Guess you're a day late and about fifty pounds short." That hurt worse than any punch he could have thrown. He brushed by me and opened the door. "I want those papers signed the next time I see you."

"Goddamn you, Avery. You want out? Well, you can have out, but it's gonna cost you. And last time I checked, your ass was flat broke. How you gonna pay me unless you've robbed a bank in the last ten days?"

"You'd be surprised what I'd be willing to do to get rid of your fat ass. Just tell me how much it's gonna cost."

"Twenty thousand," I blurted out, picking a number I knew he'd never obtain. "You want me to sign, it's gonna cost you twenty thousand."

He didn't even flinch at the amount. "Okay. I'll see what I can do," he said and then exited the apartment.

I felt frozen with anger, disappointment, and regret. It took a couple of minutes before the reality of everything he'd said registered, and that's when I let out a roar.

"You motherfucker! I hate you! I hate you, motherfucker!" I was shouting everything I wished I'd said to Avery when he was in my face. "Broke-ass, tired-ass son of a bitch."

Before I could come up with more names, there was a knock at the door. I knew it was Avery, and this time I was going to say exactly what was on my chest.

I flung the door open and started right in. "You son of—"

"Yo!" Daryl stood there with his hands up, as if prepared to block oncoming punches. "What's going on? I heard you over here scream-ing at the top of your lungs like a mad woman." He peeked inside but only after I calmed down enough for him to be sure I wasn't going to hit him. "Is everything all right?"

"I'm sick of his shit," I blurted. "I did everything for that man. I cooked and cleaned and washed his nasty ass when he was sick. I hate him!" My bottom lip began to tremble, and tears leaked from my eyes.

At first Daryl stood there in my doorway looking at me; then he sort of nudged me on my shoulder. I looked up at him, but his eyes weren't on my face. They were roaming over my entire body, like I was on display. The funny thing is, I didn't mind it one bit because the expression on his face made me feel like he approved. Then his words confirmed it.

"The man's a fool," he said. "Mark my words. With a woman who looks as good as you, he'll be back. Or someone else will be here to take his place."

My heart began doing palpitations. Daryl's words had erased all of Avery's insults. And as if that wasn't enough, out of nowhere I felt his soft lips connect with mine. I probably should have pulled away. After all, even though Avery was filing for divorce, I was still techni-cally a married woman. Yes, I should have pulled away, but I didn't. I allowed his lips to cover mine and my tongue to intermingle with his until he finally pulled back.

Wow, that was probably the best kiss I've ever had, I thought. It was so good, in fact, that I had to catch my breath. We both stared at each other wordlessly.

I finally drummed up the courage to ask, "What was that for?"

He shrugged. "I don't know. It seemed like the right thing to do at the time. You looked like you needed it."

"I did," I said. "Can I have another?"

He leaned in again, and I closed my eyes, expecting another kiss. When it didn't come, I opened my eyes to see that he'd pulled himself back and was looking at me with a disheartened expression. I was about to ask him what was wrong, but then I heard a door opening in the hall. I peeked out there to see Benny, the young kid from the building, coming out of Daryl's apartment.

Daryl looked at Benny, then at me, and whispered, "You know, Connie, we're both in a very vulnerable place in our lives right now and going any further could complicate things."

It wasn't what I wanted to hear now that he had me all hot and bothered, but I knew he was probably right. The last thing I needed in my life was more complication. "Good night, Daryl," I said with a smile as I closed my door and went to dream about our kiss.

Avery

20

It was just about closing time when I locked the door at Cheap Sam's Furniture. Life sure takes us down strange paths, doesn't it? You couldn't have paid me a million bucks to think I'd ever walk in that place again after the way they passed me over for the position of manager, but there I was, staring across the showroom once again.

Ever since the night I met Cain, I'd been doing a lot of thinking, and I'd gained a new perspective about my life. It was time for me to stop being a goddamn doormat. I'd spent the better part of the last three years helping to build Cheap Sam's. I'd had a hand in almost everything that was on the sales floor. It was too much for me to give up and walk away without anything to show for it, so now I was back—back to claim what was rightfully mine.

"Hey, snap out of it," Cain whispered from behind me. "Get your head out your ass. You've got a job to do, remember?"

"You're right. Sorry about that," I whispered as Sam's pimply-faced son walked out of what should have been my office. I'd gotten caught up in the moment and almost forgotten my objective.

"You can apologize later. We've got work to do now. You ready? Because there's no turning back after this."

"Ready as I'll ever be," I replied with a nod, then moved quickly toward the center of the showroom. Although it was almost closing time, I was surprised that no one had even looked in our direction.

I pulled out two handguns I had tucked away in my overcoat.

"All right, ladies and gentlemen!" Cain announced as he revealed the sawed-off shotgun he'd been hiding. "This is a robbery! Hit the floor or get shot. The choice is yours."

He fired one warning round into the ceiling, and all of a sudden, everything we'd talked about and planned was no longer idle chitchat but reality. We were actually robbing my former employer with real guns, and people were screaming in fear. I had expected to be nervous, but surprisingly, I felt a surge of power pumping through my body. It was a euphoria like I'd never felt before.

I walked over and looked down at Sam Junior, who was cowering on the floor like a little bitch. I bet he wished Daddy hadn't made him manager now. I kicked the little prick in the ribs twice for good measure and laughed, only stopping when Cain swiveled his head in my direction, reminding me once again that we were there for a reason other than my personal vendetta. I had a job to do. As Cain patrolled the showroom floor, I made sure my mask was secure over my face, then headed directly to the counter in the back. I spotted Jerri lying facedown on the floor in front of her desk, and I was momentarily distracted by the roundness of her ass. I couldn't help but imagine her on all fours with me hittin' it from the back. When I noticed that she was shaking, I sort of felt bad. I had this strange urge to apologize to her for cursing her out when I quit. It wasn't her fault that those pricks had made the mistake of passing me over.

"You got the money?" Cain barked from the center of the store.

I didn't answer, but I did force myself to focus on the job at hand. I could have stared at Jerri's ass all day, but I wasn't there to sightsee. I was there to get paid. There'd be plenty of time for pussy when I got back to Cain's place and hooked up with Holly and the other girls.

"Get up," I commanded, but Jerri didn't move. "I said, 'Get up'!" I repeated, tapping her firm, round ass with my foot. She looked up at me as if to confirm that I was indeed speaking to her before she made a move. "I said, 'Get up'!"

"Okay, okay," she said, tears streaming down her face. "Please don't shoot me," she begged as she got off the floor.

"Let's go," I demanded, nudging her along with my guns until we were in front of the safe. "Open it!"

"Okay." Her hands trembled as she tried to put in the combination. Her first attempt was a bust.

"Open the goddamn safe, or I'll blow your pretty fucking head off," I said to give her some incentive to hurry.

"I'm trying! I'm a little nervous," Jerri cried out. She turned around and looked at me. "Please don't kill me."

"Open up the safe." I pointed both barrels at her, and she got the message. She quickly swiveled back to the safe, this time opening it successfully.

I removed the duffel bag from my shoulder and threw it on the ground at her feet. "Now put the money in the bag." She wasted no time following my orders. The sense of power I got from that was incredible. "Back down on the ground. Facedown."

"You got the money?" I heard Cain yell again from the floor.

I left Jerri on the floor and ran back up front, lifting the bag to show Cain. "Got it."

He nodded, and I could imagine the smile he had under his mask. "Good. Let's get the hell out of here."

We gave one last order for everyone to stay on the ground for the next ten minutes, and then we headed to the door. I noticed Cain make a move to lift his mask, but I grabbed his arm.

"No, not yet. The cameras are still on us," I warned, jerking my head upward to draw his attention to the camera above the exit. He pulled his mask back down, and we headed out to the getaway car.

"Hell yeah! We did it!" I shouted as we drove out of the parking lot toward the first of several car switches we would make in the next few hours.

"How much you think we got?"

I looked down at the bag, opening it so he could see the cash inside. "I'd say it's about thirty grand."

"Thirty grand?" Now that his mask was off, I could see the huge smile on his face. "Man, that was ingenious. I never thought about robbing a furniture store on a Sunday night."

"Like I told you, they don't make deposits until Monday, so you get the whole weekend's take. You'd be surprised how many people around here pay cash or use layaway, especially around the first of the month."

"Like I said, Avery, you're a fucking genius. I told you all you had to do was think positive and start living like you're dying."

"Yeah, you sure did."

"So, how do you feel?" he asked. "Gave you a sense of power, didn't it?" He didn't even wait for my answer. "Man, sometimes when I'm standing there with my gun in hand, I almost feel like I'm high off the adrenaline rush."

I sat there and stared at my partner in crime.

"What's wrong?" Cain asked. "Why you looking at me like that?"

"I don't know. A little overwhelmed, I guess." I looked down into the bag of money. "It's just that that day on the bridge, when you told me it was time to change my life . . . hell, even when you invited me over your house with the girls and started talking that 'live like you're dying' crap, I had no idea we'd end up doing armed robberies."

"First of all, it's not crap. It's a way of life." He actually sounded angry. "Secondly, your life, my life—both of our lives—ended on that bridge. We were as good as dead. Now look at us." Cain reached into the duffel bag and pulled out a fistful of money. "Tell me you didn't feel alive in there, Avery. Tell me the adrenaline that was pumping through your veins back there didn't make your dick hard. Tell me you ain't got thirty or forty thousand reasons to live."

This time Cain waited for my reply. I stared at the money. It would definitely make a difference in my life. "Well, partner . . ." I took out a handful of cash. "Looks like change done come," I said with a smile.

"And it ain't chump change either," Cain said, and we rode into the night, laughing all the way.

Connie

21

I was lying in bed with my eyes closed, but I wasn't anywhere near sleep. I was dreaming, though—daydreaming about that kiss Daryl had planted so expertly on my lips. As a matter of fact, I had been replaying it for almost a week: the soft caress of his lips and his tongue connecting and intermingling with my mine. Just thinking about it had me so warm inside I felt like I was going to melt. I'd never been kissed like that before—not my first kiss, not my prom kiss, and damn sure not my wedding-day kiss. To say that it was magical would not be exaggerating. It was the most accurate description I could come up with. The memory of that kiss had the power to erase the pain of my failing marriage. Whenever I felt myself getting sad about Avery, I let my imagination wander back to Daryl, and then I felt all right.

I sat up in bed and touched my lips, wishing that I could do more than fantasize about Daryl's kisses. I recalled the words he'd spoken when I asked for a second kiss: *"going any further could complicate things."* Oddly enough, instead of feeling rejected, I'd felt protected, like Daryl was stopping me from doing something I might regret. Still, I was a big girl, and what would it hurt to get one more kiss?

I pulled the covers off and got out of bed. I threw on a robe, slid my feet into my slippers, and went to the bathroom to brush my teeth. Then I strode over to Daryl's apartment and knocked on the door. I was a woman on a mission.

As the seconds ticked by and I waited for him to answer the door, I started second-guessing myself. All of a sudden I felt naked standing there at his doorstop. I looked around and prayed no one saw me, a married woman, visiting a man other than her husband—in her pajamas.

I tightened my robe and mumbled to myself, "This better be worth it." I'd barely gotten the sentence out of my mouth when Daryl's door cracked open.

"Connie?" His eyes were half-opened and he stifled a yawn. Obviously I had woken him up. He peeked his head out the door, then looked at me again. I could tell by the way he wrinkled his brow that it had dawned on him that I was in my nightgown. He asked, "Is everything all right?"

"Everything is fine. You don't have company, do you?" If he had another woman in there, I was going to be pissed. I know I didn't have a right to be, but I'd still be pissed.

"No, just me."

"Can I come in?"

"Um, yeah, sure."

I stepped forward, practically forcing my way past him.

"What's up? What's going on?" he asked, looking at my pajamas again.

I didn't know how to say it other than to be direct. "I came here to finish what you started the other day."

I think it took a minute for my words to register, but then his blank look transformed into wide-eyed surprise. "Connie, I already told you I don't think that would be such a good idea," he reasoned. "You'd had a fight with your husband. I had a bad breakup with the woman I was seeing. We were both feeling abandoned and vulnerable. I never should have taken advantage of that situation. I'm sor—"

"Will you stop making excuses and kiss me?" I stepped up to Daryl and wrapped my arms around his neck, looking into his eyes as I leaned my head toward his. I watched for his reaction to see if there was any resistance. When I saw none, I went for it. I pressed my lips against his.

I kept it brief this first time with a short, gentle kiss. When I pulled away, I searched his face once again for any type of resistance. His features had relaxed, and I took that as a sign to keep going. I kissed him again, this time slipping in my tongue.

Daryl took a step closer, simultaneously pressing his body against mine and closing the door. What I felt poking me was not resistance. Let's make that clear.

His reaction only excited me more. I deepened our kiss, exploring his mouth with my tongue and caressing the back of his head. His hardening manhood had my juices damn near dripping. All of this just from a kiss.

I felt him reach down to untie my robe, and suddenly I was no longer the one in the driver's seat. *Oh, shit*, I thought, *I only came here for a kiss*. I swear that's all I had planned on doing, but as I felt him cupping his hand over my private area, I knew I was about to get more than I'd bargained for. I was going to step over the line and become a cheating wife.

"Ohhh, Daryl." I couldn't stop myself from moaning as he massaged the wetness through my underwear and placed little kisses all along my neck.

He paused for a minute and looked in my eyes. "You sure about this?"

At this point, my heart was racing and every nerve ending in my body was on high alert. There was no turning back now. "I'm still here. Is that a good enough answer for you?"

A smile crept across his face. There was a mischievous twinkle in his eyes, as if he was thinking, *Okay then, you asked for it.*

The next thing I knew, Daryl was removing my robe and slipping my underwear down my legs. I stood there in my gown, praying he didn't try to lift that over my head. I'd lost a few pounds but not enough that I could stand naked in front of him and not feel self-conscious.

To my relief, Daryl only lifted my gown. Then to my utter shock, he lifted me off my feet. In a move I wouldn't have thought possible, he kneeled down and positioned my legs around his shoulders, and then he stood up, sliding me up the door. My head damn near hit the ceiling as I secured my thick legs around his neck and shoulders.

I heard him inhale and then exhale with an "Ummmm. You smell so good."

"Thank—" was all I could get out before he began licking, kissing, sucking, and slurping. From my spot on his shoulders, I felt like I was floating on air, getting licked and sucked on like a lollipop.

He took a break only long enough to say, "Ummmmm, and you taste good too."

I had no idea how this brotha was doing it, but he damn sure was doing it well. He had all this woman midair, using his tongue to pleasure me while he rubbed my ass cheeks like he was kneading dough. Never, ever, not never, ever, ever, ever had a man made me feel like this, and I was going to take full advantage of it.

I grabbed the back of his head like he was a steering wheel and I was the driver. It wasn't like the man was lost and didn't know where he was going, but just like a woman passenger, I still had to do a little backseat driving and guide him. It was my pleasure. It was my fantasy come true, only it was even better than I'd imagined it would be.

"Say it." I would have gladly complied, but I had no idea what he was talking about. "Say it," he ordered once again.

"Say what?" I asked, barely able to speak clearly.

"Say the word I'm spelling in your pussy."

That's when I realized that there was an art to what he was doing between my legs. He was meticulously using his tongue to place letters on my kitty kat.

There went the *D*, I realized with a moan.

Now the *A*.

"Ummmm."

The *R*.

"Ahhhhhh."

The *Y*.

A huge grin spread across my lips, and I had to bite down on one of my fingers to keep myself from screaming.

The *L*.

"Daryl," I moaned, but I guess it wasn't loud enough.

"What's my name?" he demanded, his tongue still working its magic.

"Daryl," I cried out happily as he began sucking my clit. "Daryl! Daryl! Daryl! Daryl! Dar—" I exploded in orgasm. He sucked up all my juices like we'd taken a lap around the park and he was thirsty.

Even though he'd done all the work, I felt like I'd finished a workout as well. I was drained.

He slid me back down, allowing me to place my feet on the ground.

Breathing heavily, he managed to get out, "Say it again. What's my name?"

I was leaning against the door frame, still trying to catch my breath too. "Daryl," I whispered, looking deeply into his eyes.

He gave me a peck on the cheek and took my hand. I melted. This man was a dream. It couldn't have been real. Men didn't know how to make women feel that way. At least I'd never met one who had.

Daryl had made me feel so good, and it was only fair that I returned the sentiment. I kissed him, tasting myself in his mouth as I pushed him over to the couch.

"Take 'em off," I said playfully, snapping the waistband of his pajamas. He removed his T-shirt, and for a minute I was unable to do anything but stare at his muscular torso, covered in tattoos. I'd never been with a man with so much ink, and even though I didn't need any more encouragement, it was a real turn-on.

He stood with his calves up against the couch and slid his pajamas down to his ankles. I literally gasped at the size of his Johnson. He was all man—more man than I'd ever been with—but I didn't let that stop me.

I nudged his chest gently and he fell back onto the couch. We got the formalities out of the way quickly when he sent me into his bedroom to get a condom out of his nightstand. I was so wet from his tongue workout that after I put his condom on, I slid down effortlessly onto his mini–baseball bat and went to work, rolling my hips back and forth, fast. I wasn't about to play around with it. It felt too good to waste time being timid.

I wanted to give him the same kind of rush he'd given me. I went up and down, back and forth...hell, I even went sideways, and his dick curved right with me, as if it were a custom-made fit.

I heard him groan, and then he lifted his upper body slightly off the couch. I knew it was coming then, so I tightened up around him and bounced up and down like I was on a pogo stick. "Damn, woman," he said as he pulled me down hard on him.

But that wasn't enough for me. I needed to hear him. "Say it," I ordered. "Say it."

"Connie. Oooooh, Connie, baby." He said it like I was his. Like he was mine. He said it over and over, and every time he said my name, I went faster and harder until I felt him explode inside of me. I shuddered, feeling my own delicious orgasm as he pulsated inside of me.

He had his head leaned back and his eyes closed, and he wore a smile on his face. He looked happy and satisfied, but I wasn't done with him yet. I'd come twice, and he was still on number one, so I was ready to get down on my knees and get started on his second round. I made a move to climb off his lap.

He put a hand on my arm and said, "No, lay here for a minute."

I wish I could say that after two A-plus orgasms I had lost all my inhibitions, but that wasn't the case. I was not about to put all my weight on top of this man and lay there.

He must have sensed my insecurity, because he helped me up, moved his body as far back against the couch as he could, and then patted the spot in front of him. "Come on, lay down."

I did as he asked, lying down with my back to him. He draped his arm over me and pulled me back against his body as tightly as he could. This felt like heaven. After a couple of minutes, I could hear his breathing become slow and steady. He'd dozed off to sleep... with me in his arms.

It felt so good to be lying there, cuddled up beside a man, feeling desired, that I wanted to shout to the world how good I felt, but I would start by telling Daryl. I turned my body around to face him, and he stirred, slowly coming out of his post-sex sleep. I put my leg on top of his and began rubbing my foot up and down his leg to wake him. That's when I felt something weird beneath his pajama bottoms.

I sat up and asked, "What the hell is that?"

"What?"

"This." I nudged his ankle with my foot.

"Oh, that?" He was fully awake now, but he sure looked like he wished he wasn't.

"Yeah, that," I said flatly.

"Well, I guess I didn't tell you . . . I'm on house arrest."

Krystal

22

"Have a good day, baby," I said to Slim as he released my waist. "And hurry home."

We'd just had our good-bye kiss, the one he insisted on having every morning on the stoop in front of all the cackling hens, like we were a commercial for eHarmony or something. It wasn't that I didn't want to kiss Slim. He was a good enough kisser, but I couldn't have cared less about what the peanut gallery on the stoop thought. My concern was that one of these days Daryl was going to walk out and see us kissing.

Yes, I still had the hots for my ex, despite being engaged to a man I loved, a man who would lay the world at my feet. Believe me, it wasn't like I wanted to feel this way about Daryl, but he had this hold on me, mentally and physically, that he probably didn't even know he had.

"I will," Slim replied flirtatiously. "I gotta get back home to finish what you started this morning. I don't know what's gotten into you lately, but I like it."

There were a few snickers from the peanut gallery, but I didn't care. Sure, I'd woken his ass up at six o'clock this morning, and I fucked his brains out for the next two hours too. I'm not ashamed of it. I was horny as hell. I got that way whenever I dreamed about Daryl making love to me, and well, that seemed to be happening every night lately. Add in the fact that he was living in such close proximity, and I felt like I was losing my mind.

"You, baby. You've gotten into me deep and hard," I told him with an equally naughty grin on my face. I couldn't see their faces, but I was sure the stoop crowd was losing their minds. Slim and I loved teasing these horny old bats. "You know this is all yours whenever you want it."

"That's right, 'cause you know Slim always has what you need."

"That's right, Daddy. You always have what I need." I ran my hand across his package for all to see. It didn't take long for a bulge to appear through the thin material of his summer trousers. *Now that, bitches, is what I'm working with.*

He kissed me again and said, "I left something for you on your pillow."

"A little blue box I hope?" I wanted to get to my apartment so bad I almost jumped out of my skin. I loved those little blue boxes he gave me. I don't mean to sound shallow, but I could wake up to one of those blue boxes every day. Forget the man, just give me the present.

"If it is a little blue box, I got something for you when you get home. Something even better than what you got this morning."

"Look, you better stop talking like that or I might not make it off the block," Slim warned. It was kind of cute the way he kept glancing in the direction of the neighborhood gossips to see if they were listening. It felt good to know my man was proud that I was his.

"Go ahead and handle your business, baby. I'm not going anywhere. I'll be right here waiting for you when you get back," I said.

"Butt naked in pumps?"

I could feel the women's eyes wander toward me, so I decided to give them the show they were looking for. "Butt naked in pumps, baby, with a can of whipped cream in one hand and K-Y Jelly in the other."

"Aw, shit now," Slim said. "Lemme get outta here so I can hurry up and get back. I'll be home around three."

"I'll be waiting." I shooed him away playfully, but not before he planted another kiss on my lips.

"I love you," Slim said as he walked away.

"Love you too." I stood there for a moment, marveling at how far Slim and I had come in our relationship. I couldn't believe he had actually taken the leap to get us our own place. And if that wasn't enough to show how serious he was about spending the rest of his life with me, I had this huge rock of an engagement ring to prove it. So what the hell was wrong with me that I still couldn't stop thinking about Daryl?

My mind wandered to the blue box that Slim said he had left on my pillow. Maybe that would help me forget Daryl. And even if it didn't, I knew it would make me feel good.

I headed back into the apartment building, eager to get the box. For some reason, the fates had decided they were going to fuck with me, because just as I walked into the lobby, Daryl came out of the stairwell. As always, he looked good, wearing slacks and a polo shirt. I caught a glimpse of the Jewish star pendant I'd bought him, and instantly I wished we could turn back to those happier days.

He froze for a moment when he saw me. As we stood there staring at each other, I could feel butterflies in my stomach and moisture between my legs. There was something about being in close proximity to that man that turned on my waterworks. I half smiled, wishing that I could drag him into my apartment and fuck him until I was raw inside.

Unfortunately, it didn't take him long to snap out of his fog and remember the reality of our situation. A frown darkened his face as he headed in my direction. At first I thought he was going to curse me out or maybe even raise his hand to me, but instead, he brushed right past me as if I weren't even there.

"Daryl, wait," I said as I grabbed his arm.

He turned around, jerking away from me. "What?"

I exhaled, allowing myself a few seconds to try to put my words together. "I think we need to talk."

He sucked his teeth and glared at me. "You wanna talk? How about the fact that you had a fiancé the entire time you were making me think that we were going to be together? We don't have nothing to talk about, Krystal. Actions speak louder than words, and I got your message loud and clear."

"I know, I know," I replied, lowering my head. "I'm sorry. Once again I fucked up, but we still need to talk. Set some ground rules."

"Ground rules for what?" He relaxed a little, uncrossing his arms and letting them fall by his sides.

"Me and you."

He laughed. "There is no me and you. You're engaged to be married. You live with your fiancé. The two of you need to go and live happily ever after and leave me the fuck alone." He tried to walk off again, but I grabbed his hand this time, caressing it.

"What if happily ever after includes you?" I knew I was taking a shot in the dark, but I also knew that most men thought with their dicks. Daryl may have been smarter than most men, but he was still a man, and I had yet to meet one who could resist what I had to offer—no matter how mad I'd made him. "We can make this work if we want to," I explained. "And nobody's got to get hurt."

"Is that right?" he sneered as he pulled his hand out of mine. "What exactly are you suggesting? A threesome?"

That might be fun, I thought but ultimately said, "No, silly. You two have way too much testosterone for that." I was hoping my joke would break the tension a little, but no such luck. He was still glaring at me hatefully. I pressed ahead anyway, determined to break down his wall. "What I'm suggesting is an arrangement between you and me. We may not be able to be together twenty-four-seven, but you have to admit, nobody has chemistry like me and you."

I could see in his eyes that he was contemplating my idea. There was a glimmer of hope, so I continued, "Slim spends a lot of time away from home, and well...think about it. Do you think it's a coincidence that we ended up living together in the same apartment building? Don't you see? It's fate."

He put up his hand to interrupt me. I was kind of glad, because I had been working so hard to convince him I felt like I was about to start rambling. And no matter how much I wanted him, I did not want to beg. That is not a good look.

"So, that's it?" he said. "You want me for sex? And on top of that, you want me to play second fiddle to him and lurk in the corner like some punk? Ain't no way in hell that's gonna happen."

Oh, my, this was not turning out the way I had intended. I definitely hadn't meant to offend him. Appealing to his manhood wasn't working. Maybe Daryl was different, I decided. Maybe he needed romance.

"Baby," I said, trying a new approach. "You can't deny that we have something special. You can't deny how we make each other feel whenever we're together."

I reached for his hand, but he took a step back to increase the distance between us. "I think you forgot who the hell you're dealing with," he said. "I'm no jump-off. I don't share women. He can have you. I've moved on."

I tried again to reach for him, but he threw my hand off his arm as if he were throwing away trash. I refused to accept the thought that he was really through with me. I mean, why else would he have been blowing up my phone like he did? Daryl was just playing hard to get as far as I was concerned. I guess he thought I needed to be punished, but I was still confident that he would eventually give in.

Maybe I wasn't using the right words to get my point across. Like he said, actions speak louder than words anyway, so I placed my hands on his cheeks and looked into his eyes, prepared to take action. I pressed my body against his and began molesting his mouth with my tongue.

"Stop it, Krystal," he said, although it wasn't easy with my tongue working its way down his throat.

"You know you want me, Daryl," I breathed out heavily, then mashed my lips against his.

"Damn it, Krystal! Stop!" He gave me a little shove. "I don't want you. I've found somebody ten times better."

"I'm not letting you go!" I didn't give a damn what he claimed. I knew we were meant to be together. I did a little jump up in the air, wrapping my arms around his neck and my legs around his waist.

"What the fuck is going on in here? Get your hands off my woman!"

Shit! I thought my heart would bust out of my chest when I heard Slim's voice. I immediately released Daryl, letting my feet hit the floor.

I turned around, prepared to apologize. After all, he'd caught us in the act. But then I noticed the look on his face and realized there was still hope for me. See, he wasn't looking at me at all. His eyes were burning with rage, but it was all directed at Daryl. Slim was staring him down, breathing hard, and clenching his fists like he was about to go postal on Daryl's ass.

In a nanosecond, I knew what I had to do to save myself and my relationship. I reared back and slapped Daryl as hard as I could.

"Get away from me!" I screamed as I scrambled across the lobby into Slim's arms. "Did you see that, baby? Did you see that? He tried to attack me! He was gonna rape me."

"What! What the hell are you talking about?" Daryl massaged the spot where I had slapped him. "Why did you hit me?"

Looking back on it now, I know I should have been ashamed of myself, but at the time, I was acting on survival instincts. I was between a rock and a hard place, a position that only a snake could slither out of. Call me a snake if you want to, but I had to do what I had to do.

The look of betrayal on Daryl's face bothered me, but not enough for a confession. I'd make it up to him later.

"You should kick his ass, baby. Get him!" I cried into Slim's chest.

"Are you out your fucking mind?" Daryl spat.

"No, but you must be out of yours if you think I'm gonna let you get away with that foul-ass shit right there," Slim shot back. I felt him grab my arms, moving me aside so that he could go after Daryl.

"Baby, baby, wait!" I said, planting my feet and keeping my position in front of Slim. "It's not even worth it. The only thing that's gonna happen if you go after him is you ending up in jail." I nodded my head in the direction of the stoop ladies, who were all standing behind us, looking like they were ready to enjoy a show. They would watch the fight and love it, but those heifers wouldn't hesitate to talk to the cops after it was all over. Slim got my meaning and backed down a little, but he didn't like it one bit.

"I ain't gonna let some punk-ass nigga do my girl like that and—"

"Punk-ass nigga," Daryl repeated, taking a step toward us.

"That's ri—"

I cut off Slim's words with an eruption of loud crying. "Please, Slim, I can't lose you. I'm okay. I just wanna go inside," I wailed, putting on an Oscar-worthy performance.

"It's okay, baby. I'm here," Slim comforted me. He turned to Daryl and pointed a finger at him. "You one lucky muthafucka. Believe that. Next time you ain't gonna be so lucky." Slim wrapped his arms around me to escort me to the stairway.

I looked back at Daryl over my shoulder. He was standing there in utter confusion.

"Krystal, are you for real? You really gonna get down like this?" Daryl's eyes questioned me as well. "You ain't got nothing to say?"

He should have left it alone, because now I had to throw one last bomb so Slim wouldn't get suspicious. "Yes, I do have something to say," I replied. "I got a man, so keep your fucking hands off me!"

Benny

23

"Hey, son. Look, Pam is stopping over tonight, so if you don't mind, I'ma, you know, need you to make yourself scarce," Pop said as he entered the kitchen, where I had made myself a sandwich and popped open a beer.

I had just finished working on my blog, and I was about to go into the living room to settle in for the night and watch a movie. Needless to say, my pops telling me to get lost did not sit well with me. "What if I do mind? This is my house too," I said, probably in a more harsh tone than I'd meant to. But why did he have to throw a monkey wrench into my plans just because he had plans? Why couldn't they go somewhere else to handle their business? Why the hell couldn't they go to her apartment? *Uh, maybe because she's a thirty-five-year-old whore who lives with her momma.* Of course, I would have never said that out loud to my father, but that's how I felt.

"I understand," he said, "but you are the one who said that you feel a little bit uncomfortable when my lady friends come over, so I figured you wouldn't want to stick around."

Standing there with my plate in one hand and my drink in the other, I knew that in the end, it didn't really matter how I felt about it. Pam was coming and I was leaving. I slammed my plate and glass down on the counter. Brushing by my father, I mumbled, "If you could keep it in your pants once in a while, then maybe we wouldn't have to go through this."

"Excuse me, young man? I don't know exactly what it is that's got you feeling all big and bad, but you better watch it. At the end of the day, I'm still your father and this place is in my name."

"Yeah, well, maybe I should see about getting a place of my own."

On that note, I exited the kitchen quickly in case he felt like proving that he was still the man of the house. I knew better than to come at him like that, but I was twenty-one years old now, a grown man. I wasn't that same nerdy kid he loved bragging about, and sooner or later he needed to recognize that.

I went into my room, grabbed my knapsack, and then headed for the front door, figuring I'd go to the library or catch the train to Starbucks. In the living room, I called out, "I'm out. Call me when you get finished screwing!"

As I walked down the hall, I thought about knocking on Daryl's door. Other than our fishing trip, we hadn't hung out since my birthday, and to be honest, the fishing trip was a little awkward because I kept thinking about those books. To top that off, Pop ended up inviting himself to come along. He never came out and said it, but it seemed like he didn't like Daryl very much lately, so the conversation between them was always forced. At first I thought it was because Pop was jealous of how much time I spent with Daryl, and I'm sure that had something to do with it, but now that I'd seen those books at Daryl's place, I wondered if maybe he had picked up on something about Daryl that I hadn't.

I still didn't know what to make of those books. Was dude gay or bisexual? And if he was, had he turned that way after being locked up in jail, or was he born that way? What the hell made someone like that? As confused as I was, though, I still considered him a friend—perhaps even my best friend. He was the first real buddy, other than my father, that I'd ever had. I didn't want to lose that friendship. As long as he kept his hands to himself, he was still cool with me.

As pissed as I was at Pop, I decided I didn't feel like dealing with my confused feelings about my friendship with Daryl either, so I headed out of the building. I'd only gotten halfway down the block when I heard the worst sound a black man could hear in New York City.

Whoop-whoop! That's the sound of the police.

I turned to see a squad car rolling up beside me. "Hey, son, whaddya got there?" the officer on the passenger's side asked. He was staring at my backpack.

"Books," I said and kept walking, praying they would leave it at that and go bother someone else. I did not need this right now. My dad had already made it clear that he was running things and I was still a kid. Now the Man was trying to fuck with me. Did I have *punk ass* written on my forehead or something?

"Books, huh?" the officer mocked as the squad car rolled slowly beside me. "Well, why don't you stop walking for a minute and let me talk to you about those books?"

"Is that a request or a command?" I snapped, tired of being told what to do by everyone. That was definitely the wrong move because now the cop was pissed.

"I'm a muthafuckin' cop," he spat. "What the hell do you think?"

The car stopped, and the cop jumped out of the passenger's side. I knew better than to keep walking now or else I might end up with two warning shots in my back.

"Some of the neighbors say there's a lot of what appears to be drug dealing going on around here."

"Oh yeah? Then why are you wasting time talking to me when you got drug dealers to catch?" I should have lost the attitude, but somehow I couldn't.

He shot me a sharp look. "Who's to say I ain't already caught me a drug dealer?" He turned to his partner, who was now exiting the squad car, his hand on his holster. "I mean, he could pass for a drug dealer to me. What do you think?"

Cop number two shrugged, playing along with his partner. "Um, I don't know. Looks too pussy to be a gangbanger. I'd go with a lookout."

Officer Hard-Ass turned back to face me. "I'm going to ask you to allow me to see that backpack of yours."

By now there were a couple of bystanders watching New York's Finest try to punk me. Something about that made me boil inside. "I ain't lettin' you see shit. I know my rights."

"First of all, you ain't got no rights around here. This is a known drug area, which gives us probable cause to search your bag. Now, assume the position, dirtbag." Before my last word was finished, the cops had slammed me against a concrete wall. The driver pinned my hands behind my back while the other cop proceeded to go through my bag.

"You say you got books in here, huh, son?" He was breathing heavily as he fished around through my bag. Stupid son of a bitch probably got off on harassing brothers on the streets. "Well, this sure doesn't look like a book to me."

I looked over and saw him pulling the gun out of my bag. *Fuck!*

The cop who had me hemmed up against the wall asked, "What do you have to say about this?"

There was so much running through my head. I'd never been in trouble before, and I'm sure the cops thought if they used enough force they could scare me into saying anything. But I remembered the advice I'd gotten from both my father and Daryl. It was good advice that every black boy growing up in the inner city should learn. I turned my head and said to the cop, "I ain't got nothing to say other than I want my phone call."

Being in that police precinct felt like being on an episode of *The First 48*. The cops had secluded me in this little room with nothing but a table and three chairs for most of the night. I figured the other two chairs were awaiting a couple of officers to come in and do their good cop/bad cop routine.

"Here's that soda you wanted."

I looked up to see a male detective coming through the door with a can in his hand. I figured he would be playing the good cop. Behind him I saw one of the arresting officers, the one who had pinned me against the wall. Bad cop for sure.

"Thanks," I replied as the officer slid the can across the table to me. I wanted to tell him that I'd asked for the soda six hours ago. He sat down in one of the empty chairs. Bad cop stayed standing, doing his best version of an intimidating scowl.

"Let's not play games here," good cop said. "I know you're not some gun-toting thug. Like you told Officer Jenkins here..." He looked at bad cop. "There were books in the bag. We've checked you out. You're a college kid. A good kid. No record. It's probably not even your gun. You're probably holding it for somebody, right?"

I was more than just a college kid. I was a smart kid who knew better than to say anything to them besides "I want my phone call," which I repeated again for about the hundredth time.

Bad cop shot off, "Give the little fucker a phone call so we can get somewhere."

Good cop, of course, obliged. "What number you want me to call?"

"He's probably calling his mommy," bad cop taunted under his breath. "That's what they all do."

"For your information, my mother is dead," I said before rattling off the number for good cop to dial.

It rang several times, and I found myself saying a prayer that it wouldn't go to voice mail. I was terrified. Having never been in trouble before, I had no idea what I was supposed to do if the "I want my phone call" tactic didn't work. I guess then I'd have to demand a lawyer.

Just when I thought no one was going to answer, I heard, "Hello?"

"Daryl?" My voice cracked slightly. I'd been keeping my poker face on pretty well, but hearing Daryl's voice almost pushed me over the edge.

"Yeah, Benny. What's up, man? You sound weird."

"I got arrested," I replied, getting straight to the point. "On gun charges. They found a gun in my bag."

The first thing out of Daryl's mouth was "Don't say shit!"

"I haven't," I replied on the verge of tears.

"You didn't fire it off or anything, did you?"

"No."

"Good. Sit tight and don't say nothing. Where they got you at? They haven't sent you to Central Booking yet, have they?"

"No, I'm at the precinct right around the corner from the building. Daryl, don't tell my pops."

There was hesitation, and then he said, "Okay, cool. Don't worry. I'm on my way."

There was a click in my ear, and I felt like my lifeline had been cut. Something about having someone on my side there, even if it was only by phone, had made me feel secure for a few seconds. Now I felt like a surfer with a bleeding cut out in an ocean filled with sharks.

I guess the cops felt an urgent need to squeeze something out of me before Daryl got there, because they kept pressing me to talk while we waited for him.

"Come on, kid. Wouldn't you rather be home with your girlfriend getting laid than sitting up in here looking at my ugly ass?" good cop said.

"Fuck it! Let his dumb ass keep his mouth shut," bad cop interjected, glancing at his watch. "It's a little past six. The Central Booking bus will be here in an hour. He'll be somebody else's girlfriend once they ship his ass over to Rikers Island. Bet he's a bitch before dinner."

I have to admit, that one almost got to me. The thought of going to jail...I couldn't imagine anything worse. Pop would probably never talk to me again. Shoot, forget about jail. He probably would have killed me for being picked up in the first place. That's why I had called Daryl instead. Considering the fact that he wore an ankle bracelet, he'd obviously had his own brushes with the law, so I knew he couldn't get on my case but so much.

After a tense half hour, the door opened and an older uniformed officer with a white shirt walked in. My hands started shaking because I was sure the Central Booking bus had arrived.

"Captain," good cop and bad cop greeted him.

His only words were, "Let him go."

I think everybody in the room did a double take, including me.

"Captain—" bad cop started.

"I said let him go," the captain repeated.

"But he has a—"

"It's not up for discussion. It's an order," the captain stated with plenty of bass in his voice.

Then realizing he'd basically punked his officer in front of me, he lightened his tone a little. "He's a college kid...trying to do the right thing. We've got no case."

"Do the right thing?" Now good cop had to add his two cents, and he wasn't sounding so good anymore. Matter of fact, he was starting to sound a little pissed. "This son of a bitch had a loaded nine-mil—"

"Let him go. You can't win this one. It's not worth the trouble," the captain said, then left the room.

Good cop and bad cop exchanged furious looks. I wondered how many times they'd been through this before—not that I really cared. After the way they'd harassed me, it was good to see someone put these two bitch-ass cops in their place.

Good cop took his sweet time getting up from the table and escorting me out of the room, but he finally did, and Daryl was the first person I saw when they took me to the front lobby. I walked over and gave him a quick hug with a pound on his back. He was standing next to a dark-skinned black man, who was wearing an all-white dashiki and turban. He was also wearing a Jewish star similar to the one Daryl always wore.

"Benny, this is Brother Israel. Brother Israel was instrumental in having you released."

"Thank you," I said, offering my hand in appreciation, although I had no idea what was going on.

"You are most welcome. Always a pleasure to help a striving young brother." Brother Israel smiled.

"Come on. Let's get out of here," Daryl said.

I looked back at the two cops staring at me. He didn't have to tell me twice. Shoot, I never wanted to see the inside of that place again.

We headed to the elevator and rode it down to the street level, where I walked out of the precinct on legs that were still a little shaky. Once outside, I saw about ten or twelve men dressed similarly to Brother Israel. I was introduced to them and thanked Brother Israel again for his help before he and the other men entered a van and pulled away.

"What the hell did you say to get me out?" I asked.

"Not what I said, but what Brother Israel said." Daryl laughed.

"Which was?"

"That you were on your way to the police station to turn in the gun through the amnesty program."

"The what?" I asked.

"You know, the program where you turn in guns from the street, no questions asked."

"And they let me go on his word?"

"Well, it didn't hurt that you had a college ID in your wallet. But the truth is, this plan wouldn't have worked if it wasn't for Brother Israel threatening to call the media and have every Black Israelite in the five boroughs outside that station protesting within an hour. We were about to go Malcolm X on this joint, Israelite-style."

I was touched. "For real, he would have done that for me?"

"No, he would have done it for me, because I told him that you needed my help and that you were a good kid and one of my best friends."

"Best friends, huh? Wow, that's one of the nicest things anyone has ever said to me." I looked over at him and said, "Thanks, Daryl, for getting me out. You're a good friend."

"Yeah, but I'm also a fool. I never should have given you that gun, and you can be damn sure I ain't giving you another one. You're never going to carry a gun again. By the way . . ." Daryl dug into his pocket and pulled out an envelope, which he handed to me.

"What's this?"

"It's your voucher for your free video games. You know, the voucher you were turning in the gun to receive." He rolled his eyes as we turned the corner, the apartment building now in sight.

I slowed my pace when I saw my father sitting on the stoop. For the first time ever, I would have loved to see those gossiping old hens out there instead.

"There's my dad," I said. "Do you think he knows?"

Daryl shook his head. "I don't know, man, but I guess we're about to find out."

Avery

24

I pulled up in front of my old apartment building feeling like a brand-new man. The new suit I was wearing, not to mention my brand-new Mercedes-Benz convertible and a pocketful of money, might have played a little part in that, but the fact that I had gotten rid of a bunch of deadweight from my life, aka Connie and my job at Cheap Sam's, had much more to do with it. Even though the divorce wasn't final yet, I felt free. I felt good. I felt happy. I was starting to abide by Cain's "live like you're dying" creed, and it was working out even better than I could have expected.

We'd done four more robberies since we held up my former place of employment, pocketing almost $150K in cash. I couldn't wait for Cain to get back from the Cayman Islands so we could get back to business. He was down there depositing our most recent score into the corporate accounts he'd set up for us. I had to give it to him: the man had thought of everything. Once the money was deposited in our accounts, it would be readily available through debit cards and wire transfers. Heck, I even had my new Mercedes leased to the phony company, along with my new apartment over in Forest Hills.

As much as I loved the money, I think I loved the excitement and the rush it gave me even more, which was why I couldn't wait to hit our next spot.

"Well, lookie here, lookie here," I heard someone say as I stepped out of my car. As usual, the hens were out front clucking away. "Is that Avery Mack? Well, I'll be damned if you don't look open-casket ready. When's the funeral?"

The three other women on the stoop laughed at the comment as if they'd never heard anything funnier. I almost felt bad for them. I looked damn good, and these dried-up old heifers were only making jokes because they knew I'd never get with one of them.

"If you stepping up in here looking this good, you must be looking for Connie," Nancy, the queen of the stoop, said.

"No, actually," I corrected her, "I stopped by to see my daughter." It was true that I was there to see Krystal, but I sure wouldn't mind if Connie saw me looking this good and driving this car. Plus, I happened to have a big chunk of the money she said it would cost to get her to sign the divorce papers.

"Oh. Well, that's good, because Connie ain't here no way."

She gave the other women a knowing look, which set off a chain reaction of eye rolling and snickering. They obviously wanted me to think they knew something I didn't. It's not like I really cared about those broads or what they knew, but I'm only human. I wasn't about to let curiosity eat me up all afternoon and ruin my Saturday.

"Where is she?" Seconds after I said it I regretted it. The last thing I wanted was for them to be telling Connie I was over here inquiring about her.

"You know I don't like gossip, and I'm not one to participate in gossip of any form or fashion," Nancy started and I wanted to laugh. "But the fact that your wife got all fresh and fly and then headed out with the man in 3B, that ain't gossip. That's the truth."

She looked to her cohorts, and they burst out laughing, giving each other high fives like they had won some type of victory against me. I hate to say it, but it pissed me off. I was not sure why, though, because there was no way I was jealous of Connie—what she might be doing or who she might be doing it with.

To prove it to those women—and myself—I said casually, "Oh, Daryl," shooing my hand. "They probably went to the gym to exercise."

Nancy smirked and turned to her girls. "Maybe he didn't hear what I said, because I said Connie got all dressed up, looking all fly, and then left with the man. I didn't say nothing about her wearing a jogging suit or shorts and a T-shirt. She was wearing makeup and most likely a big girls' thong."

There was more hysterical laughter from the stoop crowd. I decided that Nancy was probably exaggerating, jealous that Daryl hadn't paid her no mind.

Nancy continued her comedy routine. "Oh, but if you say they're out exercising, Avery, then who am I to disagree?" The other women hung on to her every word. "What woman wouldn't want to exercise with a man like Daryl Graham... in three-inch heels, no less?"

The cackling started again. That sound was becoming like fingernails down a chalkboard, yet I stood there, acting unfazed. I refused to let these women think they were getting to me.

"So what? She went out to lunch with him. They're friends." I took a step toward the entranceway.

"Friends, huh? Okay, if that's what you want to call it. Besides with you two getting a divorce and all, it probably doesn't matter to you anyway."

"Divorce?" Nancy had said the magic word. I stopped in my tracks. I was surprised these women knew about that. Connie must have been out broadcasting it. I wondered how she'd broken the news to the women. Were they the listening ear when she needed a shoulder to cry on, or had she been out there joking and cackling about it? Maybe she felt as free as I did.

"Yeah, you two are getting a divorce, aren't you?" Nancy pressed.

Without responding, I opened the door to head into the building. That's when I heard one of the women say, "Speak of the devil. Here they come now."

Curiosity got the best of me, and I turned to see Connie and Daryl walking toward the stoop. She was all up in his face, laughing and blushing. She didn't even notice me standing there.

"Honey, if that's the devil, then I'ma try my best to earn me a ticket to hell," another one mumbled. "If you ask me, Connie traded up."

"Connie!" I called her name before I had time to stop myself. I don't know how the hell she didn't fall flat on her face in the high-ass heels she was wearing. Where did she even get those fire-red patent leather shoes? They must have been new, because she sure hadn't worn anything like that around me in years. Guess I wasn't the only person who was making a change.

I had to admit, though, she looked good. Looked like she'd lost some weight too—not that it was enough to change my mind about her, but she was starting to look like her old self.

"Avery," Connie greeted me unenthusiastically. "What's up?" she said and then took her next step past me like she was stepping over trash.

"Where you been?" I asked.

Connie stopped and looked at me like I was gum on the bottom of her new shoes. "Daryl and I went out to lunch, if it's any concern of yours. Didn't you ask me for a divorce?"

"Speaking of which..." I reached into my suit jacket and pulled out a thick envelope. If she didn't want to bother being civil, then I might as well get right to the point. I handed her the envelope. "It's half of what we talked about. I'll have the other half when you sign the papers."

Not too long ago, I would have expected her to start crying, begging me not to divorce her, but this time, she just tucked the envelope into her purse and said, "My attorney is looking over the papers," and then kept it moving. "I'll be in touch in about a week or two. Have a nice life."

It felt like I was being dismissed right in front of all those gossiping heifers, who were hanging on every word like they were watching a soap opera. They obviously couldn't wait to start running their mouths about what was going on between Connie and me... or Connie and Daryl... or whatever.

Speaking of Daryl, he'd stopped at the bottom of the steps and waited while Connie and I had our little exchange. Now he was standing there looking like he was dude from the Old Spice commercial. I was divorcing Connie, but something about this guy parading her around like she was some sex kitten pissed me off.

"You sure spending a lot of time with my wife," I snapped at him.

"Soon-to-be *ex*-wife" was his slick-ass reply. "And well, have you taken a good look at her lately? Somebody has to do it."

"What's that supposed to mean?" I asked as he came up the stairs.

He got in close to me as if he were about to share some deep wisdom, and then he said, "What it means is that you had a beautiful wife, a real good woman, and you fucked up." He looked over at Connie and allowed his eyes to roam her body from head to toe, his eyes lingering on her ass.

I wanted to punch him. He was lucky I'd promised Cain I'd lay low while he was out of town. Next time, he wouldn't be so lucky.

"You fucked up real bad," he said, then placed his hand around Connie's waist. He looked over his shoulder and winked before disappearing into the building with Connie, which for some reason infuriated me.

Krystal

25

I hadn't been able to sleep in days and it was starting to show. The bags under my eyes were bigger than some of the purses Kim Kardashian carries. It was getting so bad I couldn't even stand to look at myself in a mirror. I needed sleep badly before all this ugly became permanent.

I'd decided to go out to the park and play some handball like I used to do in the old days. I was hoping that the physical activity would tire me out enough so that I could at least get in a good nap. Heading back to my apartment all sweaty now, I planned to take a warm shower and crawl under the covers.

I didn't want to admit it to myself, but my lack of sleep was due to the incident with Daryl last week. It had me physically and mentally out of whack. I still couldn't believe I'd accused him of trying to rape me. Of all the excuses I could have come up with, that one had to be the worst. The fact that Daryl could hardly even look at me and definitely wouldn't talk to me now was driving me crazy. It didn't seem like anything could tear my thoughts from him—except maybe those blue boxes Slim left behind, and those seemed to be coming a little less frequently all of a sudden.

"Uggggghhhh!" I kicked a can on the sidewalk. If only there was something I could do to let Daryl know how bad I felt about that little stunt I pulled. But what words could I possibly say to make him understand? Even if I had the right words, it wasn't likely I could get him to listen to me anyway.

I rounded the corner near my building, and like every other day, I saw Nancy, Pam, and Ms. Bertha—the three Wicked Witches of the

West as I called them behind their backs. They were gathered around the stoop with their eyeballs peeled, looking like buzzards in search of a carcass. What new juicy bone of gossip were they tearing apart now, I wondered.

Nancy saw me coming and called out cattily, "Your daddy was here looking for you."

"He's gone now, though," Pam said with a smirk as I approached the stoop. "Got run off by the man from 3B."

"What?" My voice jumped an octave higher. Why would Daryl and Daddy get into it unless . . . ? *Oh, God, I hope Daddy didn't hear that he tried to rape me.*

"What happened?" I asked.

"You ain't heard? Your stepmomma is stepping out with the man from 3B," Nancy announced, more than happy to spread the gossip. Had it been any other news, I might have played along, but I wasn't about to listen to this bullshit.

"Stop lying," I sneered.

Nancy raised her hand and testified, "If I'm lyin', I'm dyin'."

Although I felt like she'd hit me in the solar plexus, I stood up tall and scoffed, "Y'all really need to get a life." Meanwhile, my heart was pounding. I didn't know whether to laugh or to scream.

No way would Daryl stoop that low to mess with Connie . . . would he?

I was barely up three steps past their little huddle when I heard one of them say under her breath, "She think she all that since she got engaged to Slim."

"Well, from what I saw, Miss Goody Two-shoes ain't so good. Slim might be falling for that ol' bull, but I know better. I saw her tonguing Daryl in the hallway the other day. I know what she told Slim, but I saw what happened, and these eyes don't lie," Pam whispered loud enough for me to hear.

"Say what?" Nancy replied.

"Mmm-hmm. She's already cheating on him and they ain't been engaged a month. She ain't shit."

I couldn't believe these brazen heifers, talking about me within earshot like I wasn't even there. I didn't give a damn if there was some truth to it. I turned around as I pushed open the front door and threw a remark over my shoulder. "You bitches need to mind your business. And I know you ain't talking, Nancy, or you either, Pam, 'cause you two the only ones around here who don't know that y'all sharing the same man. And your ass is married, Nancy." There was a long silence, and everyone but Nancy and Pam lowered their heads. "Now, y'all want something to talk about, talk about that."

Once I closed the door behind me and was out of sight of the Wicked Witches, I buried my face in my hands. I was devastated by what they'd said about Daryl and Connie, and tears fell freely from my eyes as I walked to my apartment.

He wouldn't do that, would he? He wouldn't mess with Connie just to get back at me. I'm the one who's vindictive, not him. He wouldn't do that to hurt me. Would he? Oh, God, between the lack of sleep and now this, I was an emotional wreck.

I went into my apartment and flopped down onto the couch. Angry tears were still falling. Why would Daryl want to hurt me this way?

With tears still blurring my vision, I pulled out my phone and typed in Daryl's number. I sent him an angry text: a little birdie told me that ur fucking my stepmom connie. how could you?

I'd sent him several texts since the incident in the hallway and he hadn't responded to any of them, so I was shocked when my phone beeped to alert me to an incoming text. I wiped my eyes and read this response: connie! have u lost your mind?

I dashed off an angry reply: no but u must have if it's true. if u were trying to get back at me for what happened with slim in the hallway the other day this is not the way.

His response came fast: if ur with slim why do you care who i'm with?

I had to read that one twice. What did he mean by "with"? Was he saying he was actually with Connie, or was he talking about being with someone in general? Either way, I didn't want to think about him being with anyone but me. I had to convince him that we were meant to be together.

I texted back: 1st she's my stepmother and i hate her. 2nd i'm a very jealous woman. 3rd i love you. 4th i don't think i can live without u. Plain and simple, that about wrapped up how I felt.

It took him a while to respond this time, but I felt relief wash over me when I read his text: why don't u come up.

I couldn't type a reply fast enough: really? do you mean it?

He replied: as long as you put something sexy on.

My heart leaped with excitement. I texted back: you ain't said nothing but a word. give me five minutes.

I rushed to the shower, perfumed up, and threw on one of my sexiest Victoria's Secret negligees with a matching thong. I touched up my makeup and freshened up my lip gloss, then put on a pair of stilettos. Putting a London Fog coat over my negligee, I headed out to win back my man. I was so excited I was already moist.

I knocked on the door four times before Daryl answered. "Who is it?" he called through the door, sounding a little irritated.

"It's me."

Finally, Daryl cracked the door an inch. Even so, I could see Connie's fat ass peeping over his shoulder. I almost lost my lunch.

"Can I help you?" Now his voice had a whole lot of attitude.

"Yes, can *we* help you?" Connie opened the door all the way.

I stared blankly at him for a second, trying to grasp what was going on. Had he set me up? Did he tell me to come over just to humiliate me?

"What is she doing here?" I blurted out.

Connie countered with, "The question is, what the hell are you doing here?"

"You...you played me," I said sadly to Daryl. I felt like such a fool standing there in my negligee. That bastard had probably had a good laugh with Connie, telling me to come over in something sexy.

Yet he still played dumb, like he had no idea what was going on. "I didn't do nothing to you," Daryl said, sounding perplexed.

"He's right, Krystal."

I recognized Slim's voice right away. I turned to see him walking over from the stairwell, and I swear it was like I saw our whole relationship flash before my eyes. "He didn't play you," Slim said. "You played yourself, you dumb ass."

"Slim, I—Wha...?" Shit. How was I supposed to lie my way out of this one? It wasn't like I could accuse Daryl of attempted rape, considering how I was dressed and the fact that Connie was standing right beside him. Having no clue what I could say to Slim, I finally just went with, "How did you know I was here?"

"It's a funny thing about those text messages. They sure can get people into a lot of trouble if they get sent to the wrong person." He held up his phone, reading from the screen, "First, she's my step-mother and I hate her. Second, I'm a very jealous woman. Third, I love you. Fourth, I don't think I can live without you."

Oh no! My heart sank. He was right; I was a dumb ass. I was so upset before that I must have mistakenly typed in Slim's number instead of Daryl's without even noticing it. How the fuck could I have been so stupid?

"Slim, baby, this is all a misunderstanding. You see, I was only trying to see if this bitch Connie was messing around behind my father's back."

Slim looked down at my stilettos and my bare legs, and his face twisted into a look of pure hatred. "Bitch, I am so sick of your lies."

I started sputtering desperately, "Slim, baby, you know you always got what I need. Baby, you gotta listen to me."

"Yeah, I always got what you need all right, but that's coming to a stop too. You can forget ever getting one of these from me again." He reached into his pocket and pulled out one of his little blue boxes. I almost jumped out of my skin when he threw it at me. I tried to catch it, but the box opened in midair and its contents flew out, covering my face, hair, and overcoat with white powder.

"What the hell is that?" Connie turned to Daryl, but his attention was on me.

"Cocaine," Daryl said sadly, finally turning his head toward Connie. The disappointment in his eyes was more than I could bear. "She's back on cocaine."

"Back on? This bitch has been a junkie for years. The day I met her she damn near freebased an eight ball by herself," Slim said.

"Wow...is that why she's been looking so out of it lately?" Connie asked.

I wanted to crawl into a hole somewhere and die. My secret was exposed—and it wasn't just that I was addicted to cocaine. The saddest part was that truthfully, my relationship with Slim had only lasted this long because he kept me supplied with coke. I know it sounds pathetic, but the thing that hurt the most was knowing that Slim would no longer be bringing me those little blue boxes.

Slim stepped up to Daryl, his face twisted into a grimace, and pointed his finger in Daryl's face. "Dude, I don't like you and I'm gonna tell you like this: stay away from me and mine." Then he turned to me. "Get your ass down these stairs."

I moved like my life depended on it. Maybe I could save this relationship after all.

Avery

26

My man Cain sure knew how to live life to its fullest, and I was now totally convinced that his way was the best way. It had only been about five or six weeks since that day we met on the bridge, but I'd totally changed my life around. For the first time in five years, I was financially stable. I ate in the fanciest restaurants, wore the finest clothes, drank the finest spirits, and fucked the finest bitches.

There was nothing I couldn't accomplish if I put my mind to it. I'd proven that earlier in the day, when Cain and I took down a pawnshop in New Jersey for almost two hundred grand in cash and another hundred grand in jewelry. It was our largest score to date, and the first one I'd planned entirely by myself. Cain had praised me so much when we got back to his place you would have thought I discovered a cure for cancer.

I was supposed to be out celebrating with him and the girls at some club in Long Island, but I hadn't left Queens yet. I'd made a detour over to my old building to see Connie. It might have seemed like I was going to my old building more than I had when I lived there, but it wasn't even like that. I wasn't sniffin' around trying to see what Connie was up to with that guy Daryl. Hell, if I wanted her, she'd be mine. After all, technically she was still my wife. Anytime I came by, it was strictly business. This time she'd called me up to let me know that her lawyer had approved the paperwork and that I needed to drop off the rest of her money. It just so happened that I had a pocketful of cash, so I was bringing her what I liked to think of as my ticket to freedom.

As I rode the elevator up to the third floor, I wondered if Connie was with that asshole from 3B again. I couldn't forget my last visit and the way that smug bastard had acted. I didn't know who the hell he thought he was, but I had something for his ass this time if he tried to embarrass me.

The elevator door opened and I heard, "Well, well, well." It was Daryl. That chump had the nerve to look me up and down with this irritating smile on his face. "And where are you headed looking all spiffed up?"

"Man, that ain't none of your business. I came to see my *wife.*" I didn't want her anymore, but I still felt the need to remind this dude that Connie was mine. "Why? You got a problem with that?"

A puzzled expression crossed his face. I'm sure he could feel what I already knew: I was not the old Avery Mack and I was not to be fucked with. "Ex-wife, isn't it? *Wife* is not exactly an accurate term for a man who filed for divorce."

I was not about to back down. "Yeah, well, we ain't divorced yet, which means she's still my wife."

"Your wife or not, Connie is my friend. We're close like that, so don't be coming around here upsetting her." He looked me up and down again like he was waiting for me to jump. Was this dude trying to bait me into a fight?

I straightened up and puffed out my chest. "You may have all these people around here thinking you're Mr. Big and Bad, but I don't scare so easy. Until our divorce is finalized, Connie Mack is my wife and I'll come see her anytime I want. Don't let me have to tell you again."

He sucked his teeth and said, "Or what?"

"Or else it's gon' be my last time saying it." I pulled my suit jacket back, revealing the piece I kept tucked in my pants. "And then I'm done talking. You feel me?"

That slowed his roll for a second. No doubt I'd caught him by surprise. "You threatening me?"

"Like I said, I'm done talking."

Things were getting pretty tense in that hallway. It felt like we were only a few more insults away from an all-out fight. It was probably a good thing that Connie chose that moment to open her door.

"You ready?" she asked, stepping into the hall. Her eyes went from Daryl to me as I discreetly allowed my suit jacket to fall over the gun. "What's going on out here?"

"Nothing. Just discussing a couple things," Daryl said, still staring me down. Then he turned to Connie. "You look beautiful."

"Thank you," Connie said, but the expression on her face said she understood our "discussion" wasn't exactly friendly.

She turned to me. "Avery, what are you doing here? And don't give me that crap about coming to see your daughter like you did last time, because she lives on the first floor, not the third."

I could see old boy snickering, and I wanted to pull out my gun and shoot him right there. Since I couldn't do that, I did something else that I knew would piss him off.

"I came to talk to you, if you don't mind," I told Connie as I walked toward her. "Can we go inside?"

"Ah, where the hell do you think you're going?" he asked, sounding like a whiny bitch. I was about to put his ass in his place, but Connie did that for me.

She raised her index finger. "Just give me a second with him, will you, hon?" Without waiting for his response, she stepped aside to allow me into her apartment. You know I had to give old boy a grin as I walked in and closed the door in his face.

"What did you need to talk to me about?" Connie asked.

I couldn't help but notice that the way she folded her arms across her chest made her cleavage look even bigger. When I saw her the last time, I was a little shocked to see how good she was looking; now I was every bit of amazed. She was really trimming down in all the right places.

"I came to give you something." I reached into my jacket, pulled out the envelope, and handed it to her. "It's the rest of the money I promised you. Plus a little more."

She pulled the money out of the envelope and shuffled through the bills. "Oh my God, Avery. How much is this?"

"It's thirty grand. I wouldn't put it in the bank all at one time or the government might make you pay taxes on it," I said, chuckling at my own little joke.

"Avery Mack, where on God's green earth did you get this kind of money?"

"I got promoted," I told her. I hated to lie, but what was I gonna do, tell her I was an armed robber? Eventually I'd tell her I'd started a new business with Cain, but for right now I'd go with the planned lie. "You're looking at the new operations manager over at Sam's Long Island warehouse."

She raised an eyebrow and squinted at me with skepticism. "And now you can tell me the rest of the story, because this is a lot of money practically overnight."

"They gave me a nice chunk of change as a signing bonus."

She gave me a look that said she thought my story was bullshit. "You expect me to believe Cheap Sam's Furniture gave you a signing bonus and a promotion?"

"It's true." I handed her one of the business cards Cain had printed up, but she dropped it as she took it from my hand. She bent over to pick it up, and well, I must say she was looking pretty good.

"I have to give it to you, Connie. Your ass is looking good," I said because I hoped it would distract her from asking any more questions—and because it was true. I gave her a confident smile, the kind that used to melt her in the old days, but I swear it wasn't on purpose. It was more like a reflex. You know, when a man sees something sexy his body automatically responds. Hell, whether or not I was divorcing her, she was still a woman, and she was looking good.

The expression on her face was not one of pleasure or surprise, but more of disbelief. "Are you coming on to me?"

"Would that be so bad? After all, we are married, and I still love you."

She rolled her eyes. "Yeah, well, you should have thought about that before you decided to walk out on me."

"You might be right, but did you ever think about the fact that my leaving is what motivated you to lose the weight?"

Connie turned away, probably because she didn't want me to see it on her face that I was right. "Anyway," she said, "I've still got about twenty pounds to lose. It's not coming off as fast as it did when I first started, but I'm getting there."

"Well, I'd love to help you out there," I said seductively, taking a step closer. She tried to step back, but the entryway was a tight space. There was nowhere for her to go. "I mean, think of the work-outs we could have." I felt myself getting hard, something that Connie's body hadn't done to me in a long time. I tried to tell myself it was just leftover adrenaline from our last robbery, but the truth was my soon-to-be ex-wife was turning me on.

"Losing weight is not only about exercise and working out," she said, sounding nervous. "It's also about eating right and—"

I cut her off with a kiss. It landed on her cheek but only because she turned her head. I had tried to kiss her lips. "As far as eating right, let me take you out to dinner. I hear that new joint over on Merrick Boulevard specializes in salads and all this organic stuff."

"And since when do you eat organic food?" she asked, leaning her body away from me.

"Like I said, I'm trying to help you out. What do you think?"

"I think it's too little too late, Avery. I appreciate the offer, but I got all the help I need right outside that door. Now, can you give me some space?" She placed her hands on my chest.

I felt my competitive spirit rise. "Connie, that guy ain't doing nothing but using you. Trust me. I know guys like him. After he gets what he wants, he'll be in the wind."

She raised a hand to cut me off. "You don't know a thing about him."

"No, Connie, I know everything about him. It's you who doesn't know anything about him—or me, for that matter. I'm not the same old Avery." I pressed my weight against hers as I forced our lips to meet long enough to make sure she remembered. "And I'm not going to take no for an answer."

I stepped back, and the expression on her face told me everything I needed to know. She now understood who and what I'd become.

Benny

27

I'd just put on my shoes and was about to head out the door when Pop walked in looking worn down. I hadn't seen him much the past few days because he'd been doing a lot of overtime.

"Looks like you had a long day."

"Yep, a very long day," he said as he flopped down into his recliner. "You going somewhere?"

"Me and Daryl are going out for a couple of drinks."

Now he didn't only look tired, he looked irritated. Lately it seemed like he got a funny look on his face every time I mentioned Daryl's name. I kind of understood it, I guess, because before Daryl came around, Pop and I used to spend much more time together.

"Sit down, son."

I wanted to tell him I was in a rush, but his tone was pretty serious, so I sat down on the couch, hoping he would make it quick. I was supposed to be over at Daryl's fifteen minutes ago.

"I ran into Clyde tonight," he said, and then I knew this would not be a good conversation. Clyde was my father's cop friend who worked at the local precinct.

When Daryl and I had run into Pop on the stoop the day I got picked up for gun possession, everything seemed fine. I mean, he wasn't exactly friendly to Daryl, but he definitely didn't know anything about my arrest, or else he would have flipped out. Enough time had passed since then that I thought I was in the clear. But now that he was mentioning Clyde, I was pretty sure Clyde must have somehow found out and told him about the gun.

I tried to play it off. "Oh, cool. How's Clyde?" Inside, I was shaking like a leaf.

"What the hell were you thinking about, son?" Pop said, sounding disappointed.

"Pop, I—"

He blew up. "A gun? What the fuck were you doing with a gun?"

"Look, it was all a misunderstanding. Daryl took care of it anyway, so there's nothin' to worry about." I said this casually, hoping it would calm him down, but that was a mistake. It only seemed to make him madder.

"Oh, Daryl took care of it, huh? Who the fuck is he to be taking care of my son?" His voice went up a few decibels. "From now on, I don't want you hanging out with Daryl. That guy's bad news."

Before I even knew what I was doing, I jumped up from the couch and yelled at my father, "You're not going to choose my friends! I'm a grown man!"

Now it was his turn to jump up. He got right in my face. "So you're a man now?" He laughed. "Men take care of themselves. You couldn't take care of a goldfish if I left the food on the counter."

I shot back with, "Why don't you just admit what this is about, Pop? You're jealous 'cause I'm spending time with Daryl instead of you."

He didn't answer, but a look flashed across his face that told me I'd struck a nerve. I kept going. Maybe it was mean, but I couldn't help myself. I was pissed that he wanted to keep me away from Daryl.

"You wanna know why I like spending time with him? Maybe it's the fact that you keep treating me like a kid when I'm a man! That's the difference between you and him. He treats me like a man."

My father stood there momentarily, his chest heaving as he glared at me. I couldn't tell if he was hurt or if he was trying to stop himself from beating the shit out of me. When he finally spoke, his voice was low and calm. "You know what, son? I've lived my entire life for you. I've only wanted what was best for you, but maybe I've gone about it the wrong way. So guess what? I'm done. It's time you started making your own way."

"And I'm supposed to be sad about that? That's all I've ever wanted was for you to let me live my own life and make my own decisions."

In spite of the attitude I was throwing at him, he remained calm. "Fine, and while you're living your own life, maybe you should do it somewhere else, because as long as you live under my roof, you're gonna abide by my rules. When can I expect your stuff to be out of here?"

The look he gave me was a challenge. He knew I didn't have anywhere to go. He also knew I didn't have a job. I'm sure he thought that threatening to kick me out would scare me, but he was wrong. I was not going to end my friendship with Daryl, no matter what he said.

"I don't have an exact date," I told him, "but trust me, it's gonna be sooner than later."

I stormed past him and marched out the front door, making sure it slammed behind me. Had I stayed in that house with him a minute longer, I might have packed my stuff up right then and there. I needed to cool off, and I damn sure needed a drink. I headed to Daryl's.

Under his roof I have to live by his rules. Fuck his rules, I thought as I knocked on Daryl's door.

"Hey, Benny, come on in." Daryl opened the door wearing his robe, probably so that it would be easier for me to take off his ankle bracelet before we left.

I walked inside in a huff. My adrenaline had kicked into high gear. I needed to relax before I exploded. "You got any beer, man?" I didn't even wait for him to reply before I changed my mind. "As a matter of fact, scratch that. You still got that tequila?"

"Yeah, in the kitch—"

I was already in the kitchen before he finished, going through his cupboards in search of something that could take the edge off.

"Bingo!" I found what I was looking for. Opting for a small juice glass instead of a shot glass, I filled it halfway and chugged it down as I made my way back into the living room. Daryl was watching the game on TV. With a bottle in one hand and a glass in the other, I sat down on the couch.

"Dude, are you drinking that shit straight?" he asked.

"Uh-huh." I downed a huge gulp that damn near burned a hole in my throat. "Yeah, it's straight," I said with a cough.

"Benny, that's fucking tequila. What's wrong with you?"

"My dad, that's what's fucking wrong." I took another swallow, and it didn't go down as hard this time. "I'm so sick of his ass. He doesn't understand..."

Daryl got up and stood over me. "Look, man, I know it's rough being a grown man living under your father's roof, but he is your father and you gotta respect that. Some of us don't have a dad, Benny."

"I know, but he doesn't get it. He's stuck in the Stone Age, and he wants me to be there with him, but I can't let him hold me back anymore."

That made Daryl laugh. "Hold you back? He may put up some roadblocks, but the man's not holding you back. He's your father. He puts a roof over your head, food in your belly, clothes on your back. What's he holding you back from? I wish someone would hold me back that way."

"From you!" I admitted, standing on my feet. I took one last gulp of tequila, emptying the glass. It went down much smoother this time. I'd become immune. I set the glass down on the table and looked Daryl in the face. "He's trying to hold me back from being around you," I said more quietly now.

"From me?" There was a nervous laugh.

"He doesn't like you, Daryl. You'd have to be blind not to see it."

"Nah, I can see it. I been meaning to talk to him about it too." Daryl kind of shrugged. "It's just that so much shit has been going down with Connie, Avery, and Krystal that I haven't been able to deal with little stuff."

"Little?" I was kind of taken aback. Did Daryl view our friendship as something little? Maybe it was the alcohol giving me courage, but I decided to go for it. "He's trying to keep us apart, Daryl. He's trying to keep us from being together."

Daryl's face became flushed and his eyes got big. "What do you mean, *being together*?"

"Just what I said." I took a step closer. Before I knew it, I slipped my hand in his robe and leaned in, my lips headed for his.

"Whoa! Whoa! What the hell are you doing, man?" Daryl took a step back from me.

I moved forward, closing the gap between us. He seemed scared, but I wasn't—not anymore at least. It was time to stop hiding in the shadows.

"Come on, man. It's me and you here. You don't have to pretend anymore, Dee. No need to act like you don't know what's going on. Hell, evidently even my dad sees it."

This time Daryl put up two hands and sort of ran away from me backward. "Whoa, wait a minute. If you're saying what I think you're...Hold up. You and your dad's got this thing all—Benny, man, are you saying...?"

Daryl couldn't get a complete sentence out to save his life. Maybe he didn't know how to express his feelings, I thought. I couldn't blame him. I'd been keeping mine sort of bottled up too ever since I was little.

Daryl took a deep breath and seemed to gather himself. "Benny, I'm going to come out and ask you this: Are you gay?"

I thought for a few seconds. "I don't know what I am yet, but what I do know is how I feel whenever we're together." I stepped closer to him, keeping my eyes locked on his as I moved in yet again for a kiss.

"No, no. There is no *we*. There's no *together*." He hurried away from me, tripping over the coffee table. "What I mean, Benny, is that you a cool cat. Any girl would be—" He stopped and thought for a minute. "Or any man—or whatever—would be lucky to...you know...with you. But dude, that's not for me. I like women."

"I know you like women," I told him. "But I know you like men too." I pointed over to his bookshelf. "I've seen your books: *Both Sides of the Fence, Invisible Life*. I've also checked out those videos you had lying around here last week: *Six Degrees of Separation*."

Daryl laughed. "You've got it all wrong. Connie brought that video over here for us to watch. And those aren't my books. I mean, they're my books, but I was just reading them because my little brother is gay. I was trying to get some sort of insight so I would know how to deal with him...his situation. He was going through a rough time when I came home from jail."

I was starting to sober up way too soon. Daryl was doing a lot of chuckling, and he had this weird, uncomfortable expression on his face. Was he not ready to come out of the closet yet, or was he truly rejecting my advances? I wasn't sure which, but I was getting sick to my stomach just thinking it might be the latter. Something told me the tequila wasn't the only thing straight in the room.

"Come on, Daryl. You did time in jail. You mean to tell me that you never—"

"Never!" he was quick to affirm. "I've never been with a man, and I never will be, Benny."

I almost threw up right then and there, and it didn't have a damn thing to do with all the tequila I'd downed. "Oh, fuck." I turned away, my face burning with embarrassment.

Daryl put a brotherly hand on my shoulder. "Come on, man. There's nothing to be ashamed of. There are a lot of gay people in the world," he told me. "I'm just not one of them."

I couldn't even turn around to look at Daryl as I headed for the door and barged out of his apartment the same way I'd barged in. I didn't know if I'd ever be able to look him in the eyes again—or myself, for that matter.

Connie

28

I'd been thinking a lot about Avery lately. Not about being with him or anything like that, because as far as I was concerned that phase of my life was over. The kiss he gave me the other night was enough to make me sure of that. I was more than happy with the way things were progressing with Daryl. Still, Avery's actions were very troubling. He'd changed. There were no *ifs*, *ands*, or *buts* about it. I couldn't put my finger on it, but there was something about his demeanor that didn't sit well with me—that and his newfound wealth. I'm not sure what that was about, but he'd made too much money too soon for me not to be suspicious. I knew Avery well enough to know that he would never give me that much money if he didn't have a hell of a lot more stashed away somewhere. I'd tried to talk to Daryl about it, but anything concerning Avery seemed to be a sore spot with him. Not that I could blame him with the way Avery was popping up every few days.

Nancy and the stoop ladies speculated that Avery had hit the lotto and was trying to hide it from me until the divorce was final. I could definitely see him doing that, but when I searched the New York State records for recent lottery winners, his name was nowhere to be found. I would have to see about Connecticut, New Jersey, and Pennsylvania too. I'm not ashamed to say that I was checking because if he hit the lotto, I damn sure wanted my half, no matter how weird he was acting.

I glanced at the clock and realized I didn't have time to be worrying about whether Avery was hiding assets. I was already late getting off to work. I made one last sweep of the room to make sure I hadn't left anything behind, then rushed to the door. If I was lucky, I'd still be able to catch the bus.

Before I could turn the handle, there was a loud banging. I screamed as I opened the front door to see five uniformed police officers and a few plainclothes cops standing there with guns drawn, pointed at me. My hand flew to my breast, trying to keep my heart from beating out of my chest.

One of the plainclothes cops grabbed me and slammed me against the hallway wall and the rest of them stormed my apartment.

"What's going on?" I asked with tears falling from my eyes. I'd never been so scared in my entire life. I received no answer from the cop who kept me pinned with my face to the wall.

I heard, "Clear!" coming from inside my apartment, and only then was I turned around to face the officers who'd come back out.

"Sorry, Miss. We didn't mean to scare you," one of the suited men said. "I'm Detective Wilson. We're looking for Avery Mack."

"Avery? He's—he's not here." I'd been expecting them to say they were at the wrong place. It had even crossed my mind for a second that maybe they'd meant to bust into Daryl's apartment, but no way did I think that they were looking for my soon-to-be ex-husband. I couldn't imagine what they wanted with him. Maybe he'd seen or heard something. At this point, I still wasn't putting two and two together.

"Are you Mrs. Mack?"

"Yes," I whispered as it started to dawn on me that Avery might not have won the lottery after all.

"Well, Mrs. Mack, we have a warrant for your husband's arrest, along with a search warrant for your apartment." He looked toward one of the other men, who removed a piece of paper from his pocket, unfolded it, and showed it to me. I saw the word *warrant* on it and Avery's name, but how in the hell was I supposed to know a real warrant from a fake one? I didn't have any experience with this type of thing.

I took a breath and gathered enough courage to speak up. "Well, like I said, Avery isn't here. He moved out. He doesn't live here anymore."

"We're still gonna go ahead and execute the search warrant." The one who spoke this time was much more of a hard-ass. He got in my face and growled, "Mrs. Mack, let me warn you that if—"

I raised my hand, cutting him off quick. "Oh, no need to warn me. By all means, do what you gotta do. Search your heart out." I was not about to have them accuse me of being uncooperative, or even worse, of hiding Avery. I'd been a ride-or-die chick all my life, but if it came down to me or Avery, he was ass out. Whatever kind of mess he was wrapped up in now, he was on his own the day he asked me for a divorce.

As I moved out of the way, the cops began to file back into my apartment.

I leaned against the wall, folded my arms across my chest, and waited. The hallway was starting to get crowed with nosy neighbors. How embarrassing. Even Daryl was standing in front of his door. I wished he would come over and place his arm around me or something, but I understood his reluctance with him being on house arrest.

Turning to one of the cops who waited in the hall with me, I asked, "What did Avery do? What are y'all looking for?"

One of the suited-up men looked to the other for approval to answer my question. Once given the nod, he said, "Mrs. Mack, your husband is wanted for questioning in relation to a string of eighteen armed robberies."

I wanted to laugh. Eighteen robberies? Even if they had the right man, Avery hadn't been gone long enough to commit eighteen robberies. And as much trouble as he had paying his share of the bills when we were together, he damn sure wasn't robbing anybody then. I told the cop, "Obviously you've got the wrong man. Avery's been working at the furniture store, barely making enough to pay his share of the bills around here for the past two years. He just finally got a promotion."

The cop corrected me. "Until he quit under duress."

"Avery quit his job?" I asked.

"As a matter of fact, we believe his former employer to be one of his victims. There's no question it was an inside job. Only a person who worked at the store would have known they keep that kind of cash on a Sunday or where they kept the safe."

"And know the surveillance system," the other cop chimed in.

I opened my mouth, but nothing came out. I shook my head, which was already rattling from everything the authorities were telling me.

Oh, God, I thought as reality finally set in. *That's where the money came from. And that's why he didn't want me to deposit the money... Oh, shit! The money's in there!*

All of a sudden, I didn't want them going through my apartment anymore. "Um, is this going to be quick? I'm already late for work."

"It might be a good idea if you call in," an officer suggested.

"Yes, okay, sure." I sighed, knowing there was no way out of this. How the hell could Avery be so stupid?

I went into the kitchen and called my boss with the excuse that I had a stomach virus. It might have been a lie, but I sure did feel sick to my stomach as I sat at the kitchen table, waiting for them to finish their search. The whole time I sat there, I was praying none of the cops would look in the cookie jar, where I'd rolled up the cash and hidden it under a layer of Chips Ahoy.

My prayers were answered when a detective finally said, "We do thank you for your cooperation, Mrs. Mack."

"No problem at all," I said as I signed the form he'd given me, listing the items they were taking as evidence. The cookie jar was not among them.

"And Mrs. Mack, if you hear from your husband, please let him know that it's in his best interest to turn himself in. If we find him, it could get... messy."

The police weren't out of the apartment a good minute before I picked up my phone to call Avery, not sure if I was going to warn him or cuss his ass out. I would decide that when I heard his voice. I didn't finish dialing, though, because there was a knock at the door. I threw the phone down as if it were on fire, certain that it was the cops at my door again. If I opened the door with the phone in my hand, they might think I was helping Avery to elude them. I'd watched enough *Law & Order* to know that wasn't good.

I straightened myself out and took in a deep breath as I went to open the door. Through the peephole I saw Daryl, and every muscle in my body relaxed. I unlatched the door and collapsed in his arms. All the tears I'd been holding back were pouring down my face now, soaking his shirt.

"What the hell is going on? What was five-o doing here?" He closed the door, then took my trembling hand and walked me over to the couch.

"It's Avery. The police are after him. They say he's been doing armed robberies." Even as I said it, I still couldn't believe it, but somehow Daryl wasn't at all surprised.

"Yeah, I guess it all makes sense now," he said.

"What makes sense?"

"The new clothes, the new car—and the gun he damn near pulled on me the other day."

"What gun?"

"The other day when he was here, Avery threatened me with a gun."

This was getting stranger by the second. Had I ever really known my husband? "You didn't tell me that."

"I'm a big boy," Daryl said. "I can take care of myself. But I wasn't about to push him, because he had the look."

"The look? What look?"

"I really can't explain it, Connie, other than to say in the street, people carry guns every day, but most of them are just for show because the person doesn't have the guts to use it." He pointed at his eyes. "Other people don't care. It's like they're dead already and they don't have anything to lose. You can see it in their eyes. Avery didn't have those eyes when I first met him, but he does now."

I started to cry again because I knew that what he was saying was true. I had seen a change in Avery, and now Daryl was saying he had noticed it too. Avery was in serious trouble.

"Oh no." I stood up and started pacing. "I need to call him."

"Whoa, hold up." Daryl stood up. "You can't just pick up the phone and call him. You don't know if your phone is tapped."

I took in Daryl's words. As crazy as they sounded, I realized they could be true. "You're absolutely right," I agreed. "I'll go find him and tell him in person."

I began frantically looking for my purse. I wanted to find Avery before the police did. No black woman wanted to see her man— current or ex—go to jail.

"Hold up, Connie. Calm down. I'm not letting you go look for him." Daryl managed to grab hold of me and rest his hands on my shoulders. That's when it sank in that I'd kicked back into wife mode. My emotions for Avery were transparent.

"I'm sorry, Daryl," I apologized. "I—"

He shook his head. "Connie, you don't have to apologize. You have a good heart. I know you don't want to see anybody hurt or in trouble, no matter what they've done to you. That's why I care about you so much."

Hearing those sweet words almost made me forget about Avery.

"Look, let me handle this. I'll go talk to Krystal and let her know what's going on. Let her go deal with her old man. You sit here and get yourself together, okay?"

Daryl walked me over to the couch, where I sat down, feeling far more relaxed. I pulled him down next to me.

"No, you and Slim don't get along, and if he catches you down there with her, it's gonna be a fight," I said. "I'll go talk to her. It's about time the two of us had a talk, woman to woman, anyway."

Nancy

29

I thought his ass would never leave, I thought when Charles finally left for work.

I didn't bother walking him to the stoop to put on our usual good-bye-kiss routine, because my mind was on other things. I couldn't wait to get to Ben's so he could take care of the throbbing between my legs. I'd been thinking about getting some ever since I woke up in the middle of the night after an erotic dream starring me and Ben. It had me so wet that for a second, I'd even considered waking up Charles's snoring ass and climbing on top of him. We'd stopped having sex together a long time ago, though, and the thought of doing it with him had practically the same effect as a cold shower. I rolled over and tried to go back to sleep, counting the hours until I could get out of the apartment and get me some.

Once the kids were off to school, I didn't even bother to get dressed. I threw on my housecoat, slid on some flip-flops, and then exited my apartment like I was busting out of jail.

I took the stairs up to the third floor, peeking out of the stairwell before I exited. Charles and I might have had an understanding about the state of our marriage, but I didn't see any reason to advertise that to every nosy fool in the building. I liked to keep my visits to Ben as discreet as possible, so I didn't necessarily want to be seen knocking on his door still dressed in my nightgown. Fortunately, the halls were empty.

I knocked on the apartment door but got no answer. After a second try, the door cracked open.

Ben stood at the door, half awake and wearing nothing but a pair of boxers. He must have worked the night shift.

I looked past him into the apartment and asked, "Is Benny around?"

"He's not here," he answered, sounding annoyed. At first I thought he was still pissy with me about the engagement ring thing, but then he said, "He's probably sleeping at a friend's house."

Obviously things between him and his son hadn't improved, and I was not about to make the same mistake bringing up that subject again. Best to get right to the sex, because I had urges that needed to be taken care of.

"Good. You're not planning on wasting any time then, are you?" I followed him into his living room, losing clothes on the way.

"What's that supposed to mean?" he asked, barely noticing that I was also naked now.

"I've been thinking about you all night. I need you, baby." I pressed myself up against him.

Unfortunately, my eagerness was met with a frown. Now that I was up close and personal I could see sadness in his eyes.

"What's wrong, Ben?"

"I'm stressed!" he barked, making me flinch.

I stepped away from him to be on the safe side. "Hey," I said. "I don't know what's wrong with you, but you don't have to take it out on me, you know."

He didn't respond. Didn't even look my way. I probably should have left, considering how rude he was being, but I was horny as hell, and I didn't want to leave until I at least tried to get some. Maybe I needed another approach.

"Well, it looks like you need to de-stress, then. Lucky for you I know a few really good relaxation techniques." I led him to the couch and made him sit down. I slid his boxers down around his ankles, and then I assumed my favorite position, on my knees in front of him.

Usually Ben loved it when I gave him head. I'm damn good at it if I do say so myself. It's a power trip for me, knowing that when I have a man inside my mouth, I'm in complete control. Shoot, I can do tricks with my tongue that most hookers don't even know about. I know how to drive a man crazy.

Unfortunately, after a few minutes using some of my best techniques, Ben was still barely hard.

I stopped my tongue action and looked up at him. "Uh, hello! Is something wrong? We've got a slight problem down here."

Ben looked down like he was surprised to see me there. I swear to God, if I hadn't spoken up, that man might have forgotten that I was even in the same room with him, let alone going down on him. That shit right there was a blow to the ego for sure. But instead of making him feel as bad as I felt now, I decided to let it slide. It was obvious something had his mind really fucked up. I could lend him my mouth later, but for now it looked like he needed me to lend an ear.

"You all right?" I asked.

"Huh?" he said absentmindedly. "Oh, uh, no problem. It was just feeling good is all."

Who did this man think he was fooling? I sighed and then slid up from between his legs to sit next to him. "Your mouth might be saying that, but your dick says otherwise." I twisted my lips and pointed at his limp member.

"I'm sorry, baby," he apologized, finally sounding like his mind was here in the room with me. "Benny and I had an argument and he's been gone a few days. I haven't heard from him, and I have no idea where he is." He closed his eyes and leaned his head back on the couch.

"It's gonna be all right. He'll come back, and you two will work it out." I kissed his cheek. "You and Benny are closer than any father and son I've ever met."

"Yeah, we were once," he said with a sigh. "Until that punk-ass pretty boy in 3B stole my son."

I wasn't quite sure what he meant by *stole*, but my gossip-girl instincts told me there was a juicy story behind this. I couldn't resist. I had to dig for details. "You really think Daryl *stole* him?"

"Maybe that isn't the right word, but ever since he moved in, he's had some kinda hold over Benny. He acts like the guy's a damn superhero or something. Like he can do no wrong."

I thought about the girls on the stoop—myself included—who sat out there every morning waiting for Daryl's fine ass to walk by, and I couldn't help but think that I kinda understood Benny's obsession with this guy. Daryl had this magnetism that was irresistible. Of course, I couldn't say that to Ben. He was obviously feeling rejected by his son, and as his dutiful girlfriend, I had to listen—even if all I really wanted to do was get back to work between his legs.

"So what if he can fight and knows how to play video games?" Ben continued. "There's a hell of a lot more to being a role model. He wasn't around when Benny had the flu or when he broke his arm skateboarding. He damn sure wasn't the one who made coffee and sat at the table all night when Benny had to study for finals."

"I know that's right," I replied. I could see him loosening up as he got this off his chest, and I hoped it was only a matter of time before he was relaxed enough to get busy with me.

"Maybe I'm being paranoid, but I think he's trying to sabotage my relationship with Benny. For all I know, he's the one who gave Benny that gun."

His last words kind of pricked my conscience. I was the one who'd told him that Benny had been arrested for gun possession. I wasn't trying to rat Benny out or anything, but I felt it was information his father needed to know. If it hadn't been for me, Ben might never have known his son was in trouble. Now I wished I had never said anything, because they were fighting and I wasn't getting any action. I needed to help them make up somehow, because it looked like I wasn't going to be having sex again until they did.

"Well, have you asked him where the gun came from?"

"Nope," he answered. "He's barely been talking to me lately. Every time I see him he's on his way out to be with Daryl. We definitely don't talk the way we used to."

"You know, Ben, that's kinda normal. Most teenagers stop talking to their parents at some point. Maybe Benny's doing it a little later than most kids," I suggested. "Maybe it has nothing to do with Daryl."

Ben gave me a skeptical look. "My son is not most kids. He wouldn't stop talking to me for no reason. It happened right around the time he started hanging out with this guy."

"Well..." I leaned my back against the couch and folded my arms over my chest. "If you really want to know what's going on in your kid's life, you could do what I do when they're not talking."

"Oh yeah, and what's that?" he said with a smirk.

For a second I wanted to smack him because the sarcasm in his tone said he thought I was the last person who should be giving parenting advice. I mean, just because his son was a mini-Einstein didn't mean he had to judge me. My kids were constantly getting into trouble at school. Did that make me a bad mother?

I sucked my teeth at him but continued anyway. All I cared about at that moment was setting his mind at ease so he could relax and make me cum.

I asked, "When was the last time you searched his room? Or looked through his computer?"

"Search his room?" he said in that same dismissive tone. "I've never done that before, and I'm not about to start now. Who goes checking up on their twenty-one-year-old kid?"

"Shoot, I don't care how old my kids get. I'm gonna always be up they ass, checking up on them. You never know what kids can be up to these days."

He gave me a look that said, *Yeah, and a lot of good that does your bad-ass kids.* It's a good thing that my kids were not something we usually discussed or Ben and I would have ended our affair a long time ago.

"Well, the more I think about it, you're right. He does seem to be spending an awful lot of time with Daryl. Seems like every time I see Benny he's either with Daryl or he's talking about Daryl." What I was saying wasn't even really true. I'd never heard Benny talk about Daryl. Benny was like any other kid who walked by us on the stoop. If he spoke to us at all, it was only to say hello and keep it moving. I was only trying to get back at Ben for insulting me as a mother. Shoot, I stayed married to an asshole for the sake of my kids. If anything, I deserved a mother of the year award for that.

"You better check on your son, Ben," I insisted. "You never know what these young people are up to these days. If he's carrying a gun, he could be selling drugs or even using them."

He snapped his head in my direction. "What did you say?" Finally, I'd gotten his attention! I had to basically accuse his son of being a drug dealer to do it, but hey, can I help it if Ben pushed me that far?

"Get the hell out of my house," he hissed, his eyes filled with rage.

"Oh, calm down. I'm just trying to be one hundred with you. It's better you find out something like that on your terms versus—"

"I said get the hell out." He got up and put his boxers back on.

A laugh rose up deep from my throat. "You can't be serious. You are not about to put me out of your apartment, Ben. 'Cause you know if you do, it's gonna be a long while before you get some of this again."

"Please," he said. "The pussy's not that good. I'm pretty sure you'll miss me way before I miss you."

"You son of a—" I was breathing so hard I couldn't even finish my sentence. I was furious. I got up off the couch, cursing under my breath as I put on my nightgown and housecoat.

I slipped into my flip-flops and then stood there watching Ben as he paced the floor. Bastard didn't even try to apologize.

"Benny wouldn't use drugs, would he?" he mumbled as he paced.

I didn't answer him because he wasn't talking to me anyway. He was talking to himself, worrying about his perfect son, wondering if what I'd said was true. Obviously my words bothered him. Served his ass right. He never should have pushed me so far.

Since I was basically invisible to Ben at this point, I followed behind him when he stormed out of the living room and headed to Benny's room.

Who's the crazy one now? I asked myself as I stood in the door-way and watched Ben doing exactly what he acted like I was a fool for suggesting. He was searching Benny's room from top to bottom.

"Shit!" he yelled when he lifted the mattress and found nothing.

He flopped down in the chair by Benny's desk. Poor thing looked drained. I took a chance and stepped into the room.

"Ben, check his computer," I said quietly.

Ben looked toward his son's desk and then back at me. If what he said before was true, he'd never violated his son's privacy, and he was obviously struggling with it now. The way he looked at me it was almost like he was waiting for me to give him permission.

"If he's in some kind of trouble, don't you want to know about it?" I asked.

He looked at me with sad eyes. "I have no idea how to work this damn thing. When I need to send an e-mail, Benny does it for me."

"Move the mouse," I said, walking over to where he sat. I put my hand over his and then placed it on the mouse. He didn't stop me.

As soon as Ben moved the mouse, the black screen gave way to the screen saver. It was some sort of slide show with little pictures inside bubbles that kept floating onto the screen. Ben exhaled sharply as if someone had punched him in the gut. It wasn't hard to figure out why when I took a closer look at the screen. Inside every single bubble was a picture of Daryl.

"What the hell?" Ben said when he could finally speak. He started clicking the mouse wildly, as if that would make the pictures of Daryl go away. The screen saver disappeared, and in its place was the default Microsoft desktop background.

"What do I do now?" he asked.

"Let me try," I said, taking the mouse from him. I saw an icon on the desktop that was marked BLOG. I'd done enough snooping around on my kids' computer to know that a blog was the closest thing to a diary nowadays. It was the best place for Ben to find out what was really going on in his son's head. I clicked on the icon.

A page appeared on the screen and we both began to read.

Every day my feelings are getting stronger. I can hardly keep my eyes off of him when we play basketball. Sooner or later one of us is going to have to make a move. Maybe I should have done it the other day when we were watching a movie together. I won't let any other opportunities pass me by...

Ben made a sound like a roar. "What the fuck? He's trying to turn my son gay!"

I was already regretting the fact that I'd opened that blog for him, and I only felt worse when he picked up the computer screen and smashed it to the floor. Then he picked up the tower and did the same. I let out a scream but stood there speechless. I'd never seen this side of him before.

"I'm gonna kill him. I'm gonna kill that son of a bitch." Ben went into his bedroom and threw on some clothes; then he charged toward the hallway like a raging bull.

"Wait! I'm going with you." It didn't take a rocket scientist to know where Ben was heading. I couldn't blame him for being pissed, but I didn't want him doing anything that would get him locked up.

I was right on Ben's heels as he made a beeline to Daryl's apartment and started pounding on the door. "Son of a bitch! Open this fuckin' door!" Lucky for Daryl, he opened the door before Ben kicked it in.

Ben started in immediately. "You son of a bitch, running around this place like you're God's gift to the world. You are not going to do this to my son, you pervert!"

In spite of Ben's rage, Daryl stayed pretty calm. "Uh, look, man," he said. "I don't know what the hell you're talking about, but you better take a step back, brother."

"You've been planning this all along, haven't you? You bastard!" Ben was trembling as if it was taking everything in him not to put his hands on Daryl. I just prayed that he could contain himself, because once he got started, he'd kill Daryl or maybe get himself killed.

"Yo, you need to calm down," Daryl said. "You've got it all wrong."

"You calm the fuck down! I knew you were gonna be a bad influence on my son, but I had no idea you were such a perverted bastard, trying to turn him gay."

I heard locks clicking and doors opening and turned to see Connie and a couple other third-floor residents looking at the scene going down. Usually I was the one up in everyone else's business, but now I sure wished those nosy fuckers would mind their own. They were hanging onto every word like they were watching a damn soap opera. Ben continued screaming like there was no one else around but him and Daryl.

Finally Daryl put his hand up to stop Ben's tirade. He said, "Now I see what this is about." He looked like he actually felt bad for Ben. "Look, you're obviously having a hard time accepting your son's sexuality, but I'm telling you, it's not my fault your son is gay."

"My son is not gay! He's confused, and it's all because of you!"

"Ben, your son is gay. You're going to have to accept that sooner or later."

"You son of a bitch! You told him I was gay?" Benny's voice had come out of nowhere.

Ben and Daryl both fell silent, and I turned to see Benny stepping off the elevator, looking at Daryl with fire in his eyes. "I can't believe you. You call yourself my friend, and then you out me to my pops and half the building without even talking to me about it?"

That's when I knew the shit was really about to hit the fan.

Krystal

30

It was a little after noon when I finally dragged my ass out of bed and into the bathroom. Slim had said he'd be home a little after three, and he made it clear he wanted our apartment clean when he walked through the door, so I figured I'd better get started. The last thing I wanted was for him to do to my right eye what he'd already done to my left.

Thank goodness the swelling had gone down and all I had left was a black mark under my eye. I still couldn't believe he'd done this to my face. Most people would say I should have bolted right after he made it clear that he wouldn't tolerate any more of my shit with Daryl—and right before he took out his frustration on my face—but I didn't see leaving as an option. Either I could take the well-deserved ass whipping and pray things got better or be out on the street, homeless with a habit. As far as I was concerned, that was a fate far worse than death. So I chose to take the ass whipping and all the BS that came with it with one concession: It didn't matter how much he hit me as long as I had my little blue boxes to take away the pain. Slim, for whatever reason, was glad to oblige my request.

On the counter next to the sink, I saw that Slim had left a box on top of my makeup bag. It was smaller than normal, but it was enough to get the job done until he came home. Slim had been making the boxes smaller lately in order to control my use, therefore controlling me. I went to move it so I could get out my concealer and hide my bruise, but having the box in my hands was enough to get my juices flowing. I was so ready for that first toot of the day. It was always the best. Putting on makeup could wait.

Unfortunately before I could get the top off the box and enter my own personal heaven, there was a knock at the front door.

"Who is it?" I snapped when I got into the living room, not bothering to look out the peephole.

"It's me, Krystal. Open up."

Dammit. As if I wasn't already in a funk, hearing Connie's voice only made me feel worse. Stupid bitch probably wanted to rub it in my face that she was screwing Daryl. She was the last person I felt like dealing with, especially when I was itching to get a hit.

I looked out of the peephole and saw her fat face looking all anxious. "What the hell do you want?" I yelled through the closed door. I had much better things to do with my time than talk to my stepmonster. I wanted this bitch to go away in a hurry.

"Krystal, open the door. It's about your father." She was known for being a drama queen, but there was something in the urgency of her tone that told me I'd better hear what she had to say.

"You better not be wasting my time," I told her as I opened the door. "What do you need to tell me about my father?"

As soon as she saw me, her hand flew to her mouth. "Oh, my goodness, your eye! Slim didn't do that to you, did he?" She actually sounded concerned.

I guess I should have put that concealer on before opening the door. It wasn't that I really cared what Connie thought, but I didn't need her telling the whole building that Slim hit me. "If it's any of your business, I hit my eye on a doorknob. Now get to talking so you can go on about your business and get out my face."

Glancing down at my hand, she saw the blue box. She shook her head, looking like she wanted to say something, but I gave her a scowl that let her know she'd be wasting her breath.

"Get to the point," I said.

"Krystal, the police were at my place today..."

I practically jumped down her throat. "Bitch, I know you didn't call the cops on my father, 'cause if you did—"

She stopped me. "No, but they had a search warrant, and they were looking for him."

It took me a second, but then I started to laugh. "You know, I don't know what you're up to, but I'm not stupid. And this ain't funny. Did Daryl put you up to this?" I went to close the door on her, but she stopped it with her hand.

"Look, Krystal, this is not about Daryl," she said more forcefully. "It's about Avery. I'm trying to help your father, so stop playing games." She looked over her shoulder, then back at me. "And I don't think this is a conversation you want to have out in the hallway. Are you going to let me in so I can explain or what?"

I glared at her for a moment, wondering what I should do. Half of me hoped she really was playing some stupid game because then I could just beat her ass and be done with it. But if it wasn't a game and Daddy was really in trouble, I needed to know what was going on. I stepped aside, allowing her to enter.

I had barely shut the door behind her when she blurted out, "The police are looking for Avery with regard to some armed robberies."

I was laughing again. As serious as she sounded and as serious as she looked...my father? Armed robbery? No way in hell.

"You couldn't think of anything better than that to come down here and try to cause drama in my life?" I leaned in close, trying to intimidate her. "Why are you really down here, Connie? What? You went by Daryl's and he wasn't there? Came running down here, trying to see if you'd catch him with me?"

"Puhleeze," Connie said, looking unfazed as she shooed her hand at me. "Look, I'm not lying about this. Why would I? My being here has nothing to do with Daryl. Your father could be in big trouble, but if you don't want to take my word for it, fine! Just leave Daryl out of it because he wants nothing to do with you."

I rolled my eyes and looked her up and down. Could Daryl really have chosen her fat ass over me? That thought bothered me, but I couldn't let her know it. "Don't act like you don't know that Daryl and I have a relationship," I said.

She came back at me with, "You mean *had* a relationship. I'm well aware that back in the day you and Daryl used to see each other."

"Back in the day? Ha! More like yesterday. You saw how I was dressed when I showed up at Daryl's place the other day. Did that look like someone who *had* a relationship with him?" I was hoping she couldn't see through me, but my stomach was churning at the thought of her and Daryl together. Shoot, it had been bad enough when she was my father's wife. This was a hundred times worse.

"Whatever, Krystal." She turned away from me. I could tell I was getting to her, so I kept twisting the knife.

"You don't believe me, do you?"

"It doesn't matter what I believe. He's my man now. You and him are history."

I wanted to smack the smirk off her face.

"Look," she said, "can we finish talking about your father? You really need to give him a call and let him—"

I broke in and questioned, "What do you think about that ankle bracelet he's wearing these days?"

Her eyebrows shot up. Obviously she was surprised that I knew about the ankle bracelet.

"Now, how would I know about that if Daryl and I weren't together recently?" Her mouth dropped open, but she was speechless. I continued, "It sure gets in the way when you're fucking, doesn't it? I started using it for leverage. You should try it sometime. Since he's your man." I thrust my hips a couple of times for emphasis.

I could see her bottom lip trembling. She was boiling inside but trying her best not to convey it. "I did not come down here for this" was all she said. It sounded like her voice was about to crack.

"I know, but since you're here, I might as well tell you." I laughed. "Who did you think he was visiting out in the Hamptons? Or didn't he tell you about that either?"

"That was you out there?"

"Every day, all day, three times a day." I was determined to send her ass back to her apartment in tears. "Why don't you ask him about that Jewish star he wears and who bought it for him? It's a sign of our love, Connie. He never takes it off because he never wants to forget where it came from."

Surprisingly she still had more fight left in her. She regained some strength in her voice and said, "Maybe Daryl hasn't been totally honest with me—and you got the response you wanted because I'm pissed—but there is one thing I can be sure of: he hasn't fucked with you since that day in the hall."

I smirked. "How can you be so sure?"

She glanced down at the blue box in my hand. "Because he doesn't fuck with junkies. And it's pretty evident to everyone in the building that you're a junkie." She shook her head. "You know, it's a shame. You used to be cute, but you really need to get yourself together 'cause you look like shit. And I ain't talkin' about your eye."

With a smirk, she headed to the door. She opened it and then turned back to say, "Oh, and you might wanna call your father and give him a heads-up before you dive headfirst into the blue box. It'd be a shame if he got shot by the cops because you were too high to pass on a message."

Avery

31

After my daughter called to tell me that the cops were looking for me, I panicked and went to hide out at a small hotel in New London, Connecticut. Cain, on the other hand, was as calm as ever. He looked at it this way: crimes happened every day in New York, so the cops were pretty overloaded. Cain said that as long as we laid low for a while, they'd forget all about us. Thank goodness he'd made it very clear from the start that we wouldn't be robbing banks, post offices, or any government buildings, which would have turned the feds on to us. Since we'd kept all our jobs local, all we had to do was take a nice long vacation and then move our operation to another state far enough away that our MO wouldn't be noticed.

My hotel was near the Foxwoods casino, and after three days of gambling, my money was running low. That's why I was relieved to be heading to Cain's house, where we could re-up our funds and discuss a strategy for the future. I was thinking that Jamaica would be a nice place to visit. We'd made a small fortune in the past few weeks, so I would be traveling in style—everything first-class and top-shelf. Hell, maybe I'd even invite Connie to go with me.

Unfortunately, when I pulled in front of Cain's house, my vacation fantasy was interrupted by what I saw in front of me. I watched in confusion as a woman planted a FOR SALE sign in the front yard.

I threw the car in park, turned off the ignition, and hopped out, running to catch her before she got in her car.

"Excuse me, ma'am. Is this property on the market?"

With her hand on her car door, she turned and looked back at the sign, which was the obvious answer to my question. No doubt she was thinking about how stupid I was, but then she looked at my Mercedes and her eyes lit up. I knew that look. Back when I was a mortgage broker, my mouth watered plenty of times when I thought I had a rich prospective buyer on the hook. Too bad for her I wasn't interested.

"Uh, yes. It's new on the market. Are you interested in buying?" She was already reaching for her business cards. I decided to stop her before she tried to waste my time with a long-winded sales pitch.

"Actually, I know the owner, and I had no idea they were selling," I said bluntly.

She tucked the card back in her purse, not bothering to hide the disappointment on her face. "Oh, yeah, well, Mrs. Melinsky wanted it on the market as soon as possible."

"Mrs. Melinsky?" Who the hell was Mrs. Melinsky? "I'm talking about Cain, the guy that lives here."

"Oh, you mean the gentleman who was leasing the home. He's not here."

"Leasing?" That was news to me, and it wasn't good news. I had a bad feeling in the pit of my stomach. "He didn't own this place?"

"Oh no." She shooed her hand at me. "He was just leasing the house. He was a good tenant, though. Unfortunately, he had to leave town. Something about his job. Paid up his lease three days ago and moved out."

"Moved out?" I almost lost my lunch. This couldn't be happening. Cain wouldn't do this to me. We were kindred spirits, right? I was still trying hard to convince myself that everything was going to be okay.

"Yes, that's what Mrs. Melinsky said. He moved out, and he didn't leave a forwarding address."

Shit! Shit! Shit! Shit! I had to get into that house.

"You know what? I think I am interested in this property." Without any real plan in my head, I started walking toward the front door, my heart beating ninety miles per hour. "Anyway, can I see the inside?"

"Yes, yes, of course," the woman shouted, following me. I couldn't see her face, but she probably had a big-ass grin.

She opened the door and then stepped aside, allowing me to enter. My heart dropped into my stomach when I walked in and saw my worst nightmare come true. The house was completely empty, not even a piece of paper left behind on the floor.

"Now, this is five bedrooms, four baths..."

Ignoring the woman, I raced straight to the study, where I felt some relief when I saw one picture still hanging on the wall. Rushing over to it, I pushed the painting aside and entered the combination to the safe.

"Shit!" I roared after finding the safe as empty as the house. "It's gone. Goddammit, it's gone."

"What exactly were you expecting to find?" I was startled to hear the woman behind me. I'd almost forgotten she was there.

I shook my head and said quietly, "Nothing. Nothing at all." I brushed by her, leaving the safe wide open.

"Does this mean you're not interested in the house?" she called out as I left.

I dialed Cain's number as soon as I got outside.

"Hello," Cain answered.

I let out a sigh of relief. "Cain, thank God. Where are you? I'm at the house. They say it's not yours."

"Well, Avery my boy, technically it isn't. It was a lease to own, but I decided I didn't want to own it anymore."

"Okay, fine, I can live with that," I said calmly. Cain always seemed to have that effect on me. I was sure he had some plan to fix this that he hadn't told me about yet. "Where are you?"

"I'm with the girls. We're headed out of the country to a place where there aren't any extradition laws to the United States. I suggest you do the same. The police are taking this whole thing a little more seriously than I would have thought. It seems they feel holding someone against their will and locking them in a broom closet is kidnapping."

I was a little bothered that he had left without telling me and now he wasn't inviting me to join them, but whatever. I was a grown man, and I wasn't about to start whining about it. "No problem, Cain. I'll get out of town. All I need is my share of the money."

His answer shocked me. "You've already gotten everything that's coming to you, man."

"What?" I yelled into the phone.

"If you recall, you were the one who insisted we had to rob your former employer. I told you it was a bad idea, but no, you had to get revenge on them."

I said nothing because he was speaking the truth, but I had an idea where he was going with this.

"Well, it seems your insistence that we rob your former employer has brought the heat down on us, forcing me to leave the country. And that, my friend, is going to cost you your share of the money," he said, his voice no longer sounding calm, but rather seething with anger.

"Are you crazy? We're talking about damn near a half a million dollars. I earned that money. I want what's mine."

I heard him laugh. "If it was yours, you'd have it and I wouldn't. Now, like I was saying, I'm heading out of the country, and if you were smart, you'd do the same."

"With what?" I asked, no longer yelling, because I knew it would do me no good. He wasn't going to change his mind. It was definitely every man for himself at this point. "Cain, man, I'm broke. I gave all my cash to my ex so she'd sign the divorce papers." I beat my hand on the steering wheel. "You have all the rest of my money." The stress was so bad that I was on the verge of tears.

"Well, Avery," he said in this cool, detached voice, "I guess you only have three choices: You can turn yourself into the cops, leave the country like me, or take your black ass back to that bridge and jump. Whatever you choose, it was nice knowing you."

"Nice knowing me?" I repeated. Did he really think I'd let him get away with this? If I was going down, I was damn sure gonna take him with me.

At least that's what I was about to threaten him with before he said, "Oh, and for the record, my real name isn't Cain, and you won't find one fingerprint in that house." With that, he disconnected the call.

"Cain!" I yelled, still holding the phone to my ear.

Son of a bitch! I threw the phone down on the seat next to me.

What the hell was I supposed to do now? If Cain had skipped town, then things must be really fucked up. What if he knew more than he was telling me? What if the cops were closing in even as I sat in front of Cain's house?

I looked up and noticed the real estate agent standing in front of her car. She was staring at my car and talking on her phone. That scared the shit out of me. For all I knew, she was calling the cops. I threw the car into drive and got away from that house as fast as I could. I didn't know where I was going, but one thing was for sure—I had to find a way to get some money in a hurry and get the hell out of New York.

Connie

32

I'd been tossing and turning all night, unable to sleep for more than a few minutes at a time before I woke up again, mostly from sexual frustration. It was even harder knowing that Daryl was across the hall with the prescription I needed to calm me down and put me to sleep. It would have been so easy to get up, knock on his door, follow him to his room, and lay down in his bed, but I couldn't do that. Unbeknownst to Daryl, I'd placed him on pussy punishment for not telling me the entire truth about his relationship with Krystal. Don't get me wrong. He did come clean, and technically he really didn't lie. He just omitted the truth, but he also had to be taught a lesson if we were going to move forward. The problem was that I was suffering too.

Four days seemed like a reasonable amount of time to punish him, and we were at the end of the third already. I was thinking about granting him—or perhaps myself—an early parole. By three o'clock in the morning, I'd fully committed to his release. I slipped into my robe and snatched my keys off the nightstand, then headed out of the bedroom.

I almost jumped out of my skin when I heard a rustling and saw a shadow move near the living room sofa. The shadow rose, and I grabbed the lamp off the nearby coffee table to protect myself. I just prayed that whoever had broken into my apartment didn't have a gun.

"You better get the hell out of my apartment. I've already called the police," I lied threateningly, hoping that would be enough to scare away the intruder.

"Connie, please. It's just me, Avery."

It took me a minute to get myself together and make sense of what was going on: my estranged husband was hiding out in the dark in my living room. I flipped on the light switch.

"What the hell are you doing here? And how'd you get into my house?" I shouted. I could have killed him for scaring me like that. "I changed the locks."

"I lived here for almost four years," he said. "You think I don't know how to break into my own house?" He looked in the direction of a window that faced the back of the building. "How many times have I told you to lock that window? All I had to do was climb the fire escape."

He had yelled at me about that at least a thousand times during our marriage, but that still didn't make it right for him to come through the window in the middle of the night. This was *my* home now, not his. "So you broke into my apartment for what, to prove a point?" I lifted the lamp like a bat.

"No, no," he said, holding up his hands in a defensive posture. "I needed to talk to you, and with everything that's going on with the cops, I didn't wanna take a chance and walk through the front door." His eyes kept shooting around the room, as if he half expected the cops to jump out of their hiding place at any minute. "I was trying to keep the heat off of you. But I also didn't want to scare you, so I thought I'd just crash on the couch until morning when you woke up."

"And you didn't think waking up to you sleeping on my couch would scare me? What if I had company? Daryl could have been here."

"I saw the pretty boy staring out his window like he'd lost his best friend, so I knew he wasn't over here. And if he had been—well, I have something for his ass." The smirk on his face was eerie.

I stood there staring at Avery. It was like looking at a stranger. Long gone was the man I fell in love with and married. The man sitting across from me was like a piece of steel, cold and hardened.

"Avery Mack, what have you gotten yourself into?" I was still holding the lamp, but I lowered it to my side.

"Over my head, Connie. I've gotten in over my head, and now I'm just trying to keep my head above water. Did the cops really have a search warrant?" he asked, walking over and standing close to me like he thought he might get some sympathy. Not a chance.

"Sure did," I said flatly. "And they tore my place apart when they executed it."

He lowered his head. "I'm sorry. I really am. I'm sorry about everything, Connie."

I rolled my eyes. Of course he was sorry—now that he was in trouble. He was probably just looking for a place to hide. The sad thing was, the old me would have taken him back, no questions asked. The new me, however, was demanding an explanation.

"Is it true what the cops are saying about you, Avery?"

He took a long breath and hesitated. I wasn't about to let him off the hook, though.

I put my hand on my hip and said, "You can either answer me or you can leave now."

"I don't know," he said. "What exactly did they tell you?"

I looked up at his dead eyes and shook my head. It was obvious Avery was fishing to see how much the police knew. He had no intention of telling me the truth if I didn't already know it.

"They said you robbed Cheap Sam's Furniture and you've been involved in other armed robberies. They've got a task force just for you."

"Shit!" He turned away from me as if he needed a moment to himself.

"Avery?" I walked around so that I could be face-to-face with him. "It's true, isn't it? What they said is true." His silence was his answer, but I wanted him to say it. "Answer me, dammit."

"Connie, please don't ask me questions unless you're ready to deal with the answers. The less you know the better."

Now it was my turn to go silent for a minute. When I finally spoke up, I told him, "You gotta turn yourself in or they're gonna kill you."

"You can't kill someone who's already dead." I wanted to ask what that meant, but he continued, saying, "I'm leaving the country anyway. Gonna get a fresh start, and I want you to come with me." He took a step closer. "I need you to come with me."

"Huh?" He was talking crazy.

"We'll go to Jamaica. You know how you're always talking about Montego Bay and how much you love it there. We'll go stay for a month, then check out Barbados. We can island-hop until the heat cools down. It'll be fun. You'll see." His voice was becoming more animated, but he still had that dead look in his eyes. I couldn't tell if he was serious about taking me out of the country, but it didn't matter anyway. Even if I wanted to, I couldn't do it. It was way too late for our relationship to be rekindled.

"Avery, I'm not going to leave the country with you." I paced over to the window, turning my back to him. "I'm not going to be a fugitive, and I'm not gonna live like one."

"Connie, it's a woman's place to be with her husband." He walked over and started rubbing my shoulder.

"You seem to be forgetting that we're in the process of a divorce," I snapped. I didn't know where his head was at, but he was acting as if he hadn't broken my heart, and it was really starting to irritate me.

"We're not divorced. Not yet anyway. The paperwork isn't filed. Right now you are my wife...'til death do us part. I still love you, Connie. Let me prove it to you."

I spun around and looked at his face, which showed no emotion. "You don't love me, Avery. You're saying it, but you don't feel it."

"Yes, I do."

He looked so pitiful. I truly felt sorry for him. I gently placed my hands on his cheeks. "Right now, you're just scared and you don't know what to do. You're looking for a safe place, but I'm not it. Not anymore."

He moved my hands off his face not so gently. "Don't let that nigga get between us, Connie. Come with me."

"Avery, I wish you the best, and I pray to God you get out of this mess, but I'm not going to leave the country with you." There really wasn't much else to say. Avery and I were definitely not on the same page. I loved him once, but he'd gotten himself into something that I couldn't save him from—and I wasn't willing to risk my own freedom for him. "I think you better get going. The last thing we need is for the cops to come back around and find you here."

"Yeah, you're right," he said with a sigh. "But this isn't the last time we're gonna talk about this."

I didn't waste my breath on a reply. We could go around in circles discussing it forever, but one thing would never change: I wasn't going anywhere.

"There is, however, one thing I need before I go."

"What's that?" I asked.

"I need that money I gave you."

"Excuse me?" I raised my eyebrows.

"The money I gave you last week. I need it back. Otherwise I can't leave the country."

"Uh, Avery, I would give it to you if I could, but . . ."

"But what?" he said, his voice a mixture of fear and anger.

"But I . . ." My words trailed off. I didn't want to tell him the truth.

"Don't tell me the cops found it. If—"

"No." I knew I had to tell him the truth because I could see how on edge he was, pacing and sweating. "I gave it to Daryl to hold." I said it so quietly I was practically whispering.

"What? You gave my money to that chump?" He exploded. "What is he, your pimp? I didn't give you that money for you to give to some nig—"

"Don't call him that!" I yelled. "And I gave it to him to hold. I got freaked out when the police came. I mean, I thought I knew you, and I didn't want to believe them, but they were talking robbery, and you were dropping thousands like it wasn't nothing. I was scared. I didn't want them coming back with another search warrant and finding that money. Then I'd be an accomplice or something."

I thought my argument made sense, but Avery was so far gone at this point that he had no sympathy for me. He didn't care about what I'd been through with the police. All he could think about was that I had no money to give him.

"So you gave my muthafuckin' money to that clown?" He shook his head in disgust. "You didn't even let my side of the bed get cold before you probably had his ass up in here, huh?"

I wasn't going to acknowledge Avery's question. The way he was acting, he didn't deserve to know anything about my relationship. I just folded my arms and looked at him like I was unfazed.

"You do know he's fucking my daughter, don't you? Do you have any idea how ridiculous that makes you look?"

If Avery wanted to cut deep, he had. Yeah, I knew about Daryl and Krystal—after the fact—but hearing it was still like a knife in my heart. I couldn't let Avery know he was getting to me, so I struggled hard to keep my game face on.

He shook his head. "And obviously you don't care. Well, I don't either. I don't care who the bastard is fucking. All I care about right now is him having what's mine."

Something inside of me wished that Avery was talking about me, but I knew he wasn't. "Where are you going?" I asked Avery as he stormed to the door and opened it.

"I'm going to see Casanova. I need that money!"

That's when I saw him remove a gun from his waistband. I could finally see what Daryl had seen. It was clear to me he would do whatever it took to get what he wanted, no matter the consequences.

Nancy

33

"Good morning, Benny," I said warmly. I was surprised to see him, because ever since it came out that he was gay, he'd been keeping a very low profile. I hadn't seen him in at least a week.

He barely acknowledged me with a grunt as he stumbled up the stoop carrying a paper bag. He looked like crap, but then again, that's what staying out all night drinking will do to you, which was what I was sure he'd done.

"Hey, Benny, tell your daddy I said hi."

My words weren't meant to be sarcastic. In fact, they were meant to be just the opposite. I didn't want Benny telling his father I was acting all stink, especially since I was hoping to reconcile our relationship, which had gone south ever since he found out his son was gay. Ben wasn't even talking to me these days, and boy, did I miss him. Since we'd been apart, I was starting to realize just how much I cared about Ben. He was more than just a side piece for me, and it was really starting to bother me that we weren't on speaking terms. I was hoping that if I could help him and his son mend their fences, it would put me and Ben back on the right track.

Judging from the smirks on the faces of the women sitting around the stoop, me trying to make nice with Benny was a lost cause. Nonetheless, I tried one more time.

"Tell him I said don't be a stranger and that I might bring him by some pie." I was sure his father would know exactly what type of pie I was talking about—sweet, creamy Nancy pie.

Benny stopped and turned, wagging his finger as if he wanted to say something. Instead of speaking whatever was on his mind, though, he just rolled his eyes and then continued into the building.

"Humph. I guess someone has a problem with you 'cause that boy is usually polite," Bertha, the stoop's elder stateswoman, stated from her perch on the top step. The other ladies sitting and standing around the stoop laughed.

I waved my hand at the door to let them know his little attitude didn't faze me. "Don't pay him no mind. He's probably drunk. I bet that bag he's carrying has a fifth of vodka in it. Besides, he's just mad 'cause he thinks I had something to do with his daddy finding out he's gay."

Bertha gave me a knowing glance that made me want to recant my statement. "Um, Nancy, if I'm not mistaken, you did have something to do with his daddy finding out he was gay."

I glanced around at all the eyes accusing me. "Well, yeah, maybe I did," I admitted sheepishly, "but he don't know that for sure. Far as he's concerned, his friend from 3B outed him." I folded my arms, hoping that would be the end of it.

"Speaking of 3B," one of the women chimed in, looking at her watch. "Where the hell is he? Shouldn't he be out here by now? I don't know about the rest of you, but I haven't fed my kids yet, sitting around waiting on him."

Truth is, none of us had done much of anything. It was almost eight thirty in the morning on a Saturday, and we were all doing what had become a habit ever since Daryl Graham moved in: we were waiting for the 3B show. Usually he was right on schedule, coming out for his morning run every Saturday at eight on the dot. Lately, Connie had been following behind him like she was a tail growing out of his ass, but that didn't stop the rest of us from sitting around every weekend to get a look at the hottest man ever to grace the stoop.

Thank goodness we weren't disappointed, because a few moments later Daryl strolled out of the building. Even better, he was alone for the first time in weeks. Apparently the rumors about him and Connie being on the outs were true. If she was out of the picture, that made him available and fair game. That's why the stoop was even more crowded than usual this morning. Every able-bodied woman within a two-block radius was itching to take Connie's spot. You could put me at the top of that list, despite the fact that I had a husband—and a fireman that I'd been sexing for the past three years. Shoot, just because Ben was giving me the silent treatment didn't mean my hormones were on vacation.

Mmm-mmm-mmm, that man is so fine, I thought, admiring the way he looked in his tight white wife beater and New York Knicks jogging suit. It seemed like the sun got a little brighter as soon as he appeared.

"What's up, ladies?" Daryl flashed a smile as he stood on the sidewalk and began stretching.

"Morning," we all replied like a love-struck chorus.

Daryl always did warm-ups before his morning run, but this time something seemed different about his jumping jacks, deep knee bends, and squats. It was like he was putting on a special show just for us. Well, actually, like it was just for me. I swear he was smiling directly at me. I couldn't remember him ever making eye contact with me the way he was this time. He bent over to touch his toes and looked right at me to make sure I was watching. Maybe it was just because Ben hadn't been sexing me lately, but I couldn't tear my eyes away!

"Whew, it's hot out here already," he said, wiping his forehead.

I'm feeling the same way, I thought, *but it's not the weather that's making me hot.*

I watched him remove his Knicks jacket, and then to my surprise—and probably the disappointment of every other woman on the stoop—he tossed his jacket in my direction. "Hey, Nancy, can you hold onto this until I get back?"

"Uh, sure," I said, clutching it to my chest. Everything in me wanted to hold it up to my nose and sniff it. If I could have, I would have thrown him my panties in exchange.

"Thanks." He flashed me another million-dollar smile before taking off down the block. I watched him, my eyes glued on his ass, until he disappeared into the park entrance. When I came out of my trance, I felt the stares of the other women on the stoop. I quickly surveyed their faces, seeing the same thing in each: pure jealousy.

"What?" I said, barely able to contain a smile. I glanced down at the jacket like it was a well-deserved trophy. I wanted to hold it up and scream, "Victory!"

"Ummm, don't you have a husband?" one of the women asked with annoyance in her tone.

"A husband and a *his*tress," Bertha added, sitting back and crossing her arms indignantly over her huge chest. "I guess she wants every decent man for herself."

I gave Bertha a fleeting glance. I couldn't believe that of all the women on the stoop, she was hating on me. I thought we were friends.

I turned to my supposed friend. "First of all, Bertha, what I do is none of your business," I said with a sister-girl roll of my neck. "But even if you could have him, what would you do with someone as young as Daryl?" Bertha had to be pushing seventy.

Bertha stood up, running her hand through her gray hair and shaking her ample hips. "Honey, just because there's snow on the roof doesn't mean there ain't fire in the furnace. You wanna know what I'd do with a young buck like him? What you think I'm gonna do? I'm gonna fuck his ass just like you—only better. That's what I'm gonna do." Bertha gave us all a good thrust with her hips, and the entire stoop burst out laughing. I loosened up and laughed right along with them. And why shouldn't I laugh? I was still the one holding Daryl's jacket.

"Girl, I heard that," I said. "But for the record, I didn't know he was gonna give me his jacket to hold."

"Mm-hmm, sure you didn't," another woman mumbled as she dragged herself off the stoop like a loser walking away from the racetrack. "Guess I can go feed my kids now . . . Right before I take a cold shower."

The rest of the women and I chatted it up for a while longer as we waited for Daryl to return. We talked about some of the characters passing by, as well as the characters we had living right in our apartment building. I tried to avoid the subject, but Benny and his father kept coming up.

"I kind of feel sorry for him," one of the women said in reference to Benny.

"Yeah," I agreed. "That boy's been drinking away his sorrows ever since he came out the closet."

Bertha had to get her two cents in again. "He didn't come out the closet. His daddy pushed him out—along with your help—right in front of your boy Daryl." For some reason, Bertha was really on my case today.

"He is not my boy, Bertha." *Not yet anyway,* I thought.

"Shh. Here he comes," someone whispered in warning.

"I can see." I turned, picking my fingers through my hair in an attempt to give it some style. All of our back and forth banter came to a halt as he walked up.

Sexy, sexy, sexy. That was the only word to describe this hunk of perfection as he stood there drenched in perspiration. Hell, I would have worn his funky sweat like perfume if I could have. How in the hell did Connie ever give him up?

"Good workout?" I asked.

"It was. You should join me sometime," he replied.

I thought he was just making polite conversation until he leaned in closer and added, "Come up to my place sometime so we can discuss it."

When he pulled back, I searched his eyes in an attempt to determine if his invitation was serious.

"You want me to come up to your place?" I asked to confirm for myself and to make sure the rest of the stoop heard it.

"You heard me. Come check me out sometime so we can discuss a workout schedule." He took his jacket and headed up the steps.

"You want me to come up to your place?" I repeated.

"Why do I feel like I'm talking to a parrot all of a sudden?" he joked.

I couldn't help but ask, "But what about Connie?" I was not trying to have an issue with her. Even though she'd lost weight, she still had me by a few pounds.

"Don't you worry about Connie. You let me worry about her fat ass," he said with a wink. The entire stoop went silent.

Okay, so maybe it was a little offensive to hear him calling her a fat ass, but hell, let's keep it real. When a man as fine as Daryl asks you to meet him upstairs, you're willing to overlook a few minor character flaws.

"Then I guess I'll see you in a few," I announced, wishing I could fast-forward time and go upstairs at that moment.

He was barely out of sight before the old hens started pecking.

"For a woman who prides herself on discretion, that was not discreet at all," Bertha said.

"What are you trying to say? We're just gonna talk about working out," I insisted, but the women erupted in laughter. I wasn't fooling anyone, including myself.

"Girl, do you even hear yourself?"

"Yeah, what do we look, stupid? We all know what you're going up there for," Bertha said. "But like y'all say, I ain't mad at ya. I'm just mad it ain't me."

"I heard that!" another woman agreed and gave Bertha a high five.

I spent the next fifteen minutes trying to convince them that I was not going up to his place for any hanky-panky, but it was useless. They weren't going to believe it any more than I was. We all knew damn well what I intended to do when I was alone with Daryl. Maybe Ben had done me a favor after all by cutting me off.

Our good-natured joking was interrupted when Slim and Krystal came barreling out the door and busted through our group like there was only half an hour left to cash in the winning Powerball ticket.

"Excuse me, what's the damn hurry?" I shot off, but neither of them said anything. They just ran down the block.

A few minutes later, they came riding past us in a shiny Mercedes. They actually circled the block three times before disappearing.

"Isn't that Avery Mack's car?" one woman asked.

"Uh-huh." Bertha nodded. "Her daddy sure does spoil her, letting her ride in his car like that."

"Didn't I hear you say the other day that the cops were looking for him?" the woman continued.

"Mm-hmm, sure did. Probably looking for that car too." I shook my head.

"You know that girl ain't got no damn sense. What kinda school-teacher dates a drug dealer anyway," Bertha said. "Humph."

"A drug-addicted one," I concluded. "He's got her ass so strung out. That boy's gonna be the end of her one day."

"She's too damn pretty to be so stupid," one woman said.

"Her and her daddy," I replied.

"You know, I could have sworn I saw her daddy creeping out back last night," Bertha added. "But Mister told me to get my nosy-ass head from around that damn window and mind my business before someone blows it off." She chuckled. "I took that as good advice, but now I wish I had seen who it was for sure."

"You know, I can believe it was him. Now that he's robbing folks and got a little money, Connie might be letting him in the back door. I bet you that's the reason why her and Daryl broke up. That Avery always did have a spell on her," one woman speculated.

"Well, I'd love to stay here and chat it up with you ladies a little longer, but I got a meeting in apartment 3B." I winked. "So, ta-ta, ladies. I'll see y'all later."

I loved rubbing it in their faces that I was about to go live out what for the past few months had been a fantasy for each of us. There was nothing but hate for me out on the stoop, but if those heifers hated me now, then this afternoon, when I strolled outside glowing from head to toe, they would absolutely despise me.

"Have fun," someone called out sarcastically.

"Yeah, don't do anything I wouldn't do," Bertha added.

"Don't worry. I will," I shot back as I opened the door. Just the thought of wrestling naked with Daryl was making me moist. I was about to show him things he'd never seen before.

I walked into the lobby and froze. Connie was standing by the mailboxes, staring at me as if she knew exactly what I was up to.

"Hi," I said, lifting my hand in a weak greeting.

"Hey." She nodded curtly and headed for the door.

I was thankful that she wasn't headed up the stairs but also concerned about whether Bertha and the rest of the haters outside would keep their mouths shut about my little rendezvous with Daryl. So for good measure, I hung out in the lobby for a minute or two, just in case. When Connie didn't come stomping back into the building, I headed for the elevator.

As I rode up to the third floor, I realized that Connie might not be the only person I ran into on my way to Daryl's. What if I saw Ben? After all, he lived on the third floor too. This wasn't the first time I'd snuck into a man's apartment in this building, but it was definitely turning out to be the most stressful.

What would I say if I ran into Ben? Part of me thought, *Who cares? It's not like I belong to Ben, and besides, he's not talking to me anyway. It would serve him right to see me going into another man's apartment.* But the truth was I did care. All of a sudden, I wasn't sure I could go through with this rendezvous with Daryl or if I really even wanted to. As much as I talked a good game in front of the girls, that's all it was—talk. Sure, being with Daryl was a nice fantasy, but if I was being honest with myself, I was more in love with Ben than I was with my own husband. Being with Daryl would be cheating on Ben, and I didn't know if I could do that.

As it turned out, I did meet Ben on the third floor, but it didn't go down anything close to the way I'd imagined it. The third-floor hallway was filled with a cloud of thick, black smoke that came billowing into the elevator as soon as the doors opened. I staggered out, confused and frightened. All of a sudden, Ben came out of nowhere, guiding me toward the staircase door and away from danger.

Connie

34

I could feel Nancy's eyes on my back as I retrieved the mail from my mailbox and walked out of the building. It wasn't hard to tell she was up to something from her lack of eye contact and uncharacteristically timid behavior. I didn't pay her much attention, though, because I had other things on my mind—like the fact that my crazy, gun-toting ex-husband had broken into my apartment the night before to confess his undying love and to plead with me to go on the lam with him. Of course, I turned down both offers, only to find out that his main objective was to get back the money he'd given to me. To say he didn't take it well when I finally admitted that Daryl was holding the money is an understatement.

I was still kind of in shock over the whole incident. I couldn't believe that he'd actually had the balls to break into my place, then storm into Daryl's apartment with a gun, threatening to kill him if he didn't give him my money. It was touch and go there for a minute, but Daryl gave him what he'd been asking for and Avery was gone. I just hoped the whole incident didn't come back to haunt us one day.

When I brushed past Nancy and stepped outside, I heard one of the hens out there whispering, "Oh, Lord, speak of the devil," loud enough for me to hear. It was obvious my name had just been on their tongues. It was safe to assume that Nancy had been out there instigating. If this was any other day, I would have given these broads a real piece of my mind, but I didn't have time for their pettiness. So instead of going off on them, I decided to take the high road. Besides, if I stayed out on the stoop and made small talk, one of those gossiping fools would eventually spill the beans and I'd know exactly what had been said about me.

"Hello, ladies. How's everybody doing?" I leaned against the concrete banister halfway down the steps and thumbed through my mail.

"Oh, we're all just fine," Bertha answered. "How you doing? I'm sorry to hear about your recent split."

I waved away her comment. "Thank you, Bertha. Don't you worry about me. I might be big, but I always land on my feet. Besides, breaking up with Avery might be the best thing that ever happened to me."

"Avery?" Bertha looked even more confused than usual. "I wasn't talking about Avery. I saw him creeping around the fire escape to your place last night. I know what was going on with that. I was talking about your breakup with Daryl."

And that's when the lightbulb went off in my head. They must have noticed I'd been keeping Daryl at a distance the past few days, and Bertha must have seen Avery when he snuck into my apartment last night.

"Daryl." I let out a laugh. "Oh, you really don't have to worry about that. We're fine. As a matter of fact, we're better than fine." I looked over my shoulder and lowered my voice. "And as far as Avery's concerned, he just wanted me to give Krystal his car keys." No way was I gonna tell them about his demand for my money.

Marie, one of the ladies from the second floor, said, "So you and Daryl are good, huh?"

"Mmm-hmm, I just had him on pussy punishment is all." I straightened up and smiled. "But I think it's about time for him to get off punishment."

"Oh, I'm sure he's on his way to doing just that." Marie looked at the other women and snickered. They all wore similar smirks on their faces.

I wasn't quite sure what she meant by that, but I could tell when someone was taking a jab. My first instinct was to whip her ass, but after last night's confrontation with Avery, I didn't think I could handle any more stress.

I turned my attention to Bertha. "What is she talking about?" I asked.

Bertha raised her hands and lowered her head at the same time. Without making eye contact, she said, "Look, Connie, I'm really not trying to get involved in your personal business, so maybe you should be taking this up with your man."

"Yeah, maybe you should take it up with him right now!" Marie said excitedly, prompting every woman on the stoop to laugh. Bertha shifted in her seat and cut her eyes at Marie the way a parent looks at a child who's been misbehaving in public.

"What, Bertha? I was only making a suggestion." Marie lifted the palms of her hands as she proclaimed her innocence. This ignited another round of laughter, pissing me off even more.

"Will somebody tell me what the hell is going on?" I'd lost my cool. I could no longer sit there and wait for them to spill the beans. I was ready to pull out a sharp object and cut the damn can open!

I shifted my head, surveying each woman on the stoop and looking for the weak link. None of them looked like they were going to crack. These heifers were a tough bunch, and they were damn sure loyal to each other.

We were at a standstill with me feeling like the outcast up against a group of mean girls. They looked like they were determined to torture me. I was ready to play hardball by threatening to tell some of their secrets, but a loud, blaring sound came from inside the building, startling us all. A few seconds later, Nancy burst out the front door with five or six other tenants on her heels.

One of them screamed, "Fire! Fire! The building's on fire!"

"Somebody call 911," Nancy sputtered as she ran toward us.

With our little rivalry forgotten, all of us on the stoop remained frozen for a few seconds, watching in shocked confusion as people ran out of the building.

DeLisa, whose apartment was on the first floor, was the first one to finally react. "Oh my God! My kids are in there!" She jumped up from the stoop and ran into the building.

"Where's it at?" Bertha asked as she was jostled from her seat on the top step by tenants rushing out of the building.

"Somewhere on the third floor," Nancy said, panting and panic-stricken. We looked up in the direction she was pointing and saw smoke pouring out of a third-floor window.

I shouted in a panic, "Oh my God! That's Daryl's apartment!"

I made a move toward the door, but Nancy grabbed my shoulders. "No, Connie, it's not safe."

"No, you don't understand. Daryl's up there."

"It's okay," Nancy said calmly. "Ben's up there too. He's a fireman. He'll know what to do." She took my hand, and it comforted me for a second until I realized how much she was trembling too.

Benny

35

I sat on the roof, feeding the super's pigeons and finishing off what was left of the bottle of Hennessy I'd been nursing ever since I came back to the building. I hadn't been up there in a while, but for years the roof had been my sanctuary whenever I had an argument with Pop. There was something about being on the roof alone with those birds that helped me put things into perspective. I was there now because I was trying to figure things out, not with Pop, but with Daryl.

Thanks to a night of drinking, I'd finally gathered the courage to talk to him about the day Pop found out I was gay. I wanted to tell him that I knew he wasn't to blame and to make sure there were no hard feelings between us.

I hated to admit it, but it was partly my own damn fault that Pop found out. I figured that out when I saw my computer smashed to bits. That's when I knew that Pop had read my blog. I'd never protected my stuff with a password because Pop was so ignorant when it came to computers. He barely knew how to turn the damn thing on. Who would have thought he'd find a way to access my blog? Turns out I forgot to factor in his meddling bitch of a girlfriend, who Pop admitted later was the one who opened it for him. So now I knew who had been doing most of the detective work into my personal life, and I wanted to apologize to Daryl.

Truth is, part of the reason I blew up on Daryl that day had nothing to do with Pop. It was about how he rejected me when I came on to him. I was hurt and humiliated by the rejection, and more importantly, embarrassed, so it just made my anger ten times worse when I saw him with Pop. Now I just wanted to be around him again, to hear him say that our friendship was still intact even though I'd tried to come on to him.

Unfortunately, when I knocked on his door this morning, things didn't turn out how I'd planned. Daryl wouldn't even let me into his apartment. He barely stuck his head out the door to say, "Listen, Benny, I'd love to have a drink and sit down and talk, but can we do this another time? I'm kinda busy right now."

"Look, man," I said, "I want to make sure you and me are cool. I'm only asking for five minutes of your time." I didn't think that was too much to ask from your best friend.

"We cool, man. Listen, why don't you hit me up later tonight? I really don't have five minutes right now." He looked over his shoulder, but I couldn't see what was in there because the door was only cracked open a little. Whoever was in there with him, he damn sure didn't want me to see.

I thought I was cool with being friends, but the thought of him with someone else—plus all the alcohol in my system—set me off. I stuck my foot in the door so he couldn't close it on me, and I tried to grab the doorknob "Why the fuck are you trying to play me? Just fuckin' let me in! I gotta talk to you!"

Daryl pushed my hand away. "I'm not trying to play you, Benny. I'm busy."

"Bullshit. You don't wanna have a fag in your apartment, isn't that right?" I'm embarrassed to say it, but I felt like I was about to start crying.

"That's not true and you know it. Now, let me finish up what I'm doing here, and we'll talk tonight."

"Fuck you, you fake-ass Israelite. I'm not gonna kiss your ass anymore." I had to get out of there before Daryl saw my tears. I flipped him the bird with both fingers and headed for the stairs. At the time it had felt good cursing his ass out, but now I was sitting on the roof, regretting the argument. I only wanted things to go back to the way they were before I let my feelings about Daryl be known.

My plan was to go back down to see him once I'd sobered up. I threw some more feed to the pigeons, thinking about what I could say to make up for the way I'd acted a little while ago. That's when I heard the fire alarm go off.

At first I figured it was a false alarm. We had a couple families in the building with some bad-ass kids, and it wouldn't be the first time one of them set the alarm off on purpose. But after a few minutes, I got concerned when the alarm didn't stop. I heard a commotion down on the street, and I went to the edge of the roof to check it out. It looked like half of the tenants were outside, most of them looking up at something that scared the shit out of me. There was smoke billowing out of a window a few floors below where I was standing.

I don't know if it was the alcohol giving me false courage or the fact that I was a fireman's kid, but I chose to head back into the building instead of going down the fire escape. I felt an obligation to make sure everyone was out. I knocked on every door on the fourth and fifth floors, but it looked like the tenants had already evacuated. Things didn't get scary until I entered the third floor, where the hallway was full of smoke. My heart nearly stopped when I saw that the door to Daryl's apartment was open and a coughing figure was stumbling out.

I screamed out Daryl's name as I rushed down the hall. Instead of Daryl, I found my father, leaning against the doorjamb with a fire extinguisher in his hands.

"Benny, don't go in there. The fire's out," he coughed.

He dropped the fire extinguisher and reached out to me. I could feel from the weight of his body against mine that he was too weak to walk on his own, so I guided him to the stairs and down to the first floor. In the lobby, we were met by four firemen rushing into the building.

My father called one of them by name. "Richards, fire's out, but we've got a DOA in 3B."

"Got it," Richards said.

My father's words were so unfathomable that it took a while to figure out what he might have meant.

"What do you mean DOA?" I finally asked as I followed Pop out of the building.

"He's dead, Benny. Daryl. He died in the fire," he said as he sat down on the sidewalk.

I pointed an accusatory finger in my father's face. "You're lying. He's not dead. He can't be dead. I just spoke to him fifteen minutes ago." We'd argued in the past, but I'd never directly challenged my father's words, never called him a liar. But he had to be lying. There was no other explanation—at least not one my heart was ready to accept.

Pop stared at me for a couple of seconds, his soot-streaked face full of pity. He finally spoke in a caring, fatherly voice. "I'm sorry, son, but he is. He's dead."

"No!" I screamed. I felt the urge to reach out and strangle my father, and having no place to channel all that rage, my arms flailed about wildly. "If he's dead, then you killed him, because he was alive last time I saw him."

Pop stood up and put his hands firmly on my arms. He said forcefully, "Benny, calm down. You're talking crazy. I didn't kill that man." He was speaking to me but looking around at the crowd, as if he wanted to make sure the bystanders heard his denial.

I squeezed my eyes shut and shook my head, wishing I could make everything go away. "Yes, you did. You knew how I felt about him and you killed him. I'll never forgive you for this."

Pop sounded more angry than fatherly now. "Son, don't say that! I didn't kill him. He was already gone by the time I got inside his apartment."

"You're a liar!" I tore free from his grasp and forced my way to the stairs. "I have to see him!"

"Benny! Goddammit, don't go up . . ." My father's voice faded as I ran up the stairs two steps at a time. There was no way I was letting him stop me now. I couldn't accept reality any other way than to see for myself.

He can't be dead. He can't be, I kept repeating as I raced to the third floor. I'd just seen him in the hallway a little while ago. I'd just argued with him about nothing.

"Hey! Stop!" a firefighter yelled when I caught up to them on the stairs near the second floor. They were carrying heavy equipment that slowed them down, so I easily sprinted past them to the third floor.

Stepping into the third-floor hallway, I was overwhelmed by the smoke still lingering in the air. It sent my lungs into a coughing fit, and I had to stop and catch my breath before I made my way down the hall to Daryl's apartment. At the entrance, I looked down and saw the fire extinguisher my father had dropped there. Seeing it sent a wave of panic through me as my brain finally registered that this was real.

I stepped into the apartment. Considering how much smoke had been pouring out of the place, it didn't look as bad as I had expected—until I got halfway into the living room.

"No, no, no…" I dropped to my knees as I looked up at my friend's lifeless body. He was slouched over on the sofa, his face and body burned beyond recognition. The gold chain and Star of David he always wore still hung from his blackened neck. I don't know how long I sat there sobbing before I felt a hand on my shoulder.

"Son."

I turned to see my father standing behind me. The firemen and a couple of uniformed cops were right behind him. "Come on, Benny. Let's go."

"No! Get off me!" I shook his hand off my shoulder, then turned back to Daryl's charred body. "I wanna know why, Pop. He was my friend. I was gonna come back down and apologize to him, and now he's gone. Why?"

My father took me by the shoulders and tried to lift me up, but I couldn't leave the spot I was in. It was like Daryl's soul was pulling me toward him. I managed to get close enough to barely touch what was left of the electronic bracelet that cuffed his ankle.

"Young man, you could be tampering with evidence." I turned to see a police officer giving me an order. "You're going to have to leave."

At this point, the room was beginning to fill with more men in uniforms.

"As a matter of fact," the officer said to me, "I'm sure the detectives would like to speak to you downstairs." He looked at my father. "You as well, sir."

Pop gently tugged me by the elbow, and the officer led us out of the apartment. I was still in a haze of confusion as we retraced our steps back down to the first floor. I was in such a state of shock that I didn't know what to feel, but when we stepped out onto the stoop, a hysterical, ear-piercing scream from someone in the crowd shot right through my haze and broke my heart.

Krystal

36

"Noooooooooooooooooo!" I screamed so loud that my throat felt raw. I must have looked like a woman possessed, because that's how I felt when Pam, one of the stoop regulars, told me Daryl was dead.

Not ten minutes earlier, I'd felt like I was on the top of the world, the wind blowing through my hair as Slim and I cruised back to the building in my new convertible Benz. The car was given to me as a going-away present from my father, who I hoped was lying on some tropical beach with a fruity drink. He'd sent me a text promising me that he'd be back when the heat died down. I was glad to hear that he was safe and even happier that the text also said Connie had the keys to his Benz, which was now mine.

I still couldn't believe the cops were after him and he had to leave town under the cover of darkness, but there wasn't anything I could do about it at this point except pray he was safe. In the meantime, I was damn sure going to enjoy riding around town in a car that cost more than I made in a year. Oh, and I was definitely going to make sure all the gossiping heifers in my building saw me riding around in it. That's why Slim and I had circled the block a few times before we went joyriding that morning.

Slim was as happy about the car as I was. In fact, he'd been pretty happy in general lately, which was such a relief to me. Things between us had gotten much better lately, and he'd even stopped bringing up Daryl all the time. It's amazing what a little passing time and a couple of good blow jobs will do. Don't get me wrong, Slim still didn't like Daryl, but at least now I didn't have to constantly worry about him trying to take Daryl out. Well, that's what I thought before I saw the scene in front of my apartment building.

Before we rounded the corner to go back home, I had planned on having Slim drop me off right in front, so I could stroll past all the ladies and rub it in their faces. But it turned out there was no way we were getting anywhere close to the building. It looked like all hell had broken loose on the block. There were cop cars, fire engines, and ambulances all over the place.

"What the hell is going on?" I asked Slim.

Slim kind of shrugged his shoulders, looking unconcerned. I didn't understand how he could be all calm, cool, and collected. Everything I had in this world was in that apartment—along with the man who still had my heart. I don't think Slim had even brought the car to a full stop before I hopped out and ran toward the crowd.

"Yo, I'm going around the block to find somewhere to park!" Slim yelled at me.

"What the hell happened?" I asked a woman who was standing in the back of the crowd.

"There was a fire. A man got killed."

"Oh my God. Who got killed?"

The woman didn't even look at me. She was too busy gawking at all the action on the sidewalk. "I don't know," she said. "I just heard someone got killed."

I turned to Pam. I knew she hung out on the stoop all the time. If anyone would know who was dead, it would be one of the gossip-mongers from the stoop.

"Who got killed?" I asked her.

Pam turned to me with this glint in her eyes, like she didn't give a shit who died—she was just proud to be the one with the informa-tion. "The pretty thug, you know the one with the nice body and the beard that everyone been talking about."

It was as if my heart stopped beating and everything around me went into slow motion. There was only one man who fit that descrip-tion. "You mean Daryl Graham?" I tried to tell myself she couldn't be right. Daryl couldn't be dead.

"Yeah, I think that's his name. Damn shame too, because he was so—"

She never got to finish her sentence because I started screaming at the top of my lungs. I swear it felt like I lost consciousness for a second, because I don't remember moving away from Pam, but the next thing I knew, I was pushing my way through the crowd.

As I stumbled around trying to come to grips with the news, a terrifying thought entered my mind. If Daryl was really dead, could Slim have had something to do with it? Sure, we were doing well lately, but Slim obviously hadn't forgotten about my affair. That very morning when we drove by Daryl on his jog, Slim had pointed his finger at him like it was a gun, saying, "Bang, nigga, you dead." At the time, I'd ignored it, but now I was scared that maybe he hated him enough to have him killed.

I ran toward the stoop when I saw two familiar faces, Benny and his father.

"Oh my God, Benny, is it true? Is Daryl really dead?"

Benny stood there like a zombie, saying nothing. I grabbed him by the shirt collar and shook him violently, but even that didn't get a reaction.

"Goddammit, Benny, answer me!"

"Benny's in shock, Krystal," Ben Senior answered for his son. He sounded exhausted. "And yes, Daryl's dead."

I stared at Ben's face for a minute, refusing to accept his words. It was like I was waiting for him to tell me he was joking. When he didn't say anything else, I turned back to Benny and said, "Please tell me he's lying."

Benny spoke for the first time. "It's true, Kris," he whispered with lifeless eyes. "Daryl's dead. I saw his body myself."

My hands eased off of Benny's collar and fell to my side. My knees gave out, and I slumped down to sit on the sidewalk. Through trembling lips I cried, "He can't be dead. I haven't had a chance to apologize yet."

Benny sat down next to me. "I know. Me neither." He reached out to hold my hand, and we cried together.

"How'd he die?" I asked. Part of me was afraid to hear the answer.

"His apartment was on fire," Benny responded, his tears now uncontrollable. "He was burned up in a fire."

A fire. Just like my mother. What a horrible way to die. I felt my stomach tighten and my morning's breakfast rise into my throat as I thought about what Daryl must have gone through. And Benny...the poor kid had seen the body.

"Oh my God. I could have stopped it," I cried.

Suddenly Benny's face transformed from a look of grief to something closer to anger. He looked up at his father, then said to me, "This wasn't your fault, Kris."

Benny's father sat down on the other side of me. He said, "No, this wasn't anything more than an accident."

I shook my head adamantly. "You don't understand. This wasn't an accident. This was a murder, and I know exactly who did it."

At that moment, I felt someone's hands on my shoulders, and I looked up to see Slim still calm, cool, and collected in the midst of the chaos surrounding us.

"So what'd I miss?" he asked. "Y'all look like somebody died around here."

Nancy

37

The morning after Daryl's death, the building was quieter than usual as I made my way down to the stoop. There was a lingering smell of smoke that was mostly concentrated on the third floor, but there'd been no serious damage except for Daryl's apartment. The cops had roped off 3B, but we were all eventually allowed back into the building late that afternoon. A lot of residents had still chosen to go stay with friends or family somewhere else. My husband took the kids over to stay at his mother's place because he got sick of waiting around on the sidewalk. A few of the regulars from the stoop stayed around long enough to get some of their things but then left. One of them said she couldn't stand the thought of staying in a building where someone had just died. I understood where they were coming from because it was a little eerie thinking that Daryl had burned up in that fire, but I wasn't about to go somewhere else and miss all the action.

Only Ms. Bertha was on the stoop when I walked outside. I could see from the tired look on her face that yesterday's activity had taken its toll on her too. It looked like she hadn't gotten any sleep. Not that I could blame her. I hadn't gotten much myself. Daryl's death had taken its toll on everyone in the building. We hadn't known him long, but in the little time he lived here, he'd made a big impact on our lives. Never again would we sit outside on the steps and wait to see his fine ass jog by. Yeah, I was gonna miss that for sure.

I wished that I could close my eyes and see an image of Daryl in his Knicks sweat suit, stretching on the sidewalk before his run. Instead, I kept replaying yesterday's scene, when they wheeled his body out on a stretcher to take it to the morgue. There's nothing like seeing a dead body to remind us all that life is short and we never truly know when the end is coming.

"Going somewhere?" Bertha asked, looking up from her morning coffee to check out my outfit. Instead of my usual morning attire of slippers and housecoat, I was wearing my Sunday best, including a hat and a curly wig.

"Yeah." I nodded. "I thought I'd head over to First Jamaica and listen to Bishop Wilson preach."

"You're going to church?" she said with wide eyes, looking like she thought the church might catch fire when I walked through the door. That pissed me off. I wasn't the biggest churchgoer—mainly only for holidays and funerals—but Bertha had some nerve because she wasn't much better.

"Yes, Bertha, *I'm* going to church. You got a problem with that?" I placed a hand on my hip and stared at her hard.

She twisted up her lips but was smart enough not to insult me again. "No, I don't have a problem with it," she said. "I'm just surprised is all. I need to be going over there with you." She gave me an apologetic shrug that put her back in my good graces.

I exhaled. "With all that happened yesterday, what do I have to lose by going? I'm not sure if I'd call it salvation or not, but I'll take whatever I can get for as long as it takes. I just don't want to end up like—"

My words got caught in my throat, and I was surprised to find my eyes starting to tear up.

Bertha finished my sentence. "Like Daryl."

"Yeah," I said through the lump in my throat. "You didn't see when they wheeled him outta here yesterday, Bertha. It was enough to change your life."

"Oh, I saw him," she said somberly, shaking her head. "That was the saddest thing I ever saw, and I've lived me some years and seen a lot of things. That boy was nice, a real gentleman. He didn't deserve that." She stared off into the distance for a few seconds and then looked up at me, her mood suddenly lifted.

She said, "Oh, by the way, you owe me ten dollars."

"Owe you ten dollars for what?"

"I told you that fire was suspicious. Daryl's death wasn't an accident."

"What? Where'd you hear that?" I eyed Bertha skeptically. She'd been known to make up her own truths, so I knew better than to believe her without verifying her sources first.

"That's what Connie told me when she came back from the precinct last night."

While the firemen were working inside to secure the building, a few detectives had hung around outside, talking to all of us residents on the sidewalk. They were pretty slick, making it look like simple conversation when they were really investigating. I actually felt kind of stupid, because I'd been right there, running my mouth about everything I knew about everyone in the building. You know, stuff like who was sleeping with who and who had been arguing lately. For me that was just everyday gossip. I didn't even realize the cops were using me to gather evidence until I watched them ask Ben, Benny, Connie, Krystal, and Slim to go down to the precinct for some "routine questioning," as they put it. I might not have run my mouth so much if I had realized it was a murder, not an accident.

Now I was bothered by two things: the fact that I had given up so much information so easily and the fact that Bertha had gotten the 411 before me.

"Bertha, are you sure?" I asked.

"Mm-hmm," she said proudly, obviously relishing the fact that she was one up on me and ten dollars richer. "But that's not even the good part. Guess who didn't come home from the precinct last night?"

She didn't even give me time to try to guess before she told me, "Your girl Krystal and her boy Slim."

"Shut up!" I felt that familiar rush that always accompanied some really juicy gossip. "You don't think...?"

"Look, I don't make the news, I report it. But any fool can see when five people go down to the police station to be questioned about a killing and only three return, someone's in trouble."

I had to admit her logic was sound, but I didn't want to give her the satisfaction of thinking I was hanging onto her every word. If I did, I'd never hear the end of it. "Hmph! That don't mean nothing. Maybe they just went to a hotel or snuck in here after you went to bed."

Bertha's look of pride disappeared.

"I don't care what you say, Bertha. I believe deep down that girl loved Daryl. She wouldn't do anything like that to hurt him. You don't remember the way she used to look at him?"

"Mm-hmm, I sure do," she said. "But I also remember the way Slim used to look at him too. I'd never seen that much hate and jealousy in a man's eyes. If looks could kill, Daryl would be dead."

"Daryl *is* dead, Bertha."

She lifted her finger and made a check mark in the air. "Exactly my point!"

I shook my head at her foolishness. I thought I loved gossip, but this woman was taking it to the next level. "I hear you, Nancy Drew, but before you start pointing the finger, you better make sure Slim did it. Last thing you wanna do is start accusing Slim of murder. We all know what he's capable of, and neither of us wants that. Hell, we don't even know for sure that Daryl was murdered."

A male voice came from the sidewalk. "I do!"

We turned to see two people getting out of an unmarked police car that might as well have had POLICE written all over it. Well, at least now that everything had calmed down it was obvious to me that they were cops. Why couldn't I have been that observant yesterday when I was giving up all that information? One of the cops was a tall white man, the one I spilled my guts to yesterday, and the other was a brown-skinned woman who flashed her badge as if we couldn't tell they were five-o from a mile away.

"I told ya he was murdered." Bertha tapped my leg excitedly. When I finally nodded my head in acknowledgment, she stuck out her hand and said, "Gimme my ten dollars."

I shoved her hand away. "Have y'all arrested the killer, detective?" I asked, testing Bertha's theory on Slim and Krystal.

"Not yet, but we've got some good leads, Mrs. . . . ." The man turned to me, looking upward as if he was about to pull my name out of the air. Instead, he flipped through his notepad to find it. "Mrs. Williams, isn't it? Nancy Williams?"

"Yeah." I tried to sound confident, but inside I was scared to death. Why did this guy remember my name, and even scarier, why was he back here looking like he had more questions? When I was talking to him yesterday, I had been too embarrassed to tell him I was on my way up to Daryl's apartment right before the fire broke out. How was that going to sound after I'd already told him I was married? I might not have cared what the girls on the stoop thought, but I wasn't trying to look like a slut in front of a total stranger. Now I was afraid that one of those jealous bitches might have said something to him, and now he was back, trying to pin a motive for murder on me. But then he spoke, and I realized the detectives were here for a very different reason.

"Well, Nancy, you were really helpful yesterday, and I was hoping you could help us again, you know, fill in a few of the missing pieces."

Shit, shit, and more shit! They were gonna haul my ass down to the precinct like they'd done the others. I mean, I felt bad that Daryl was dead, but I sure as hell didn't want to go with them and then be pegged as the building's snitch.

Before I could try to talk my way out of it, Bertha spoke up. "Oh, please. Y'all don't need any help. You already got the killers down at the station, don't you? Everyone knows Krystal and Slim had something to do with that fire."

"Oh, really? Why is that?" the female detective asked, pulling out her own notebook.

"Because right before the fire, the two of them came busting out the building like the world was about to end. Ain't that right, Nancy?" Bertha winked, then nodded her head like she'd just spoken the gospel.

Even though it was Bertha who was running her dentures, the female detective looked to me for confirmation. "That true? You saw them running out of the building?"

My eyes shifted to Bertha, trying to send her a message to shut her trap. I looked back to the detective, who was waiting for my answer with pen poised over her paper, ready to take notes.

I realized these cops weren't going away without some answers. Like an idiot, I'd already shown them yesterday that when it came to info about the folks in our building, I was the one to go to. There was no way they'd believe me if I told them I didn't know anything all of a sudden. "Look," I answered reluctantly, "I don't know if they're guilty or not."

The male cop raised his eyebrows and said, "But . . . ?" letting me know they weren't going to accept a half-assed answer.

"Fine," I said with a sigh. "It *was* kinda strange the way they came barreling out the building like they were running from a fire."

"Who knew they really were?" Bertha said with a laugh. She folded her arms as if she'd stated her entire case. "So, you gonna arrest them now? If you need me as a witness, I'll testify."

The female cop turned to Bertha and spoke slowly, like she was talking to a senile person in a nursing home. "Well, ma'am, I'm not sure we're ready for an arrest, but I can promise you we'll look into it. Right now we have a few other leads we're looking at."

"Really? Like who?" Bertha asked.

The cops glanced at each other in a way that said Bertha was working their last nerves. She was a little too damn eager to know everything. I, on the other hand, wished we could hurry up and get this over with.

Instead of answering Bertha's question, the male detective turned to me. "Mrs. Williams, can we talk to you privately for a second?"

Bertha made this grumbling noise, like she was insulted they didn't come to her. What the fool didn't know is that I would have been happy to change places with her. I followed the detectives away from the stoop toward their car, but fortunately, we didn't get in.

"How can I help you?" I leaned against the car, not because I felt relaxed, but because my knees were so wobbly I needed it for support.

"Well, for starters, do you really think Slim and Krystal had something to do with the death of Mr. Graham?" the male detective asked me. Unlike yesterday when he made it seem like we were just having a conversation, now he was all business.

I thought about his question and shrugged. "I don't know. I guess. I mean, there are probably other people who didn't like him. It's not like I was close to the guy and knew everyone he hung out with. Maybe he had beef with lots of people . . . but yeah, as far as the tenants in the building, I guess they're at the top of my list." *Shit!* Why was I rambling? I'd already said way more than I wanted to. My big mouth was going to get me in trouble if I didn't learn to shut up.

"Listen," I continued, "I'm not like Bertha. I'll help you, but I ain't testifying about shit. If what you say is true and Daryl was killed, I don't wanna be next on the list, especially if we're talking about Slim."

"Why's that? What's so badass about him?" the woman asked.

"He's a drug dealer. A murdering drug dealer from what I've heard." There I went again, speaking without thinking. The problem was, once I'd said it, I couldn't take it back. Now the cops would pump me for even more information about Slim—a man I'd just admitted was capable of murder.

"Interesting. You sure about that?" The female detective raised an eyebrow at her partner as he continued to write in his pad. "We ran his name and nothing came up."

Oh, hell. I'd already practically dug my own grave, so why not keep talking? Maybe he did really kill Daryl. At least if they arrested him for it, then I'd be out of danger. I asked, "Did you run it down south? He doesn't sell around here anymore, mostly in Virginia, I think. I'm pretty sure he has a record down there, and he definitely sells drugs. Of that I'm sure."

The male detective closed his notebook and reached out to shake my hand. "Thank you. You've given us a lot to think about."

I shook his hand and then looked over to Bertha, who I knew was damn near about to soil her Depends waiting on me to bring her back the scoop.

The female officer put a hand on my shoulder and said, "I know this isn't easy, but you're doing the right thing. If you could help us out a little more by being our eyes and ears in the neighborhood, it would be appreciated."

Oh my God. This kept getting worse for me. "Why me?"

"I don't know, Nancy," the male said, suddenly all chummy again. "You seem to tell it like it is. And something in my gut says you're the right person for the job. But if my gut's wrong, we can talk to your friend Bertha over there. She seems real cooperative too."

We all glanced over at Bertha, who was practically drooling on herself, waiting for a chance to get in on the action. As much as I didn't like talking to the cops, I couldn't help myself. I was not about to lose my top spot on the stoop by letting her outscoop me.

"No," I told him, "your gut's right. Bertha doesn't have a subtle bone in her body." Something told me today wasn't the day I was going to go see about saving my soul. It was more like the day I was going to be playing with the devil.

The female officer spoke up. "Well, then, while we've got you here, there is one other neighbor we'd like to ask you about." She glanced over at her partner, who was frowning. Whatever she was about to ask, he was not on board. Neither was I once I heard what she wanted to know.

"What do you know about your neighbor, Ben Wilkins, from 3C?"

I tried my best to hide it, but her question sent a chill down my spine. "Um, what about him?"

"How well do you know him?"

I stared at her for a second, trying to read her body language. Did she already know about me and Ben? Maybe she did and she was trying to see if she could catch me in a lie. Or maybe she didn't know anything at all. I couldn't tell from her poker face what she did or didn't know, so I tried to be as vague as possible in my answer.

"He's a nice man. I have a lot of respect for him. He's been raising his son alone since the boy was in elementary school."

As the detective was writing all of this down in her notebook, her blank expression didn't give away anything about her thoughts, so I came right out and asked her, "Why? Do you think he killed Daryl?" I didn't think she'd say yes, but if she did, at least I'd be able to warn Ben that they were looking at him.

"We're not sure yet," she said. "We heard from some other tenants that he'd had a pretty heated argument with the deceased. Almost came to blows."

Despite our recent disagreements, I felt a need to protect Ben. "Oh yeah, they had an argument, but it was nothing. Just a misunderstanding. And it wasn't like he was the only one who argued with Daryl. Hell, him and Slim got into it physically. Avery Mack and him had words too. And there were those gangbangers he ran off from the building when they were attacking Benny."

"Oh, so you were there when Ben and Daryl argued?" It was the first time the male detective had spoken up in a while. The bad thing was this: He was frowning when his partner first brought up Ben, but now he seemed more interested in hearing about him. All because of me and my big mouth. Well, I was going to have to keep talking now to make sure they stopped focusing their attention on Ben.

"Yes, I was there for it," I confirmed, "but like I said, it was just a misunderstanding. It wasn't anything to kill someone over."

"What was the fight about?" the female cop asked.

Dammit. I was getting sick of this. "Um, I don't know. I didn't really see the whole thing," I lied.

"I see," she said, narrowing her eyes like she didn't believe me. "Well, do you think he's capable of murder?"

I straightened my shoulders and spoke confidently. "No, I don't think he's capable of murder. The man's a New York City fireman. He saves lives; he doesn't end them. Just because Ben argued with Daryl doesn't mean he murdered him."

The female detective gave me a skeptical look. "No, it doesn't necessarily mean that, but I think we all can agree that Ben Wilkins didn't like Mr. Graham. And who knows more about setting a fire than a fireman, right?"

I opened my mouth but then realized that she was trying to put words in it, so I closed it and thought for a second before I spoke. "Look, all I know is that Ben Wilkins is a good, decent man. He's a 9/11 hero and the one who put out the fire so it didn't spread. I think everyone in this building owes him a debt of gratitude. If you need to know anything else about his situation with Daryl, I think you should talk to him."

"We already did," she said. "Somehow he doesn't seem to remember the details of his disagreement with Mr. Graham. But don't worry. We're going to get to the bottom of this."

Krystal

38

The morning after Daryl's death, I woke up in pain. Everything hurt—my head, my back, and of course, my heart. I still couldn't believe that he was dead, and I didn't want to believe what I'd suspected and what the cops had confirmed the night before: Daryl was murdered.

I was grateful to be in the bed alone as I lay there with tears flowing freely down my face. Slim had gone out as soon as the sun came up, saying he had things to take care of before he headed back down to Virginia. I usually hated it when he was away, but this time I was looking forward to having a few days apart, both to mourn Daryl's loss and to give Slim a chance to cool off. He'd been in a pissy mood ever since they dragged us down to the police station for that group interview last night. They didn't interview us individually, and the questions weren't even that deep, but being in such close proximity to the law was enough to have Slim on edge. If he saw me crying over Daryl now, he just might kick my ass.

As you can imagine, Slim wasn't exactly heartbroken over Daryl's death. He probably figured that with Daryl out of the way, he had nothing left to worry about when it came to me. The truth was that even before the fire he had nothing to worry about. As long as Slim kept providing me with those little blue boxes, I would be his for life. It wasn't really a question of me loving Slim or Daryl better because cocaine was my one true love.

I sat up and stretched, then headed over to my dresser to get something to numb the pain. The familiar blue box was there waiting for me, and I felt instantly more relaxed at the sight of it. I scooped up some of the white powder in my fingernail, placed it underneath my nose, and inhaled. A pleasurable chill raced through my body and put a smile on my face. What a great way to start off the day.

I heard my phone chirp on my night table, so I took one more hit and went to pick it up. It was a text from my father.

hey sweetie. just checking in on you.

I'd sent him a quick text the night before to tell him about the fire and Daryl's death, but I guess he hadn't had a chance to answer until now.

I texted back: yeah daddy. I'm good. everything okay on your end?

i'm fine. just enjoying the sun.

At least the sun was shining in his life. There was nothing but doom and gloom this way. I really was glad to hear that my dad was doing well.

wish i could be there. I was fishing for an invite. I would love to get out of this place for a while.

so do I, but this is no place for you right now. and i'm way too hot.

i understand.

It took a while for his next text to come through, and for a minute I thought maybe our conversation was done. Then I read his next text and wished he had ended the conversation.

so how's Connie holding up?

Just the mention of her name sent me back to the dresser for another hit. I hated when he asked about that bitch. I thought about not responding at all but thought better of it. I had no idea where my father was. The last thing I wanted to do was piss him off and have him stop communicating altogether.

I sent him another text, cursing Connie the whole time. Why the fuck did he care how she was?

she's mourning daryl, daddy. let it go.

It took a while before he replied. I think he hated Daryl as much as I hated Connie.

He finally sent this back: She'll get over him.

I doubt it.

He had no idea the hold Daryl could have on a woman. He obviously didn't want to argue the point with me, though, because he quickly sent back a good-bye.

love you. gotta go.

I stared at the screen, hoping I hadn't pissed him off too much. I was about to text an apology when I was startled by a loud knock at my door.

"Who the hell is pounding at my door like you the damn po-po or something?" I said as I went to check the peephole. Putting my eye to the door, I realized there was a good reason why they were pounding like the damn po-po—because they were!

I took a step back from the door and put my hand over my chest like it might slow down my racing heart. My eyes darted around the living room, checking every table and chair to make sure Slim hadn't left anything lying around that would get us into trouble. The cops knocked again, which made me jump.

"Uh, who is it?" I called through the door.

"Ms. Mack, it's Detectives Thomas and Anderson. We spoke briefly last night. We'd like to ask you a few more questions."

I considered refusing to open the door, but that thought disappeared quickly. The best way to draw the attention of the cops would be to piss them off, and I did not need any more headaches in my life right now.

I slipped my cell phone into the pocket of my sweatpants and opened the door just a crack.

"Yes?" I asked.

He flashed his badge, although there was no need. I definitely recognized him from the night before. "I'm sorry to bother you so early in the morning, but we'd like to talk to you some more about Daryl Graham and the circumstances surrounding his death."

"I thought we answered all your questions last night."

"You did, but some new information has come to our attention, and we'd like to clear it up without dragging you back down to the station."

There was no denying the threat implied by his tone. If I didn't cooperate now, they were going to bring me back to the precinct. Considering how much coke I had in my system at the moment, I really didn't want to be in a building filled with cops. "What do you want me to do?"

He glanced down at the chain on my door and said, "For starters, you could invite us in so I can explain. This really won't take long at all."

I sighed in defeat as I unlatched the door to let them in. Slim was going to kill me later if he found out I'd let them in without a warrant, but shit, what choice did I have? Besides, in some little corner of my heart, I wanted to help them punish Daryl's killer.

"Thank you," the detective said as he and his partner came in. I closed the door and offered them a seat, but they both declined.

"Is your boyfriend Slim around?" the female cop asked as she searched the room with her eyes.

"No, he's at work. Why?"

"Just wondering." She picked up a picture off an end table and showed it to her partner. "This you and your mom?" she asked.

"Yeah, she died a few years ago," I answered, wishing I could tell that bitch to put down my mother's picture.

The male detective got in on the small talk act. "Oh, sorry to hear that," he said. "You look like her. She was pretty."

"Thanks." I gave him a half smile, wishing I could tell them to hurry up and get to the point.

"So you said your boyfriend's at work. What kind of work does he do?" the female cop asked.

I gave her the answer I always used when someone asked about Slim. "He's self-employed."

She stopped poking around my shit and sat down next to me on the sofa. "Doing what?"

"Is this why you're here? To harass me about my boyfriend's profession?" A nervous laugh escaped my lips. The female detective stared at me intensely without a word. If she was trying to make me more nervous, it was sure as hell working.

"What, do you think we killed Daryl or something?"

That put a smug smile on her face, like she'd accomplished her goal of making me paranoid. Stupid-ass cop was on a power trip.

"No," she said. "To be honest, I think you loved him—as much as someone like you can love another human being."

"What the hell is that supposed to mean?" I looked up at her partner, expecting him to check her, but he only stood there.

"I think you know exactly what I mean." She gave me a knowing look that made me very uncomfortable. "By the way, what's that on your lip?"

"Huh?"

She pointed at my mouth. "Right there. The white powder on your lip."

"There's nothing on my lip." I quickly wiped my mouth on my sleeve. There was no doubt in my mind that both of them knew exactly what the white powder was.

"Not anymore there isn't. I think you got it all now," the male cop said as he sat down on the other side of me. At least he didn't sound sarcastic like his partner. I hated cops in general, but I decided he was the lesser of two evils.

"Why are you really here?" I asked the male detective.

Even though I'd turned my back on her, it was the female cop who laughed out loud and answered me. "I was asking myself the same thing." She stood up from the couch and said, "Let's get the hell outta here, Thomas. You know I don't do well with junkies. I've got a good mind to lock her ass up for possession."

I felt beads of sweat break out on my forehead as my heart rate skyrocketed. What the hell was going on here? Had they really come by to talk about Daryl or was this about drugs? With the coke that I'd already snorted that morning, I was having trouble focusing my thoughts to figure out how I was going to talk my way out of this. As it turned out, I didn't have to, because the male detective got a text that distracted them both.

"Shit, what else can go wrong?" he said after he read the text.

"What's up?" his partner asked.

"That's the M.E. office. The family's already down at the morgue, trying to claim the body. They must have some pull, because they're about to throw him on the table, then turn him over. If we want a thorough autopsy, we gotta slow them down, because it looks like they're planning on cremating the body."

His partner screwed up her face, making her even uglier than she already was. "Let me make a call to my contact at the M.E.'s office. See if I can slow them down long enough for us to get there. I'll meet you at the car." She threw a glance in my direction as she went to the door. "Now you know why I send my kids to private school, Thomas. With a teacher like her as a role model, the kids have no chance but to fail."

After she left, her partner turned to me and shrugged. "She used to work vice. She can spot an addict a mile away."

"Well, there aren't any addicts around here." I straightened my back and tried to sound indignant, but it must not have been convincing because he shook his head and chuckled.

"Look, let's just get to the point, okay? I didn't come here to waste my time."

I folded my arms and clamped my mouth shut.

"Krystal, we've interviewed quite a few people from the building, and more than one of them said they heard you saying that you know who really killed Mr. Graham."

"I have my suspicions."

"Are those suspicions based on fact, or are they fantasies brought on by the cocaine you sniffed before we arrived?"

I was getting sick of these cops harassing me about my habit when they should have been focused on a murder. "Dammit, did you come here to hassle me or to find out who killed Daryl?"

"I'm twenty years homicide, not vice. I'm here to solve a murder."

"All right, then," I said, thinking he was done.

"But I will not be made a fool of," he added. "If you commit a crime in front of my face, I will arrest you. Fair enough?" He gave me such a serious look that I knew, nice guy or not, he was not to be fucked with.

"Okay. You wanna know who killed Daryl?"

He pulled out a pad to take notes and looked at me expectantly.

"It was my stepmother. Connie Mack."

He lowered his notepad without writing a thing. "Are you jerking my chain?"

"Hell no. Who'd you think I was gonna say? My boyfriend Slim?" I laughed, but when I glanced in his direction, I was met with cold eyes that shut me up.

"Hey, I know what you think of Slim," I said. "Your partner wasn't exactly subtle about her feelings. Slim didn't do it, though. Connie did. Shoot, I would have thought you guys were already looking at her. I mean, isn't it obvious? Once a murderer always a murderer."

He cocked his head to the side like he had no clue what I was talking about. "We've run a check on every person in this building. She's never had as much as a traffic ticket."

I sucked my teeth. "That's only because no one would listen to me six years ago when I told them she killed my mother. And now look what's happened. She's fucking Daryl, and he dies exactly the same way my mother did. I'd call that suspicious, wouldn't you, Detective?"

You should have seen the look on his face. He was so confused that I could have knocked him in the head, taken his gun and badge, and he wouldn't have even noticed.

"How come this is the first I'm hearing about this? Why didn't you say anything last night?"

"Uh, you mean aside from the fact that she was sitting right there in the room with me? I mean, no offense, Detective, but I wasn't about to speak up in front of a room full of people. In case you haven't noticed, folks around this neighborhood aren't too fond of speaking to the police."

Instead of being insulted, he softened his face and said, "I understand. But you're talking to me now because you really loved Daryl and you want his killer brought to justice, right?"

Damn, this guy was good. Just like that, I was no longer mad at him. In fact, I was close to tears as I admitted, "Yeah, I loved him."

He patted my hand. "I'll take a look at your claims about Connie Mack, but you do understand I'm gonna need a little more to go on than your word, right?"

"Wait right here," I said, then jumped up and ran into my bedroom. I brought back a scrapbook full of newspaper clippings about my mother's death and handed it to him. As he flipped through the pages, I asked, "How many suicides do you know that involved a fire?"

That was not a rhetorical question. I took a brief pause, allowing him to reply, but he didn't. He couldn't. I could tell by the look on his face that he'd never dealt with a suicide by fire in his entire twenty-year career.

He looked at me with sympathy in his eyes, but I could tell he still wasn't entirely convinced. "You bring up an interesting similarity, but these articles say your mother was also found to have very high doses of prescription drugs in her system."

I rolled my eyes and spat, "Drugs that Connie probably force-fed to her before she set the fire!"

He stood up from the couch, and I figured that was the end of it. He was going to write me off as paranoid just like all the other cops did when my mother died, and fat-ass Connie was going to get away with murder again. At least that's what I thought until he asked, "Do you mind if I take these articles with me?"

"Does this mean you're going to look into it?" I asked.

He hesitated for a minute like he was still trying to decide, and then he said, "I can promise you that my partner and I are going to leave no stone unturned in this investigation. First thing I'm going to do when I get back to the station is see if I can get my hands on the files from your mother's death."

I had to grip the sides of the cushion to stop myself from jumping off the couch and shouting, "Hallelujah!"

"Thank you. Thank you so much. That's exactly what I needed to hear." I wiped happy tears off my face.

He headed to the door and then turned to look at me one last time before he left. "You know, Krystal, I think you might wanna get yourself into a program."

A fresh wave of tears streamed down my cheeks. "That was the last thing Daryl said to me too."

"Then maybe Daryl Graham was smarter than any of us will ever know."

Connie

39

When I heard a knock on my door, I was already on my fourth bottle of Febreze. I'd been spraying it everywhere, hoping to get rid of the smell of smoke that lingered. The spray was masking the odor, but it wasn't enough to get rid of it. The smoke had settled into my couch, in the carpet, in the walls. If I couldn't get rid of it soon, I didn't know what I was going to do. I sure couldn't live in an apartment where the smell would be a constant reminder of the nightmare I'd been through.

I set down the Febreze and went to the door. Without checking the peephole, I flung open the door and said, "Detectives, come on in. I've been expecting you." It was Thomas and Anderson, the two lead detectives I'd met the night before when they took us to the precinct. It was supposedly so they could ask questions about the fire, but it turned out to be little more than a free fried chicken dinner. I sure hoped they were more serious about investigating Daryl's death today.

Obviously the way I greeted them wasn't what they usually experienced when they knocked on someone's door. They gave each other a confused glance.

"You've been expecting us? What are you, some kind of psychic?" Anderson asked.

I laughed and told her, "The girls on the stoop told me you'd been questioning everyone. I figured it was just a matter of time before you made your way to me." I gestured for them to sit on the couch, and they settled in. Their clothes would probably be reeking of smoke by the time they left. "Have you made any progress in finding Daryl's killer?"

"Some," Detective Thomas said. "But we're still in the beginning stages of our investigation. We're trying to eliminate possible suspects from our list. This, unfortunately, brings us to you."

I might have been expecting them to show up, but I sure as heck hadn't been expecting them to say that. "Am I a suspect?"

"Right now everyone's a suspect. Considering your close relationship with Mr. Graham, I hope you can understand why we'd like to speak to you and scratch you off our list as quickly as possible," he said.

I felt tears welling up in my eyes at the mention of our relationship. It had only been a day, but I missed Daryl so intensely that hearing his name set me on edge. I still couldn't believe they considered me a suspect, but I was willing to do whatever it took to make sure they arrested someone for this hideous crime.

"I'll tell you everything I know. I just want you to find Daryl's killer," I told him as I slumped into the armchair before my knees gave out.

Anderson jumped in, sounding much less sympathetic than her partner. "I'm glad to hear that because we talked to your stepdaughter, and—"

"Oh, God. Here we go. I knew this was coming," I said. "What has Krystal accused me of now? Murdering Daryl the same way I murdered her mother?" I had to laugh to keep from crying. This whole situation was so absurd. I never could have imagined my life would get to this point.

Thomas, who was busy taking notes, didn't say anything, but I saw him smirk like he thought the theory was as stupid as I did. Anderson was looking at me with raised eyebrows, though, and I realized she had taken Krystal's accusations seriously. She was waiting for me to defend myself.

I shook my head. "She must be driving you all crazy, pushing to have me arrested. I should have known that she'd bring up her mother's death. She's been trying to pin that woman's death on me since the day of her funeral. She brings it up every chance she gets."

Anderson said, "Yes, she did bring it up. What concerns me is that you didn't. Don't you think you should have volunteered that information at the precinct last night?"

I definitely didn't like Anderson's tone. This woman was one hard-ass cop, probably looking at this case as her chance to prove herself. Well, she was not about to use me to get ahead.

"Excuse me," I started with no intention of speaking respectfully. "My boyfriend had been burned up in a fire, and you had us sitting down at the precinct, waiting for two hours. Then you talked to me for five whole minutes, and you expected me to volunteer that BS? You have got to be kidding me."

"So, you're saying that Krystal's accusations are BS?" Anderson asked, stating the obvious.

"Of course I am! Her mother died in a fire. My boyfriend died in a fire. I don't see how that points a finger in my direction. Shit, people die in fires every day."

I had to get control of my emotions in a hurry, because I could see from Anderson's expression that she was reading something into it.

I turned to Detective Thomas, who seemed to be the more reasonable of the pair. "You guys aren't taking that bitch Krystal serious, are you? She's been talking this crazy stuff for years, and as you can see, no one's ever charged me with anything. I didn't kill that woman. She committed suicide."

"We're trying to get to the bottom of this, Connie, and the only way we can eliminate you as a suspect is to ask you questions. We're just doing our job—and that job is to find your boyfriend's murderer." His voice was calm and reassuring, and I felt my pulse relaxing.

"I know," I told him, "but I didn't have anything to do with that fire. If you don't believe me, call Sergeant Acosta of the Second Precinct in Nassau County. He'll tell you. I was at work that day."

"We already have. He's sending over the file. Hopefully that will clear some of this up."

I was kind of taken aback by that. These two were seriously pursuing this angle if they'd already contacted Nassau County about me. That damn Krystal had been a thorn in my side for so long. Why the hell couldn't she have been the one in that fire yesterday?

Anderson jumped back in to ask, "Why don't you tell us why your stepdaughter is so adamant about you being her mother's killer?"

"I was having an affair with Krystal's father. She's always claimed that I murdered her mother to get her father, but she's got the story all wrong."

"Really? Well, why don't you tell us the right story, then?" Anderson said, still sounding like she had some kind of problem with me. This woman sure took her bad cop image seriously.

I released a heavy sigh and then told them the same story I'd repeated to the Nassau County detectives all those years ago when Krystal first brought up this bullshit. "I didn't need to get rid of anyone to get Avery. He'd already told his wife he was going to divorce her to marry me, but he had no idea the woman was so unstable. She couldn't take losing him. She had some kind of breakdown and took an overdose of valium."

"Tell us about the fire," Anderson said.

I wanted to tell her to read it in the damn report when it came from Long Island, but there was no sense in antagonizing her. "She doused her comforter in WD-40 and placed a lit candle at the other end of her bed. She was already dead from the pills by the time the bed caught fire. All of this was in the report, but Krystal refuses to believe it. She can't get it out of her head that I did it."

"I see," Anderson said. "And what does her father say about all of this?"

Damn, I was hoping they weren't going to mention Avery. These two were in homicide so maybe they didn't know about the robberies, but I sure as hell didn't want them asking me questions about it. The last thing I needed with everything else going on was to be linked to Avery's criminal activities as an accomplice or something. It was in my best interests to make it very clear that I'd distanced myself from him.

"Her father...ha! Well, Krystal got her wish after all because we broke up a few months ago. Our divorce will be final in a couple of weeks."

"Sorry to hear that," Thomas said, surprising me with his kindness. "I've been divorced. It's not easy."

"No, it isn't," I said, feeling a little less like I was in the hot seat. "But I got lucky. I met Daryl. He was the best thing that ever happened to me." This brought on a fresh wave of tears.

Anderson still wasn't ready to back off. "You make it sound like everything between you and Mr. Graham was great," she said. "But I hear you two weren't even on speaking terms the day before his death."

I nodded and shrugged, refusing to let her think she was intimidating me. "I wasn't talking to him. He lied to me."

"Is that why he was on pussy punishment?"

I stared at her without answering. In my head, I was cursing those nosy bitches on the stoop with their big mouths.

"I'll take that as a yes," she said with a smirk. "Is that why he called you a fat ass?"

She thought she had caught me in a lie. I couldn't help but smile. "No, that's not why he called me a fat ass. He's always calling me fat ass."

Thomas looked up from his notepad. "And you didn't take offense?"

Anderson seemed happy that her partner had finally chimed in on her side. She stressed his point by adding, "Someone called me a fat ass in private, let alone in public, I'd want to kill him."

I burst out laughing. "Take offense? Is that what all this is about? You think I killed Daryl because he called me a fat ass? First of all, I'd never hurt a hair on Daryl's head, let alone kill him. And even though what we had wasn't long-lived, I loved him."

"Loved him, huh?" Anderson said doubtfully. "Maybe the feeling wasn't mutual if he was running around calling you a fat ass."

I shook my head. This woman just wouldn't let up. "That was his pet name for me."

Anderson frowned at me like she thought I was feeding her a load of crap.

I couldn't wait to break this one down for her. "Yes, people called me fat all the time, but Daryl took the power from the word. When Daryl called me fat, it wasn't F-A-T. It was P-H-A-T. Pretty, hot, and tempting, which I am."

"And you really want us to believe that?" Anderson asked.

"You can believe it or not," I replied. "It's the truth."

Anderson folded her arms. She looked pissed off, like she was sick of trying to get me to tell the truth. Well, I guess it was time for me to give her what she wanted—the raw, uncensored truth.

"Excuse me for a minute," I told them. "I have something you should see."

I headed to my bedroom and returned a few moments later with proof in hand. I gave the DVD to Anderson. "Maybe this will convince you."

She looked down at the disc. "What's this?"

"It's a private video Daryl and I made, buck wild and naked. Watch it. He refers to me as his phat ass at least thirty-five times. Oh, and you can have that one. I've got another copy."

Anderson looked at her partner, then threw the DVD onto the table. She finally looked ready to back off a little. The silence in the room was so awkward that I almost felt embarrassed for her. I decided it was a good time to help her out a little bit, steer her in another direction now that I'd shot down her flimsy theory about me.

"Look, I promise you that you guys are barking up the wrong tree...with both Daryl and my husband's former wife. Between you and me, you might want to look into my stepdaughter's boyfriend."

Anderson and Thomas shared a pointed look. This was obviously not the first time they'd heard this.

"And what reason would we have to do that?" Anderson asked, trying to play dumb. I was sure the stoop ladies had already been flapping their gums about everyone, including Slim.

"You haven't heard from the curb? Slim and Daryl couldn't stand each other. Slim even threatened to kill him. I would have expected him to be your number one suspect."

It wasn't long before we wrapped things up and the detectives were heading out my front door, leaving me with their last words: "We'll be in touch."

Krystal

40

Have you ever had that uncomfortable feeling that you were about to walk into a place you really had no business being? Well, that's how I felt as I walked up the steps of the J. Foster Phillips Funeral Home for Daryl's wake. This was the last place I wanted to be—and the one place I had to be. I owed that much to Daryl. I'd never had the chance to apologize to him, so the least I could do was show my respects to his family now that he was gone.

When Slim and I walked in, I stopped in my tracks, thinking we had accidentally stumbled into the wrong wake. The place was jam-packed with people from every walk of life: black folks, white folks, bougie folks, hood folks, and quite a few famous people. I took Slim's hand and was about to walk out until I saw Nancy, Bertha, and the rest of the stoop crew huddled in a corner, whispering and pointing at some woman who looked a lot like Foxy Brown.

An usher approached us and handed me a program. One look at the picture of Daryl printed on the front and my knees buckled. It took everything I had not to break down right on the spot. The usher gave me a sympathetic nod as he held out his hand in a gesture for us to be seated. Of course, there really weren't many seats left with the place being so full.

"Slim, I'm going to see if I can find us seats near the front," I said.

Slim kind of rolled his eyes and said, "Whatever." He leaned against the wall in the back of the room. "I'm gonna stay right here."

I let him stay put and headed to search for a seat for myself. I could have used a little support during the wake, but I wasn't about to argue with him. If things were reversed, I don't know if I could have sat through one of his ex-girlfriend's wakes. I gave him credit just for sticking around—even if he was only making an appearance to squash the rumors about him having something to do with Daryl's death.

I found an empty chair between two women, who were both staring straight ahead, dabbing away tears from their eyes. Looking in the direction they were staring, I saw the closed casket with a framed photo of Daryl on top, and I had to reach for a Kleenex of my own. I couldn't believe that Daryl was really dead. I would never get the chance to make things right between us. All of a sudden, I was itching to take the blue box out of my purse and do a line to ease my pain.

The funeral director asked everyone to get settled so they could start the memorial service, led by none other than Bishop T. K. Wilson, one of the most influential preachers in all of New York. Everyone in Queens knew who Bishop Wilson was, but what surprised me was that when the bishop spoke about Daryl, it sounded like he knew him personally. How did Daryl, a Hebrew Israelite, become a close personal friend of a Baptist preacher?

As the memorial proceeded, I had to ask myself the same question over and over: How well had I really known Daryl? I reflected on the time we'd spent together and realized that he spent a lot of time listening to me but not much time talking about himself or his past. When his mom, brother, and sister got up to speak, it dawned on me that I'd never even met them. Daryl never talked about introducing me to them, so I just assumed they weren't close. But now, hearing the way they talked about him, it seemed like he had a great relationship with his family.

I was even more surprised when the infamous New York rapper Buck-Fifty read a poem he'd written in Daryl's honor. He called it "The Thug You Could Take Home to Your Momma." Again, I was left feeling like this famous rapper knew Daryl personally—and I had never really known him at all. Who was this man whose death had summoned a crowd as if Barack Obama himself were delivering the eulogy?

By the end of the wake, I was more confused than ever. I made my way through the crowd to find Slim in the same spot where I'd left him.

"Thank God this thing is over. Can we please get the hell outta here now?" he said as soon as he saw me.

"Okay, babe. Let's just go up there and pay our respects to the family and then we can leave."

"I'm not going up there." He shook his head. "I don't know those people, and I didn't particularly like their son."

"Hush." I slapped his arm and looked around to make sure no one else had heard him. "You know why we have to make an appearance. We talked about this earlier."

"No, you talked about it. I only agreed because you were giving me head at the time. Now, all we gotta do is sign that book up front to prove that we were here."

"But..." I stood my ground even though I couldn't deny that Slim was right. We could have signed the guest book and headed out. Truth was, I wanted to meet Daryl's family. I wanted to know if they'd ever heard of me. Had Daryl loved me enough to tell them about me, or was I some big secret?

Somehow, I think Slim sensed what I was thinking. "If you wanna go up there for some other reason, that's on you, but don't be expecting me to be happy about it." His tone was nasty, and I knew what he was threatening.

Him not being happy meant no more blue boxes anytime soon, and it didn't matter how well I sucked his dick. I wasn't sure if I could deal with that, especially when I desperately needed something to dull my pain.

Speaking of pain, my heart ached even more when I turned and saw Connie all hugged up with Daryl's mother and sister like she was part of the family. A flash of jealousy, accompanied by a whole lot of anger, raced through me, and I started trembling. That damn Connie had to be the biggest phony I'd ever seen. I swear she was determined to ruin my life.

"Yeah, you're right. Let's get the fuck out of here," I said to Slim.

"Yo, look at Benny over there with his pops. Poor kid's really broken up over this, huh?" Slim said in what almost sounded like a sympathetic tone. He was a hard-ass most of the time, but Slim did have a soft side that he let me see once in a while.

I turned to see Benny, standing in line to walk by the casket, crying on his father's shoulder. "Yeah, he looks like he lost his best friend," I said.

We stood there for a minute, watching the raw grief and emotion that Benny was displaying. I don't know what Slim was thinking, but I was wishing there was some way to take away Benny's pain. Hell, I wished someone would take my pain away. Of course, that's when I thought of my best friend in the little blue box in my purse. I needed a hit badly.

I turned to leave and almost ran right into Connie. She'd moved from the front of the room without me even seeing her, like some damn sorceress or something, and now she was in my way. She had the nerve to be smiling at me as she wiped tears from her raccoon eyes. I had to resist the urge to slap her.

"What are you, the grieving widow?" I asked her curtly.

She looked me dead in the eyes. "You know what, Krystal? You have absolutely no class. You are pathetic."

"I know you ain't talking about class. Not you, the woman who was screwing Daryl and my father at the same time." Her jaw tensed up, and I could tell she was trying to keep it together.

I really wanted to see her lose it in that place in front of all those people, so I kept trying to push her buttons. "Oops. Was that supposed to be our little secret? 'Cause I've told damn near everyone who will listen."

"Kris, this is not the place." Slim tried to push me on, but my feet stayed planted.

"You're right, babe. Don't worry. I'll be nice." I gave him a pacifying smile, then turned back to Connie. "Have you heard from my father?"

"You might wanna listen to your boyfriend. This is not the place or time to talk about this." She tried to walk past me, but I stepped in her way.

I knew I should have shut my mouth and left well enough alone, but I couldn't help myself. I needed an outlet for all the pressure building up inside me, and she was as good a target as any. "You don't wanna talk?" I taunted. "Well, maybe I should go talk to Mrs. Graham about the similarities between Daryl's death and my mother's."

Connie's yellow face turned red as she checked left and right for eavesdroppers. Oh, how I wished Nancy and her crew were standing closer.

"Now, I asked you a question. Have you heard from my father?"

Aside from the fact that I was enjoying Connie's squirming, I really did want to know if she had any news about my father. I hadn't heard from him in three days and I was starting to worry.

"No, I haven't heard from Avery since he broke into my apartment and forced me to give him the money back from our divorce settlement."

Slim interrupted us. "Um, Kris, maybe we should be getting outta here."

Without looking at him, I raised my palm in his face. Most of the time, I let him be the one in control, but even he knew better than to get in the way when it came to my father.

I glared at Connie. "You need to stop exaggerating. You know my daddy didn't force you to give him anything."

"Krystal, your father is not the man you think he is."

"No, thanks to you. I'm sure any trouble he's in now has something to do with you."

She still refused to back down. "Nope, he's a fugitive from the law, and whether you want to admit it or not, it's his own damn fault. And as far as me hearing from him, he knows better than to call me. If I know him, he's probably somewhere in some foreign country right now, blowing that money he took from me."

I waved my hand, dismissing her accusations. "Anyway, just tell him that I'm looking for him if he calls or something."

"Don't worry, I will," she said. "Right after I call the police."

"Let's not talk about police because there's plenty I could say to them," I shot back. Of course, I had already spoken to the cops, but she didn't know that and neither did all the people in the room, who were about to find out.

I was about to tear into her ass loud enough for everyone to hear what I believed in my heart of hearts to be true when Slim grabbed me. "Um, Krystal," he said through gritted teeth.

"What, Slim? You're hurting me." I slapped his hand off the back of my neck and turned to face him.

"Po-po, nine o'clock."

I turned to my left to see Detective Thomas and his partner, who didn't like me too much. I immediately thought of the cocaine in my bag.

"Shit," I cursed under my breath.

"What's the matter? I thought you had so much you wanted to say to the cops. Here's your chance." Connie sounded almost gleeful, like she knew what was about to go down.

My instincts told me to run, but a quick check of the exits showed that there was a cop stationed at each. I glanced over at Slim, who had a deer-in-the-headlights look on his face. He hated cops for obvious reasons and had recently told me that he felt the cops had been watching him more closely. The way the detectives were striding across the room now with a few uniformed officers following them, I knew it had been a huge mistake not to leave when we had the chance.

Benny

41

I was so relieved to have Pop with me for support as I stood in line waiting to pay my final respects at Daryl's casket. I wiped away my tears and blew out a long, slow breath, trying to get my emotions under control. It seemed like I'd been crying for days, ever since the fire. No, actually I'd been crying for about two weeks, ever since my father found out I was gay and I blamed it on Daryl.

Fortunately, Pop and I had had plenty of time to talk over the past few days so things between us had improved, but it was killing me to know that I'd never get the chance to make things right with Daryl. If it weren't for Pop, I might have done a header off the roof into the street. I mean, I was seriously depressed, and Pop was the only reason I was still standing. He'd always been there for me, but this time he was there for me in a way I would have never expected. He was there as my friend. Sure, we'd always been close, but we were never friends in the traditional sense of the word. He didn't always value my opinion. He was the father and I was the son, and what he said was the law. We weren't equals.

After Daryl's death, I'd spent a few days in the apartment, getting over the shock of the fire and talking to Pop almost nonstop. We talked about our feelings in a way that we'd never been able to. When my mother died, I was really young, and I think my father thought he was protecting me by keeping things from me. Since then, I guess we'd developed this sort of habit of not really addressing our emotions. But after the traumatic events of the last two weeks, I decided I couldn't keep things bottled up anymore. It didn't make sense to me to be anything but open and honest because we never know when it will be the last time we talk to someone. I guess Pop must have felt the same way because he really opened up to me.

We talked about my mother's death and what it was like for him to raise me without her. I'd always appreciated everything that Pop did for me, but hearing him talk about it this way made me see how much he'd sacrificed to give me a good life. He admitted to me that he was in love with Nancy, and if it weren't for me, he might have tried harder to get her to leave her husband. The only reason he didn't was because we all lived in the same building and he didn't want me exposed to that kind of drama.

Our conversations finally got around to the source of all the tension between us lately. Pop said he didn't understand how I could be attracted to men, but I told him there was really no way I could explain it any more than he could explain what made him like women. In the end, he said he loved me and would accept me as I was, and that was enough for me. We healed a lot of pain in our relationship in the time we spent together.

One area we really didn't talk too much about was my friendship with Daryl. The only thing Pop said was that he still had his doubts about Daryl's intentions toward me. As for me, I could barely even speak Daryl's name without breaking down, so we stayed away from that subject. My emotions were still so raw. It would be a long time before I got over the loss of my best friend. That's why it was a good thing I had Pop to lean on at the wake.

"Come on, son. This way." He handed me a tissue, then placed his arm around my shoulder, directing me forward in the line to greet Daryl's family near the casket. "You okay?"

"Yeah, I'll be all right. It just hurts, that's all." I wiped my eyes and lifted my head, but a glimpse of Daryl's photo on top of the casket caused a fresh wave of tears.

"What the hell—?"

For a second, I thought Pop was mad at me for crying over Daryl, but he wasn't even looking at me. I followed his gaze and saw what had caught his attention.

The police were rushing in from the back of the room. I recognized the homicide detectives who'd interviewed us the day of the fire. They were headed toward Slim and Krystal, who looked pretty damn scared. Connie was there too, but she had this weird look on her face, like she was amused by their arrival. I didn't know what was happening, but I had a bad feeling.

Everything that happened after that was a blur. Instead of stopping by Slim and Krystal, the cops kept going. Slim looked at Krystal, and I swear I could see every muscle in their bodies relax now that they knew the cops weren't there for them. Connie's smug look was replaced with confusion. The astonished crowd parted for the cops like Moses parting the Red Sea. They were headed toward the line that Pop and I were standing in, and suddenly I was the one feeling tense.

I heard Pop say, "Don't resist and don't say anything without a lawyer."

"Uh-huh," I answered, and just like that they were upon us, hands on their waistbands like they were ready to draw their guns. Pop raised his hands in the air, and I followed his lead. After the worst two weeks of my life, this was definitely not the way I wanted it to end.

"Benton Wilkins," Detective Anderson said loudly, "you are under arrest for the murder of Daryl Graham."

I heard the crowd in the room react, and the noise sounded like a thousand angry bees. I was too dazed to make out what anyone was saying.

The detective spun Pop around, jerking his arms behind his back and slapping on handcuffs. I wanted to protest, to say they were hurting him and that they had the wrong man, but I couldn't form the words. I watched in stunned silence as they led Pop out of the room.

"Benny, could you use a ride?"

I felt a hand on my shoulder and turned to see Detective Anderson standing next to me. "Where are they taking him?" I asked.

"Down to the station. Eventually he'll be taken to Central Booking. I can take you down there if you'd like."

"Yeah, take me down there."

*   *   *

An hour later, I was sitting in a tiny room alone at the 113th Precinct. Detective Anderson walked in carrying a cup of coffee and a can of Coke. She sat down and slid the Coke across the table that separated us. I felt her eyes on me as I opened the can and took a long swig.

"Your father's in a lot of trouble, Benny," she said when I put down my drink. "If you know anything, you should tell us so you can help him."

I leaned back in my chair, feeling scared and confused. I'd been sitting there expecting someone to come in and tell me they'd figured out they had the wrong guy and they were letting Pop go. But now Detective Anderson was making it sound like Pop was guilty. What the hell was going on? Was this some trick they were playing on me, trying to get me to implicate my father just so they could close their case? Well, I was not about to play their game.

"I don't have anything to say until I get a lawyer."

She chuckled. "Been watching *Law & Order* reruns lately, have you?"

"I don't watch a lot of TV, but I know my rights, and I want a lawyer."

She looked down at her coffee, shaking her head. "For what? You're not the one under arrest." She lifted her head and looked me dead in the eyes. "Your father is."

I didn't know how to respond. No one ever tells you what to say beyond "I want a lawyer."

This was the best I could come up with—"Well, then he wants a lawyer too."

"To be honest, Benny, your father gave up his right to counsel."

Why in the world would Pop do that? It couldn't be true. "You're lying. That doesn't even sound right. He's the one who told me not to talk to you without a lawyer."

"I'm sure he did. I'd tell my son the same thing. But once we showed him all the evidence we had against him, he must have said the hell with a lawyer."

I stared at her, at a complete loss for what to say next.

Anderson softened her tone a little and said, "Benny, your father confessed. Truth is, you can go home if you want to. I just wanted to know if you had anything to say before we sent him down to Central Booking."

"What are you talking about? He confessed to what?" I'd heard of good cop/bad cop, but she was taking it to new extremes. Did she really expect me to believe this crock of shit she was trying to hand me, that my old man up and confessed to murder? For the first time in a long time, I laughed.

"Benny, I know it's hard to believe, but your father confessed to the murder of Daryl Graham."

"I don't know what you're trying to do, but it's not gonna work. I know my father would never confess to a crime he didn't commit."

"Believe me, you're not the only one who's shocked. Our case was good, but I'll admit it was mostly circumstantial—until he confessed. Now it's a slam dunk. This case might make my career."

"Well, congratufuckinglations. I don't care what you say. I'm not buying it. I know my Pop didn't confess." I shook my head, still refusing to believe what I was hearing.

She said, "I can get you a copy of his confession if you'd like. We've got it all on tape."

I rolled my eyes.

Anderson kept going, probably trying to see if she could get me to crack. "He said he did it because Daryl turned you against him and made you gay. Is that true?"

My stomach lurched. I hate to say it, but even with all the bonding we'd done over the last few days, there was still a nagging suspicion in the back of my mind. Was it just a coincidence that Pop was at the scene of the crime before anyone else? And since then, he'd claimed he was cool with my sexuality, but he never said he was cool with Daryl. Now Detective Anderson was making me wonder if there was a reason he'd never said that. Could he really have hated Daryl enough to kill him?

"Did he—" My voice cracked, and I couldn't go on because I refused to break down in front of her.

She stared at me as I tried to process the news. "If it's any consolation, I'm sorry, Benny."

"I wanna see him," I mumbled. If he had confessed I had to hear it from his own lips.

"Sure. He wants to see you too." She stood up, gesturing for me to follow her out of the room.

I could barely catch my breath as I walked down the hall behind her. She took me into another small room, where my father sat handcuffed to a chair beside Anderson's partner, Detective Thomas.

Pop and I stared at each other until finally Detective Thomas got up and said, "Anderson, why don't we give them a minute alone?"

Anderson turned to me and asked, "You gonna be all right?"

I nodded, and the detectives left me alone with my father. Our staring contest continued until Pop finally broke the silence.

"Have a seat."

"I'm okay standing."

All of a sudden, it was hard to look at him.

"Did they tell you I confessed?" There was no remorse in his voice. Like it was no big deal. Like it was easy to take a man's life.

"Yeah, they told me," I said as the tears began flowing down my face. "Why, Pop? Why would you kill him? I thought we were past the whole thing about me being gay. I thought we were good."

"We are good, son." That's all he said. No explanation, no apology. Nothing. He was my father and I loved him, but I was seriously starting to hate him.

"You told me you didn't kill him!" I said through angry tears. "How could you? He was my only real friend."

Finally my father's tough exterior broke and I could see real emotion on his face. "Benny, can't you see I did this for you? I'm trying to protect—"

"*Protect me?* How the fuck is this protecting me?"

He glanced toward the two-way mirror in the room. Obviously the detectives were watching this whole thing. "Sit down, son. Let me talk to you. I can explain."

"We've got nothing to talk about." I walked over to the door and banged on it three times. "Let me out!"

"Benny, please! Let me talk to you, son."

As the detective opened the door, I turned to Pop and said, "We've got nothing to talk about. And for the record, I am no longer your son."

Connie

42

I heard Nancy pounding on Ben's door long before I stepped off the elevator and actually saw her. In one hand she held a foil-covered dinner plate, and with her other hand she was banging on the door like she'd lost her mind. I wasn't surprised to see her, because she'd been delivering plates to the Wilkins's household pretty often since the fire, but I'd never seen her so worked up about it.

She took a break from pounding to yell, "Benny, I know you're in there. I can hear you on the other side of the door. Please let me in. The food's gonna get cold."

"Lay it down outside the door," I told her. "He'll take it when you leave."

I knew from experience that Benny was still too shell-shocked to want company. I'd been leaving a plate at the door for him every day since his father was arrested to make sure the poor kid was eating. Yesterday was the first time he'd opened the door and took it from my hands, and even then, he couldn't bear to make eye contact.

"I'm trying to make sure he's okay," Nancy said, sounding sincerely worried.

"I know, but he's not ready for help just yet. His world's come crashing down around him, and he's still trying to make sense of it."

"He sure ain't the only one. Between Daryl's death and Ben's arrest, I'm barely holding it together myself." Tears were welling up in her eyes, which kind of surprised me. She was taking this whole thing much worse than I would have expected, considering she had a husband downstairs. I wondered what he had to say about all the plates of food she'd been delivering lately.

I reached out and put a hand on her shoulder. "Hey, Nancy, it's gonna be all right," I said, even if I wasn't sure it would be.

"It's not true what they're saying about Ben, you know. He didn't kill Daryl." She wiped her tears and looked at me. "I know he confessed, but he didn't do it."

Wow, now that's what I call a ride-or-die chick. She really cared about Ben more than I would have guessed.

"I hope not, Nancy. I'm gonna keep him in my prayers."

"Thank you. I appreciate that. How you holding up?"

I shrugged. "As well as can be expected, I guess. One minute I'm fine; the next I feel like jumping out my window." I sighed. "I'm thinking about moving out of state. Maybe out to California or down to Florida. I just know I wanna get far away from here."

"I know exactly how you feel. I wish I could get away too. If I didn't have those kids, I'd be your roommate," she said with a grin.

I placed one hand on my hip. "Uh-uh, girl. You couldn't be my roommate. You talk too damn much for me. I'm moving to get away from the drama, not create it. I can see you now, running the West Coast version of the stoop news."

She laughed along with me. I was glad to see she had a sense of humor about it.

"That may be true," she said. "But at least I don't lie like some of the sisters out there on the stoop." We both knew she was talking about Bertha. "Seriously, though, Connie, if you do move, go somewhere that you're going to be happy."

"Trust me, I'm planning on it."

"Good."

She looked at the door and said, "Well, I guess you're right. I'll just leave the plate out here and Benny can come get it later." She put the plate down and said, "It was good talking to you, Connie."

"You too." When she walked away, I fished in my purse to find my keys. When I turned around to head into my own apartment, I glanced down the hall toward 3B. That's when I noticed that the door to Daryl's apartment was open. Curiosity got the best of me. I walked to 3B and peeked my head inside the open door.

"Hello?" I called out. I wasn't about to go any farther. The living room was a black charcoal mess. Regrettably, there wasn't anything to be salvaged other than some really good memories. "Anyone in here?"

"Can I help you?" A voice came from one of the bedrooms. Detective Thomas walked out into the living room. "Connie, everything all right?" he asked when he saw me.

"I saw the door open. I just wanted to make sure it wasn't one of the kids trying to vandalize the place. Not that there's much to vandalize."

"No kids; just me, recanvassing the crime scene."

"I thought this case was closed," I said.

He stepped out of the apartment to continue our conversation in the hallway, away from the smoky odor. "My captain and the DA seem to think so. As far as they're concerned, this case is a slam dunk. Score one for the good guys."

"And you don't?" I studied him. It was pretty obvious something was bothering him. His whole demeanor was off.

"Nope. The pieces are all there, but it just doesn't feel right."

"Really? You don't think Ben did it?" I was confused. My curiosity was definitely piqued.

He stared at me for a few seconds, no doubt contemplating how much information he should share with me. I guess he decided he could trust me, because he kept talking. "I never thought he did it. Still don't, but that's not my call."

"Then why'd you arrest him?"

"That was my partner's bright idea. Anderson had found out Ben Wilkins was some sort of accelerant specialist for the fire department, so she thought, why not see if this guy brought his work home with him? She went and talked the DA into issuing a search warrant."

I was kind of amazed that he was going into so much detail. This was not your average cop. It seemed like he was probably breaking every rule in the book talking to me this way, but I got the sense he was getting things off his chest. Like he was feeling bad about locking up what he thought was the wrong guy. He seemed to really care.

"You didn't believe he was guilty, but you went along with it anyway?" I asked.

He shrugged. "Why not? Anderson is my partner. She's backed me on a lot worse plays than this. I figured worst case scenario, we search the place and eliminate the father and son as suspects. Except Anderson was right. The father did bring his work home."

"What do you mean?" I asked.

"Preliminary tests showed an accelerant was used in the fire, and we found the same base components in his apartment. I still had some leads I wanted to follow a little further, but with the evidence we had and the history between Daryl and Ben, the DA put a stop to it and issued an arrest warrant right away."

I was shocked. What reason would Ben have to keep accelerants in his apartment? I guess you never truly know your neighbors.

"I'm not a cop, but that sounds like a pretty strong case against Ben," I said.

He laughed. "Not really. It's all circumstantial until the final test results come back. DA will never admit it, but we didn't have any probable cause for the search warrant. Truth is, any first-year law associate might have been able to get the search thrown out, which pretty much would have killed our case. Well, until he confessed. If he had lawyered up, he'd be in his apartment right now, but this idiot goes and confesses on tape."

"No offense, Detective, but you sound like you're taking this awfully personal."

He sighed. "I am taking it personal. I didn't become a cop to lock up the wrong person—not knowingly anyway, and my gut's telling me this guy's innocent."

"You sound pretty sure of that."

"Damn right, I'm sure of it. The confession was all wrong. I've been interrogating people for over twenty years, and I've never seen anyone agree with us so much. Anderson might as well have written the confession herself and signed it."

"What are you going to do?"

"Officially, I'm not going to do anything. Unofficially, I'm going to solve Daryl Graham's murder and get Ben Wilkins out of jail."

He sounded sure that he'd be able to do that. For Ben's sake—and Benny's—I sure hoped he could.

"Well, if I can be of any help, let me know."

He chuckled, which I have to admit I found a little unsettling. "It's funny you say that, Connie, because my next stop was to your apartment to ask you a few more questions."

All of a sudden I had this feeling that sharing all that information with me had been some sort of trap, and I'd fallen right into it.

"Questions about what?" I asked, hoping my nerves weren't too obvious. "I've told you everything I know."

He screwed up his face in a frown. "Really? Then how come you neglected to tell me about how jealous your estranged husband was of Daryl?" I was stunned silent. "I think you've been holding out on me, Connie. And I can't say I'm happy about it."

"I wasn't trying to hold out on you," I muttered. "I just didn't think it was important."

"Is that so? Well, I was talking to Bertha Dunbar on the way in, and she seemed to remember him sneaking around the fire escape the night before Mr. Graham's death. You wouldn't know anything about that, would you?"

I hesitated, wondering how much he really knew. He couldn't possibly know about Avery's visit to my apartment, could he? I felt cornered, but I still didn't want to have to tell him the whole story.

"Don't even think about lying to me anymore, because if you do, you're taking a trip down to the station in handcuffs for all your neighbors to see."

I raised my hands in surrender. "Okay, okay, I'm sorry. I'm not gonna lie to you. Avery did come by my apartment that night . . . Well, technically he broke into my apartment."

Thomas still had an impatient look on his face. Obviously, I wasn't going to get away with telling him anything less than the whole story of Avery's visit to my apartment.

"I swear. He was looking for the divorce money he'd given me so he could get out of the country. I don't know if Bertha told you or not, but Avery is a wanted man."

"Wanted for what?" He started to write in that damn notepad of his.

I searched through my bag for one of the cards the detective had given me the day they searched my home. I handed it to him. "Armed robbery, I think, but I'm not really sure. You might want to talk to Detective Ryan over at the Major Crimes Unit."

He glanced down at the card, then stuck it in his pocket. "Did you give it to him, the money he was looking for?" he asked.

"Yeah. And that's the last I saw of him. I swear." I raised my hand. I knew I was taking a chance, but I chose not to tell him about Daryl being involved with the money because it would open up another can of worms.

"How much money are we talking about?"

"About twenty thousand."

"Twenty thousand! Cash?" Thomas didn't look happy when I nodded. "Damn, he's probably long gone by now." He scribbled something else on his pad, then asked, "He hasn't tried to contact you, has he?"

Once again, I hesitated and he said, "Don't play games with me, Connie. You won't like how I play."

"He texted me last week, but I didn't text him back," I said adamantly. "Here, look for yourself." I took my phone out of my bag and showed him the text.

"Is there anything else you're not telling me?" He stared at me, trying his best, I suspect, to read my body language.

"No," I said. "I think I've told you just about everything you need to know."

Krystal

43

"Oooohhhh, shiiiiiiiiiit!" Slim let out a long moan, arching his back before collapsing on top of me.

I had to laugh. When he first climbed into the bed, he'd promised he was going to put it on me, but from the way he was struggling to catch his breath, it was fair to say that our roles had been reversed. I was definitely the one who put it on him. A huge grin covered my face. I loved it when I had that effect on him.

"You okay?" I kissed his perspiring neck, then nudged him off of me. He rolled onto his back and stared at the ceiling like he'd just seen the heavens.

"Uh-huh, I'm great," he heaved between breaths. "And you?"

"Wonderful. Only one thing could make it better." I rose up onto my elbow and reached for the blue box on my nightstand. I sat up and quickly snorted two hits; then I leaned against the headboard with my eyes closed to enjoy the rush.

Okay, so maybe I closed my eyes so I wouldn't have to see the dirty look that I knew Slim was giving me. He hated when I did coke after we made love. He said it "cheapened the experience." When I was feeling particularly annoyed, I wanted to tell him that his performance was what cheapened the experience, but of course I never did. What I couldn't seem to make him understand was that making love was always nice, but a couple of hits of coke made it so much better.

I dipped my fingernail into the box and took a few more hits. By the time I did one last hit and put the lid back on the box, Slim was snoring. The coke had me wide awake, so I considered waking him up for round number two. He was usually pretty irritable when I woke him up out of a sound sleep, though, so I turned on the TV instead.

A few minutes later, my cell phone chirped, signaling that I had a text message. There was only one person who'd be bold enough to text me at this time of night—my father. I was so happy to see his name on the screen, because it had been a while since he'd contacted me, and I was starting to worry that I'd never hear from him again.

I looked down at Slim and was relieved to see that he was still asleep. He had warned me repeatedly not to talk or text my father until the heat died down, so he would have flipped out, maybe even taken away my phone to prevent me from responding. I couldn't understand why he was so worried about it. What were they going to do, arrest me for texting? It wasn't like I knew where my father was or anything.

hey baby girl, my dad had texted.

hey daddy. did you get my text the other day?

I had texted him about Ben's arrest. Seeing poor Benny's face when they handcuffed his father made me think about how much I missed my own father. I couldn't stand not talking to him, so I waited until Slim went out for a while and then I sent Daddy a message. He and Ben had been friends, so I thought he'd want to know about his arrest.

what's this about ben being arrested for daryl's murder? Daddy asked.

he wasn't just arrested. he confessed!

It took him a while to respond. He was probably just as shocked as everyone else in the building that Ben was capable of murder.

Sounds like ben and i have gotten ourselves into a lot of trouble recently. who would have thought?

I felt like crying. Given Slim's choice of careers, I'd always kind of had it in the back of my mind that he could be arrested one day, but never in a million years would I have predicted it would be my father running from the law. And now it looked like Ben Wilkins was a murderer. It felt like the whole world had been turned upside down, and it scared me.

I texted Daddy: please be careful.

i am. have you put together that list?

He'd asked me to compile a list of countries without extradition laws to the United States. I had some names, but I was trying to make sure most of them were countries I could visit.

yes. it should be finished in the morning.

good. i need you to do me another favor.

anything. what is it? I was hoping it might involve going to meet him somewhere. I really missed him.

i left some stuff in the trunk of the car. can you have slim get rid of it?

Sure. you want me to put it in grandma's basement?

His reply came back lightning fast: no. just have slim throw it away. it's mostly trash.

That was a little puzzling. My dad was somewhere on the other side of the map, and he was concerned about the cleanliness of the trunk of his car. It wasn't even his car anymore. He gave it to me. What did he care if it was dirty? I hoped it didn't mean he was planning on taking the car back from us.

you sure it's all garbage? i think i saw some boots in there the other day.

just clean it out. i'm not coming back unless i'm in a box.

Those last few words hit me kind of hard.

please don't talk like that.

sorry. just make sure you clean out that car.

i hear you. is there anything in particular you want me to throw away?

NO, EVERYTHING! GET RID OF EVERYTHING!

Dang. Was he yelling at me via text? Before I could ask him why he was so worked up about this, he sent another less angry text: please do that for me. don't question me. just do it.

ok. i'll take care of it.

thanks. while you're at it why don't you have the whole car detailed.

ok.

After that, there was such a long pause that I thought maybe the conversation was done. But then my phone chirped again with a text that pissed me off.

how's connie doing? have you been checking up on her for me?

"Goddammit," I mumbled to myself. "Why does every conversation have to end up being about her?"

I shot him off an angry text that would hopefully put an end to his obsession with that bitch.

that woman doesn't deserve your concern. she's still mourning daryl. you need to forget about her.

Right after I hit send, I was startled by Slim's voice. I must have woken him when I was talking to myself. "What the hell are you doing? I know you're not texting your father."

"Huh? Oh no, baby. I was just updating my Facebook status to 'deeply in love.' "

Nancy

44

I hadn't been out on the stoop other than to enter or leave the building for a few days. Not too long ago, I was the queen bee out there, sharing in all the latest gossip and enjoying every minute of it, but now that Ben's arrest was the topic, I didn't have it in me to go out there. I was in too fucked up a place for all that. I still hadn't wrapped my head around the fact that Ben had confessed to killing Daryl. Didn't think I ever would. Sure, Ben wasn't short in the ego department, in or out of the bedroom, but he was a good person, a good man. The Ben I knew was not a murderer. I believed that with all my heart.

There was something else I knew in my heart: I truly loved that man. I'd been trying to deny it for a long time. Tried to convince myself that what we had was nothing more than a convenient affair. It had taken me watching him get hauled away for me to admit to myself how I felt. But I loved him, and I needed to show him how much. That's why I'd spent the better part of two hours on three separate buses traveling to see him.

"Have a seat anywhere you'd like," the guard said.

Truthfully, there was no place where I'd "like" to sit. Rikers Island's visitation room was the last place I wanted to be, but it was either go there or sit at home and go stir-crazy with unanswered questions and unvoiced feelings.

I looked around the room and prayed the look of disgust wasn't too apparent on my face. I'd never in my life been to a place like this, and I prayed to God that I would never have to come back. Of course, that would depend on the outcome of my visit with Ben.

"What the hell are you doing here?" Ben asked when he walked into the visiting room wearing an orange jumpsuit. It went without saying that I preferred his fireman's uniform over this getup, but Ben still looked sexy as hell to me.

"I don't know," I told him. "I'd seen pictures of the place on television. Thought I'd come and check it out for myself firsthand. What about you? What are you doing here?" I smiled, trying to make light of the situation even though I wanted to cry at the sight of Ben in his jailhouse garb.

"I know we talked about visiting the islands together, but this isn't the island I was talking about," he shot back, cracking a smile. I was surprised he was able to joke about it. Surely there hadn't been much to laugh about in this place.

"All jokes aside, Nancy," he said, getting serious. "What are you doing here?"

I shrugged. "I was worried about you. I had to come check on you."

"That's my girl. You're really down for the cause," he said with a chuckle.

"Mm-hmm, maybe I am." I forced a smile, but it didn't fool him.

"What's wrong?" he asked.

Rather than answering his question, I asked him, "How you holding up in this place?"

He sat down slowly like an old man. Had only four days zapped him of all his vibrant energy? Or were those jailhouse tales of the new guy getting raped actually true? "It is what it is," he said flatly.

Seeing him in this condition was heartbreaking. I couldn't sit here and make small talk with him, so I let my emotions go where they wanted to. Through my tears I asked, "Why, Ben? Why did you confess to killing Daryl? I know you're not that type of man. You couldn't have done it."

"You calling me a liar, Nancy?" He sat back in his chair and glared at me.

His reaction really confused me. I would expect someone to be angry about being accused of murder, but he seemed more upset about being accused of lying. It was weird. Something else was going on here, and I wasn't going to give up until he told me what it was.

"I wanna know why you're doing this."

He pressed his lips together, as if to say, *You can't make me talk.* I leaned back in my chair and folded my arms, raised my eyebrows, and stared him down. He was being stubborn, but I could be too. At this point, it was a battle of wills to see who would surrender first. Ben did.

"Okay, you're right," he finally said.

"What do you mean, I'm right?"

I guess I'd raised my voice out of frustration because he leaned in and shushed me. "Keep your voice down." He smiled at the guards who were looking in our direction.

"Right about what?" I whispered it this time.

"I didn't kill Daryl."

Now things were getting interesting.

"Then why are you here? Why would you say you killed the man if you didn't?"

"Because I know who did, and I'd rather it be me in here than him. I have to protect him. It's my job."

"Oh, please. Your job is to put out fires, not take a bid for some murderer. I mean, who are you indebted to like that, Ben? Who are you protecting?" And that's when it hit me. There was only one person Ben would protect with his life.

I took a deep breath and then exhaled slowly, trying to wrap my head around this whole surreal experience. "You're doing this for Benny, aren't you?"

There was a silent pause, then he nodded. "Look, I confessed to the murder. Live with it, because that's my story and I'm sticking to it."

Now I was even more confused. "Benny couldn't have. He wouldn't have. He and Daryl were..." I almost fixed my lips to say, "lovers," but the verdict was still out on that one. I didn't want to go bearing false witness—which was exactly what Ben was doing. "You can't take the rap for this, Ben. How do you know he did it anyway? Did he tell you he did it?"

Ben glanced in the direction of the guards again, but they weren't paying us any mind. Thank God, because if they had been, Ben might have clammed up, and now that I had him talking, I needed to know everything.

"No, he didn't tell me. I just know."

I shook my head. "Not good enough, Ben. You could spend the rest of your life in jail, thinking you're protecting your son, and you don't even know that he really did it."

"He did it!" Now he was the one getting loud. He caught himself and calmed his tone. "Remember when I used to take Benny upstate on the Fourth of July?"

I nodded. I'd hated that holiday ever since Ben and I began our affair, because it meant he would be out of town with his son.

He continued, "One time on that trip, I showed him how to make homemade fireworks."

"So what? Daryl died by fire, Ben, not by fireworks."

"No," he said. "It wasn't the fire."

"Ben, you're not making any sense. I'm worried about you." I was starting to think he could plead temporary insanity.

"When they were interrogating me, the cops revealed some of the evidence they had. I think they were just trying to scare me into confessing."

"Well, I guess it worked, didn't it?" I said. "I still don't see how any of this convinced you that it was Benny."

"The fire was set to cover up the murder. Daryl was already dead when the blaze started."

That was tragic, but I still wasn't getting his point. I guess he could see from my face that I was confused because he continued his explanation.

"The fire investigators said the fire was started with kerosene and graphite."

"Okay . . . ," I said, still not putting the pieces together.

"The homemade fireworks Benny and I used to make were made with kerosene and graphite."

Okay, now it was becoming clearer.

"When the cops searched my place, guess what they found?"

It felt like my heart stopped as I finally understood the whole picture. "Kerosene and graphite," I whispered breathlessly.

"That's right. And now that you have this information, what conclusion do you come up with?"

"That either you or Benny killed Daryl," I said, speaking words I never dreamed would come out of my mouth.

"Bingo. And if I didn't do it . . ."

I swallowed hard. "Then Benny had to have done it."

"And I'm not letting my son spend the rest of his life in prison. He's got too much going for him. So I killed Daryl Graham. That's my story, and I'm sticking with it." He leaned back. "Now leave it alone, Nancy."

"Do you really expect me to leave it alone while the man I love sits in here and rots?"

Ben's eyebrows rose. "What did you just say?"

"You heard me. I said I'm not going to leave it alone."

"No. Before that. The part about the man you what?"

Suddenly it dawned on me that I'd confessed my love to him. And I didn't regret it one bit. "I said, *'the man I love.'*" I reached for his hand across the table. "I've never met anyone like you, Ben, and hearing what you are willing to do for your son, that only makes me love you more."

Ben looked down at our intertwined hands, then up into my eyes, but he never said the words I wanted to hear: *I love you too.* Part of me understood. He was in jail and it looked like his only son was a murderer, so there probably wasn't much room in his heart for mushy emotions right now. But I had to believe that if he was out of jail— like I hoped he would be one day soon—he would tell me he loved me too.

Getting past the awkward moment of silence, Ben said, "Please, Nancy, promise me you won't say anything."

I stayed silent.

"If you really love me, you won't interfere. Let me do what I have to do."

Did he realize what he was asking of me? He was asking me to let him go to prison. He was asking me to give him up. "I don't know what I'm going to do right now, Ben," I said, and that was the truth. "You must really love that kid of yours to be willing to do something like this."

"I do with every ounce of my being."

"Well, I can't sit by and watch you throw your life away. I'm not making any promises, but I think I know somebody who can help us."

I saw a glimmer of hope in his eyes, which told me that even though he'd do it for his son's sake, Ben did not want to go to prison.

I visited with Ben until they had to damn near kick me out. We were allowed one good-bye kiss, and I was still holding onto the memory of that kiss as I took my seat on the bus from Rikers Island headed to Queens Plaza. Halfway through the ride, I took out my phone and called the only person I could think of to ask for help.

"Hello."

"Detective Thomas, this is Nancy Williams. You were right. Ben Wilkins didn't kill Daryl Graham, but it's possible I know who did."

Krystal

45

The Mercedes was parked out in front of the building with the top down when I walked outside to see Slim off on his trip. He was going down to Virginia to take care of some business. Although I was sure I'd eventually miss him, I couldn't wait to have some time to myself to chill out and get high—the latter of which I planned to do extensively, thanks to the two-week supply of blue boxes he'd given me. Yep, it was gonna be a good two weeks.

I leaned over the passenger's side door to kiss him good-bye.

"Oh, shit. Just what I don't need," he said under his breath.

I straightened up, a little insulted that he hadn't kissed me back. "What, Slim?" He didn't reply, didn't even look my way because his eyes were glued to the rearview mirror. I turned to the rear of the car, hoping to catch a glimpse of whatever it was that he saw. It didn't take but a second to realize what had caused his reaction.

An unmarked police car had pulled up behind the convertible. The next thing I knew, there was a second marked car pulling up behind the first one. I knew something serious was about to go down when a third cop car pulled up alongside us, blocking Slim in. My fears were only confirmed when Detective Thomas and another very serious-looking white cop sporting a crew cut got out of the first car. They approached us, followed by at least six other cops, who looked like they were ready for business. My only hope was that, like the arrest at the wake, they weren't looking for either of us. Unfortunately, that wasn't the case this time.

"Good afternoon, folks," Detective Thomas greeted us. The crew cut cop was on the driver's side, and Thomas was behind me on the passenger's side. The other cops had spread out in various positions around the car.

"What do you want?" Slim asked in a tone that sounded a little too cocky to me. The fact that he never carried drugs or anything illegal in the car when he traveled probably had him feeling confident—too damn confident, if you asked me.

"We can start with your license and registration," Thomas said.

"For what? I haven't even moved."

"No, you haven't," Crew Cut chimed in. "But the keys are in the ignition and you're sitting behind the steering wheel. In the state of New York, that makes you a driver. So can I have your license and registration, please?"

Slim rolled his eyes, then reached for the glove compartment. Every cop surrounding the car tensed, ready to blow his ass away. I sighed thankfully when he lifted up his wallet for everyone to see.

"Here," Slim said, handing Crew Cut the paperwork.

He studied Slim's license and the registration like he'd be taking a test on it later that afternoon.

"By the way, real nice ride you got here." Thomas stepped up to the car, inspecting it as if he was about to make us an offer on it. "Where'd you get it?"

"My father gave it to us," I answered nervously.

"Your father's Avery Mack, isn't he?" Crew Cut asked. I didn't like the idea that he knew who my father was, and the disdain in his voice made me think he knew something about my father's latest activities.

"And who exactly are you?"

"Oh, that's right. You two haven't met," Thomas said. "This is Sergeant Ryan of the Major Crimes Unit. He's been looking for your father for a while now."

"Yes," Ryan said. "And you haven't returned any of my calls, Ms. Mack, so Thomas offered to bring me over here to talk to you. Nice of him, wasn't it?"

Slim and I shared a frightened glance, then looked at the cops silently.

This bold motherfucker Ryan opened Slim's door. "Now that we've been officially introduced, why don't you join your girlfriend on the sidewalk so we can have a little chat?"

Slim stepped out of the car and made his way to my side. I wondered if he was thinking the same thing I was thinking: What the fuck did the Major Crimes Unit want with us? Slim had assured me that his little criminal enterprise was way off the New York police radar.

"You folks mind if we search the car?" Ryan asked.

"You got a warrant?" Slim replied.

"Your paperwork says this car is registered to a man who's wanted for major crimes. I can get a warrant here in fifteen minutes," Ryan said. He was all in Slim's face. "Do I have to get one, or are you going to make this easy?"

"I never do anything easy," Slim responded, folding his arms.

Of course, you know the peanut gallery on the stoop was growing by the minute. When I first came out of the house, the only one there was Bertha. Now there had to be fifteen people on our stoop and half a dozen in the windows.

"What do we have here?" Thomas had been leaning over the convertible looking in.

Slim's face went pale and his voice cracked. "Hey, you can't touch that. I didn't give you permission to search the car."

My knees almost gave out on me when Thomas turned toward us holding an empty blue box. He ran his finger along the inside and then held it up for us to see the layer of white powder.

"Didn't need permission," Thomas said. "It's a suspicious package in plain sight. That gives us probable cause to search the vehicle."

Thomas handed the package to Ryan, who turned and spoke to the two officers standing near the back of the car. "Search the car completely. I want everything bagged and tagged. Oh, and I'll be getting a search warrant for their apartment. I got a feeling we're going to find enough in there to send someone away for a long time." He was looking directly at me as he spoke. I got an instant chill when I heard him.

Benny

46

I'd just made a quick trip to the liquor store, and when I returned to the building, I could hear the laughter and joking halfway down the block. Those damn cackling, conniving, low-life wenches on the stoop were half the reason I hadn't been out of my apartment in over a week and a half. I swear their gossip seemed to be even more vicious than before the fire, especially now that they had my father's arrest to talk about. It had gotten so bad they didn't even bother to stop the conversation when they saw me on the corner. They didn't care that I was hurting inside and trying to get through the day. I suppose they were all competing to take Nancy's spot as queen bee now that she was no longer hanging out there with them.

When I got within a few feet of the stoop, they finally decided to show some common sense and stop talking, but they couldn't have been more obvious about it. It was like the needle had been snatched off a record as every single voice came to a complete halt. Whatever they had been saying about me must have been pretty bad because not one of the hags could even make eye contact with me as I walked up the stairs. Since when had any of those broads ever been speechless?

Once inside the building, I could hear them start up again. I couldn't make out what they were saying, but I could imagine the hateful words, and that was bad enough. I didn't know how much more of this I could take. It wasn't like I had the money to move out of the building, and I couldn't hide inside forever. Sooner or later I'd have to start going out again, and I wasn't about to walk through that gauntlet of gossipers every single time. I made up my mind right then and there to put an end to it.

Straightening my shoulders and taking a deep breath, I went back out on to the stoop. They turned to look at me, and again all conversation came to a screeching halt.

"You ugly-ass bitches got something to say, then say it to my face! Otherwise, keep my motherfucking name out your mouth!" I waited for a response, but not one of them opened her mouth. "Now, y'all have a nice day." I left them with their jaws hanging open and stormed back into the building.

Back in my apartment, I sat down on the sofa, trying to fight back tears. As much as they deserved it, I felt bad about the way I'd spoken to them. It wasn't in my character to be that disrespectful—at least I wasn't that kind of person before Daryl's death. Ever since then, the pressure building inside of me was almost too intense to bear. I was becoming someone I didn't want to be. I wished I could turn back to a more innocent time, before I met Daryl, when Pop and I were close and life seemed simple.

My eyes locked in on a picture of my dad in full uniform, and I felt my heart swell with sadness. I wanted to hate him more than anything in this world for what he'd done, but I couldn't. He was my father, and I missed him. He was the one person I used to be able to turn to whenever I had a problem. But now who did I have? Pop had taken everything from me, including himself. How fucked up is that? I had no one. I was completely alone, and I had nothing to live for.

With tears streaming down my face, I went into the bathroom and opened the medicine cabinet. I clumsily knocked things out of the way, letting them clatter from the cabinet into the sink, until I found what I was looking for—Percocet.

I carried the bottle into the kitchen and set it down on the table while I scribbled out a note.

> *To whom it may concern:*
> *I can't take it anymore. The guilt of Daryl's death and the incarceration of my father have made life unbearable. I want*

*everyone to know that the blame for Daryl's death is squarely
on my shoulders. I'm sorry.*

Benny

It was my hope that once they found my note, it would cast doubt
on Pop's confession and they would release him. He'd be mad at first,
but hopefully he'd be able to live out the rest of his life in happiness.
Who knows? Maybe he could retire and move away somewhere with
Nancy and be happy. I knew I was ready to go to a happier place.
Hopefully I'd see Daryl there.

I opened the bottle of Percocet, emptying the contents into my
hand. There looked to be about twenty or so left from a thirty-
day prescription. From what I had read, twenty was plenty. Then I
reached for the bottle of Hennessy that I'd purchased specifically for
this purpose. When the guy at the liquor store put it in the bag for
me, he said, "Enjoy." I doubted I'd even taste it going down. I'd only
bought it to speed up this whole process, to get it over with.

My heart was beating so hard that it took me a minute to determine that the loud thud I'd heard wasn't my heartbeat, but instead
a knock on the door. The first person that came to mind was Nancy.
She'd been trying to get me to talk to her ever since Pop was arrested.
I twisted the cap off the bottle, figuring Nancy would get the hint and
go away. But it wasn't her.

"Benny, open the door. It's Connie. I got a surprise for you."

"Connie," I said softly.

In the past week and a half, she had been the only one, other
than Nancy, who'd come to see about me. She'd brought me food
and lent a listening ear when I let her in, which wasn't often. She'd
been so nice to me, hadn't questioned or judged me once. She only
listened. Considering how she felt about Daryl, she could have
hated me because of what Pop did. But she never said one bad word
about Pop, and she showed me more kindness than I felt I even
deserved.

I put down the Hennessy and poured the pills back into the bottle. Had it been anyone else, I wouldn't have bothered answering the

door, but after the way Connie had been there for me, I had to at least say good-bye.

When I opened the door, I saw something that made the hairs stand up on the back of my neck. I took a step back, closing my eyes to see if it was just a mirage. When I opened them, he was still standing there next to Connie.

"Daryl?" I asked the man. He had dreads pulled back in a pony-tail and a little less facial hair, but even behind those sunglasses he was sporting, he looked just like Daryl.

"No, this isn't Daryl." Connie laughed. "This is Rodney, Daryl's brother. They do have one hell of a family resemblance, don't they? Almost made me pee in my pants when I saw him at the wake."

My mouth hung open. I couldn't find any words to express what I was feeling as I stared at this person who was the spitting image of the man I loved.

I swear I almost started crying when Rodney stepped up and gave me a warm hug. "So you're the guy my brother was always telling me about. I've heard a lot about you, Benny." He stepped back and smiled.

"Really?" I was surprised that Daryl had even mentioned me to his family. Just that little bit of information lifted my spirit.

"My brother really liked you, man. He said you were one of his best friends. He just never told me how handsome you were."

I glanced at Connie, who had a satisfied smirk on her face.

"Thanks." I could feel myself blushing, and I lowered my head. I would have loved to return the compliment, but I was still a bit flab-bergasted by the mere sight of him.

Connie leaned in and whispered, "Daryl had been thinking about hooking you guys up, you know." She pulled back with a grin on her face. I couldn't help but smile too. Now, that was something I hadn't done in a long time.

"Anyway, Rodney, I'm gonna leave you in Benny's capable hands. I'm sure you two will find something to talk about."

Was she really going to leave me alone with him? "Where are you going?" I asked, trying not to sound panicked.

"I have to go pack. The movers are coming in a couple of days, and I still have more than half my place to box up. Rodney here wanted to talk with you, so I'll leave you two alone."

"You're really moving, huh?"

"Aint nothing here for me, Benny. Not anymore." She glanced over at Daryl's apartment sadly.

"I can relate. I'm planning on checking out myself," I said, thinking about the pills I'd left in the kitchen.

"Who knows? Maybe you and Rodney can check out together."

Poor Connie. She had no idea what she'd just said. I hoped she'd forgive me later for committing suicide.

Connie gave me a hug and a kiss on the cheek. And then it was me and Rodney and an awkward silence at the front door until he spoke.

"I'm sorry. I know this is a little weird. I didn't think she was gonna drop me off on you like that."

"I know, but it's okay. I'm not doing anything." *Other than killing myself, that is.*

"Do you mind if I come in?"

"Ah, you know, my place is really a mess . . . ," I said awkwardly.

"No problem. Why don't we go have a drink somewhere?" Rodney suggested.

I shoved my hands in my pockets and thought about it for a second. Sure, Rodney was cute, and he seemed nice, but I doubted Connie had told him everything about me. Once he learned the truth, he would probably run, and I didn't think I could bear it if one more person left me.

"I don't know about that. I mean, I'd love to get to know you better, and I'm sure there are lots of things about your brother we could share, but—"

"But what? I know you loved my brother, Benny. He loved you too, just not in a romantic way. I think he would have wanted us to be friends."

I shook my head. "Nah, I'm sorry. I can't."

He was persistent. "Oh, come on. Let's have a drink and shoot the breeze about my brother. I really miss him. Don't you?" We were both silent for a second, lost in our own private thoughts about Daryl. "Besides, it's my birthday. Daryl told me that he went with you on your twenty-first, so you owe me at least that much. Everybody needs somebody to hang out with on their twenty-first birthday."

I smiled as I thought about how I'd used the same tactic to convince Daryl to spend my birthday with me.

"Is that a yes?" Rodney said, playfully jabbing me in the arm.

"Before I say yes, there's something I've got to tell you. Something that might change your mind about having that drink with me." I couldn't even finish the sentence without my eyes welling up with tears.

"What's that?"

"My father's the one who killed your brother." I took a step back just in case he decided to swing. "He killed him because he thought Daryl turned me gay. I'm sorry. It was all my fault."

Rodney looked down at the ground and blew out a long, slow breath; then he looked up at me. He lifted his hand, and I tensed up, expecting a slap in the face. Instead, he placed it gently on my cheek. "I know. I was there when your father got arrested, Benny. Me and my family have made our peace with God about that. The rest is up to the court system. We don't blame you. I'm just sorry that you don't have your father and I don't have my brother."

He leaned in and gently kissed my cheek.

"You ready for that drink now?"

I wiped the tears from my eyes. "Let me go clean up some stuff in the kitchen, and I'll be right out."

Krystal

47

I had never been so scared in my life. I put my hands together, got down on my knees, and prayed to God for the first time in years.

"Please, God, if you can somehow get me out of this mess, I will never, ever use drugs again, I swear. And I'll go to church too. In Jesus's name I pray. Amen."

I got up off my knees and sat down on the chair in the interrogation room, wondering how much longer the detectives were going to make me wait. It had been almost an hour since that hard-ass Detective Ryan read me my rights, then drilled me about Slim and his operation. I tried to be strong, but when he showed me the blue boxes they'd found in our apartment, I threw Slim so far under the bus he might not ever get out from under it. I hated what I'd done to Slim, but at this point, it was either him or me, and it damn sure wasn't gonna be me. I just hoped the DA cut me a deal to go to one of those drug programs like Ryan had promised instead of jail.

"You know you're in big trouble, right?" Detective Thomas entered the room, followed by his female partner, Detective Anderson. Neither one of them looked happy, and Thomas sounded pissed.

"What are you talking about? I've been cooperating. I already told Detective Ryan everything I know. He's trying to get me into a substance abuse program."

"I wouldn't be worrying about going to a program yet if I were you," he said, sitting across the table from me. "What I'd be worried about is this."

Anderson handed him a brown paper bag and he dumped out its contents. At least a dozen aerosol cans rolled across the table.

"What's that?" I asked.

"We'll get to those in a minute." He picked up a plastic bag containing a knife. "Do you know what this is?"

"Uh, yeah. It's a steak knife. Most people use them to cut their food." What the fuck was going on here? I was still scared, but now I was becoming a little irritated. Why were they bothering me with this bullshit that had nothing to do with my drug use?

"I believe this particular knife was used to end Daryl Graham's life. We'll know for sure in a couple of days."

"So that's what Ben used to kill Daryl?" I asked. "What's that got to do with me?"

"Is that what Ben used?" Anderson mocked me angrily. "Somehow I doubt it. We found this bag in the trunk of your car."

"No fucking way!" I swallowed so hard one might have thought I had a bowling ball stuck in my throat. Now I was starting to see where they were going with this, and I did not like it one bit. "You don't think that I . . . no fucking way."

"We got the final lab report back this afternoon on the cause of that fire. It turns out that the accelerant used to start the fire was WD-40." He picked up one of the cans that had rolled off the table and stood it up for me to see the label. It read, WD-40.

"My—My mother was burned with that." I lowered my head to the table so I didn't have to look at the detectives, the knife, or the aerosol can anymore. If there was ever a time I needed some cocaine, this was it.

"Hey, I think she's getting it now, Anderson," Thomas said to his partner before turning his attention back to me. "You are getting it, aren't you?"

Yes, I was getting it, but that didn't mean it made any sense.

"I thought you found the cause of the fire in Ben Wilkins's apartment. He confessed, didn't he?"

"Yes, we did find kerosene and graphite in his apartment, both of which are key components of WD-40, but WD-40 has a distinctive residue signature when it burns. A signature that was prevalent at the Graham crime scene. I'm not sure why he confessed, but Ben Wilkins didn't kill that man. None of our evidence supports that. I'm sure it would have been overlooked if it wasn't for my partner's instincts," Anderson said.

"And your text messages," Thomas added.

"My text messages?" God, I didn't like the sound of that at all. Slim had warned me about text messaging, and I always blew him off. "What are you trying to say? You think I killed Daryl?"

"No, I'm trying to say that your text messages led us to the evidence we needed to solve Daryl Graham's murder," Thomas said.

I stared at them both blankly. I'd already come to my own assumption, but I damn sure wasn't ready to express it. "I don't understand. Can one of you explain to me what the hell is going on?"

"We knew it was only a matter of time before your father contacted you, so Detective Ryan got a warrant to tap your wireless phone," Thomas explained. "And bingo! What do you know? Your dear old dad contacted you, and for some reason, he seemed real concerned about you cleaning out the trunk of that car."

"Now, would you like to explain to me why we found evidence in your car?" Anderson asked.

They kept saying my car, but it wasn't my car. It was my . . . "Daddy," I said under my breath. I think that once they said the knife was found in the trunk, my subconscious mind knew the truth, but it took a while for me to acknowledge it. Daddy killed Daryl. That's why he wanted me to clean out the trunk of his car. He wanted me to get rid of the evidence.

"Oh my God!" I shouted. "Daddy killed Daryl."

"You do realize there's a good possibility he killed your mother too?" Anderson said, sounding almost like she was enjoying herself.

I shook my head adamantly. "I don't believe that."

"I'm not asking you to. I'm just asking you to be honest with yourself. If you loved your mother and/or Daryl, you owe it to them to bring their killer to justice, even if it's your old man."

"The hell with them. You owe it to yourself," Anderson said.

"Because if you don't help us, I can promise you the DA is going to lock your ass up for aiding and abetting a fugitive. Oh, and we've got plenty of proof of that."

I ignored Anderson and turned to Thomas. "Do you really believe my father had something to do with my mother's death?"

He nodded. "I did a little research. At the time of her demise, your father was worth about two million dollars. He was going to have to split that with your mother, plus pay her alimony. It would have been a pretty tough nut to swallow considering the lifestyle he was living at the time. With your mother gone, he didn't have to split a thing. So yes, I think he did it."

I wanted to crawl under the table, curl into the fetal position, and never get up. My whole world had been shattered. How was I supposed to move on after news like this? All those years I'd been blaming Connie for my mother's death, and it was devastating to learn that it was Daddy who killed her. It was her death that made me what I was today—a damn drug addict. Everything that was wrong with my life was all Daddy's fucking fault.

"I want him arrested," I said to the detectives, my voice as cold as ice.

Thomas answered, "Of course. So do we. And you can help us get him, Krystal."

"Tell me what I have to do. I want that fucker to pay for what he did to my mother. And to Daryl."

Thomas pulled my cell phone out of his pocket and slid it across the table to me. "We need you to keep in contact with him. This way our techies can track him."

I was skeptical. "I don't know if I can talk to him without cursing him out now."

Anderson rolled her eyes. "Damn junkies can be so weak," she said.

Thomas shot her a warning look and she shut right up.

He turned to me and said, "We really need you to do this, Krystal. The text messages your father has been sending came from several different countries in the Caribbean, but until he stays in one place for an extended period of time, we can't dispatch the local police force to pick him up."

"Of course, we have to hope he lands in a spot where they have an extradition treaty with the US," Anderson added, letting me know that they were aware of the list of safe countries I'd compiled for him. All of a sudden, I realized that there was still a possibility they'd try to prosecute me for aiding a fugitive.

"Look, I need some kind of guarantee that the DA won't be pressing any charges against me. I want some kinda deal," I said.

Anderson sighed, and Thomas nodded at me. "I'll see what we can do about that," he said. He looked down at my phone. "In the meantime, send your father a text."

I picked up the phone and typed: daddy, where are you? slim is acting crazy and i want to get away. can i come see you, please?

Connie

48

I followed the movers out of the building as they carried the last two boxes from my apartment. I'd made the decision to put all my stuff in storage until I decided where I was going to finally settle down. I was pretty sure I'd be on the road for a while, so my next stop was to liquidate all my accounts, including my IRA and my 401(k). For now, I intended to travel the world. Montego Bay in Jamaica would be my first stop.

"So you're really going through with it, huh?" Bertha asked. She was in her usual spot on the stoop, along with a couple of the other girls. Ever since Nancy had stopped spending time out there, it seemed that Bertha had become the new mouthpiece for the group.

"I sure am," I replied.

"You just up and quit your job, packed your shit, so you can travel the world?"

"Mm-hmm. That about sums it up," I said. "All I know is I can't stay in this building anymore after everything that's happened."

"I know what you mean. Matter of fact, I think I'm gonna stop drinking the water."

I gave her a puzzled look.

One of the other stoop ladies asked, "Bertha, what the hell are you talking about?"

"I'm not drinking the water 'cause there's something wrong with it," she said in a very stern tone that had me rather concerned. "There has to be because everyone in this building has lost their damn mind."

Everyone on the stoop laughed, except Bertha, who kept a straight face. "Seriously, Connie, I been thinking about it a lot."

"Thinking about what?"

"Ever since Daryl moved in, haven't folks been acting crazy? Think about it now." Bertha sat up in her chair like she was preparing to deliver a speech. I sat down on the step to listen for a minute.

"To start with, every woman with a slit from eighteen to eighty-five had been sitting out here on this stoop like we'd lost our minds just to get a glimpse of him. Most of us got halfway decent husbands and boyfriends sitting right upstairs, but we couldn't miss seeing the man in 3B. And that includes me."

"I know that's right," came from one of the other women on the stoop.

"Hell, I burnt up dinner one night staring at his fine ass down here," one of the other sisters said.

"You weren't the only one," Bertha said, pointing at Pam, who nodded. "And that was only the beginning of the craziness. Look at what happened to Benny. One day he's an awkward college kid; now he's out of the closet with a boyfriend—Daryl's brother, of all people. Now ain't that some crazy shit?"

"Bertha, being gay doesn't make him crazy," I said in Benny's defense.

"No, but it sure drove his daddy's ass crazy, didn't it? Confessing to a crime he didn't commit. Try to tell me that ain't crazy!" Bertha laughed and we all joined in. "Speaking of his crazy daddy, did you hear?"

"About him being released from jail?" I said. "Yeah, I heard. He knocked on my door the other night. Thank God they let him out."

"No, not that. That's yesterday's news," Bertha said, obviously proud that she was the one with the latest scoop. Yeah, she'd definitely taken Nancy's place. "Did you hear about him and Nancy?"

I shook my head. "What about him and Nancy?"

"Ben and Nancy are getting married. She asked her husband for a divorce and moved into Ben's apartment."

"Get out! What about the kids?" Usually the gossip on the front stoop didn't interest me much, but I have to admit that news floored me. After such a long time, I never thought Nancy would leave her husband. Hell, I never thought Ben would propose. I guess after so much tragedy, people start to rethink the choices they've made in their lives, and they start making changes.

"Her kids are both teenagers. You think they didn't know what was going on with their parents? I heard they told their mother they just want her to be happy," Bertha reported.

"Well, I'm glad to hear Nancy's happy."

"Me too," Bertha replied. "You hear anything about your ex-husband and stepdaughter?"

"Now, talk about crazy." I chuckled. "The police came by asking if I'd heard from Avery yesterday. They seem to think he's out of the country and long gone. And no one has heard from Krystal."

Bertha added what she knew. "Well, she ain't at Rikers Island. I called over there to see."

Pam laughed and said, "Leave it to you, Bertha, to be making a call like that."

"Mm-hmm. You know that's right! Ain't no shame in my game," Bertha said proudly, then shared the rest of her information. "A lot of people think she's in some type of witness protection program after the way she snitched on Slim. I know his boys have been around asking if we seen her."

"What a terrible waste," I said just as my cab pulled up. "Well, y'all, that's my ride to the airport." I stood up and picked up my suitcase.

"You take care of yourself, Connie," Bertha said.

I bent over and hugged Bertha and then waved to the rest of her news crew on the steps.

"Don't worry. I will."

Epilogue

I watched Connie from the shadows of Rick's Café in Negril as she casually searched the pool area for a lounge chair. She found one by the Jacuzzi, took off the colorful sarong she was wearing, and set it down on the chair. I couldn't take my eyes off her. She looked absolutely mesmerizing. She'd firmed up and lost even more weight since I'd left New York. She'd also cut her hair shorter in this remarkable style that I really liked. She was thick and fine just the way I liked my women.

I'd been following her ever since her plane landed in Montego Bay three days ago. I'd purposely kept out of sight, hiding in the shadows to make sure she hadn't been followed by the police. I wasn't even sure she knew I was around. The plan was that she would enjoy herself on the island until I felt it was safe to contact her. If there were cops in the area, I sure hadn't spotted them, so I was about to make my presence known.

I took one more look at the love of my life, then stepped over to a secluded section of the cliffs, taking off my knapsack. Inside were the last remnants of who I used to be, along with five of the six disposable cell phones I'd purchased before leaving the States. I'd already gotten rid of the phone I'd been using to text Krystal. Despite how I felt about her, I knew she couldn't be trusted. My source back home had told me about her and Slim's arrest. I almost felt sorry for Slim. The only thing she truly cared about was herself and that damn cocaine. Predictably, right after her arrest, she began blowing up my phone with text messages. I didn't have to be a rocket scientist to understand that she was working with the police. I wasn't about to fall into that trap, so I tossed the phone over the railing of the cruise ship I'd been traveling on for the past two weeks.

A friend of mine once told me that cruising was the best way to travel. Coincidentally, he was the same friend who sold me a new identity in the form of a passport, birth certificate, and Social Security number. For ten thousand dollars, I had become a whole new person. Well, it turned out that not only was it the best way to travel, but it was also the best way to hide out in plain sight. Vacationers didn't care if a nuclear bomb went off back home as long as the drinks were flowing on the ship. The crew members were busting their asses so hard to keep guests happy that they couldn't have cared less about me and the troubles I'd left behind, which suited me just fine. It was also a great way to confuse the cops because I only turned on the cell phones when I disembarked from the boat. Right now I'm sure they thought I was somewhere in the US Virgin Islands.

I reached in the knapsack and picked up the phone that was marked with the number three. I'd written a number on each phone, designating it for a specific purpose or person. Phone number one was the phone I'd been using to text Krystal and Connie. It was somewhere at the bottom of the Caribbean now. Number two was used to call Connie's disposable. Phone number three was the phone I was using right now, and phone number four was my miscellaneous phone used to check flights, call cabs, and so on. I hadn't used numbers five and six yet.

I dialed phone number three.

"Hello," a male voice answered.

"Hey, it's me," I replied. "Any word?"

"Yeah, there's still a warrant out, but the cops have moved on to other cases."

"Good. Thanks."

"No problem. You be safe."

"Always." I hung up and turned off the phone. This would be the last time I spoke to him. He had been paid well to keep his mouth shut, but unfortunately I wasn't in a position to trust anyone anymore.

I needed to verify what he'd just told me, so I picked up phone number four and dialed a number I'd committed to memory.

"Homicide. Captain Blake speaking."

Don't ask me why, but I stood up straighter as I spoke, trying to sound as proper as possible. "Good afternoon, Captain Blake, this is Theodore Andrews with the *Amsterdam News* in Harlem. We spoke two weeks ago about Daryl Graham's murder. We're running a follow-up piece on black-on-black crime, and I was hoping to see how the case was coming along."

There was silence on the line; then I heard Blake clear his throat. "We've issued a nationwide fugitive warrant for one Avery Daniel Mack, along with an APB. Our investigation leads us to believe he's traveled out of state or maybe even out of the country. If he's still in the New York area, our best hope is to pick him up on a quality-of-life crime from here on out, but don't quote me on that last line."

"I won't. Is it possible for me to speak to the lead detectives on the case?"

"Well, to be honest, I really wish you wouldn't. They've got a pretty large caseload right now, and we've got them assigned to those Rego Park murders."

"I see. Well, all right. Thanks for your time, Captain." I turned off the phone and felt my whole body relax. It was good to know the cops had moved on. I actually felt free for the first time since I'd left New York.

I placed all of the phones back inside the knapsack, then tossed it into the ocean before heading down the cliff toward Connie. She was standing by the rail with her back to me, watching the world famous Negril sunset.

"Beautiful, isn't it?" I whispered, pressing against her and wrapping my arms around her waist.

She spun around, and the startled look in her eyes quickly gave way to a smile. She threw her arms over my shoulders and hugged me tightly, pulled away slightly to look in my eyes, then fell against me and squeezed me again. Neither one of us said anything, but the two of us standing there, with our arms tightly around each other, communicated so much. I wish I had a picture of that moment.

We kissed deeply and passionately. When we finally broke apart, I looked into her eyes and said, "I love you."

She looked up at me, her eyes shining with tears. "Oh, Daryl, I'm so happy we're finally together again. I love you too."

"I can't believe our plan actually worked."

"Neither can I."

We fell back into another embrace. There was no need to say anything further. We'd gone through so much together that it was enough just to be in each other's arms again.

If I had to do it all over, I would have never answered the door for Avery that night. But when I looked through the peephole and saw Connie standing there next to him, I couldn't stop myself. I was already upset because Connie had cut me off in the sex department and refused to spend the night in my apartment. Seeing her standing out there with her not-quite ex-husband at three in the morning had my blood boiling. My intention was to take my anger out on Avery's ass. What I didn't anticipate was that he'd already have a gun drawn when he walked in the door.

"Where's my money, nigga!" He pointed the gun directly at me.

"What the fuck are you talking about? And don't point that gun at me!" I yelled, matching his intensity with my own.

The look on his face was one I'd seen in the streets before. It told me to proceed carefully because he would not be intimidated. Whatever was going on in his head, he was desperate—and desperate people are capable of anything.

"I'm talking about my money. The money that my wife gave you." He glanced over at Connie, who was standing by the closed door, looking terrified. That was when the picture became clear. I should have known when she put the money in my safe that he'd come looking for it at some point.

"Give him the money, baby," Connie said. "At least then we'll be rid of him."

Avery whipped his head around and said to her, "You will never be rid of me, Connie. Don't you ever forget that." Then he looked back at me. "But yeah, gimme my money." He was sweating like a fiend waiting for his next fix. I knew things could go wrong in a heartbeat, and I didn't want anything putting Connie in danger. I needed to get him out of there fast.

"A'ight, man. It's in here," I said, walking toward my bedroom. He followed me there and hovered over me as I opened the safe. For a second I considered trying to take him out, but Connie appeared at the entrance to my room, so I erased the thought from my mind. Last thing I wanted was for her to get shot by accident.

I thought everything was going to be okay when I handed him the stack of bills and he headed toward the door. I was going to let him leave to make sure Connie was safe, but in an hour he would be running from more than just the police. One phone call and half the brothers I knew on the street would be after his ass.

Standing in the doorway, he turned toward Connie. "Last chance. We can be in Montego Bay by tonight."

She rolled her eyes. "Avery, you might be in jail tonight. Now, you got what you wanted, so get the hell out of here." She pointed at the door.

"You really gonna choose him over me?" He was waving the gun at me as he spoke.

"I don't have to choose between the two of you, because I don't want you, and I love him. Can't you get that through your thick head?" She folded her arms defiantly and tilted her head toward the door in a gesture that said it was time for him to leave.

I knew she wasn't trying to provoke him, but Avery's face turned beet red and the look in his eyes turned from anger to that of a man possessed. He was not in a good place, and with the way he was holding that gun, neither was I.

"Oh, is that right?" He pointed the gun directly at my chest. I could tell by his facial expression and body language that this motherfucker was really about to shoot me. "Well, if I get rid of him, then I guess you're not gonna have any choices at all, are you?"

Connie started to tremble. "Avery, don't do this," she pleaded. "Please. You're in enough trouble as it is."

"That's exactly why I can do it. I'm already at rock bottom." Instead of shouting, his voice was calm and tranquil. "I can't go any further down. I ain't got shit to lose."

He turned the gun sideways like he was some type of gangster.

Everything after that happened in a flash. Avery never got the chance to pull the trigger because out of nowhere, Connie pulled out a knife and stabbed him in the back. She didn't kill him, but he was so surprised by her actions that he dropped the gun, staring at her in astonishment.

He let out a howl like a madman and tried to lunge at Connie. This was exactly what I was trying to avoid, her being in danger, so I did what I had to do to protect the woman I loved. I gave him one swift kick that sent him sprawling onto the floor. Once he was down, I snatched the knife out of her hand and jumped on him, stabbing him in the back over and over until I felt my rage subside. Avery was no longer moving.

When I looked up, Connie was trembling and sobbing as she held the gun with two hands, pointed at Avery's head.

I reached up and gently took the gun from her. "Hey, it's over," I said. "He's gone. He can't hurt you anymore." I placed the gun on the coffee table, and she fell into my arms, weeping uncontrollably.

I led Connie to the sofa and sat with her, holding and rocking her until she finally calmed down. It was a long time before either one of us spoke.

"We have to call the police," she finally said, staring at Avery's lifeless body.

"No police," I said, looking deeply into her eyes to make sure she understood how serious I was.

"What?"

"If we call the police, I'm probably going to jail for a very long time."

She shook her head adamantly, almost as if by doing so she could make the whole situation disappear. She spoke in short bursts. "No, this was self-defense. Avery's a wanted man. You were protecting me. I'll tell them that."

I chuckled at how naive she was. "Baby, I'm on parole, and I got two strikes against me already. With my record, they'd throw me in prison on principle."

She refused to hear me. "No!" she insisted more forcefully this time. "It was self-defense! Hell, I'll tell them I was the one who did it."

I took her hand and stroked it gently. "And I love you for being so loyal, but you gotta be realistic about this. Are you really gonna tell them you did it?"

She nodded firmly.

"That sounds good," I said, "until the cops ask why you stabbed him so many times in the back."

Her eyes got wide as she understood how easy it would be for them to poke holes in her story.

"Cops are lazy, Connie; they aren't stupid, especially not homicide detectives. They're going to know you didn't do it. I was so damn pissed I'm sure I broke a couple of his ribs when I jumped on him. I don't think they're going to believe you have that type of brute strength."

She lowered her head. "You're not going to jail for this, Daryl. I refuse to let that happen."

I covered my face with both hands, wishing it was as easy as she was making it sound. We were in deep trouble. "I'm not even sure they'll believe it was his gun," I said. "Both of us touched it. You probably wiped away all his fingerprints when you held the gun to his head."

"Oh, God, I wasn't even thinking about that. Daryl, I'm sorry." Her tears started up again, so I pulled her against me and began rocking her.

I wanted to kick Avery's dead body for putting us in this situation.

"Connie," I whispered when she had quieted down. "I have to make a decision."

She looked up at me, her eyes still shining with tears. "What is it?"

"I won't let you try to take the rap for this. I just have to decide if I'm going to face the judicial system and go back to jail, or if I'm going to disappear."

Her mouth fell open, but no words came out for a long time as she processed the situation. When she finally spoke, she had made a decision of her own. "Well, if you decide to leave, I'm going with you."

"No, I'm not going to let you ruin your life, Connie." I got up from the couch and started pacing, trying to avoid the pool of blood on the floor. "You have no idea what it's like living on the run."

I checked my watch. An hour had already passed. If I was going to leave, I'd have to do it soon. My parole officer was coming for a home visit at noon.

"Why don't we just get rid of the body like they do on TV?"

Her suggestion shocked the hell out of me and stopped me in my tracks. I turned slowly toward her and said, "You're joking, right?" The expression on her face told me she was dead serious.

"Where the hell would we get rid of the body?"

With that same determined look on her face, she laid out her plan. "I'm sure Avery's car is around here somewhere. We could put him in it, then drive out to Long Island. Set him and the car on fire."

The idea of disposing of the body and saving myself from a prison sentence was definitely appealing. I considered her plan but couldn't see how we would get away with it. "Not gonna work," I told her. "Too many cameras around this building."

"Not around back," she said. "That's how Avery got into my house. From the fire escape. Cheap-ass landlord put fakes in the back."

"It still wouldn't work. We carry him down that fire escape, someone is bound to hear us or see us. One person might not be noticed, but two people carrying a dead body sure as hell will. You know how nosy the people in this building are. Someone is gonna call the cops." I looked at the mess around my feet and added, "Besides, my parole officer's coming tomorrow at noon. We'd never be able to clean up all this blood by then."

She looked down at Avery's body and then back up at me with tears flowing down her cheeks. "I'm not giving up, Daryl. I won't lose you."

I sat down beside Connie and held her tightly, thinking it might be the last time I would have her in my arms. We were in deep shit, and it didn't look like there was a way out. Once my parole officer showed up, I was on my way to prison for sure.

"I wish we could get away from here," I said with a sigh. "You know, take off before they even find the body."

She sat up and looked at me hopefully. "Why don't we? Let's just go, Daryl. Let's go now."

I gave her a sad smile and kissed the top of her head. "We can't, baby. I'm wearing an ankle bracelet. That signal would bring the cops over here before we even made it onto a Greyhound bus. Besides, even if we got away somehow, we'd spend the rest of our lives on the run. I can't let you live that way."

She fell back against the couch, looking defeated as she stared off into space, probably trying to come to terms with the truth of our situation. "Too bad we couldn't make it look like you were the one who died in here," she said after a while.

"Yeah, that would be something, wouldn't it?" I agreed. "Then I could slip out of the country and you could meet me on some romantic island where we live happily ever after." It was easier to go along with the fantasy for a few minutes than face the reality that I would soon be behind bars.

It was as if we were writing a script for our own Lifetime movie. She leaned her head against my shoulder and continued the story: "We could start a fire to cover up the evidence. I bet no one would even question his identity if he was wearing your Star of David."

"It would be better if he was wearing this." I lifted my leg, revealing the monitoring device. "I've watched Benny take this thing off enough times. I bet if I put my mind to it I could remove it and put it on your ex."

She was silent for a minute, then turned to me with a look in her eyes that said maybe this was more than a story we were telling each other. A smile crept up on her face, and I felt myself grinning too. I had no doubt we were both thinking the same thing.

"Nah. It wouldn't work... would it?"

"I don't know; it might," Connie said. "If we plan it out a little better, it just might work. Worst case scenario, it would give you a hell of a head start on the police."

"Along with the eyes and ears in the building who will help steer the cops in the wrong direction." I felt a glimmer of hope growing inside me.

Connie leaned over and kissed me. "Let's do it. Let's be done with this place and make a life for ourselves somewhere else. You and me. Bonnie and Clyde."

It took a while, but she finally convinced me that we could make it work. For the next two hours, we meticulously planned our escape from New York. We devised ways of staying in contact while I was gone; we discussed how she should speak to the police, and more importantly, how we were going to trick everyone into thinking Avery's body was mine.

Connie came up with the idea that we should use WD-40 to ignite the fire. It was the same substance that started the fire that killed Avery's first wife. Using it to start this fire might send the cops on a wild-goose chase, trying to connect the two deaths. It was genius as far as I was concerned. Connie was a hell of a lot more sneaky than I would have given her credit for.

As it drew closer to daybreak, we put our plan into action. We both changed out of our bloody clothes, which I placed in a bag along with the gun. Then I spent the next hour dismantling my ankle bracelet and placing it on Avery's corpse, and Connie drove out to Long Island and purchased one can of WD-40 from twelve different 7-Elevens. When she came back, we put Avery's body on the couch, put my Star of David necklace on him, took his keys, and sprayed WD-40 around the whole scene. If everything went as planned, the blood evidence on the floor would be destroyed by the flames.

As an extra precaution, we decided it was important for people in the building to see us, so that if the cops started asking questions, nothing would raise any red flags. My legs were shaking like crazy when I went down to the stoop to go on my usual morning run, but somehow I managed to play it off. I even flirted with Nancy a little before I headed back into the building.

Connie was pacing the floor in my apartment when I went back upstairs. She ran to me and squeezed me tight, then stepped back and said, "No turning back now. I love you."

One last kiss and then she was gone. I waited until I was sure she would be safely downstairs with the other ladies on the stoop before I went into action. I peeked out into the hallway to make sure that my escape through the back of the building wouldn't be seen. No one was around. I shut my door and made my way over to the couch, standing over Avery's body, where I took a deep breath and started to say one final prayer for his soul.

That's when Benny knocked at my door.

I swear I thought Benny could hear my heart pounding as I leaned on the door to keep him from entering the apartment. Thank God for the alcohol I smelled on his breath. If he had been sober, he probably would have pushed the door open, and then the whole plan would have blown up in my face. I don't think I'd ever been as scared as I was at that moment. When he finally stormed off, I shut the door, locked it, and fell to my knees, barely able to catch my breath.

It took me a minute to get my head straight, but then I realized the clock was still ticking. My parole officer was due in a few short hours.

One more check in the hallway to be sure it was clear, and then I did it. I lit a match and threw it on the floor. The WD-40 ignited instantly. I grabbed the bag full of bloody evidence and bolted down the hall into Connie's place. She'd left the door unlocked for me so I could climb down her fire escape in the back of the building. By the time I heard the fire alarm go off, I was already halfway down the back alley. My next stop was the river, where I dumped the bag of evidence, and then on to my friend, who would sell me a new identity.

As I took Connie's hand now and walked down the beach in this tropical paradise, I still couldn't believe we were together again. I'd spent the last few weeks worrying and waiting, and now it looked like we'd actually pulled it off.

We walked along the shore with our bare feet in the water. It was nice to be with her again. Nice to enjoy the woman I'd fallen in love with. Maybe one day all of that other stuff would be a distant memory, like waking up from a bad dream that you only half remember.

"Did you talk to my mom before you left?" I asked.

"Yeah, I went by her house," she told me. "She's fine. Told me to tell you she loves you. And to be careful. She understands if you don't call for a while."

Other than the dude who sold me my identity, and who had been paid very well to keep his mouth shut, my mom was the only person who knew the truth. I couldn't leave with her thinking I was dead. It would have devastated her.

Connie was worried about me going to see my mom before I left the country. She didn't think it was wise, but my feeling was this: My mother was the only person on earth I could trust with this information. And I turned out to be right. My mother played her part to a T. She rushed down to the morgue with my lawyer to claim Avery's body as her son's. She used some excuse about me being an Israelite and needing the body within twenty-four hours. Thanks to her, the coroner rushed the autopsy, and my mother had the body cremated an hour later, destroying any chance of further DNA testing in the future.

"So, is everything straightened out with Ben?" I asked, still feeling bad that he'd had to spend any time behind bars over this. Why he confessed to the murder was still a mystery to me, something I'd probably never understand. I was just glad that in the end, Connie was able to talk the detective into taking a closer look at her ex-husband, and the detectives were smart enough to follow the trail we left to the trunk of Avery's car. Once again, Connie deserved the credit. It had been her idea to keep a spare key when she gave the car keys to Krystal.

"Yes, thank God," Connie answered. "He and Nancy are getting married."

"We got him out of jail and now he's willingly entering prison?" I said with a laugh.

Connie punched my shoulder playfully. "Nancy's not that bad!"

I took her hand again. "No, seriously, I'm happy for them. It's a hell of a lot better than it could have been."

"Amen to that." She stopped walking and pulled me in for a kiss. "So, my love, we've made it to paradise, but where do we go from here?" she asked

"I've got a villa with a private beach in Discovery Bay waiting for us. We'll stay there for a week, then jump on a repositioning cruise that's sailing to Europe and the Greek isles. I know you like Jamaica, but there's too many people from back home that travel here. I think Europe's a safer bet. How does that sound?"

"Sounds great. But then again, living with you in a shoe would sound great to me."

Reading Group Guide

DISCUSSION QUESTIONS

1. Krystal said Daryl was the one that could get it anytime. What is your opinion of their relationship, past and present? Do you believe everyone has "the one"?

2. What did you think about the stoop crew? Do you know any women who love to gossip as much as they do?

3. Have you ever had a neighbor you wanted to sleep with?

4. Who was your favorite character? Why?

5. Did you figure out that Benny was gay? Did you think Daryl was gay?

6. Connie blamed her weight gain on stress. Why do you think she was able to lose weight once she met Daryl?

7. What would you do if your husband asked for a divorce in the manner that Avery did?

8. What did you think were in Krystal's little blue boxes at first?

9. What were your thoughts about Cain and his "live like you're dying" philosophy?

10. Do you think Avery ever really loved Connie?

11. Who was the most trifling character in the book?

12. How did you feel when you read the fire scenes? Were you sad that Daryl was dead?

13. Were you shocked when Cain left Avery high and dry?

14. Who did you think killed Daryl?

15. Were you happy with whom Benny ended up with?

16. Carl Weber calls Daryl Graham "the thug you can take home to your mother." Would you agree?

17. Were you surprised when you read the Epilogue?

18. Do you feel sorry for Avery? Do you think all the characters got what they deserved in the end?

19. Would you consider this a mystery?

20. There are parts of Daryl's past that are never revealed. Would you like to see more of this character?

Carl Weber takes readers
back to church in

The Choir Director 2:
Runaway Bride

with some hard-earned lessons in
love, faith . . . and betrayal.

Please turn this page for a preview.

Aaron

1

My stomach was full of butterflies when I poked my head into the sanctuary from the side door. The church was packed from wall to wall with folks dressed in their Sunday best, and Bishop T. K. Wilson stood at the altar with Bible in hand. It wouldn't be long before the bishop gave the church organist the signal to play, and we'd be heading out to the pulpit ourselves. In all honesty, I couldn't believe how nervous I was. I mean, technically this should all be a cinch. It wasn't like we hadn't practiced this whole thing last night. Besides, I'd mounted that pulpit hundreds of times before as the choir director. But none of that could stop my nervousness.

I glanced over at my mother and my aunt Bertha, who were sitting in the front row pews. They'd traveled all the way from Virginia to be here for this very special occasion, and the look of pride on my momma's face was priceless. I don't think she had a clue just how much I loved her.

I pulled my head back into the room feeling like I was going to pass out from the anxiety. The butterflies in my stomach felt like they had morphed into bats. I turned to Ross Parker, my lifelong friend and the newly appointed business manager for our church choir. He was sitting on the small worn-out sofa about three feet away from me.

"You okay? You don't look so hot," he said, looking down at my hands, which were shaking visibly.

I took a deep breath, hoping that might calm my stomach. I could feel the bile at the back of my throat. "I don't know. I feel like I'm gonna be sick," I said.

Ross stood up and closed the short distance between us. "Dude, you're getting married in about five minutes. It's a big step. Everyone has last-minute jitters before they tie the knot. I bet Tia's out there thinking the same thing." He reached over to the table and picked up a can of Sprite. "Here, take a sip of this. It will calm your stomach."

I did what I was told, my hands trembling as I took small sips from the can. "I don't know, man. Look at my hands. I don't think I've ever been this nervous. Am I doing the right thing?"

Ross took the soda from me, placed it back where it had come from, and then turned to me. As he straightened my collar and adjusted my tie, he looked me dead in the eye and asked, "Do you love her?"

I looked back into my friend's dark eyes and nodded. "Yeah, man. I love her more than anything in this world. If any woman is my soul mate, it's Tia."

"Well, if that's the case, what are you worried about?"

I made a gesture in the direction of the sanctuary where so many people were waiting for the opulent ceremony to begin. "I didn't want a huge wedding. As far as I was concerned, we could have gone down to city hall and gotten married by the justice of the peace," I said.

"Oh, that would have worked out well," Ross said with a laugh. "Besides the fact that you're the choir director in this church and Bishop would have killed you, every woman wants a big wedding, man. They want their special day. You know that." He laughed again. "Besides, when that music starts playing, all this nervousness is gonna go away."

No sooner did he speak than the sound of the organ music filled my ears, signaling that it was time. I gave Ross this *So what do I do now?* look as I lifted my still trembling hands.

"You were wrong," I said.

He shrugged his shoulders. "Aaron, you'll be fine."

I dropped my hands to my sides and shook my head. "I'm still nervous. I don't think I can go through with it."

"Man, if you don't get your behind out there..." He pointed at the door. "Do you know how beautiful she must look right now, standing outside the church waiting for you?"

He'd finally said the right thing. An image of Tia flashed through my mind, and I knew there was no way I could leave her at the altar. I really did love her and wanted to marry her. I exhaled loudly and shook my arms to release the tension, announcing, "Okay, let's do this."

Ross gave me a final once-over to make sure nothing was out of place, and then he patted my shoulder. "You look good. You ready to get married?"

I nodded, taking a deep breath to steady my nerves, then walked out the door into the sanctuary. As I stopped to look at the crowd before ascending the steps in front of the altar, I felt Ross's hand on my shoulder.

"We out here now, bro," he said. "Ain't no turning back."

I looked at him over my shoulder and said, "Wasn't trying to turn back, my man. Just stopping to pinch myself to make sure this is actually real and not a dream."

"Oh, it's real a'ight. Now get your butt up there."

I continued up the steps on wobbly knees and didn't stop until I was in position next to Bishop Wilson.

"You all right, son?" Bishop asked.

"Yes, sir, Bishop. I'm good to go." I nodded nervously as I looked out at the crowd.

The bishop studied me momentarily, then said, "I've never met a man who wasn't nervous on his wedding day, including myself."

Ross said with a chuckle, "He's fine for now, Bishop. Let's just speed this up a little before he changes his mind."

"Well, then, let's do that, Brother Parker." Bishop Wilson turned and nodded to the organist again. On cue, the music changed and another, more majestic song began.

I stood at attention, still nervous but with a feeling of excitement too, as I looked toward the doors at the back of the sanctuary. Every head in the church turned to see the first of four women being escorted down the aisle and into their positions at the altar. Each wore a formfitting blue dress with white trim. They were escorted down the aisle by my groomsmen, who wore black tuxedos and blue vests.

The last bridesmaid was being led by John Nixon, or Pippie as we called him. One of my friends from Virginia, Pippie wasn't the most attractive brother you'd ever wanna meet, but he'd been there for me when no one else was, including Ross. That's one of the reasons why I'd asked the bishop to give him a job upon his recent release from prison. Being the janitor at First Jamaica wasn't what I would call a high-achieving job, but Pippie was grateful.

Once everyone had taken their places in the front, all eyes were on the matron of honor, who happened to be none other than First Lady Monique Wilson, wife of the bishop. It was no surprise that Tia chose her to be the matron of honor. She'd been a good friend to both me and my wife-to-be.

To distinguish her from the bridesmaids, Monique wore a hat made out of the same material as her dress—which was custom-made to accentuate her very large breasts and rather grand rear. If she was anyone else, I would have sworn she was trying to upstage Tia, but I knew Monique well enough to understand that she wasn't doing anything but being herself. She was definitely like no other first lady you'd ever meet.

Monique took her place across from Ross, and then I knew the time had come. The flower girl had dropped her last petal, and the doors to the church sanctuary had closed. I glanced over at my mother, who blew me a kiss as she stood with the rest of the guests, and the first strains of the "Wedding March" began.

So far, everything had gone just as I expected, and the butterflies in my stomach had settled—that is, until the time stretched on into a second and third repeat of the "Wedding March" and still no sign of my bride. I felt the butterflies taking up flight again.

I glanced at the bishop, who was looking at me with raised eyebrows. I shrugged. Bishop turned to Ross, who also shrugged.

We all looked to the first lady.

"Where is she? I thought she was going to ride in the limo with you guys," I whispered to Monique.

"She did," Monique whispered back. "She stayed in the limo with her brother when we got out. I sent the driver back to get them right before I came through the doors."

"Then where is she?"

I glanced over at my mother and then at the crowd. People were starting to get restless, some sitting back down and others mumbling their confusion to each other, looking around as if they'd find the bride somewhere other than coming down the main aisle. I'm sure everyone was wondering the same thing I was: Where was my bride?

God, this can't be happening. Tia wouldn't leave me at the altar, would she?

"Everybody just relax," Ross said to the group assembled in front. "You know how women are. She'll make her grand entrance and get the reaction she's hoping for. Just chill."

I tried to buy into his confidence. "Yeah, man. Yeah, you're right," I said, loosening up my shoulders and then cracking my neck.

Once again, I turned my attention to the closed sanctuary doors. By now the organist was on her fourth or fifth repetition of the "Wedding March."

Finally, the sanctuary doors opened. I felt a momentary rush of relief when I spotted Tia's brother Kareem. He was the one escorting Tia down the aisle to give her away.

There was a collective sigh of relief from the crowd, and my heartbeat slowed down a little, until I saw Kareem striding toward the front—alone. The noise from the guests in attendance was no longer a whisper, but more like a frenzied buzzing. I didn't pay attention to them, though. I was focused on Kareem. As he got closer, I could see the expression on his face, and I knew it meant nothing good.

He came up the steps and stood in front of me. "Look, Aaron, man, I'm sorry." Dude could barely look me in the eyes.

"Sorry about what?" I gave a nervous laugh.

"She's gone," Kareem said.

"What do you mean, she's gone?" Bishop's voice was barely above a whisper, but he was still clearly taking charge of the situation. I was glad for that because I sure couldn't. As weak as my knees felt, I was lucky I was still standing.

"She's gone as in she's not here. She's not at the church," Kareem answered.

I looked to Monique. "You said she rode in the limo."

"She did," Monique said, looking confused.

"Then what—where…?" I couldn't even finish my sentence. I grabbed my forehead as I felt a splitting headache coming on.

"I'm sorry, man. She left." Kareem apologized again. "I don't know what to tell you."

I stared off at nothing in particular. "Tell me she's coming back. That's what you can tell me. I thought she loved me. I thought she wanted to marry me."

What was I supposed to do now?

About the Author

CARL WEBER is the *New York Times* best-selling author of over a dozen novels and short stories. A lifelong reader, Weber wanted to write stories about ordinary people who have crazy things happening in their lives. Now, when he's not connecting with readers through his books and his two bookstore chains, Urban Knowledge and Beach Reads, Weber is finding new talent for his own publishing company, Urban Books.

Weber graduated from Virginia State University with a bachelor's degree in accounting and has an MBA in marketing from the University of Virginia.

You can learn more at:
www.carlweber.net
Facebook: http://www.facebook.com/AuthorCarlWeber
Twitter: @IamCarlWeber